Critical

CAROLE NELSON DOUGLAS

Author of the Midnight Louie and Irene Adler mystery series

"Douglas is the master of the well-told tale."
—*Booklist*

"You never know what madness and mayhem you'll find in Douglas's mysteries, but you can be sure it will be wild, witty, and utterly irresistible."
—*The San Francisco Chronicle*

"A saucy style and a delicious sense of humor."
—*The New York Times*

And raves for her new urban fantasy series

DELILAH STREET:
PARANORMAL INVESTIGATOR

BRIMSTONE KISS

"Filled with kisses and kick-ass action. . . . Douglas's dishy style complements the twisty plot."

—*Publishers Weekly* (starred review)

"All of the dark, dangerous, and unique paranormal elements readers seek, along with the passion, love and exciting temptations that add spice to the mix."

—Darque Reviews

"A wonderful second Street urban fantasy . . . *Brimstone Kiss* is a magical mystery fantasy tour."

—Alternative Worlds

"Douglas has populated her Post-Millennium Las Vegas with the most outrageous and outlandish cast of supporting characters this side of *The Wizard of Oz*. . . . The rich details and inventive mysteries in *Brimstone Kiss* completely submerge you in the story."

—SciFiGuy

"Another fabulous job of drawing the reader into the story, making them feel as if they are a part of it."

—Bitten By Books

DANCING WITH WEREWOLVES

"Spectacular style . . . Douglas spices the action with fabulous characters: Quicksilver, Delilah's protective dog; Cin-Sims (Cinema Simulacrums), dead celebrities re-created via science and magic; the oldest living vampire in Vegas, once a famous aviator; and Cocaine (aka Snow), a devilish albino rocker. Readers will eagerly await the sequel."

—*Publishers Weekly* (starred review)

"A wonderfully written story with a unique take on the paranormal."

—*New York Times* bestselling author Kelley Armstrong

"A captivating storyline and some of the most unique supporting characters around."

—Darque Reviews

"Fabulous!"

—*New York Times* bestselling author Sherrilyn Kenyon

"A smartly written, plot-driven, original novel that deftly combines the elements of fantasy, mystery, and romance to the well-sated delight of the reader."

—*Midwest Review of Books*

"Charming, witty, and utterly imaginative. A pure delight! Captivating characters, a new spin on the supernatural, simply delicious."

—*New York Times* bestselling author Heather Graham

"An entertaining urban fantasy that rivals that of Kim Harrison and Kelley Armstrong. The protagonist jumps from the frying pan into the fire as she tries to stay one step ahead of her enemies and those who want to use her. . . . A mystical delight."

—Alternative Worlds

"In *Dancing with Werewolves,* there aren't just scary things under the bed, but in it, too! Carole Nelson Douglas invents an amazingly rich world of shadows come to life. . . ."

—Award-winning author Nancy Pickard

"What a thrill ride! . . . A fascinating combination of romance, mystery, fantasy, and paranormal. . . . Douglas has definitely created a character and a setting that will keep readers coming back for more."

—The Romance Reader

"Award-winning Douglas turns her hand to the urban fantasy genre, creating a savvy and highly inquisitive new heroine. This first-person narrative follows Delilah Street's journey into a creepy and dangerous new world, where telling friend from foe is not so easy. A wild new ride!"

—*Romantic Times*

"Crisp and edgy. Delilah's voice came through loud and clear, a perfect mix of hard-nosed reporter and small-town girl. . . . *Dancing with Werewolves* is a wonderful addition to the paranormal genre."

—BlogCritics

Don’t miss any of the adventures of Delilah Street!

Dancing with Werewolves
Brimstone Kiss

Available now from Pocket Books/Juno Books

CAROLE NELSON DOUGLAS

VAMPIRE SUNRISE

DELILAH STREET:
PARANORMAL INVESTIGATOR

POCKET BOOKS
NEW YORK LONDON Toronto Sydney

Pocket Books
A Division of Simon & Schuster, Inc.
1230 Avenue of the Americas
New York, NY 10020

This book is a work of fiction. Names, characters, places, and incidents either are products of the author's imagination or are used fictitiously. Any resemblance to actual events or locales or persons, living or dead, is entirely coincidental.

First Juno Books/Pocket Books paperback edition December 2009

JUNO BOOKS and colophon are trademarks of Wildside Press LLC used under license by Simon & Schuster, Inc., the publisher of this work.

POCKET and colophon are registered trademarks of Simon & Schuster, Inc.

Cover design by Lisa Litwack; cover art by Gordon Crabb; background photo by flipchip/lasvegasvegas.com

Manufactured in the United States of America

10 9 8 7 6 5 4 3 2 1

ISBN 978-1-4391-5677-3
ISBN 978-1-4391-6689-5 (ebook)

For Summer and Secret,
the silver and golden ladies
who crossed the Rainbow Bridge
during the writing of this book

VAMPIRE SUNRISE

Meet Me, Delilah Street

EVERYONE HAS FAMILY issues, but my issues are that I don't *have* any family. My fresh new business card reads *Delilah Street, Paranormal Investigator,* but my old personal card could have read *Delilah Street, Unadoptable Orphan.*

I was supposedly named after the street where I was found abandoned as an infant in Wichita, Kansas. (I guess I should just thank God and DC Comics it wasn't Lois Lane.) I've googled and groggled (the drinking person's search engine) the World Wide Web for Delilah Streets and not a single bloody one of them shows up in Kansas.

Whoever my forebears are, they gave me the Black Irish, Snow White coloring that is catnip to vampires: corpse-pale skin and dead-of-night-black hair. By age twelve I was fighting off aspiring juvie rapists with retractable fangs and body odor that mixed blood, sweat, and semen. Really made me enjoy being a girl.

My growing-up years of group homes in Wichita are history now that I'm twenty-four and on my own. I had a good job reporting the paranormal beat for WTCH-TV in Kansas—until a jealous weather witch forecaster forced me out.

Now I'm a freelance investigator in wicked, mysterious post–Millennium Revelation Las Vegas. Vegas was wicked, of course, long before the turn of the twenty-first century brought all the bogeymen and -women of myth and legends out of the closet and into human lives and society. Now, in 2013, Vegas is crawling with vamps and half-weres and all-werewolf mobs and celebrity zombies and who knows what else.

My ambitions are simple.

One, staying alive. (Being turned into an immortal vampire doesn't count.)

Two, being able to make love in the missionary position without having panic attacks. (Whoever thought someone would *aim* for the missionary position?) Position hadn't been an issue until recently and neither had sex. I've finally found a man I *want* to make love with, ex-FBI guy Ricardo Montoya—aka the Cadaver Kid. He's tall, dark, handsome, Hispanic, and my brand-new horizontal ambition. He has my back—and my front—at every opportunity.

And three, tracking down "Lilith Quince"—my spitting image—to find out if she is a twin, double, clone, or simulacrum. Or if she is even alive. Seeing her/me being autopsied on *Crime Scene Instincts V: Las Vegas* one rerun-TV night in Wichita brought me to Sin City in the first place.

Lucky me, Lilith became the most desirable corpse ever featured on the internationally franchised show. I knew Millennium Revelation pop culture and taste tended toward the dark—now I know *how* dark.

When the *CSI* cameras showed a discreet maggot camping out in a nostril that held a tiny blue topaz stud like my very own, Lilith's corpse was dubbed "Maggie" and a fantasy franchise was born. Maggie is the It Girl of 2013: Maggie dolls and merchandise are hot and so are bootleg Maggie films, outtakes, and my hide, if anyone could snag it—dead or alive. One werewolf mobster almost did already.

At least ambition number four is now a done deal: identifying the embracing skeletons Ric and I discovered in Vegas's Sunset Park just after I hit town and just before the town hit me back, hard.

I discovered more than Ric and corpses in Sunset Park. I found an ally who has heavenly blue eyes and is seriously gray and hairy. That's my dog, Quicksilver. He's a wolfhound-wolf cross I saved from death at the pound. He returns the favor with fang, claw, and warm, paranormally talented tongue.

(I have a soft spot for dogs—especially since Achilles, my valiant little Lhasa apso in Wichita, died from blood poisoning after biting a vampire who was trying to bite me. Achilles' ashes rest in a dragon-decorated jar on my mantel, but I haven't given up the ghost on him.)

That mantel is located in the Enchanted Cottage on the Hector Nightwine estate. Hector rents it to me cheap because, as producer of the many worldwide *CSI* franchises, he's presumably guilty of offing my possible twin on national TV.

When Hector's *CSI* show made Lilith Quince into a macabre international sex symbol, he inadvertently made me, Delilah Street, a wanted woman. Not for myself alone, mind you, but for the naked and dead image of another woman, who may not be dead.

Hector doesn't have a conscience, just a profit motive. He's banking on my finding Lilith or becoming her for his enduring financial benefit.

The only thing Hector and I have in common is loving old black-and-white films. The Enchanted Cottage is based on a setting from a 1945 movie. A shy-to-the-point-of-invisible staff of who-knows-what supernaturals run the place, and I suspect it's supplied with the wicked stepmother's mirror from *Snow White*. Although it's been mum with me so far, I do see dead people in it.

The most complicated beings in my brave new world are the CinSims. Cinema Simulacrums are created when fresh zombie bodies illegally imported from Mexico are blended with classic black-and-white film characters. The resulting "live" personas are wholly owned entertainment entities leased to various Vegas enterprises.

Hector and Ric blame the Immortality Mob for the brisk business in zombie CinSims, but can't prove it. Hector wants to wrest the CinSims from the mob's control into his. Ric aches to stop the traffic in illegally imported zombies. It's personal—he was forced to work in the trade as a child.

I'd like to help them both out, and not just because I'm a former investigative reporter crusading against human and inhuman exploitation. My own freedom is on the line from several merciless and downright repellent factions trying to make life after the Millennium Revelation literal Hell.

Luckily, I have some new, off-the-chart abilities simmering myself, most involving silver—from the silver nitrate in black-and-white films to sterling silver to mirrors and reflective surfaces in general.

Which reminds me of one more sorta sidekick: a freaky shape-changing lock of hair from the albino rock star who owns the Inferno Hotel. The guy goes by three names: Christophe for business, Cocaine when fronting his Seven Deadly Sins rock band, and Snow to his intimates. He seems to consider me one of them, but no way do I want to be.

While thinking of my lost Achilles, I made the mistake of touching that long white lock of Snow's hair. The damn thing became a sterling silver familiar no jeweler's saw or torch can remove from my body. Since it transforms into different pieces of often-protective jewelry, it's handy at times. I consider it a variety of talisman-cum-leech.

That attitude sums up my issues with the rock star–hotelier, who enslaves groupies with a one-time mosh pit "Brimstone Kiss."

Then I discovered *why* those postconcert kisses are so bloody irresistible . . . and Snow forced me to submit to his soul-stealing smooch in exchange for his help in saving Ric from being vamped to death. This kiss-off stand-off between us is *not* over.

I've been called a "silver medium," but I don't aim to be medium at anything. I won't do things halfway. I intend to expose every dirty supernatural secret in Las Vegas, if necessary, to find out who I really am, and who's been bad and who's been good in my new Millennium Revelation neighborhood.

Chapter One

DEAD TIRED, I headed "home" in the early evening Las Vegas Strip traffic. Instead of sugarplums—or even three cherries in a slot machine window—other, far less delightful, images danced in my head.

I was only two days of sleep deprivation past an endless night fighting Vegas's hidden ancient Egyptian underworld of bloodthirsty supernaturals. My cup of nightmares was sure to runneth over for weeks with visions of zombie mummies, hyena carcasses, and vampires in eyeliner.

Even worse would be visual reruns of Ric chained to a dungeon wall under the Karnak Hotel, victim of a vicious suck-fest. That was the ancient Egyptian vampire empire's version of waterboarding as they sought the secret of his ability to raise the dead.

Now my investigative partner was out of the Karnak's supernaturally infested bowels and alive, barely, in a high-rise suite at the rival Inferno Hotel. In an hour, Ricardo Montoya had gone from the pit of Hell to the heavens, or the Vegas version of both.

Following Ric's and my separate life-threatening investigations at the Karnak, I was alive but iffy on the matter of my soul and sanity. Ric was in a coma—possibly more dead than alive—and possibly possessed of a more compromised soul than I was.

I'd been too frantic to do anything but hover over Ric for hours and was finally heading home under doctor's orders to "freshen up" before returning to his comatose side.

Good advice.

Getting myself together enough to drive my big black '56 Caddy, Dolly, through brassy Vegas Strip traffic forced me to focus. My heart felt a faint *ping* of security when the Nightwine estate's iron side gates opened automatically to admit us.

After parking Dolly near the carriage house, I could hardly wait to enter my soothing rental digs and start to feel human again. In a city built on flash and flesh, *un*human seemed the dominant life, or death, form.

I headed for the Enchanted Cottage, then stopped. Its Hobbity front door formed a gray wooden frame for something black-and-white and silver all over that stood before it, blocking my way. Yes, this "something" was also "someone" I welcomed seeing. My favorite CinSim.

"Godfrey!" My voice quivered with mingled grief and joy.

"My dear Miss Street," he began in the brisk tones of that fine actor, William Powell, playing the ultra-competent *My Man Godfrey* in the 1936 romantic comedy film classic. "How splendid to see you alive and well and back on the premises."

Godfrey was my landlord's butler and looked more than double my age. He was actually three or four times it, depending whether you counted birth dates or film dates. Godfrey was as formal as an English tea caddy, but he'd been my first real friend in Las Vegas. That he was a Silver Screen movie image imposed on a zombie body "canvas" made him no less dear to me.

"Where is our Master Quicksilver?" he asked, worried and glancing behind me.

That's what an old-school butler like Godfrey called my

adopted hundred-and-fifty-pound dog: "Master Quicksilver." Godfrey honored my canine companion by addressing him as he would a young male human. Quicksilver indeed had awesome qualities above and beyond the ordinary dog.

Godfrey's always amusing formality helped me focus even more. Stiff upper lip and all. Right.

"Quick's fine, Godfrey. I left him guarding Ric at the Inferno."

"Ah." Godfrey's pencil-thin black mustache twitched ever so slightly with sympathy. "I understand Mr. Montoya is secure and doing well in Christophe's magnificent establishment."

I noticed Godfrey hadn't described Ric as he had me, "*alive* and well."

"How do you know what's . . . happened?" I asked.

"Word gets out," he murmured, as discreet as ever.

"'Word.'" My stress-dulled mind grabbed that one piece of mental flotsam and clung to it.

APPARENTLY, "WORD" HAD been thorough enough to make everyone I knew uncomfortable with the "alive" designation for Ric's current state.

That kicked me back into reliving the nightmare of Ric's rescue. I saw our war party retreating quickly through a trail of downed Egyptian warriors, attack mummies, and hyenas as the underground River Nile became one of the rivers of Hell flowing beneath Snow's Inferno Hotel.

Snow's security head, Grizelle, a six-feet-something black supermodel type who can turn that catwalk strut into the stalking stride of a six-hundred-pound white tiger, had borne Ric's unconscious body along so fast she was out of sight.

Snow, acting fast like the big shot he was, had already

arranged a state-of-the-art hospital suite in the hotel. No outsiders would know what had happened to Ric. The Vegas bigwigs involved wanted news of a rival supernatural vampire empire at the Karnak kept secret.

I was just as eager to keep Ric's one paranormal power private.

When I caught up with Grizelle at the hotel's forty-second-floor high-roller penthouses, I'd found Snow's designated hospital site was the bridal suite. *Ouch.*

Snow always played Mr. Discreet, but, like the scorpion, his every move could bear a sting in its tail. My "bridegroom" might never awaken.

I couldn't carp about the setup.

Ric was soon ensconced in a hospital bed so accessorized it resembled a Bowflex home gym. He had twenty-four-hour guards and nursing care. As he slept, blood dripped around-the-clock into his circulatory system, an oddly vampiric process.

That last memory of him made me shudder now.

"MISS STREET." GODFREY gently broke into my dark trip down bad-memory lane. "You're not here to brood, but to rest, recover, and change clothes. Please go inside and do that."

"Oh. Yes. Yes, Godfrey." I looked down at the shopping bags dangling in my hands. "Thanks for packing me some things to use at the Inferno. I'm going right back, of course. Directly back."

"Of course." He used that agreeable tone that didn't quite gibe with what he just said. "I'll wait here until you're safely inside."

"Getting pushy, are we, Godfrey?" I smiled. "I'm supersafe on Nightwine's ultrasecure estate. I'm just not safe alone inside myself right now."

I let Godfrey feel useful. He took and slid my key card into the door slot, nodding good-bye as I shuffled my boot-clad feet over the threshold. Everything inside looked the same, but seemed oddly alien.

I felt like I'd been on a two-day bender—like Ray Milland in *The Lost Weekend*—although alcohol hadn't been my downfall. Since I work freelance, weekends don't have the significance for a 24/7 on-call snoop like me that they hold for the forty-hour-a-week wage slave I used to be.

Life in post–Millennium Revelation Las Vegas is one long—one might even say eternal—Lost Weekend anyway. Before the millennium turned, party-hearty Vegas was full up with social vices . . . drinking, dicing, doing anyone and any illegal substances in sight.

Me, here and now, I'd just OD'ed on fighting supernatural crime. I ached from ankle to angst, but mostly I was mentally sucked dry.

I'd left the Enchanted Cottage thirty-six hours earlier a relatively well-adjusted woman with a mildly important mission . . . handling a rogue CinSim at the Inferno Hotel. That was more a public relations assignment than a serious case for a fledgling paranormal investigator.

Here I was coming home a virtual zombie, a husk who'd danced cheek-to-cheek with sex and death and destruction and—even more blasphemously—perhaps given life.

When I left my fairy-tale digs I hadn't anticipated meeting a particularly iconic CinSim: Humphrey Bogart as "gin joint" owner Rick Blaine in the 1942 film classic *Casablanca*. Who wouldn't want to share a bar with Mr. Noir Guy, even if he was just a CinSim?

Once placed, CinSims are chipped to stay where put, within a room or a set range of so many feet. They are property on loan. One of them strolling off assigned premises, even in their home hotel, was big news.

Wouldn't you know it was tough-guy Bogart/Blaine who'd wandered from his proper place in the hellfire bowels of the Inferno Hotel? He'd made it all the way to the ground-level bar. There he'd asked for me, Delilah Street. Well, he didn't exactly ask for me, personally.

He'd muttered about a woman of my description: "black and blue." That's me on a police blotter—black hair, blue eyes. Add a funeral-lily pale complexion and red lips and you have Snow White wearing Lip Venom gloss.

Since my "summoning" then and my exhausted return now, my attire had gone from a midnight-blue velvet gown among my personal vintage clothes collection to an armored catsuit fit for a sixties James Bond movie action climax.

The steel-studded, patent-leather suit and crotch-high flat-heeled boots I wore, sans the black mail hood, were unnaturally light and tight and adapted to the wearer's physical dimensions, permanently.

At least Grizelle said so.

That's why I'd worn the thing home under a jersey caftan. The suit moved like muscle with my weary body and kept me upright, thanks to spandex and some possibly supernatural spell known only to Snow.

For all its creepy flexibility, the outfit felt as hard as a scarab's shiny carapace. Inside it my joints creaked as if cased in concrete. My mind felt duller than a battle-worn sword and my heart heavier than a black hole filled with lead.

How odd that instead of a weapon I now toted something as trivial as a Prada shopping bag loaded with my clothes from my original dress-up outing to the Inferno.

I pulled out midnight-blue sequined pumps—call them Dorothy Gale in mourning—and matching evening bag, and a tiny but significant container of Lip Venom plumping gloss.

All very chichi, yet to me the limp blue velvet vintage gown draping the crook of my arm was now about as attractive as a vamp-drained corpse.

I let it slide to the floor with the shoes and bag as soon as I crossed the cottage threshold, the beginning of my personal safety zone.

There was no place like the Enchanted Cottage for R&R.

My landlord, another triple threat like Snow—TV producer, film buff, and morbidity entrepreneur Hector Nightwine—had duplicated a film set as a livable guest house on his estate.

I can't swallow the fairy tale that quaint settings create a stage for true love, as happened in that movie. Still, since the Enchanted Cottage had been recreated in post–Millennium Revelation Las Vegas, what had been merely "charming" before was now actually "charmed," in the sense of hosting a mostly unseen magical staff.

Yup, I knew that lodging me here was like reinventing *Snow White* with pixies and gnomes instead of workaholic dwarfs. The best part was these shy, often unseen creatures worked for me, not Hector.

And work they did, leaving no domestic duties to distract this kick-ass late-model Snow White from just how bad things looked for her Prince Charming.

Chapter Two

A FIRE DID a mazurka in my parlor fireplace, even though this was a simmering Las Vegas June. The parlor was a shadowed Victorian retreat crammed with bric-a-brac. I veered toward the comfort inside, drawn by the hearth flames as if they were the bloodied, beating heart I imagined pulsing inside my own body.

The lobster-tank-size plasma television in the media corner reflected my passage. I jerked to a stop and whirled to face it, my hand reaching for a weapons belt I'd left behind in the Inferno's bridal suite.

I spied only a shadow of myself, black-on-black. Or maybe my doppelganger, Lilith, was moving in that dark world I could sometimes walk into through mirrors. Even the promise of one of Lil's rare personal appearances couldn't breach my frozen self at this lost moment.

I went to the wooden mantel above the fireplace, focusing on the black glass vase embossed with the undulating form of a five-toed imperial Chinese dragon. It drew me as if it too held the magnetic warmth of a hearth fire.

With Quicksilver guarding my sleeping prince at the Inferno, my first dog waited here to welcome me home. Sort of.

Achilles' ashes rested inside the black mantel top vase. I stroked the dragon on it. Now I'd actually seen one breathing fire.

A blackened ring with a green stone was a new addition

to the mantelpiece, a gift from a strange old lady living a half-life at a Sunset City retirement village near Vegas. She'd recently acquainted me with the historic and fearsome medieval Parisian dragon Gargouille, whom I'd just met in person and in massive physical form when Snow had resurrected it from its ashes.

How's that for a brand-new Las Vegas attraction? I tried to laugh at the thought, but couldn't.

I edged down the mantelpiece to inspect an alien addition. Wow. A huge juicy muffin squatted on a china plate. EAT ME, a paper tag ordered in tiny type. Beside it, a mug of tea broadcast the seductive, steamy scent of licorice. DRINK ME, a matching tag read.

Eat me. Drink me. I grimaced at the hidden sexual and sacrificial religious undertones I now saw in those "whimsical" *Alice in Wonderland* instructions.

Muffin. Tea. How homey. I hadn't eaten in . . . thirty-six hours. My body needed this, I knew. So I took my post-battle snacks to the upholstered wing chair near the fire, setting plate and cup on a small end table.

The cranberry-walnut muffin was delicious, but I noted the taste from a distance and used the tea to wash it away until I felt refreshed enough to walk upstairs.

The tall mirror at the upper hall's dimly lit end was as dark and unseeing as an ordinary mirror, though it was made of unusual front-surface glass with a blue cast.

Nothing moved in the looking-glass now, not the ghost of a mobster's daughter named Loretta Cicereau, not my doppelganger, Lilith Quince. Not even my reflection. Did a black mourning pall now obscure the sometimes magical surface?

The cottage interior was a strange blend of an earlier century's country charm abetted by up-to-the-minute conveniences. My bed was an old-fashioned four-poster but I could hear the modern Jacuzzi bubbling in the adjoining bathroom.

I entered the bedroom to find the Enchanted Cottage shocking the patent-leather boots off me once more. Someone or something had suspended a white-linen 1940s frock from a hook beside a closet that had expanded to hold all my clothing, vintage and contemporary. Below the dress waited white lace-up oxford pumps to match. Who'd been playing personal shopper in my closet?

Pulling off my knit caftan, I sat on the dressing table stool to struggle out of the long tight boots, then stood to unfasten the supple battle suit, letting it pool like a small tarpit at my bare feet.

Except for a thin silver chain around my hips, I was nude. You don't put modern underwear beneath the clingy vintage velvet gown I'd worn to the Inferno.

Walking into the bathroom, I winced to remember my humiliating bargain for Ric's rescue, which resulted in Snow's half-stripping that gown from me. He'd somehow even relieved me of the unwanted, shape-shifting silver familiar. I'd hated accepting the familiar back after our bargain was made, but freeing Ric required every weapon I could command, even a thing I loathed.

Betray a lover to preserve him.

I shuddered from cold in that cozy, hothouse atmosphere and eyed the Jacuzzi tub's inviting cauldron of churning water. Chilled to the bone and soul or not, no way would I loll in comfort anywhere while Ric suffered elsewhere.

In the shower, I turned on the water and walked under the spray before it had time to warm.

The Enchanted Cottage got me again. Instead of the icy, punishing sleet I craved to wash me free of my Brimstone

Kiss sins, I got a welcome massage from a hot spray of water.

When I stepped back onto the plush area rug outside, the sight of the blue velvet gown hanging fresh and unwrinkled above the blue-sequined pumps I'd worn to the Inferno gave me another unwanted chill.

Whatever agency had revived and moved the outfit, I'd never wear it again. Yet . . . the cottage had never before revealed the presence of a lady's maid, although I'd glimpsed the kitchen witch and Woodrow, the grumpy garden gnome. Woodrow resented his new yard duty, cleaning up after Quicksilver. Almost three times the size of a small wolf, Quicksilver left a lot to pick up, so I was happy to have less to collect on our Sunset Park walks.

In a weird way, the Enchanted Cottage was soothing my stress by enveloping me in more magical services than I'd ever suspected it possessed.

Bemused, I dressed as it had suggested. The silver familiar ran up my torso in chain form, then whipped down my right arm to circle my wrist as a moonstone bracelet. I was so used to its body-surfing ways that I hardly felt its faint stirrings.

I eyed it askance. That Brimstone Kiss night, Snow had sworn it reacted only to me, despite having morphed from a lock of his hair. I still felt unclean from its connection to a supernatural blackmailer who'd demanded a trivial but humiliating sexual surrender.

Whatever I felt about Snow now—at the moment a noxious stew of anger, self-disgust, queasy gratitude, and confusion—I didn't seem to have become addicted to the infamous smooch. I did not harbor an ungovernable desire for another Brimstone Kiss.

That was encouraging, especially since I'd learned the

usual effect was every woman's dream . . . multiple orgasms. Call me crazy, but that was an awful thing to have foisted on you by a man, or whatever, who'd never kiss you again!

At least I hadn't suffered *that* reaction, that night or ever. Orgasms one at a time are plenty for me. Many women don't ever get even one. At least I still felt only fury from the Brimstone Kiss fiasco, not any desire for a rerun like the idol's addicted mosh-pit groupies.

The crawliest new emotion I could detect was my shame at having reacted to Snow's stagy sexual magnetism enough to be putty in his hands for maybe a minute too long. After a puberty of fighting off punk vamps drawn to my undead looks, I'd always prided myself on independence and immunity to self-serving male lust.

I stared at the innocuous moonstone bracelet the silver familiar had become. *Wait!* I kept a strand of *Achilles*' white hair in a locket.

Was there anything on earth purer to counter a lecherous rock star's long lovelocks? Pure pet love from a Lhasa's floor-sweeping snowy coat? The breed had guarded Tibet's Dalai Lamas all these centuries, tough little warrior-terriers. I could use all the mojo I could contrive.

I dug through the bedroom chest that housed my jewelry until I unearthed the locket holding a coil of white hair curled behind lead-crystal glass.

I opened the locket, removed the crystal oval, and paused. Eyeing the bracelet, I touched the soft circle of hair inside the locket. This risked bridging two beings, two species, two states, life and death. I'd been chancing that a lot lately.

A whiplash of past emotion made me again mourn Achilles' brave death in my defense. I lifted the hair to my

Brimstone Kissed lips . . . a machine-gun blast of static shock numbed my mouth.

The lock of dog hair curled around my forefinger tight enough to cut off the blood supply. Then it spun down to my wrist to twine the moonstone bracelet as if seeking a mate.

Staring, I watched the original bracelet thin into a chain. A string of silver Lhasa apso heads appeared as dangling charms. The silver familiar had produced this particular charm before, but never so many.

Again, the silver reshaped itself faster than the eye could detect, this time into an old-fashioned charm bracelet loaded with keen little items, like the weapons in a game of Clue.

I turned on the small dresser lamp to inspect them all: doghouse, ball and leg iron with lock, binoculars, wishing well with bucket, violin, top hat, mummy case, shackles, globe, scissors, chariot, anchor, high-heeled platform sandal, fan, cannon, war helmet, chair, wolf's head, and thimble.

Some of those charms seemed mighty relevant to me and my recent adventures. I shook my wrist and heard a cheerful jingle. I felt much better. Achilles' hair-lock would be my own little watchdog on duty to ensure Snow didn't retain any smidgeon of influence on the silver familiar.

I spotted my tiny Lip Venom case from the Prada bag downstairs returned to me on the dresser. I always carried the tingling lip gloss as a memory of how meeting Ric had sent me on the first girly shopping spree of my life. So *not* me.

Now the slick little container was a bigger mystery on its own. It was a physical object transported by a wandering CinSim, an object I'd unknowingly lost at what had become the scene of the crime against Ric . . . the vamp-infested underbelly of the Karnak Hotel.

Peter Lorre as Ugarte from *Casablanca* had somehow smuggled the lip gloss case to Rick Blaine at the Inferno, who then returned it to me as a message that *my* Ric was in danger. This was impossible CinSim behavior. Purchased automatons were incapable of free movement, free will, loyalty, or innovation, right?

Later I'd solve how the CinSims had violated their boundaries to smuggle me the lip gloss. Now I needed to get back to Ric, pronto. What if he woke up without me there?

I slipped the Lip Venom into a pocket. Dresses and pinafores had pockets in the forties. I grabbed a white crocheted clutch purse and headed downstairs to fetch my ID and usual items from the Prada bag.

Prada, Irma snorted. She was my inner voice and alter ego since early childhood. Irma acted as my older, more cynical sister in times of trouble, which were becoming a lot more frequent. *You are getting so upscale girly, girl! The designer shopping bags probably belonged to Grizelle, doncha think*?

I eyed myself in the hall mirror. Dressed in white from head to foot, with my pale complexion, I looked like a ghost.

As what persona, I wondered, had the Enchanted Cottage really chosen to dress me? A nurse eager to return to her patient or a bride aching to return to her groom?

Or the ghost of a woman with no soul since the Brimstone Kiss.

Chapter Three

GHOSTS WERE FOR sissies, I'd decided.

Vegas had a lot more potent supernaturals to worry about.

Dolly awaited me under the porte cochere beside my cottage. I slid into the red leather driver's seat and revved her powerful engine. Getting behind that giant pizza-size vintage steering wheel gave me the sense of power and direction I needed right now.

I tooled through the tepid evening dark to the Strip and up the fabled thoroughfare to the Inferno Hotel, a literal "hot spot" on the horizon. The sound of snapping, whipping flames under its main canopy was almost as rhythmic and soothing as the myriad fountains at the Bellagio.

My self-appointed parking valet, Manny, was demon-on-the-spot to take Dolly in hand. His orange scaly skin and gray-green teeth put off some tourists, but he adored classic cars. I was pleased to see that his Inferno uniform had arrived and he no longer wore the ancient Egyptian kilt and accessories of his former employer.

Had he still worn that Karnak costume, I might have lost it and strangled his scrawny orange throat for reminding me what had happened to Ric there.

"You all right, Miss Street?" Manny looked up from admiring the chrome-heavy dashboard.

"Sure. Fine." Easy lies were all I was capable of in public yet.

"That awesome Grizelle has been checking the entryway every twenty minutes. The Boss must want to see you bad."

He winked as I blanched. I reminded myself that I did not want to see the "Boss" in any of his incarnations, especially hotel-casino mogul Christophe, my blackmailer and Ric's rescuer. Talk about having mixed emotions.

"Be gentle with her," I told Manny as he put Dolly in gear.

"Miss Street," he rebuked, "Dolly and me are soul siblings."

This was not encouraging. The last thing I needed was a demon car.

I bumped into Grizelle as soon as I hit the lobby.

She was indeed haunting the entrance in human form, attired in the deep purple leather suit of a fashion victim.

"Any change?" I asked.

"Not with Montoya."

I'd slowed to brush past her but never stopped. Now I clickety-clicked on the black marble path through the casino carpeting, heading for the luxury tower's elevators. Her own noisy spike heels followed.

"The Boss wanted to know the moment you came back."

"So tell him."

"He's due onstage for his first show any minute. You could see him backstage."

"Sorry. Ric's bedside is my priority. Snow can see me *there*."

She stopped. "The show will be late—"

"Showbiz motto: 'Make 'em laugh, make 'em cry, make 'em wait.' Don't thank me."

I didn't want to see Snow anywhere, so leaped into the first open elevator without looking back. Treating Grizelle like a flunky was probably stupid but it made me feel better.

The bridal suite was on the forty-second floor. I stormed through the unlocked double doors to find Quicksilver panting on the other side, already sensing my approach.

Not just bright, Quick was a great big beautiful dog with all the glorious lupine features—big furry ears, big sharp white teeth, and soulfully intelligent eyes of winter-sky blue, a paler version of mine.

His huge jaws accommodated a grin but his furry brow was furrowed with questions.

"It's okay. I'm sitting with Ric tonight. You can stand down."

He trotted after me through the set of double doors into the huge bedroom anyway.

I stopped just inside, aware suddenly that Ric resembled Vegas's undercover senior citizen vampire, Howard Hughes.

Hughes lay abed atop the deserted 1001 Knights Hotel at the fag-end of the Strip surrounded by lush vampire nurses he never touched and a constant IV drip of sterile blood.

Ric reclined here, supervised by human nurses administering constant fluids and blood IVs to replace what the Karnak's ancient Egyptian bloodsuckers had drained from him for nearly a day.

The doctor said his circulatory system had slowed almost to a stop, as if he was being embalmed alive. It would take many transfusions and much time to bring him fully conscious.

Thing was, I wasn't sure that the undead vamps at the Karnak hadn't sucked the soul right out of him while they were torturing him.

Had he been clinically dead when I finally found him

and used CPR on what seemed to be a corpse? Nobody wanted me to revive him. If he had been made vampire, at least in 2013 there were ways to "live" that way

For the time being, he remained comatose. The one moment he'd opened his eyes when we were alone, I was shocked to see that one iris was now pale silver, not the hot coffee-dark Hispanic brown I loved. What was *that* about? Had Ric's near-death experience and my heart-felt second-hand Brimstone Kiss transferred a touch of my iffy silver powers?

That was another reason for my speedy return. I'd stopped en route at one of Vegas's many costume shops to buy a cosmetic pair of brown lenses with no correction.

The lenses would have been cheaper at Déjà-Vous, the vintage shop that catered to CinSymbionts, fans who dressed up as the black-and-white CinSim celebrities. I needed these contacts kept secret, and Snow owned that place.

Snow owned a lot of things in Vegas. I desperately hoped one of them wasn't me.

Ducking around the metal stands and medical equipment boxes to lean over Ric's cumbersome hospital bed, I dropped some water from the bedside table carafe onto the transparent brown lens and lifted Rick's left eyelid with my other hand.

I paused to admire the glittering silver clarity of his iris around the pupil's pinpoint black center. Silver was my medium and a hallmark of my paranormal powers. Perhaps in Ric this was a *good* sign. Or not.

Whichever it was, Ric needed to avoid unanswerable questions when he awoke. The water on the lens drew it to the moisture of his eye like a magnet. Ric's other eyelid opened for an instant.

"Nurse," he murmured, seeing my white dress and probably nothing else.

He drifted back to sleep. I preferred to think of it that way, not as unconsciousness. Not as a coma.

"The doctors," a resonant voice said behind me, "still describe his condition as 'alive.'"

I jerked upright, afraid Snow had seen me slipping in the contact lens. How easy it was to lash out in order to distract him from what I'd just been doing.

"You never believed he was still alive," I spat out as if I lived on Lip Venom. "You'd have let him be carted from that subterranean slaughterhouse as dead meat."

"If he *was* indeed dead, it might have been easier to let him come back as a vampire than what he may be now."

"Ric never settled for 'easy,' and I don't either."

"And don't I know it." Snow almost chuckled.

Every word he spoke, every gesture he made, was like screeching chalk on the blackboard of my senses. It didn't help that he was attired in his white leather catsuit for the evening's performance, with the jeweled fly reminding me how close and sexual we'd been recently.

Thanks to the Brimstone Kiss, Snow was the only man besides Ric to have seen and touched my naked breasts. That fact made my skin crawl. I suppose a lot of women would have loved getting it on with the sexy rock star, even without being under the influence of the Brimstone Kiss.

They didn't have my sexual history, or rather, lack of it.

"I'm still pissed at you," I said.

He folded his arms over his bared white chest with its lightning-strike scars that I'd been skin-to-skin with for longer than I cared to remember.

"If I didn't have a show to do I'd stay here and spar with you. Montoya is a valuable asset. It's good he's 'alive' in any sense. I'm sure your nurselike attire will comfort him, consciously or subconsciously. I'd be careful about kissing him too deeply until he's fully awake. Who knows what hidden influence you might unleash?"

He left before I could sputter at him for sounding like a spymaster weighing the life and death of an operative. Yet his hint that the Karnak vampires might have infused Ric with foreign elements chilled my anger.

I sank onto the bedside chair, taking Ric's cool fingers in mine and lowering my cheek onto our clasped hands. I didn't like Ric's prolonged coma, and I *did* fear what he might be when he awakened.

If he awakened.

Chapter Four

I PLUNGED INTO sleep, too exhausted to dread my usual nightmares. No problem. Desert scenes in living color—all muted shades of brown and beige and sage green—flickered through my fading consciousness. Not my usual crisp black-and-white Silver Screen movie backdrop at all . . .

I felt the silver familiar sidle up my side and snake down my arm. Small beads twined our clasped hands, linking them, binding us together. I tightened my fingers on Ric's hand and dreamed . . .

OUR RESCUE PARTY had fought our way to the dungeon's darkest, farthest corner. I had to push through the Gehenna Hotel werewolf pack and Christophe's Inferno Hotel security forces. They had stopped, frozen silent, intentionally blocking me from seeing what they'd found.

Only his head and forearms were visible. He lay on the naked stone floor, his wrists manacled above his head to the wall behind him. I cursed the bloody gaping hole in his neck . . . not the bite of merely one vampire, but the banquet site of an entire convention of bloodsuckers. The once-human vampires had sated themselves and left. Now a writhing sea of vermin—feeding vampire tsetse flies and leeches—served as his blanket.

They said he was *dead, dead, dead, Delilah,* and tried to hold me back. No one could stop me from falling to my knees beside him, or my frantic application of CPR, the brutal chest-pounds alternating with blasts of my breath blown into immobile lungs.

My thumping heart seized when my old-fashioned revival efforts brought Ric's eyes open for a precious instant. Had my extreme efforts triggered a faint pulse of life in his ravaged circulatory system?

Minutes later, exhausted, even I had to admit that single eyelash flutter had been a postmortem twitch. I bent to bestow what I considered the Kiss of Death on his pallid lips, a final passionate farewell.

As my lips met his, I felt a deep primal pull in my belly . . . desire or a last spasm from my recent period, which always hurt like hell? We were linked by both pain and pleasure and love and loss and maybe now even blood-bonded.

Beyond all human and inhuman hope, Ric responded, bloodstained arms lifting to seize mine and curl fresh-bleeding knuckles around them. The voices that had urged me to give up went silent, astonished.

My passionate farewell kiss had become the Resurrection Kiss. From the interlocking forks of our bodies to the marriage of our mouths and the mated mantras of the past in our minds, I could imagine liquid-silver hope running like hot blood through my veins and into my beating heart, which sensed an answering rhythm in the body beneath it.

Now his dreaming mind stirred to fill mine as I shifted past the shards of *my* dream into *his* oldest nightmare . . .

. . . AND INHALED the scent of charred cedarwood. It masked the spoor of predator tracks in the sand. The air broadcast the musk of animals with hooves and coats rather than fur. I was glimpsing a scene distant in time and geography.

That's when my dozing self realized that I wasn't simply falling asleep. I was falling into Ric's coma, dreaming his dreams. Eavesdropping on his nightmares was like watching his own personal oldie midnight movie.

THE DEVILS SLEEP inside their adobe shelter, their campfire only ashes. The great desert grows cold at night and coyotes always circle the camp, but I sleep against the warm, swollen side of Mother She-goat.

The human *coyotes,* the evil men who illegally cross the border to trade in their own kind, have noticed that the she-goat has adopted me. I hear them laughing into their tequila, threatening to slaughter her and her kids.

"Kids," they call out so I hear and can't sleep, not even in the dark and animal stink of the *corrales.* They use the *gringo* word for children. *Me. I* am one of the "kids" to be slaughtered. At least they want me to worry that I might be.

They suspect I know more English than I should, know more of everything than I should. I often overhear them dealing with the *gringos* for what I can find under the shifting sands.

The scent comes again, sweet as fresh goat milk, heavier than the cactus blooms that fade so fast within their eternal crown of thorns. Jesus had a crown of thorns. I think of the Passion of Jesus when El Demonio whips me and it is better.

"No!" a strange voice calls in my mind. *"Sweet Jesus, no!"*

This voice has a warmer, lighter tone than the shouts of the devils. I heard such sweet voices from the time before the devil *coyotes* came and took me away. I remember as far back as when I first walked. I always found toys around my *casa,* forked branches of mesquite wood I had to wrest from the dogs.

My toys. I remember laughter then, and eyes high above me, watching. Then the twigs were snatched from my small hands, scratching them. Big sandaled feet kicked sand at me, into my eyes.

"No!" the foreign woman's voice is crying, murmuring now, growing used to things as they are, as I have already done.

Small Me is bewildered. My cheeks are wet as well as stung. I touch the dry, whole hide of the lizard my stick has found, hoping another poke will awaken it to play with me.

"No. Agua!" a deep voice shouts. *"No. Agua,"* a high voice shrieks. *"No muerto."* More kicked sand makes my eyes squeeze shut. Blows hit my head and shoulders. I am *"malo!"*

I try to run away and finally do. I find only more forked branches. I can't keep my hands off them. They quiver like live things against my burning palms. They hurt me. Holding them brings curses and beatings. Yet they are all I know.

"Oh, baby, baby, no!" the odd voice in my head cries in English.

I don't fully know that language, but I hear the voice again now and understand it weeps for me. After that, the *coyotes* take me for theirs. They like what my forked branches find, the quiet, dry, dead things. The quiet dead people beneath the desert sand who walk after my pricked fingers bleed on the divided branch. They call them "zombies," and laugh.

I don't know where the visiting *gringos* take these quiet raised dead, but they pay well and ask no questions and when their light-colored demon eyes pass over me they are empty.

The Devil has a forked tongue, I heard once, but the only devils I know are here, all around me. I give them more and more of these People of the Depths, and they still don't like me.

I run away to find people who will like me, but the desert is empty and the devils' legs are always longer than mine. I am always caught and returned to the camp, thrown in with the burros they drag along and beat, and the goats they slaughter and eat.

El Demonio's bullwhip, when they find me again, is longer than the farthest Joshua tree I can see is tall. His whip has a thirty-foot-long tongue he can flick into the herds to kiss me good night. If he misses me, a four-footed friend suffers instead.

I wear pieces of the clothes I steal from the People of the Depths. The flies buzz all day. I crouch beneath shit-caked tails to escape them. I smell worse than the goats, and that keeps the devils at a distance. Even El Demonio.

Yet the night is my time. The night brings peace to the burros and goats. Some nights the sweet smell off the desert almost covers the stink.

And then *she* comes, the Virgin of Guadalupe. She wears a white gown and a blue cape. Her arms are always outstretched. I know she would wrap them around me and shelter me in her cloak, only there is no room because the cape spills forth bloodred blossoms that smell sweeter than any goat milk, sweeter even than burning cedarwood.

The flowers fall at my feet as I sleep.

Then comes bright day again and the burning sun of Hell.

No, no, no, the distant voice is chanting. *I don't want this dream. Take this nightmare away.*

I realize the Virgin is praying for me. I'll never forget the pain and beauty in her voice.

THE VIRGIN IS angry with me. No . . . sad. She no longer comes to see me. I smell only filth and blood and death. My thoughts buzz like the big blue flies that torment my friends with hides. My thoughts also swarm with anger and hatred. I look at the wood in my hands that raises the Dead day after day and think how a bigger branch would gash the devils' filthy heads. But the desert grows small brittle trees. I need metal to fell a devil, brown or white, and they have guns.

Despite them, I'm growing bigger, and hunch to hide it. *Cabro-niño,* goat-boy, they call me. Some always guard us stock when the others are gone. My escape plans now consider the comings and goings of the *gringos*. El Demonio is hardly here and hasn't used his whip on me for months. I've learned to sneak close to their sleeping place and listen. I've stolen food they don't miss, even a handful of shiny papers as brittle as cactus flowers I buried.

When I dig them up to study, the pages throng with naked people doing what goats and donkeys do to birth young. The animal young are so soft and smell sweet. I guard them as much as I can, but some are destined for slaughter and all for pain and servitude. Still, I know that these pictures do not celebrate new life but are as dirty as the looks the drunken demons slide my way. If I did not smell so bad . . .

Bastards, the woman's voice curses, sounding furious.

That can't be my Virgin of Guadalupe. She would never use such a word. But I agree. I like this voice. It is brave, as angry as the Virgin would be if she were still visiting me. I doubt the Virgin would like the strange dreams I have now. She would shower no roses on me.

For on the back of these evil pages is a beautiful colored picture showing a cigar like the *gringo* devils smoke. I can almost smell its pungent scent, and in that cigar's huge cloud of smoke appears a new Virgin.

I unearth and stare at her every chance I get by the light of the abandoned, dying campfire.

She wears no white gown and blue cape. She wears nothing but a sunset-purple skirt. Glittering bridles of gold coins circle her flanks and chest. Her hair is not hidden by a veil, but hangs long and black and glossy. No flea and fly bites mar her pale arms and face. Her skin is as white as the mountaintop snow, her smiling lips are rose-red, and her eyes are the blue of the Virgin's cloak.

I feel a strange, warm sense of recognition. I pretend the Virgin has come to me again, after all this time. She smells as clean as the night wind. My heart opens like a desert flower and my whole body feels such a heavy, alien ache that my head lolls back on my neck.

I feel her lips there, leaving a kiss despite my filthy skin. I know they're as soft as a burro's nickering lips in the palm of my callused hand.

Her lips have settled on my skin to draw from it like a horsefly, but the sensation is painless, soothing. My body basks in unthought-of happiness.

I reach up to touch my neck . . . and touch no silken hair, no smooth skin. I capture a furred, struggling form, a mouse wrapped in hairless hide.

In the ember glow I open my fist to reveal a leather-wing-wrapped bat, its eyes small black beads between tiny but donkey-tall ears. The mouth gapes wider than the Virgin's cloak, bloody fangs poised to bite again.

This vampire bat preys by night on sleeping cattle and burros and goats . . . and one goat-boy who dreams alone by a dying fire in the desert.

I release the struggling form. I live off the Dead, as the

coyotes do. This bat at least feeds off the living. The wings *whoosh* as they flap away.

A flare of light makes me gaze with horror at the fire. It's catching flame again, reaching for my beautiful Virgin's image, curling black along the edges.

I try to snatch her from the greedy tongues of fire, my fingertips swelling with instant blisters. She vanishes before my eyes, burning me as she departs: my hands, my heart, and the new dowsing rod at the fork of my body.

Jesus, Mary, and Joseph, I hear my alien voice crying for the lost Virgin, for me. *No more.*

And so I understand when I am asleep and she comes to me again, many years later and miles away, after I've long since put my desert memories in a barbed-wire-bound box.

I'd grown into forgetting her and the desert and the devils, but the bat has been at my neck again. This time it wore El Demonio's face behind an exotic mask of twin pharaohs and wanted to drain all my life and soul. This time I might sink into sleep forever.

I lie there lost, and then I sense her coming for me again as if in a dream to save me. . . .

AND THEN I struggled to open my eyes.

Ric and I were alone in the bedroom–turned–hospital room. He was still in a coma. I'd been dreaming, rehashing recent all-too-real nightmares, Ric's brutal childhood past and my anxiety for his future, not to mention my own guilt and fear about what he might have become after my intervention.

Ric's eyes remained shut, his breathing so deep and slow I had to watch his chest for a full minute to see it.

I studied our interlocked hands. The silver familiar had bridged them as we slept, adapting a form both comforting and a bit alarming to a good-girl graduate of Our Lady of the Lake Convent School.

A rosary.

Sweet Virgin Mary and Sweet No-Longer-Virgin Me!

I'd been channeling Ric's coma nightmares. His near-death experience had unearthed the trauma of his enslaved childhood. I knew Ric would rather die than betray the zombies he could be used to raise. I would rather die than see him become something he loathed.

To ensure getting him back whole and sane, he needed more than unconscious fantasies about visitations from Virgin Mothers and belly dancers, or even of his best girl in avenger mode.

I now knew I needed more too . . . expert help beyond doctors. And I knew just where to get it.

Unfortunately, it was on the opposite side of the country.

Chapter Five

TWELVE HOURS LATER I turned my hybrid rental car down a winding gravel driveway. Main roads in pricey suburban Virginia ran alongside fenced and thickly wooded acres. The impression was of farms rather than residences. All the streets had Scottish names. I was leaving Braeburn Glen Lane for a private entry.

Autumn would turn the winding driveway ahead of me into a carnival of falling colored leaves. Now everything was green and lush. The rental car nosed around descending curves until a low, sprawling house came into view.

I parked in the circular driveway before the double-doored entry and got out, smoothing my narrow navy skirt.

A heavy dark cotton suit would make me swelter in Las Vegas this time of year. Here, the summer temperature was lower but humid. I felt the film of a nervous sweat.

I'd bought this vintage suit in Wichita because I loved the 1950s details: white piqué collar and matching cuffs, eight brass horse's-head buttons down the jacket front and a singleton at each short cuffed sleeve.

The silver familiar retained its discreet default mode: twin of the so-not-me silver hip chain I bought in the crazy rush of first romance with Ric. I figured the hidden familiar was *too too* tasteful to clash with my current outfit's brassy touches.

Tough. I'd chosen this suit for this mission, for what its

color and cut would unconsciously imply to the people I wanted to see inside this pleasantly expensive house on the groomed and expansive grounds.

I even wore the Suit Era's regulation white, wrist-length gloves and carried a neat navy patent leather envelope-style pocketbook. I took a deep breath before ringing the small round doorbell button with one gloved forefinger. Avon lady calling.

I hoped they answered soon. My heart was beating like I was auditioning for the class play. A knob turned on the right-hand wood door, allowing me to glimpse the occupant as it opened slightly.

A woman. Good. She registered my gender and opened the door further. The handsome blonde looked forty-something but was probably a poster child for the Washington, D.C., "well-preserved" matron set. She eyed me quizzically.

"Is your husband at home as well?" I asked. "I have important news for you both."

My vintage apparel had subtly distracted her, causing a faint frown to materialize on her smooth forehead.

"Yes?"

She eyed my face again, hard, then silently stepped into the shadows behind her, swinging the door wide.

The entry area was paved in black marble, so the heels of my open-toed pumps made a military marching sound over the polished stone.

The living room was carpeted in deep shrimp plush wool, gorgeous and madly expensive to maintain. I almost wanted to step out of my shoes before I walked on it. Couldn't afford to lose one iota of authority, though.

Her husband was reading a thin newspaper in an easy chair, hair thinning on top to match, half-glasses perched on a strong Roman nose. Old-fashioned habits died hard in this house.

He looked up, glanced at her, then eyed me again, rising slowly.

"My name is Street," I said crisply. "I've come from Las Vegas with unwelcome news, but it's not dire."

"Ric," the woman breathed beside me.

The newspaper was flung aside, the man striding toward me.

"Who are you, young woman?"

"Street, Delilah Street. I'm a . . . professional partner of your . . . of Ric's."

"Partner?" he echoed dubiously.

"A private investigator. Sometimes we work the same cases."

"And your news?"

"He's under doctor's care but is doing fine."

"Doing fine from what?" the man asked.

I felt a hand on my bare forearm. The woman's fingers were icy. I fought a sudden, rare urge for tears. She loved Ric too.

"Our guest needs to sit down, and so do we, Philip," she told him. "Miss Street said the situation isn't dire. She's come all this way to spare us a shocking phone call. Let's not make an interrogation of this."

She ushered me to a love seat opposite her husband's chair and then paused. "I suppose we should hear the rough scenario first, then I'll get some coffee and we can relax a bit."

"No relaxing here," he grumbled, sitting again to brace sweatered forearms on his thighs and lean forward, eyeing me like a murder suspect.

The woman's sigh was almost inaudible but she sank down beside me.

"Ric was found," I began, "with many superficial wounds and one more severe . . . stab wound in the neck that wasn't fatal, although he'd lost a lot of blood."

The laundered account came tripping off my tongue with a few hesitations that, I hoped, would be taken for difficulty recounting the hard facts.

What I really had trouble doing was converting a gang vampire torture attack to something human. My instincts told me to go slowly. I had no idea what the Burnsides knew about Ric's consultancy work or even if they believed in the Millennium Revelation and the supernatural beings it had revealed. A lot of people still didn't.

"My God," Mrs. Burnside said.

She had a longer bio on Groggle than even her husband. A respected psychologist, her given name was Helena and her maiden name had been Troy. Luckily, she was beautiful enough to carry off that bit of parental hubris.

Her silky caftan's turquoise-and-purple floral print gleamed jewel-like against the yellow silk-upholstered sofa. Now I knew where Ric had acquired his polish and manners. Not a thing was out of place in this spacious formal room except for the crumpled tent of the tossed-aside *Washington Post* print edition.

"Which hospital is he in?" Mr. Burnside asked me.

"It's a . . . private facility, to keep his condition secret. We think . . . he fell into the hands of drug lords."

"It's his damn obsession with those endless Juarez murders!" Burnside told his wife, his eyes furious over the forgotten half-glasses. "What's the matter with the boy? He could have had a top FBI position here in D.C. He needs to stay out of Mexico."

Her faded blue eyes closed momentarily. "That's the problem, Philip. He *needs* to pursue old demons there."

I almost jumped. Did she mean "demons" literally?

"How badly was he injured?" she asked me.

"A lot of surface wounds on his chest and arms and face—"

"Cigarette burns," Philip Burnside spit out. "Bastards."

"And the stab wound in the neck."

"Probably happened when they captured him," he added.

"He's in a light coma and the doctors actually like that," I said. "It gives his system time to repair. It's not his physical condition I'm most worried about but his mental one."

Helena Troy Burnside was standing and nodding. "Miss Street is right. New torture is the last thing I'd want him to undergo. I've got to get out there," she told her husband. "The university jet—"

"I'll handle it." He reached for a cell phone on the end table.

"My work with Ric's case brought Georgetown a lot of good press, they'd be happy—"

"I'll handle it," he repeated. "You pack."

"Come with me, Miss Street," she said, turning to me. "You can tell me what to take for the current Nevada climate."

She was gone in a swirl of floral silk as I rushed to catch up to her. I didn't want to be left alone to answer any more questions from Ric's eagle-eyed "father."

Ric Montoya described himself as "adopted," but told me it'd never been made official. So. How should I regard this otherwise childless couple? I understood they wanted him to take pride in his heritage, not deny it after his ordeal. That's why Ric's "chosen" last name. Philip Burnside had rescued Ric as a "wild child" in a raid. Dr. Helena Troy Burnside had saved his sanity. Then they'd housed him through high school and college. Maybe they were just "the folks."

The stairs were steep but she had already vanished up them. I ran up after her, finding a bedroom with the door flung wide and her soft-sided suitcase already open on the bed.

She was used to sudden trips out of town.

"What?" she asked me. "Temps in the nineties in June?"

I nodded.

She paused to study me as sharply as her husband had.

"That ensemble would be murderously hot to wear in Las Vegas. It suited perfectly here, especially to make instant subconscious points with my ex-military husband. I see you're a clever young woman, Delilah Street. I'm glad you're a, an . . . associate of Ric's. You can take off the kid gloves now."

I blushed as I remembered my First Communion-style white cotton gloves. My outfit had been designed to imply military formality, of course, to ease me into the presence and confidence of an ex-officer.

But Mama was a high-ranking shrink, and she was even harder to bluff.

"You blush? I'm liking you more and more, my old-fashioned girl."

I hated the blush, but a Snow White complexion hides neither minor social shame nor the flush of major arousal. Ric liked my blushes too.

Helena was whipping out casual slacks and tops from her wall-long closet in quick succession. I nodded or shook my head just as fast, so she soon made an apt selection.

"I won't be able to stay long. I'll change and be right down. Philip should have arranged for the plane by now. Don't let him scare you. He's worried sick but can't show it. Needed to take some action."

I nodded and ran back down again to find her husband pacing in front of the fireplace.

"Oh, it's you. I'll drive you two to the airport."

"My rental car—"

"Papers in the glove compartment?"

I nodded.

"I'll see to it."

"I've got a return plane ticket—"

"Give it to me. I'll take care of it."

I pulled the ticket out of my purse, much easier to do without the gloves, which I stuck in the purse in the ticket's stead.

Burnside lowered his voice as I heard Helena's footsteps on the stairs. "Ric's going to be okay, isn't he? He's a tough kid. Did he—?"

I knew what he needed to know by the furtive, haunted look in his eyes he didn't want his wife to see.

"He didn't tell them anything they wanted to know," I said with all the conviction I felt in my soul. "Not a word. No matter what."

He nodded, relieved and yet guilty about that. Then he left to fetch the car around before his wife could see his troubled expression.

Helena's khaki slacks and azure silk-knit sweater set enhanced her similar coloring. It wasn't vanity, just habit. She looked cool and elegant and was watching me just as closely as I summed her up.

"How long have you gone without sleep, Delilah? That lovely pale complexion of yours looks as blue as skim milk under your eyes."

I blinked at her, too weary—and wary—to admit I was afraid of Ric's dreams.

"We'll talk on the plane," she told me. "It'll be more comfortable."

The endless drone of jet engines and those cramped rows of seats? I doubted it. Here it was so clean and peaceful I would have wanted to stay if I wasn't frantic about getting back to Ric.

At least I'd made it home to meet the parents.

Chapter Six

I HAD TO hand it to Helena Burnside.

She didn't smirk once when I was Alice-in-Wonderlanded to Andrews Air Force Base southeast of D.C. and driven up to a waiting small private jet. Shortly after we were up, up, and away as the sun sank slowly in the west. It was almost 8:00 P.M. and the three-hour time difference meant we'd chase the sunset all the way, arriving at about the same hour we'd left.

I'd gone wide-eyed when I spotted the turn-off for Andrews and don't think I blinked until we were airborne and sitting in cushy leather chairs that had more positions than a yoga class.

"You can catch up on your sleep," Helena suggested, "or we can have a drink and talk. Your call."

"We need to talk and I need a drink."

"Fine. Any druthers?"

I'd followed her to a built-in cabinet whose exotic wood doors concealed an awesome wall of branded bottles. Guess this wasn't Alice's Restaurant, as in the old song by Arlo Guthrie, but Alice's Bar.

"I'll concoct something," I said. "*Hmmm,* no white chocolate liqueur aboard for an Albino Vampire."

"This is usually a guy's plane, Delilah. No sweet girly liquors allowed. An Albino Vampire? That does sound intriguing."

Wait until she met Snow, which she would. He may

deny being a literal vampire but he *was* a money-sucking albino casino owner, so I'd named the drink to irk him.

"Vodka's a manly drink," I said, spotting a crown-shaped vodka bottle of cut and frosted glass touched with gilt. *Hmm,* this Regalia Gold was something decadently pricey the Inferno bar might feature. "I'll whip up something apropos. I seem to have a way with spirits."

Into a highball glass I poured a jigger or so of the high-end vodka—though I'd have preferred pepper vodka—and a half jigger of cinnamon schnapps, then five ounces of orange juice from an under-counter mini-refrigerator. Feeling frisky, I added two jiggers of orange-flavored cognac from a fancy little bottle. Finally, in went a scant half-jigger of rich thick red grenadine to sink to the bottom. Sweet! I did it all over again and brought the second drink to Ric's mother.

"It matches the sunset," she commented, lifting her glass. We settled into our chairs to watch the sun painting the horizon dark watercolor hues through the windows. "We should be shadowing the sunset like Sam Spade on a case all the way west."

She eyed her vivid glass. "*Umm.* Subtle yet spicy . . . for modern women like us. What will you name this concoction, Delilah? It looks like a Tequila Sunrise."

"No tequila in it. How about a . . . Vampire Sunrise?"

"Don't vampires retire to their coffins to sleep all day about then?"

"So says the legend. Let's drink to that."

We clicked rims even as I was thinking that, whenever they grabbed some shut-eye, the Karnak vampires threatened to become the major force in Vegas. They made Cicereau's Gehenna werewolves look tame.

I kicked off my shoes.

"Panty hose? Why don't you peel out of those unbearably unbreathable things in the executive washroom?"

I grinned. "How did you know I don't usually wear them?"

"No sane woman does these days."

No sane woman. I thought that over while I wriggled the hose down past the shy silver hip chain in a bathroom three times the size of a commercial jet's biffy. I'd worn nylon bikini briefs underneath the panty hose to make them slide on better, so I was still decent enough for an Our Lady of the Lake Convent School girl.

Pretty sharp lady, Irma said as I rolled the hose into a ball and washed my hands. *Watch yourself around her. We don't know where she's coming from. And she* is *a shrink. She'd frown on me for sure. Want you to dump me. You've already had me on "mute" too long.*

I won't dump you, I told her. *It's just been so stressful lately.*

Because you've been doing things you didn't want witnesses for.

That's enough! I slammed a door shut in my mind. I'd never done that to Irma before.

Yet she was right. Helena Troy Burnside had transformd Ric from a feral child before the Millennium Revelation into a secure and dedicated man in a world where nothing was certain anymore but change. She wouldn't be easy to fool.

I returned to the main cabin to find her pensively watching the sunset blaze of purple and orange turn lavender and yellow, like a fading bruise.

What should I tell her about Ric?

With his paranormally healing tongue, my wonder dog, Quicksilver, had licked Ric's skin clear of the sores from the vampire tsetse-fly bites. I couldn't conceal that ragged hole in his neck from when he served as the "catch of the day" for the Twin Pharaohs' bloodthirsty undead minions at the Karnak Hotel three nights ago.

I sat down, my calves rubbing together and giving me a mental flash of how inciting Ric would find my bare legs under this prim, uniform-suggestive suit. *I'm your stewardess, Delilah. Fly me,* as the old airline ad went.

Here I didn't even know if Ric was coming out of his coma, with or without a soul, if you believed in that sort of thing, and I was thinking about us having sex.

Helena looked away from the window to me as I picked up my Vampire Sunrise for a sip.

"How long have you and Ric been sleeping together, Delilah?"

"Ah—" I got my mind doing mental math. That would short-circuit intimate memories. "A few weeks."

She was smiling at me like the Madonna, all-wise and a bit rueful.

"I'm not exactly Ric's mother," she said, "but the relationship is close enough to that, so I don't really need to know certain things. You might want to shutter some strong memories. I do sense you and Ric share unconventional and trying childhoods. You seem to be a good match. And, no, mild bondage during sex is not abnormal, especially when the woman is terrified of losing control because of a forgotten childhood trauma. It might be just what the doctor would order. In matters of sex, if it's effective, it's right."

This "old-fashioned" girl was flushing like a red light. I could feel the heat suffusing my pale chest and face, scarlet against the white and navy of my outfit. I was vividly patriotic at the moment.

She laughed softly.

"Are you . . . psychic?" I asked. "You can read minds?"

"I always was intuitive," Helena explained, looking out the window as she sipped my "Sunrise, Sunset"-colored cocktail. The sentimental song about love and life ran through my mind, not vampires. "It was really only close observation, in the way Sherlock Holmes practiced it. His methods, as he called them, were learned from a brilliant diagnostician, a doctor Arthur Conan Doyle studied under."

"Really? The fictional Sherlock Holmes was inspired by a doctor?"

"Maybe there were always those who had millennial gifts." She sighed, perhaps thinking of Ric. "After the Millennium Revelation, I found my 'insights' became much more literal. I can 'see' high-impact or traumatic incidents from my patients' past. It's not like 'reading minds,' though." She eyed me again. "It's like surfing Web pages really fast. Skittering images and emotions. I sense a lot of upheaval in you."

"I can't imagine why," I said ruefully. "I lost my dog and my home and my job in Kansas. I'm supposed to be an orphan but I saw my double being autopsied on *CSI V: Las Vegas*. I came here to find her and found Ric instead. So far."

"You're not one to give up, I can also sense that. I do see mirror images colliding around you. And, like Ric, you had no one to nurture you as a small child. No one to hold you and keep you safe. No one to tell you that you were a pretty and smart girl, as every girl is, in some way. I suspect those raging, suppressed infantile emotions will manifest themselves in your adult powers."

"I'll have delayed tantrums?"

"Maybe not. You're a very sensible and mature young

woman, Delilah, a bit too much so. You're so demanding of yourself and others. Your relationship with Ric has been good for you but now you must concentrate on being good for Ric. I hope not, but what's just happened to him could undo the years of reclamation work I did to overcome his brutal childhood."

And she barely knew the half of it. I drove out my haunting worries about his torture at the Karnak by concentrating on something happier, another lovemaking session she really didn't want to spy on. I could sense her regard blurring and withdrawing.

"Yes, you can block my unconscious 'readings' if you concentrate," she told me, unaware that I was putting up barriers by thinking about sex with her patient-son.

Some things never change, Millennium Revelation or not. When it comes to parents and children of any age neither generation can quite bear to think of the other "doing it."

"Thanks for the warning," I said. "But, just to follow up, you say Ric is trying to overcome my, ah, position phobia about lying on my back in dentists' and doctors' offices in, um, bed?"

"He was a very bright boy who survived a nightmare childhood and underwent years of therapy. Yes, he can help you, Delilah. More important, I sense that he badly wants to."

Shoot! I blushed again. Time to get away from my intimacy issues and back to finding out what Ric is really about. Wanting to help must be our mutual weakness.

"So what *is* your relationship to Ric?" I asked.

She considered. "He's not quite a son to us. More like a beloved foreign student who came to live with us for a long time."

"Does your husband know about your expanded intuition?"

"No. Philip is a military man by profession. He must remain skeptical to maintain equilibrium. He can't even face Ric injured and in pain, not because he doesn't care but because he'd choke on helpless rage. He'd want to raid Mexico and make someone pay."

I thought hard about those awful piano lessons I suddenly remembered having at Our Lady of the Lake school to block her enhanced intuitions. Did I want to correct their assumption, that Ric had been captured and tortured while out of the country, not in Vegas? No.

"Why does Ric keep returning to Mexico?" I asked instead. "His memories must be horrendous."

"The men who held him captive then are crime kingpins now, drug lords and human and unhuman slavers. They're exploiting and torturing his people. He needs to stop them."

"I saw—" I began.

"Saw what? Oh." She drew back as if I'd slapped her.

I'd been unable to keep the image of Ric's whip-scarred back from my mind's eye.

We both sipped Vampire Sunrises, girding ourselves.

"What did he tell you about the scars?" she asked finally.

"Nothing. I saw them while he was sleeping. He keeps me—I imagine all women—from touching his back, even clothed."

She fidgeted in the cushy chair. "That's not good but understandable."

"He was just a *child*!"

"Nine when he was freed."

"Who? Why?"

"El Demonio. A fittingly obvious name," she said bitterly. "This 'demon' surnamed Torbellino now heads a dozen criminal operations all over Mexico and along the U.S. border. When Ric was captured, El Demonio was only a border-running *coyote*. Ric ran away, and when he was inevitably caught and returned, he was whipped. El Demonio had a thirty-foot bullwhip he liked to unfurl, at long distance or short."

My stomach told me I was getting nauseous. Our shared dream had made me feel the unimaginable brutality of using such force against a valuable child laborer. I just suffered from a lack of love. Ric had been hated.

"One whipping like that would have killed him," I said, amazed he was still here to talk about.

"Ric ran away and was caught, and then ran away again. And again."

"Even though he knew—? That's crazy."

"It was how he kept his spirit from being broken. If he let those men intimidate him into giving up on freedom, it would mean nothing if and when he finally got it. They call it 'fire in the belly.' Ric is probably the only person who challenged El Demonio and lived.

"So," she went on, "from what you've said, he either didn't fall into El Demonio's hands this time, or the man's henchmen didn't know whom they'd captured. If he was tortured lying on his back, as the frontal injuries you describe indicate, his identity would remain secret."

I clasped my arms against the chill I felt at her medical, logical approach to this atrocity. Perhaps to keep her motherly feelings at bay?

Even worse, I now knew that *two* demonic forces would love to recapture and try to break Ricardo Montoya yet again, this El Demonio and his associates as well as the Egyptian vampires.

She saw my goose bumps, picked up her doffed cardigan, and laid it over my shoulders. That motherly gesture nearly undid me. Nobody had touched me or my clothes that I could remember, nobody had ever dressed me until Ric started undressing me, which was another thing entirely.

Still, her words haunted me. I was supposed to be glad the Pharaoh freaks had wanted Ric's throat accessible while they tormented him with leeches and vampire tsetse flies and held a group suck party at his neck?

"Delilah, I can't glimpse your thoughts right now, but I can tell you're overdramatizing," she said softly.

Darn right.

"Your husband hasn't even the slightest notion that you're able to see into other people's heads since the millennium turned?" I asked, wondering what that would do to the trust in a marriage. Who was I kidding? In my relationship with Ric too.

"No. Washington bureaucrats only subscribe to facts. They are the most inadaptable creatures on the planet."

I wondered if either of the Burnsides knew Ric could dowse for the dead and guessed they didn't. Ric had been only nine when he was rescued and the wife began to work with him. He was only fifteen at the Millennium Revelation. He didn't start dowsing for the dead again until he was out of college and training at the FBI's Body Farm. Helena admitted her enhanced "intuitions" could be blocked. An adult Ric would surely hide his resurrected powers to avoid worrying his only parental figures, as he had concealed his disfigured back from me. The Burnsides probably thought El Demonio had kept him prisoner as a goatherd.

"Will he look the same?" she asked, visibly nervous for the first time.

I nodded. Yes, he would.

Especially now that I had sneaked that long-wear brown contact lens into the Inferno bridal suite.

He would *look* perfectly the same.

Only time and a return to consciousness would tell if he was the Ric I knew and loved.

Chapter Seven

I SEE THE Vegas entertainment scene has gotten dark and dangerous," Helena Burnside commented as the cab dropped us off at the Inferno entrance at 9:00 P.M.

Manny was there to sweep open the SUV's sliding door for us.

"Welcome back, Miss Street. I'm sorry to see Dolly has not accompanied you."

"Dolly?" Helena asked after I'd tipped Manny and we were walking inside. "And just what is that parking valet's, ah . . . derivation?"

"A low-order demon, usually harmless. Not that he wouldn't snap up a careless soul if he could."

"And . . . Dolly is a friend of yours?"

"My car. Demons love classic cars and Dolly is choice."

She eyed me hard. "You named your car Dolly?"

"She's an estate-sale cream puff, a '56 Caddy Biarritz with pointed chrome bumper bullets up front that could take out a tank nest."

"Oh? Oh. My, this town is colorful, and so are you."

"As you noted, my stuffy outfit was for the benefit of the resident D.C. bureaucrat."

"I bet you show my boy a whole different side."

"He's shown me a whole different side of myself."

"It's that way. I see. What should I expect with him, Delilah?"

By then we were in the elevator wafting upward.

"That's why I went to you. He's been healing well but is still comatose. I think his mental state needs expert addressing."

"You aren't the person he'd most respond to?"

I couldn't say that he'd already responded to me way above and beyond the call of mortality just by staying alive.

"He's gone so deep inside himself the present is lost. I think he needs to come back from his past."

"A rather profound analysis, Delilah. Thanks for getting me here."

"Thanks for coming."

We smiled at each other outside the suite.

"Bridal Suite," she read aloud from the embossed gold plaque beside the double doors. "Is this a portent of the future?"

"It's what the hotel owner had free and big enough to accommodate around-the-clock nursing care."

"A most accommodating hotel owner. Any reason why?"

"Christophe is quite a . . . prominent figure around Vegas. It's hard to know what his motives are."

"Yet you accepted his generosity."

The statement, although true, grated on my sense of independence.

"I didn't have a choice. Ric wouldn't want his condition made public and paparazzi always stake out Vegas hospitals hunting celebrities and sensational stories. Human hyenas. That could compromise Ric's government consulting work and he'd hate that."

She nodded. "So would Philip." I saw Helena gather herself, despite her formidable poise. "Well, shall we see the patient?"

"I'M SO GLAD you're back, Miss Street," a frazzled nurse said. "Our patient is getting fractious about having a sponge bath and your dog is not having any of it either."

Sponge bath? In a way that was a good sign. It showed that Ric's deeply ingrained reflexes to keep people from seeing his disfigured back were still operative.

"This is Mr. Montoya's mother," I said. "She's a doctor." So I was fudging between a medical and academic title . . .

"Dr. Helena Troy Burnside, Georgetown University." His mother extended a hand. "Thank you for taking such good care of my boy."

"Of course we would. To see such a young and handsome man so unmoving . . ." She choked up, perhaps envisioning Ric through a mother's eyes.

Helena Troy Burnside actually was doing that, but was married to sterner stuff and quashed the emotion. "Forget the sponge bath for today. I'd like to examine him first myself, then spend some time evaluating his condition."

The nurse nodded, swept open one of the double doors to the bedroom suite, and stood back.

Quicksilver waited inside, muzzle lifted over his intimidating teeth like a black awning. He thrust up his snout to verify my and the nurse's familiar scents, and assign one to Helena.

"It's okay, Quick," I told him. "Ric's mother is here to see him."

The dog backed off to the side but remained alert. Even Helena lost her eternal composure enough to sidle past, eyes averted. She'd be very steadying to distraught and disoriented patients.

Once she glimpsed the hospital bed accessorized by

metal medical equipment poles and tangled cords, she moved tensely forward, leaning over Ric.

"Delilah," she said without looking over her shoulder, "you probably keep more comfortable clothes here. Go ahead and change while I see what's what with Ric." She sank onto the chair's edge, setting her belongings on the floor and leaning forward to take his hand in both of hers.

With Helena here to fend off unwanted back exposure and Quicksilver on guard, I slipped away, yearning to switch my confining fifties clothes for low-heeled mules, low-riding jeans, and a simple knit top.

The bridal suite offered separate bedrooms for overnight relatives. I'd chosen the nearest one. I changed fast and skittered back into the main area to find Snow there. Rats! We'd arrived right between his 7:30 and 10:00 P.M. shows.

"Where have you been?" he asked.

I wanted to snap, *None of your business,* but since he was providing everything Ric needed, I bridled my tongue and thoughts.

"I fetched Ric's mother. She's a famous psychologist."

"A medium might do more good," Snow suggested. "So he's still comatose?"

I nodded.

"May I meet the mother or do you want to stand there glaring at me all night?"

Looking him over, I weighed whether a skintight bejeweled leather jumpsuit was too much glitter-rock macho for a dignified middle-aged professional woman. I finally nodded permission. It would do Snow good to meet a formidable female who wasn't rock idol bait.

He shook his mane of white hair. "I don't know whether you or your dog is the fiercer bodyguard."

"Someone who uses a white tiger for a security chief is hardly one to talk."

He passed me without further comment and entered the bedroom, me following and wondering how Ric's mother would handle a long-haired albino wearing sunglasses.

At our approach she looked up, then gave a little coo and said, "Oh, my God! It's Cocaine. I saw your farewell show in D.C. when the Sins were still touring. Helena Troy Burnside."

You could have picked my tongue off the floor and rolled it up like a very long cigarette paper.

"They were fabulous," she gurgled on. "*You* were fabulous."

Helena Troy Burnside a Snow groupie?

He smiled politely, an expression *I'd* never seen before.

"I own the Inferno now. The road life gets old. I'll get you mosh-pit passes to the show." He turned to regard me over his shoulder. "I'm sure Miss Street would love to accompany you, and her dog is all the security your son needs, believe me."

"Oh, I believe you," she answered, while I ground my teeth at their incredible coziness. Snow was a very unreliable witness on all counts as far as I was concerned.

"Meanwhile," he said, "consider yourself a guest of the Inferno, with the use of an adjoining bedroom. Anything from the hotel restaurants and shops that you need or desire may be charged to the room, gratis."

"Anything that I desire?"

She let the question hang to the point of flirtation. I supposed Snow could use that Ole White Magic anytime, on any woman. Except me.

"I desire my son's recovery," she added with a smile. "I won't need to stay long but much appreciate your princely hospitality. Delilah didn't tell me who our host was."

"She probably didn't want to ruin the surprise. She's that way. Likes to keep things to herself to tease and intrigue and enchant others."

"Really?" Helena let her clear blue gaze rest on me. It was as demandingly honest as Quicksilver's. "She's something of a magician. But then, so is a charismatic stage performer like you. If I need to stay overnight, I'll try to make your show, but I doubt I will. Ric seems to be doing well under your generous care."

He nodded and left without another glance at me, although with those dark sunglasses who could be sure?

"I had no idea," I told her, "that you were a fan."

"Oh, I wasn't. My resident fifteen-year-old boy, though, wanted to impress a girl who was, so I provided wheels and chaperoning."

"Did he—?"

"Who, Ric?"

"No, Snow."

"'Snow?' Oh, of course. A natural nickname. You must know him well."

"Can anybody really know a man who wears sunglasses all the time?"

"His albino eyes must be ultrasensitive to light."

Yeah, like the "light of truth."

"Did Snow give the so-called Brimstone Kiss to the mosh-pit groupies then?" I finally asked.

"Oh, yes. Ric's would-be girlfriend was suitably impressed. She jumped higher than all the other teenyboppers, and some pretty mature women, in fact, to snag a kiss. Funny, that reminds me that they never dated after that. Guess Ric didn't like the competition."

Or the girl had no time for fifteen-year-old Ric after getting the Brimstone Kiss. That, at least, wasn't going to happen to me. I still would rather hiss and spit at Snow than kiss him. Maybe I was exaggerating my anger to ensure my independence. Whatever worked.

I turned the conversation back to Ric. "You sound like you're not staying long."

"Don't have to. I've already established a deep suggestive state in Ric."

"You used hypnotism on him?"

"Long ago, yes. Now, I just have to draw on our common memory bank, as it were, and run the images through my mind. I'm rebooting his consciousness, you could say, overpowering the evil done to him with a speed-reading course in good nostalgia. He'll awaken and act normally soon. He'll slowly recall what happened to him only when his subconscious fully ramps up over the next several days. The shock will be muted, like a bad dream. The pain will be distant."

She bent over to lay her cheek on his hand, then straightened with a happy sigh.

"Since you've bonded with him, you should be able to do something of the sort too. Just sit by him, remembering the happy times. You can even remember the hot times." She laughed to see my latest blush. "Men respond very strongly to such stimuli. He could do worse than come to consciousness again with a wet dream. This is a bridal suite, after all.

"I'd suggest you reinstitute sex with him before he's totally himself again. That immediate and pleasant sensory memory will do more to override the ugliness than anything I can do."

Imagine. A guy's "mother" prescribing sex to his girlfriend. Helena Troy Burnside was a cool lady, just like Irma said.

She stood and gazed down on him. "I'm so proud of him. He overcame so much to become the strong, confident, well-adjusted man you fell in love with. This won't knock him down again now that he has you. Trust me."

"You're leaving? You told Snow you might not—"

"I could hardly tell a rock idol that I don't have time to accept a personal invitation to his show. I'll instruct the nurses not to disturb Ric until tomorrow."

She eyed me oddly. "I have a feeling that you can heal Ric more than I can. Sit by him for the night. I've opened his mind and senses to pleasant things. Your love is what he needs now. Don't be afraid to give it no matter what form it takes."

"But—"

"Philip will be anxious for a firsthand report. I'll catch a cab outside. This is Las Vegas. Getting in and out of town is a snap, particularly with a private plane waiting. Call me anytime to report or ask questions. I've left my card on the bedside table. Perhaps Ric will bring you home for Thanksgiving."

She embraced me lightly at the door, her smooth, mineral-powdered cheek brushing mine. For an instant after she'd left, I felt a sickening replay of interviews at the group home with prospective adoptive parents who never returned after that first meeting with me. I felt abandoned and swallowed a lump of concrete in my throat.

Get a grip, Irma told me. *Be glad she's not the clingy mother type. She's a smart one. You saved Ric's life, now you get to have him to yourself and be the light of his eyes when he comes fully conscious. Enjoy, Street! You so do not get that part of things.*

I walked to the wall of windows. The Strip was lighting up as the sun had set and blackness pooled over the valley.

It was that magic twilight time just past sunset when Vegas's garish self-advertisement felt easy and muted.

A deep breath cleared my mind and emotions but I was still tired. I put Quicksilver on guard in the main room, where his food and water dishes were kept, and walked back to the double doors and up the single step to Ric's bed.

The nurses had settled down in their rooms and one would give Quicksilver his evening walk, she told me.

That must be a sight on the Strip!

I sat in the chair Helena Burnside had left, watching Ric. His mother was confident he'd be all right, why couldn't I be? Maybe because I feared the Resurrection Kiss as much as I'd feared the Brimstone Kiss. Or more.

Chapter Eight

THE NEXT MORNING, after I awoke stiff and with tingling feet, I was booted out by the attending nurses.

With Ric in Helena's time-slowed state, I had a choice of occupations.

I could sit by his bedside day after day, waiting for something to happen, or I could do what I'd always done, push out into the bigger world and make something happen myself.

The heave-ho seemed a perfect opportunity to do some quick, minor investigating.

Most of the things that had happened to me and Ric in Las Vegas since we'd met a few weeks ago had changed our lives and almost caused our deaths.

I needed to understand what every dedicated reporter needs to know: who, what, when, where, and why.

And I knew just where to begin.

TO ANYONE REARED in the Midwest, calling upon someone at home without notice was incredibly rude.

I cringed to park Dolly's huge shiny black presence, so like a stylish hearse, outside Caressa Teagarden's Sunset City residence, all exterior shingles and peaked roof, a gingerbread cottage for the Millennium Revelation.

I neared the front door but still I hesitated to knock. When "Sun City" retirement communities cropped up in Sunbelt states more than half a century ago, they were viewed as enlightened communities that encouraged the aging population to unite in child-free environments. The oldsters would never have to worry about breaking a hip by tripping on abandoned roller skates and could travel anywhere to see their families.

The Millennium Revelation changed even that.

Nowadays "Sun*set* City" is the Shangri-la for older people. These post–Millennium Revelation communities for the aged thrive in the hammock-shaped "smile" that the warmer Lower Forty-eight states create, from North Carolina to northern California through all the temperate zones in between.

Instead of signing up for "adult living" that would morph into assisted living and then medical bed-care until death, aging people could have themselves sucked and tucked to a fare-thee-well, then sign up to live on indefinitely in a physical virtual reality state as long as their money lasted.

It wasn't that different from the previous plan, except that weird science and possibly supernatural mojo were involved.

Of course, the Sunset City owners and operators never revealed exactly *what* they were doing. It was a "proprietary" program, rumored to rely on cellular and cloning experiments by the Koreans, later snapped up by the elusive Immortality Mob.

The artificially preserved oldies but goodies were happy. Their offspring may have resented not inheriting the family estate but could look forward to an extended self-care plan also. (I hate to call it an "extended life" plan. To me, it didn't seem so much life as the illusion of it.) I guess a lot of people had settled for that even before the Millennium Revelation.

Still, my unannounced visit was Caressa's fault. She wasn't listed in any directory either by a phone number or an email address. She was also "at fault" for following me from the Wichita Sunset City to this one near Vegas. Unlikely coincidences like that were starting to make me highly suspicious.

When I'd "interviewed" her recently, pretending to follow up on our mysteriously canceled Kansas appointment earlier, I'd originally made the usual mistake of the arrogant young. I'd considered her the typical rambling old dear living in the past. She was also the only "old-looking" person I'd met in Sin City, with the exception of Howard Hughes.

Caressa Teagarden had managed to take the "mummified" look out of the museum and return it to the parlor. I admired her for ignoring the siren call of eternal youth and beauty so easily achieved today.

"Oh, it's you again, my dear girl," she greeted me after I finally knocked on her unlocked front door and she edged it open. Unlike the usual glamorous Sunset City residents, Caressa's slight body curled over a supporting cane and her pale facial skin was crossed with tiny arroyos begging for a flash flood of daily moisturizer. I can't say how pleased-pink and lovely she looked.

"I was so hoping for another chat," her raspy voice welcomed me. "Don't pussyfoot around. Come in and sit down."

Hospitality was a challenge at Caressa's place. The furnishings all looked as elderly as she did.

I'm not fat, but I am farm-girl solid. So I perched precariously on a tiny wooden rocking chair with a needlepoint seat that seemed like it belonged in a Victorian child's playroom. It was meant for adults back in the days when five feet tall was common for both men and women and thirty-five was the average life span.

"You can stop clutching that silly briefcase on a strap. Put it down."

I leaned my messenger bag beside the chair, feeling the silver familiar's charm-laden weight on my wrist as if reminding me of its presence.

"You reporters always have more questions," she told me. "Hurry them along. I take a daily afternoon nap, you know."

I let her continue to take me for what I'd been, a TV reporter, trying not to stare at the dark blue veins atop her hands.

Was her life's blood darkening and pooling in her extremities rather than running through them? Should I even be bothering this slip of shaky mortality relying on a semi-holographic appearance?

"Well?" she demanded.

"I do have questions. You mentioned your real name was Lila and you had a twin sister Lili, whom you lost track of in young adulthood."

"So? The Depression separated a lot of families and siblings."

"I may have been separated from a twin at birth," I told her.

"That is the beginning of a great story."

"Not if it's your life. They called me Delilah, after the street I was found on as an abandoned infant."

"Delilah. Most old-fashioned. Most naughty! It would have done well on the screen in my heyday, Delilah."

I gritted my teeth. Her coyness was getting as cloying as brown-sugar candy. "I saw my double on TV recently, in a bit part."

Caressa shrugged. "It's a start, but the internet is better for ambitious young people like you these days."

"She went by the name of Lilith."

"Are you accusing me of something, Delilah?"

"Knowing too much?"

"About what? Dragons?"

"We were . . . are Delilah and Lilith. You and your twin sister were Lila and Lili. Isn't that too much of a coincidence?"

"I was not named after a street," she said icily. "We took stage names, my sister and I. Both Lili and Lila were popular names in the nineteen twenties. Too popular. When my Hollywood career took off I made myself Caressa Teagarden."

I have a wordplay mind. I couldn't help musing that DElilah and LiliTH almost equaled DE-A-TH.

That reminded me of Vida, the nineteen-forties mistress of Vegas werewolf mobster Cesar Cicereau. I'd seen her in a photo with him and the daughter he'd later had murdered, Loretta, whose bones Ric and I had found in Sunset Park. Vida. Wordplay. Vida equals Avid equals Diva.

"Did you ever know a beautiful brunette named Vida?" I asked

"A woman named Vida had a bit part in *Gone With the Wind,* and then she was, *whoosh,* out of Hollywood."

To Vegas? Where she later was made into a vampire at the behest of Howard Hughes, so a glamourpuss could bite him into eternal billionairedom?

"And you never saw or heard of your twin sister again?" I asked Caressa.

"No." Her expression took on an elaborate wide-eyed overinnocent look suitable for silent films. "Only once, many years later, the same year they made *Gone With the Wind* with that gorgeous, neurotic English girl and *The Adventures of Robin Hood* with that pretty Flynn boy and *The Wizard of Oz* with that chubby girl. I could have played the Good Witch Glinda in *Oz,* did I tell you?"

She had. Apparently it was a chorus with her.

"I finally had the right vocal range, and could outtrill Billie Burke anytime."

"Nineteen thirty-nine, that was a record year for top-notch Hollywood films," I prodded her.

"Yes, well." Caressa looked miffed. "Lili sent me that ring I gave you on your last visit that very same year. She said the stone was a piece of the prop mirror from the Disney *Snow White* of 1937, and both of our careers were kaput, but if I cared to ask who was still 'the fairest of them all,' it was she. Lili. Not me, Lila."

"But you were twins."

"Not identical emotionally. And blood doesn't guarantee love. Nothing does. Rivalry and hate are easier."

"I still want to find my double, Lilith."

"Wear the ring I gave you. Maybe it'll attract Lili," she cackled. "Deal with her and see if you like it."

"You're saying the *Snow White* mirror fragment in the ring might be . . . magic? Wasn't everything simply a drawing in a cartoon movie?"

"One would think so. Lili was always a lying chit. You think sisters are a gift? *Hah!* Those animation artists worked from life. Snow White was acted by a real girl. They could have made a prop mirror as an artist's model or a promotional device.

"The mirror was a very popular character in the film. But now, who needs actors when you can manufacture CinSims? The world has gone to the dogs, my girl, and the werewolves. Watch out that you don't get bitten. Especially by film fever," she whispered.

She'd sounded just like the Wicked Stepmother disguised as the witchy crone urging Snow White to "Come, bite."

I already had been bitten by the Millennium Revelation and Las Vegas so I didn't intend to nibble on anything new. Still, I'd reexamine the cheap green ring on my mantelpiece. First, though, I needed to learn more about angels and demons.

"Last time I visited, you also claimed you were the last living descendant of a man, Jean-Christophe l'Argent, who carved gargoyles on Notre Dame Cathedral in Paris to fend off a devouring dragon that lived in the Seine."

Sacre cow! It was only when I repeated her ancestor's name that I remembered *argent* was French for *silver*. Silver was a word and a metal and a color that had a lot to do with me.

"I 'claimed'?" she challenged me. "Do you disbelieve Caressa?"

"Hardly. I came here to tell you I recently saw the darn dragon with my own eyes. Gargulie, isn't that its name?"

I'd deliberately garbled the dragon Gargouille's French name. It was pronounced "Gargooee," and had been adapted to the guardian "gargoyles" her ancestor carved to defend the holy place from the river monster.

Her eyes in their frills of wrinkled skin shone like black diamonds.

"You saw Gargouille himself? In all his glory? Aren't you the clever minx? The way you walk is hard but there may be hope for you yet, Delilah Street. Where did you see him? When? How was the old devil?"

"Where? I saw him four days ago, raised in service as a tugboat in a dark river under the Inferno Hotel."

"Yes? Y*eee*s," she purred, her transparent hand clutched into an ecstatic claw over her bony, age-freckled chest. "Dark rivers are very good for dragons. Running water is both sacred and profane."

"You said that the people of medieval France threw maidens and murderers into the Seine for Gargouille once a year. Why?"

"Could it be a dragon is a cousin to a unicorn? Thus the maiden? You were a virgin when you first started out to see me at the Wichita Sunset City, Delilah, but you aren't now. It's a good thing you didn't see Gargouille until you were no longer a maiden and are not yet a murderer. He will devour both extremes, but leaves the middle alone."

I blushed that she seemed to know my private life. Did all Las Vegas? After Ric's spectacular almost-death . . . maybe.

"Why," I asked, "were innocence and guilt sacrificed together to save the people of Paris?"

"Virtue and vice in single doses can be lethal. Nothing and no one is all good or all bad."

"It's true that the Gargouille I saw was tamed, reconstituted from his own ashes thrown into the subterranean river. The creature was resurrected, and then . . . ridden. Then it vanished under the waters, which had been shallow."

"That is only possible because half a millennium has passed since the dragon was banished. Do you remember by whom?"

"A holy cardinal," I repeated her tale, "but Gargouille's master this time was hardly holy or a cardinal of the Church."

"How do you know?"

"A modern-day rock star? Decadence is the life-form's middle name as well as lifestyle. Your day in the early-twentieth-century movies was far too genteel for that sort of thing."

Caressa's head thrust back on her scrawny neck. She laughed until I feared she'd shake it completely off.

"My day! The Roaring Twenties? Cigarettes, bathtub

gin, gangsters, and the Black Bottom? Sex, drugs, and income tax cuts? We were debauched beyond words, my dear girl. Or could be, if so inclined."

She had a point. People tend to think the "old days" were quaint antiques stored under dusty bell jars atop doilies when they were "modern" at the time.

"Don't make such a face, Delilah! You're still learning and may live long enough to benefit from it if you ask the right questions of the right sources. So. I think you know who harbored Gargouille's ashes. Dragons never die. You have seen my distant cousin, Christophe, raise one. He must not yet be a murderer if he can do that. Yes, I knew he was raising Hell, if not dragons in Vegas, why else would I come here? Tell me all the rogue is up to these days besides making that modern cacophony on a stage?"

I sat on the ridiculous kiddie-size chair, reduced to mental sputtering.

I could hardly seethe on about an extorted kiss to a crone clearly a hundred years or so old. Wild youth. I could hardly confess my fears about violating the natural order by reviving my lover with a secondhand soul kiss when I sat with a creature whose natural order had long since been outlived.

Cousin Christophe?

Not a murderer. Yet. As I wasn't. What a relief.

But a holy cardinal? Those guys were supposed to be celibate, although that didn't always happen, particularly among the Medici popes.

Christophe? Celibate? The notion took my breath away. Cocaine never slept with his groupies. Could the sexy bastard possibly be holier than *moi* now that I was no longer virgin?

Chapter Nine

ONCE I'D HAD my eye-opening interview with Caressa Teagarden, I realized that while Rick dozed like Sleeping Beauty, I could continue bopping around town putting a whole lotta loose ends together.

Now that Cesar Cicereau had decided I was too much trouble to kidnap for a "Maggie" attraction at his Gehenna Hotel, I was only vulnerable to the odd freelance entrepreneur happening to recognize me and my signature bright blue eyes. Sunglasses and occasionally wearing my gray CinSim contact lenses fixed that. How lucky I was to live in a city where "fans" turned themselves into duplicates of the black, white, and gray Silver Screen CinSims.

As Dorothy finally learned in *The Wizard of Oz,* there's no place like home.

So that afternoon I was back at the Nightwine estate sitting in the carved Gothic chair across from Hector's desk, swinging my feet because they didn't quite reach the floor. I'm sure Hector liked all his visitors feeling about nine years old.

Only one question occupied me now: how best to catch and fix the film producer's always fluttering attention.

A primmer Sharon Stone move seemed most efficient. I crossed my legs. I may not be a needle-thin femme fatale with the cool aplomb of a Hitchcock blonde but I'm not baked eggplant either.

The Fat Man perked up like a burp of morning java in the glass bubble atop a vintage coffee percolator.

"I have some complaints about the accommodations," I drawled Bette Davis style.

A gasp of indrawn breath was his first, almost musical, reaction. Then came the lyrics.

"My dear Miss Davis. I mean, Street. The Enchanted Cottage has never served as a long-term domicile before but it is a full-scale replica of the film's original set. You should be as cozy as a tick in a trachea in it."

His figure of speech recalled serial killers who left insect "calling cards" in victims' throats, so my own was fighting an automatic gag reaction. Hector no doubt cherished that as producer of the world's many *CSI: Crime Scene Instincts* forensics TV shows.

It should be noted that "forensic" meant everyone—producer to viewers—could wallow in the ooky details of death and dying in the name of educational scientific entertainment. Just as everyone could ogle the provocatively clad contestants on the many reality TV dance shows in the name of supporting the arts.

"Exactly what do you find wanting in the accommodations?" Hector pursued. "Are the accessories too vintage or too modern? The cable channels too stuffy or too racy? Is the jetted tub too big or too small? The four-poster bed too soft or too hard? The morning porridge too hot or too cold?"

"That's just it, Nightwine!" I stamped my dainty little foot—in my case a respectably large size 8—in its peep-toe forties pump.

Nightwine leaned his immense frontage as far forward as it would allow him to cop a foot fetishist's view. I had pity and crossed my legs again, swinging the shod foot in question.

"The Enchanted Cottage is *too* accommodating," I said.

"*Too* accommodating?" he demanded. "You live there virtually rent-free, safeguarded by the highest-tech security my estate can buy. Your meals and maid service are gratis. Your oversize dog can't even make a deposit without a yard gnome whisking away any offending matter. How can a damn Enchanted Cottage be too accommodating? Hedy Lamarr and Dorothy Lamour never complained."

"Sarong girls? You used the Enchanted Cottage to host CinSim starlets from the casting couches of the nineteen forties?"

Nightwine sniffed his indignation and clawed a fistful of crunchy black and white "wings" from a huge wooden bowl on his desk.

"I'm not talking CinSims, Delilah. I am speaking of the actual actresses."

Hmm, Irma said. *That would make our roly-poly bug-biting host and landlord a hundred years old. Or so.*

I studied Hector's face and beard under the purple velvet beret he affected today.

All visible hair was totally black; could be dyed. Plastic surgeons had been injecting fat into faces for decades. Given the oddly immortal cast of characters in post–Millennium Revelation Las Vegas and medical advances verging on the miraculous, Hector could well be an Extreme Senior Citizen.

"Anyway," I said, shaking my head to refuse the wooden bowl he nudged toward me, "my point is that the cottage offers me no domestic outlet whatsoever. I'm complaining that you're not making good use of me."

Of course I'd *meant* to appeal to all his worst instincts, which were ninety-nine and forty-four hundredths percent *im*pure. Ivory Snow detergent he was not.

"I have failed to make good *use* of you, Miss Street? Tut-tut. Shameless! How may I atone?"

I fluffed my hair and crossed my legs in the reverse order. I conjured a classic starlet pout by thinking of the Misses Lamarr and Lamour. Hedy Lamarr, I recalled, had made a luscious Delilah in a Technicolor epic named after both her and her leading mane, Samson. He still got top billing.

"I'm only asking for a bit part," I said. "Nothing costly. Just that Lilith cameo you promised me."

Hector Nightwine's eyes grew so dark they made the clichéd "beady" obsolete. They seemed the utter absence of color, rather than any shade. But black is the result of all color, so that made sense. I guess a black hole was the other side of everything.

Anyway, both of Hector's BB eyes glittered like lumps of coal that had just found Christmas stockings for the duration.

"Of course," he whispered. "We film an autopsy each and every day for some *CSI* program somewhere on the globe. For your appearance, I suggest we simply reverse the direction in which the corpse faces. We can leave in the single maggot although it need not decorate a nostril. The little curve below your lower lip, perhaps."

"And of course leave the clothes off? I don't think so, Hector. I hate typecasting. I don't want to play the usual naked lady on a stainless-steel autopsy table. I want to play an onlooker, a witness."

"But Lilith was—"

"A one-of-a-kind corpse, Hector. Hard to achieve in these days of media overkill. You don't want to dilute the 'Maggie' brand, do you? I recall you saying when you first broached this idea to me that my resemblance to your most famous corpse should be hinted at, should be taunting, haunting, an echo, a face in the misty night, a familiar refrain . . ."

"Like in that great classic novel and song and 1944 film *Laura*! Yes, of course. Director Otto Preminger's eternally enchanting tale of a beautiful dead girl with whom the investigating detective falls in love. Wonderful resonance! Brilliant. Lilith is 'my' Laura. How could I have not seen it?"

He had gone where I'd led. Waft a whiff of necrophilia over the media barons in these decadent post–Millennium Revelation times and you were a genius. I was ashamed to recall that Snow had suggested this very scenario of getting myself onto Nightwine's *CSI V* autopsy set. Now it was working like a charm.

"Do I need to do anything but show up?" I asked.

"What? Ah, no. Yes. I-I-I'll send fresh 'sides' to the cottage for you to study tonight. You can't think I'd use you as a mere underpaid extra? Of course I'll give you a few trifling lines. That way you'll earn my *CSI* minimum of six hundred fifty-eight dollars and sixty-three cents a day for a speaking bit role, my dear girl."

He beamed over his fistful of munchies. "Even a teensy bit part will help make you eligible for an AFTRA card, if you so desire, Delilah." He chuckled until his velvet gut shook like a bowlful of earthworms. "Then you'll be able to hold old Hector up for real dough when I want you for a spare shot."

Not my ambition. I was taking a risk even by letting Hector play on the notion that the "Maggie" corpse was possibly alive and well and on the *CSI* set. I could end up a kidnap target of Dead Celebrity profiteers again, but the film bit might also flush out Lilith in more than my mirror, from which she'd been absent recently.

AFTER LEAVING HECTOR'S office, I engineered a secret flying visit to the Inferno and Ric in the bridal suite.

He was still sleeping like a baby, except for a totally hot smudge of five o'clock shadow the nurses couldn't—or wouldn't—tame. I stroked the back of my fingers over his soft/rough cheek.

The color was returning to his Latino complexion. He was still so dead to the world after Helena's visit . . . I couldn't help remembering that well-fed vampires in their caskets always had a sinister healthy glow in the lushly colorful Hammer films.

HECTOR'S "SIDES," OR dialogue pages, caught up with me about six that evening at the Enchanted Cottage after I got back from sitting with Ric.

Godfrey brought the pink-colored papers to the cottage on a silver salver, alongside a tiny crystal glass of Madeira. They included two pages of wordless action and two freaking pages of monologue.

"It's a good thing a former TV reporter is a fast study," I grumbled to Godfrey, "or I'd never memorize this in one night."

"The master quite adores the idea of a teasing reappearance of a Lilith look-alike on *CSI V*," Godfrey said. "The Las Vegas version is his foundation show. I took the liberty of scanning the monologue before I came here and modifying a few rough edges. It's a good bit. I grew up speaking lines by masters like Dashiell Hammett, Raymond Chandler, and Anita Loos."

"*You* wrote it, Godfrey?"

"I 'massaged' it. Master Nightwine has the big ideas. I finesse the execution."

I hoped he didn't mean "execution" literally, not with modern *CSI* shows sometimes using authentic corpses nowadays.

Chapter Ten

WHEN I SHOWED up at the designated address on Pinto Lane the next morning at 6:00. I realized that the soundstage was *right next* to the Vegas coroner's facility.

Wow. There must be a sweetheart deal between the city, L.V. coroner Grady "Grisly" Bahr, and Nightwine's production company. I suppose there were cases when Hector needed additional corpses in a pinch and the morgue had plenty of unclaimed ones. It would also give the unknowns an unprecedented chance at recognition.

Visiting the morgue earlier with Ric, I'd taken the windowless beige brick building next door for some warehouse, never guessing its equally gruesome purpose.

Once inside, the building was as echoing and barren as I expected. A clerk gave me a long form to fill out. I used mostly made-up answers. I didn't want specifics of my life in Wichita or here on record. For address, I put down the street number of Sunset Park, not Nightwine's estate address, on the odd-numbered side of the road. Hector'd get my pay to me.

I'd worn my gray contact lenses and a big head scarf with a fake fringe of blond bangs. I would unveil only when and where Lilith's famous raven locks, white skin, and vivid blue eyes would blossom for the camera.

After reading my part, I knew just where I could shock and awe to greatest effect. Before I delivered my lines and my own little surprise, I planned to find out all I could about the setup.

I returned the forms and clipboard to the attractive strawberry blonde on desk duty.

"I hope this is all right," I said, sounding flustered. "This is my first real job in film." She eyed me with the disdainful pity you get only from people who really want to be in your shoes but are too proud to admit it.

"This is not 'fillum' work. It's a weekly TV show and you're being paid just one level up from an extra. The only reason you got the job is you're packing a thirty-eight."

"Ah, I'm not armed."

"I meant the bra size, honey. Producers are all the same," she added bitterly.

I checked out her armaments, not my usual routine, and saw she'd supplemented herself to a .45 caliber. No wonder she was bitter. She outgunned me and still only manned a desk. Although I'd hated my early development in that area, I'd found as an adult observer of such things that Mother Nature's sense of proportion is always best.

"Now sit down until you're called to Makeup," she told me. "Better amp up your cell phone web service; you're going to get a very numb ass. The body is the diva around here. It takes at least six hours to prep it for the camera."

"Six hours." I sounded suitably impressed and discouraged. "For a wax dummy?"

She leaned over the desk, eager to showcase her superior qualifications and straighten me out. "You're the dummy if you think it is wax. We need better than mannequins for today's reality TV audiences. Every corpse is either a tranquilized actor or a fresh corpse, in which case the family gets the blood price."

Blood price, Irma repeated. That's what Sansouci had called the killing of Cicereau's daughter and her lover.

I shivered, authentically, to hear an echo of that horrific real-life murder in this place of phony or manipulated death.

Strawberry Blonde snickered. "Hey, the fee is a grand's worth of fuel for the family tank, sister. And relatives get special footage to show at the funeral and family reunions forever and ever amen. Greatest remembrance of a loved one ever: fame."

"Can I order a tape of my . . . bit?"

"Naw, the videographers don't have time to cut custom tapes of tiny bits like yours." She really emphasized "tiny bits."

"If you're anywhere near the corpse, and as"—she eyed the clipboard—"Female Autopsy Tech Number Two, you should be visible in the background, huh, *Lillian*? Come on! Are you trying to play off that Lilith-Maggie mania thing? Lame, kid. Get an agent and new screen name when you get your AFTRA card."

"Why would I want this card?"

"For your career. If you actually say lines on a Hector Nightwine production it counts, even if they and your image end up on the cutting room floor."

I winced.

"What's the matter now?"

"That 'cutting room floor' expression takes on a whole other meaning after the Millennium Revelation."

She shook her highlighted head of laser-crimped curls. "Amateurs! God save us!"

Would-be experts, God bless 'em, Irma hissed in my ear. *They are so easy to snow . . . oops! Excuse the expression.*

I winced again as I returned to my plastic-shelled seat to kill time. Strawberry Blondness was right.

My ass would be numb in no time.

So this is show business.

"YOU'RE AS PALE as a ghost," the makeup man fretted as he eyed me in the big dressing room mirror.

He was an angular perfectionist whose spray-on tan had crystallized into the sparkling spackle of hard brown-sugar candy. While he frowned at my face, I tried to ignore the host of television "ghosts" milling behind our backs in the mirror, each clamoring for attention. Only I could see them, thanks to my newly discovered "gifts" involving mirrors.

"Keep your eyes still," he ordered.

I hadn't counted on how many corpses might haunt this *CSI V* set and associated areas, with its reputed actor and real corpses. Luckily, mirrors were confined to the dressing rooms.

"No foundation makeup," a guy with a clipboard declared. "The Great God Nightwine wants her pasty-faced. It says so right here: dead-white skin, black hair."

I'd swept off my scarf and blond bangs the minute I'd been called into Makeup, but had retained my gray contact lenses. I wasn't going to do the "final reveal" until I was on camera and it was too late for anyone to stop me. I suspected a full-out imitation of Lilith would cause a storm on the set.

"I'll redden her lips a bit, then," Mango Man said, "just so they show."

"She'll be wearing a Plexi visor in the scene," a girl assistant noted, "so her hair doesn't need doing."

"Then what the fuck's she doing in my chair!" he

demanded. "I nearly broke my back for four hours over a corpse that will not soften to the needed degree of rigor mortis. And you there, Missy Lillian. There you sit, just as God made you. Well, let God and Max Factor help you. I'm outta here."

The moving chair spun and I was ejected in the same sharp motion.

Mr. Clipboard smiled mechanically. "Wardrobe next. Just scrubs and mask."

As I followed, he frowned at the clipboard, which was nice. I was tired of being the one constantly frowned at.

"Oh, and a custom prop, I see," he crowed. "Aren't *we* special? I hope somebody already knows about this because I only herd human actors, not vermin."

He pushed me into another room where a short, stout woman ordered, "Strip to your skivvies."

"Hi," I said first. "I'm new at this."

"Stripping to your skivvies?" She rolled humorous brown eyes behind funky old frames. No one wore glasses anymore except to pose as an intellectual or a dot-com billionaire.

"I'm new at that too. Is there someplace less public—?"

"This is it. I'd stand between you and the door but you've got at least eight inches of height on me so it wouldn't do any good. Come on, you're as good as wearing a tent; that's all medical scrubs are. You'll only need to lose your top."

I peeled off my knit tee as fast as possible while the little woman stretched up to cover my shoulders with a pale green cotton hospital gown. I bent my knees to help her as she tied me up the back.

"There you go"—she checked the clipboard that had been left—"Lillian. My name's Erlene. Relax. They don't need you on set for a whole eight minutes."

To a TV newsperson used to thinking in thirty-second slots, that was an eon. I leaned against the makeup chair and ventured a question.

"I've never seen a corpse up close before, Erlene. How will this go? Does the body get rolled in first and the actors gather around?"

"Depends on the director. If he or she wants more action they make a big deal of the camera following the bod being rolled in and then the cast is all 'We gotta do this fast. STAT!' That kind of thing."

So the bodies could come from anywhere, the morgue next door, Central Casting, or . . . a secret suicide room.

"Will the body . . . smell?"

Erlene laughed heartily. "Holy corpuscles, no, girl! They're not all really dead, although the show likes that idea to get around. Those actual, dead corpses are ratings boosters. Not many volunteer for that, and even those don't smell. Most are spanking fresh; smell less than a gurney monkey. The production company needs to film the person committing suicide off-set and then being placed on set. Legal proof of the voluntary death.

"In those instances, we have a real coroner on set for the close-up on the Y-cut, forehead saw, what have you."

"Don't the actors . . . faint sometimes?"

"Listen, faking the right moves and doing them, what's the difference? You'll see. The stars on these forensics shows get paid hundreds of thousands a week. Not so a glorified extra like you, but make a good impression and . . . who knows? I see you're slotted for a little solo." She eyed the clipboard and winked. "'Know' the producer or the director, huh? That's okay. Pretty girl like you gotta play what she's dealt."

Erlene was beginning to sound like Ric's D.C. mama.

I was beginning to believe them. Being force-fed self-esteem was quite a trip.

"Say, Lillian girl," Erlene went on. I think she'd sensed my stage nerves and was trying to sound like my number one ego-booster, Irma. "These are weird props even for *CSI V.* Should play like flesh-eating beetles in Peoria." She winked at me again. "My advice is: stay cool, remember your lines, and have an agent on insty-dial. I'm gonna do you up as a ghoul to remember."

"Ghoul?"

"That's what the crew calls the autopsy-room cast members. Nothing personal, sweetie. Now hold still."

Erlene plunked a rubber headache band on my forehead with a Plexiglas shield flipped up above it. I spotted some props laid out on the kind of steel tray that normally holds surgical tools. She picked one up, an exotic silk orchid. It was one of those luridly colored and spotted varieties that look more like giant alien leeches than flowers.

Before I could protest the notion of pinning a corsage on an autopsy tech, she snapped a watch on my left wrist and held up the empty steel tray.

"Spread 'em," she huffed in a voice like a trained seal.

While I struggled to imagine what bizarre rite this was, she nodded impatiently at my hands.

I . . . spread my hands atop the tray, my fingertips making fuzzy-focus spider-leg reflections, while Erlene slapped a set of adhesive long red false fingernails on my short, naked nails.

I gazed down into the tray at my own blurry but stunned expression. What an unforeseen and nutsy problem! I'd planned to slip out my contact lenses to unveil Lilith's and my signature baby blues just as the cameras rolled.

With these scimitars on my fingers, how could I ever

pop out the lenses? Only my bright blue natural eye color would evoke Lilith. Nightwine would be furious, I would have wasted my time, and the whole stunt effect would be ruined!

I could live with that but I didn't think Hector would.

I stood there helpless, thinking madly. I was now your typically prepped actor-corpse, tied in a winding sheet, masked by clear plastic, with hands I could only hold in front of me.

Mango Man popped around the doorjamb, frowning at me as usual. "The scarlet Vampira fingerstakes are superlicious, Erlene, but wouldn't an autopsy tech be wearing latex gloves?" he asked.

"Yes, if we were going for verisimilitude," the stumpy wardrobe lady barked back. "This is one of Nightwine's wiggy 'dream sequences.' Wait a second. One . . . last . . . delicate touch of glue. There. That'd hold through the sinking of the *Titanic*.

"Just place her on her spot like a department store mannequin and hope this rookie knows how to hold as still as a corpse and say her lines when the finger of God the director points at her to come to life."

This time I was escorted onto the soundstage itself. My pulses spiked. Cables on the floor connecting lights and cameras were passé now. The set was a highly lit centerpiece glittering with stainless steel like Grisly Bahr's real autopsy chamber.

I was guided into position behind the autopsy table with a stunning view of the main event: a naked male corpse minus legs and hands. I fought the prurient urge to see just how high up the torso had been truncated. Three other gowned actors shuffled beside me, knowing their places and taking them, unlike me.

I turned away, using the heels of my hands to shove up the Plexiglas shield. I started to claw at my eyelids with the flats of my fingertips and finally expelled each contact lens. I didn't care where they landed. Contacts nowadays are cheaper by the dozen.

Luckily, actors are pretty self-absorbed, especially just before a director calls "Action." Everyone else was fussing with their hair and wardrobe too. I pulled down the shield and turned back to face the corpse.

"ACTION!" ORDERED A commanding male voice from the darkness beyond.

I jumped like a nervous racehorse, then froze. I was a media pro, dammit, at least on camera, if not as an actor. And I'd already learned some fascinating facts about the links between *CSI V* and corpses.

All I had to do was follow the other actors' actions with my blue eyes under glass. My lines didn't come until "Special Effect #1" happened: *Corpse is cut.*

That's when I was supposed to jump (and I bet I really would), look at my wristwatch, and mutter Hector's gibberish I'd memorized. Frankly, I thought the Orson Welles of Sunset Road was losing it.

I watched the surgeon's scalpel press hard into the legless corpse's shoulder to draw the left arm of the Y incision.

"Cut!" another voice from the dark shouted.

I jumped again, rank amateur that I was, but I was sure the camera was in loving corpse close-up by this time anyway.

The "surgeon" quickly stepped aside to be replaced by a costumed "double," the actor playing the surgeon.

"My God," he began, "the skin is heaving . . ."

Special Effect # 2 spewed out a spray of what I took for cauliflower florets.

"I hate it when that happens," the actor-surgeon sputtered with disgust.

I recognized my cue from the script and glanced at my wrist, absent a watch but sporting the world's ugliest orchid.

Oh, and it also hosted one slick pale macaroni of a Lone Maggot glued to a salmon-and-purple spotted orchid petal. I sensed the camera lens bearing down on me.

Are glorified extras on *CSI V* sets supposed to heave on camera? I thought not, and began regurgitating my previously meaningless lines, suddenly understanding the cockeyed genius of Hector Nightwine, if not fully appreciating it.

This would be a truly over-the-top unforgettable moment for me and Lilith and little Maggie, who also had a glorified extra role on *CSI.* Thus spoke Lillian, Tech # 2:

"Our jobs are sad and gruesome to some, yet even the hardest soul can find some guarantee of the goodness of Providence. It rests in the flowers. All our powers, our desires, our food, are really necessary for our existence, but this simple blossom embellishes life. Only goodness gives extras.

"It's all right, Doctor," I said, finishing my interminable monologue, "this small ejected creature you see here is an 'extra,' one of death's tiny unborn messengers sprouting new life from old. Our highest proof of an ultimate Providence lies born of decay on this exotic floral altar of a flower. Our mortal needs and desires make death the worm in the rose, but that which we call a rose is only nature, and the worm within its lovely folds is the future that makes even death smell as sweet."

I now recognized phrases from everything from Shakespeare to Sherlock Holmes to Madison Avenue admixed in the monologue. I almost ad-libbed my own ending. Heck, I would, combining poet Gertrude Stein with Matthew in the New Testament.

"A rose is a rose is a rose," I intoned gravely, "when it is not the least of these, a maggot."

And an ex-TV reporter is an ex-TV reporter, when she is not a ham.

A shocked silence held.

"Cut!" the invisible voice from the dark yelled again.

The general soundstage lighting amped up sunrise bright.

Blinking, I was pushed away from the corpse and rapidly guided off the set. Still blinking, I stopped, only to feel the gown and visor ripped off. Next I heard my false fingernails in expert succession pinging into the steel tray like hail, leaving a gummy residue for me to pick off at home.

"Here's your top," Erlene said. We were in the wardrobe room. I grabbed and donned my stretchy knit top, again blinding myself for a few seconds. When I pulled it down and my hair was free, she was propping my blond-banged scarf on one displaying hand.

"Better wear this and haul ass outta here. Your bit created a sensation even on set. That agent on speed-dial should be one happy fella, Lillian."

"The orchid," I said vaguely, "the maggot." She misunderstood me.

"Pros don't ask for souvenirs, even of signature scenes. The flower stays in Wardrobe and the maggot will be recycled to Living Props for use in another shot . . . if it doesn't get too old and grow too big and is destroyed."

Alas, poor Maggie . . .

I did as she said and left. The busy crew and cast didn't even notice a blue-eyed blond ingénue on an exit run. I knew Hector Nightwine had his money shot: an azure-eyed resurrection of Lilith, complete with her single trademark maggot.

And did I know if Lilith was alive or dead? No, but I'd seen that the autopsy scene process could be manipulated, by anyone, even Lilith.

It wasn't until I got home to the Enchanted Cottage and checked myself in the bathroom mirror that I spotted the tiny blue topaz nostril jewel Erlene had slapped on my nose while slamming on my autopsy shield. She could obey a clipboard instruction sheet like crazy.

That touch made me Lilith down to this betraying trademark I'd worn in Kansas and ditched weeks ago when I realized the Lilith *CSI V* corpse had sported it too.

Hector Nightwine, the Demon Director of Sunset Road, didn't miss a thing.

BY 3:00 P.M. the next day I'd put in a long shift watching over Ric and returned to the Enchanted Cottage, where the estate internal phone line was blinking a message. Nightwine was old-fashioned that way.

A jubilant-sounding Hector was summoning me to his palatial office to view "outtakes" on the giant screen hidden behind his expensive wood paneling. I was curious enough to go straight to his office in the main house for the peep show.

I don't know if he was behind the camera himself but the sequence was . . . exquisite. My Lilith features were glimpsed through the thin Lexan shield like a fugitive reflection in a moving car window. The high-tech medical spatter guard seemed almost a modern knight's visored helmet. I resembled a pale somber Joan of Arc behind it.

As I spoke the nonsensical lines the camera angles

switched between the cuts into the corpse's wan skin welling whip lines of blood to my converging face and hand. Closer and closer the camera came . . . to my vivid mouth and eyes behind the semi-obscuring plastic . . . to my pale hands with their bloody perfect false fingernails holding the orchid, which in close-up could be seen to tremble as if the petals breathed . . . to the wet, pulsing fetal curl of the modern Worm Ouroboros, the lowly maggot.

I held my breath at the morbid beauty of it and heard my own voice-over as some mystical unintelligible poem.

"Maggie lives!" Hector crowed as the segment ended.

He slammed something down hard on his massive wooden desk.

"Don't thank me. I do have my spies on the set. I heard you expressed some interest . . . no thanks, please, my dear Miss Street. I know you are the sentimental sort."

He prodded something across his desktop. I recoiled at first, thinking it might be one of his repugnantly anonymous edibles.

No. It was ultramodern, a solid block of Plexiglas the size of a notepad square. I leaned close to comprehend it. A clear cube with something inside, something embedded.

I blinked.

I saw my hand, bloody-nailed but flaunting the most perfect manicure I would ever sport. My face and blue eyes lurked behind it through a futuristic plastic veil. My long red fake forefinger nail was just barely touching the maggot atop the exotic flower, glistening like Renaissance mother-of-pearl. These parts of me were from a film still, a photo.

The orchid and the maggot—Lord, that sounded like an antiromance novel's title!—were preserved in plastic, now eternally frozen in 3-D, like those encased desert scorpions and tarantulas sold in tourist shops across the Southwest states.

"This is the numbered First," Nightwine said, his voice trembling with triumph, "of a limited edition of a million pouring out of the Mexican workshops. Fast work, eh? All yours, Delilah, for a very good job. Thanks to you, the Maggie franchise *lives*!"

I pushed myself out of the heavy chair and picked up the slick square. Its contents were only a reproduction. As in lost wax jewelry casting, the original models, floral and insect, were sacrificed to make the mold.

Nightwine was rerunning his footage, drooling.

He didn't notice me leave his office.

Thank God.

Who would believe this hardened group-home orphan who had refused to cry for herself from toddlerhood on had been brought to the brink of shedding a tear for a dead maggot?

Chapter Eleven

THAT EVENING I managed to pay another low-profile visit to the Inferno. Although the nurses had reported regularly to my cell phone that Ric was still comatose but "building up strength," I needed to check on him. At least daily. And discreetly.

I did not want to see, or be seen by, Snow, either in rock idol or CEO guise. That meant I'd be wise to avoid his associates, like the house watchcat Grizelle and even my dear friend detective Nick Charles at the Inferno Bar.

I picked 11:30 P.M., when Snow was finishing up his second show and Grizelle was nearby to beat off the nightly Brimstone Kiss groupies if the usual security couldn't handle them. I wore touristy garb from a cheap Strip souvenir shop: loose cotton slacks and gaudy white T-shirt, fanny pack, and billed cap screaming VEGAS! in living sequined color.

Not even the Invisible Man was around to pinch my scuttling butt as I made for the rear freight elevators, then switched to the main ones. I arrived unobserved except by the cruising mirrored security balls that only reported overt oddities.

Outside the bridal suite accommodations where Ric was building iron-rich blood while Helena's psychedelic "spell" kept his mind and emotions in healing suspended animation, I paused.

Hmm, Irma noted. *It's more than odd that no one is*

questioning our surreptitious comings and goings. I smell conspiracy. Is everyone pretending you're pulling the wool over their eyes because you're such a sad case these days? You are becoming the pity fuck of the whole damn Inferno Hotel staff, girl!

That hurt.

Although Irma had always told me the truth when no one else would, I shrugged off her concerns. What mattered was getting Ric through this and figuring out how to protect us both in the future.

In post–Millennium Revelation Las Vegas? Sure it was an impossible dream. So was what Ric and I had, and I was determined we would have again: life, love, and a plan to kick supernatural ass.

AS I'D HOPED, Ric had stablized since Helena had "bewitched" him. He was off all IV drips and functioning normally, though still in a deep sleep most of the time, especially at night. Even the nurses weren't on during the graveyard shift from eleven to seven, the one still on duty told me.

"He's looking good," said the heavy-set brownette, name tag "Inez." "I leave at eleven so if you wanta take over on your own, *chica* . . ."

She must have taken letting-go lessons from Helena Troy Burnside. I didn't need further encouragement. I approached Ric's bedside as softly as a cat over the plush gold carpeting. God, I hadn't been kidding myself thinking of him as a sleeping prince.

The color had crept back into his skin. Its golden brown shade only made the black of hair and eyelashes and beard stubble look more dramatic. My hormones surprised me with a surge so strong I didn't know myself. Oh, baby, you have come a long way.

The blood-infusion IV pole was gone, leaving Ric totally unattached to tubes.

Oooh, I could attach to him mucho plenty, me on top of the poor sick man and administering play CPR. *Delilah*! Control yourself. Irma was keeping quiet. This was *my* libidinous moment. And then, the demons of doubt flailed me. Maybe the Brimstone Kiss was too potent to unleash on a live guy. Maybe it would reverse itself, and Ric's state of recovery.

From loving lust I plunged back into self-doubt.

Rats. It wouldn't hurt to sit with the sick and *look.*

I AWOKE, SENSING a nightmare.

Not mine, for once.

Ric was murmuring and stirring under the covers.

I'd fallen asleep bent over in the bedside chair, my arms and head braced on the bed, even my casual clothes feeling tight and sticky.

Ric's hands and feet began twitching, as Quicksilver's will during a dream. I thought of checking with the nurses but remembered the double doors were locked, keeping us in and everyone else out.

If Ric was about to be scared conscious, I wanted to be there the moment he opened his eyes.

I turned on the bedside table lamp, the warm light putting his features into relief, like a sculpture. The small LED clock read four in the morning. I put a hand on his upper arm, but the muscle twitched away at my touch.

His limbs began flailing as he turned and coiled into the light bed coverings, moaning now, as if from remembered pain. It had to be that. The memory of pain. His body wounds were healed. Even the gaping neck wound was finally closing, the nurses had said.

Ric wrenched himself around on his side, facing away from me, the silly string ties of the hospital gown pulled loose, baring his welt-scarred back.

Gentle bed-table lamplight became a vicious spotlight illuminating the rutted surface of a blasted moon. I reached forward to pull the gown closed, sparing him even my eyes. He reacted by spinning onto his stomach. I caught my breath.

Just as I slept only on my stomach to fend off my nightmare memories of being pinned on my back by something alien, Ric must have trained himself to sleep on his back to hide the thick whip scars from any bed partner.

He'd failed to be vigilant once with me. Now, in a half-conscious state, he was exposing his whole back . . . not only exposing it but reliving the wounds that had disfigured it.

His back muscles twitched as if writhing under the cut of the braided leather bullwhip wielded by a cowardly bastard. A child being beaten mercilessly by a grown man.

"Ric, Ric," I whispered, trying not to wake him but to prod him into a comforting defensive posture again. Concealing the scars, even unconsciously, would make him feel more secure. I couldn't bear watching his body relive that brutal punishment.

I crawled up onto the bed, but could do nothing. He was thrashing too wildly. I couldn't cover him or soothe him. I could simply witness the pantomime of the invisible whipping, only one of many he'd endured as a boy.

It was as if *I* was being scourged. I flinched every time his back muscles quivered and I keened along with his moans, feeling a dark, deep Irish grief I'd never known in myself.

This was the downside of love, such total involvement

in another's pain that you are helpless to ease. I was kneeling over his brutally bared back, surprised when raindrops started dotting the rutted skin. Oh. My tears. I, who'd never cried, not even as an orphaned, unwanted child. Especially not as an orphaned, unwanted child.

Tears were storming down my cheeks. The thought of my own salt water striking even scars was so abhorrent I slapped the wetness off my face, hard to the side, so they wouldn't sting wounds I couldn't believe had ever truly sealed. I felt I was pouring fresh acid on them.

I bent to kiss away my tears, to consume my own corrosive saltwater sorrow.

Ric moaned deeply.

I reared away, horrified, rasping frantic whispers. "Ric, I'm sorry. Sorry! I never cry. I didn't mean to hurt you again."

My tears glowed on his back like drops of radioactive dew in the lamplight, in my mind. Were my *tears* cursed now, as well as my lips?

"I'll fix it! Somehow. Fast!"

I kissed along one raised furrow, tasting my salt and trying to retract it back into my body and being, suck it away. I felt like a fucking vampire. God, no. No more pain!

Ric moaned again. Oh, my God, I was right! Ric could feel every touch as it was happening twenty years ago. I sat back up on my heels, debating whether to call the nurses or call Quicksilver and use his healing saliva and tongue again, since mine were so useless and even harmful . . .

The lamplight still revealed every ugly knuckle-thick welt knotting his flesh.

Except . . . one welt had shrunken, withered flat into a thin scar line, the one my lips had traced in anguished remorse. My forefinger lightly followed the silver line. Ric moaned softly again. I blinked, feeling the alien wetness still on my eyelashes, seeing more clearly.

Had I . . . kissed away . . . a whip welt?

Only one way to know. I bent and kissed along another eight-inch soul-scar of Hell. I jerked back.

Ric's moan was more guttural as his torso writhed deeper into the mattress. I made tight fists in shared anguish as another welt shrank to a faint scar line as smooth as the untouched flesh on either side.

I held my breath, clapped my hand to my mouth to hold it in, realizing what had happened. If I was willing to inflict fresh pain on Ric I would be able to . . . to reduce his scars to ghosts of themselves, make them faint reminders only.

Trembling, I bent and deliberately traced an ugly welt with my lips and tongue, evoking another cry of pain.

Or . . .

Oh. Ric's moans weren't from pain. They were from pleasure.

I couldn't believe it. I bent to his nearer shoulder and ran my lips lightly over the first hardened ridge of flesh they felt. The thick scar melted into another faint gleam as flat as the finest silver wire.

I began teasing him. A healing kiss high along his left hip. Again below the waist. His pelvis was grinding against the sheets, his moans soft and sensuous. Back to a shoulder, the middle of his back.

The growing tracery of healed welts was like a reverse tattoo, pale on his desert dusky skin, making a pinwheel of strokes that almost resembled some primitive artwork found painted on an ancient tribal rock.

I felt a triumphant joy in my work. Somehow, I was replacing old pain with new pleasure, erasing the past and even its evidence, undoing El Demonio's deviltry. Even

Ric's brutal brush with the Karnak vampires couldn't entirely undo this night's work. The only visible scars of his indentured childhood were fading to shiny healed flesh. He'd be truly whole again.

My body was shaking slightly with the wonder of it. I was still feeling tearful but stemming that tide, half wanting to cry while I laughed, excited by my lover's having the world's most insanely literal wet dream because of me . . .

The double doors to the bedroom burst open as if a SWAT team were attacking. The bridal suite had turned from a night sanctuary of sexual healing into a predawn death trap.

Chapter Twelve

I REARED UP on my knees as Quicksilver backed in, growling aggressively, forelegs down, teeth bared. I'd kneecap anyone busting in on our reverse S&M moment too.

I frowned at the single large shadow that swallowed the threshold before the one who cast it had even entered.

And then I saw who it was. *Grizelle!*

"What are you doing?" she demanded, her green eyes looking black in the meager lamplight. "*What. Are. You. Doing?*" she repeated, stalking toward the bed on its raised step.

Quicksilver danced in front of her, poised to leap for her long black throat five feet off the floor.

"I'll eviscerate your dog if you don't call him off," she threatened, lifting a formidably nailed hand.

"Quick! *Back.*" I eyed Grizelle again. "And you get out of here. This is a private sickroom. *What. Are. You. Doing. Here?*" I parroted her with matching fury and venom.

She took a long stride forward to brace one leg on the riser and peer at Ric in the bed. I leaned over him to block her view but she was tall enough to see what she wanted to.

"So," she said. "It *is* you! You must stop your bizarre healing ritual."

"No. Why would I?"

"For every scar you diminish on your lover my master lies flayed below, his back laced with bloody stripes that keep appearing out of nowhere. I knew *you* must have something to do with it."

Stunned, I tried to piece the two bizarre scenes together. For every whip scar I kissed away, Snow received a fresh slash in the same position on his own albino back?

Truly creepy. Impossible notions ran through my mind involving Quicksilver's healing tongue and my accepting Snow's Brimstone Kiss and converting it into a Resurrection Kiss. Now maybe a Retribution Kiss had boomeranged on its dispenser?

"You must stop now!" Grizelle shouted.

For a moment, memories of my humiliating moments standing half-naked and defenseless in front of Snow burned hot in my chest and throat, an attack of emotional heartburn.

Yes! My anger against Snow almost choked me. The bastard deserved to writhe under the lash. Better him than Ric. I'd make that choice forever and ever, amen!

Then the horror of what was happening on some floor above us hit me. No creature deserved to feel all at once what El Demonio had meted out to Ric over years of abuse. I pictured Snow's skin as white and firm as Michelangelo's *David*, reproduced at Caesars Palace. I shuddered to imagine the violation, pain, and wounds it had absorbed already.

Grizelle had backed off the riser toward the door.

"The damage is mostly done," she said bitterly. "You have caused my master trouble since you came to this city and now you have made him suffer beyond belief."

I stood statue-still on the riser, glancing back at Ric. Only a few of the horrible scar ridges remained. Could I stop just short of completion without undoing all I'd accomplished?

Wasn't there a fairy tale? A girl's seven brothers had

been bespelled into swans, so she spent years weaving shirts from punishing nettles to reclaim their proper form.

Her fingers bled from the task but she didn't quite make the deadline. As she threw the nettle garments on her swan-brothers' backs, one shirt was missing an arm. One brother would wear a swan wing for an arm for all his life.

The moral? Leaving any small part of a magical task undone could have irreversible consequences. I couldn't leave Ric half-healed, still unconscious. He might never wake up but remain suspended between the pain of the past and the pleasure of the present.

I couldn't risk it.

"No," I told Grizelle. "I'm sorry, but I can't stop now."

Grizelle stopped, turned, and stood even taller in her disbelief.

"It's only a few strokes more." I sounded lame even to myself.

"My master's back is in bleeding shreds already."

"He raised a medieval dragon from its ashes. He must have some magic to overcome this."

"Not for himself."

I shook my head. "I can't stop now."

"You will."

As Quicksilver circled stealthily around behind her, I watched Grizelle shape-shift so fast that in one blink she was her human self and the next she had stretched long and low into full Big Cat form, six hundred pounds and nine feet long.

She roared, making the walls vibrate. The carnivore stink of hot tiger's breath alone almost drove me off my feet.

Her front fangs looked longer than scissor blades and her open maw as high as a human torso was wide. I'd seen enough domestic cats chasing birds to realize she was hunched to attack. One bound would do for both me and Ric.

I clasped my hands together in front of me, not praying, but calling the silver familiar to war. Would a thing made of Snow's hair defend me now? Desert him?

Twin chains sped down my arms to my palms. Achilles was in the familiar's magical mix now.

I held the most fully realized form of the silver familiar yet—a shining sword blade—in my conjoined hands.

As Grizelle's enormous white-and-black-striped, furred body sprang into the air, Quicksilver attacked her rear flank and was lofted upward by his teeth.

My mind flashed options. First I should strike for a huge gorgeous green eye, then the throat if I missed that. If she still bounded over me I'd have one last chance to rip out the belly. What a shame . . . for one of us.

I braced myself at the foot of the bed feeling her shadow fall over me.

At that instant, the Big Cat's huge body twisted and flailed in the air, falling back to the carpeting and struggling there. It was as if an invisible leash had jerked her back.

She half-shifted into human form as she writhed on the floor, snarling between any words she could get out.

"Fool!" She shook a rear leg and Quicksilver fell off, still watchful.

I saw blood seeping onto the rug from her left hip, but she disregarded it.

"*I* didn't call this off," she said in a human voice still too rough and tigerish to reassure me. "Remember that. You will pay."

She shifted back to tiger form, watching me with suspicious lowered head, then turned and stalked out, blood staining the white fur on her left flank.

I sighed and sat on the end of the bed, lowering the sword that seemed glued to my hands. It softened into twin serpents and migrated up my forearms to become upper-arm bracelets.

Quick sat down, tilted his head quizzically, and whimpered at the bed.

I turned my head over my shoulder. Ric slept on, the flat dunes of his back gleaming silver with scar tissue in the lamplight. I eyed the ugly ridges still remaining.

"My job," I told Quicksilver. I doubted even his proven healing tongue could outdo mine after the Brimstone Kiss.

He trotted away to stand guard outside the double doors Grizelle had broken. That dog never walked, just trotted or ran flat out. And after a tiger attack, he still had the stones to take up a position between it and me should Grizelle's tiger self desire any reruns.

My relieved mind oddly at peace, I crawled back up on the bed to run a forefinger along one of the seven remaining welts.

I'd been going to tell Quicksilver, "My job, my pleasure," but knowing every erased welt here would reappear as pain elsewhere made me lose my appetite for the pleasure part.

I made quick work of it, letting Ric's satisfied murmurs override the whimpers of my conscience.

Last, I brought my trembling lips to the bandage covering the wide and deep neck wound the vampires had made. Through the gauze mesh, I tasted blood, careful not to siphon any up.

This was one old scar Ric could never hide and didn't want to. It was also his oldest erotic zone. Having missed out on the forbidden thrill of high school hickies, my loving lips had made this site an "instant on" zone and didn't I feel guilty about that now.

If my Brimstone Kissed lips could "cure" this most vicious and lethal wound, the only remaining sign of Ric's being vampire bait . . .

A migraine headache from Hell assailed me with disturbingly mixed mental images and emotional sensations. I felt and saw my lips on Ric and Snow and then vampire lips on Ric in such fast succession that waves of love and hate, passion and compassion, sexual and blood lust made me shake as if being electrocuted.

The reaction's speed had jerked me away from Ric before he could be contaminated by more than a sleeping murmur of reaction.

Some places even healing intentions couldn't go.

I glanced again at the silver tracery of his back scars. He now bore a beautiful ghost tattoo and I was drained into a stupor.

I curled up next to him and went to sleep.

Chapter Thirteen

I AWOKE FACEDOWN in the bed with a warm hand slipped under my T-shirt, cupping my rib cage and primed to do likewise with my breast.

"You give great dream," Ric's voice whispered against my neck.

I rolled over to find dark eyes smiling into mine. Eyes, plural. The brown contact lens over Ric's transmuted iris covered the silver perfectly.

This incredible moment—Ric conscious and acting normally—seemed like any lazy, ordinary intimate "morning after," although we hadn't had many morning afters during our brief love affair.

And we hadn't been indulging in sex last night but a bizarre form of erotic healing. Something new under the sun popped up every day in the post–Millennium Revelation world.

How good to know that Ric's return to full consciousness was also filled with pleasurable memories to counter the horrible ones sure to return someday soon.

"What'd you dream?" I asked him, unafraid of his answer at the moment.

He looked as lazy and satisfied as a tomcat in the sun. "Your lips and mouth had developed a magic touch, Delilah. Must have been wearing that crazy, hot Lip Venom again. I came at every kiss, over and over again."

"Wow. The only way I can offer that in a waking state is we log a lot of time in the sack from now on," I joked.

"Yeah." He frowned and looked around. "Where are we anyway? Cushy, but not your or my home, sweet home."

I used his distraction to run my hand around his hip, meeting no resistance, and up his back. Meeting major resistance. His entire body bucked away.

"Time to get going." He jumped up to face me by the bedside. "What is this thing?" he asked, discovering the soft cotton straitjacket of a hospital gown hanging from his shoulders.

A tiny strawberry print was definitely not Ricardo Montoya's style. I knee-walked over the empty mattress to keep it from sliding off his shoulders. He didn't need privacy from me in the front, but he was conditioned to keep his scarred back covered and untouched.

"You've been a little sick and I'm your night nurse," I cooed to calm him down.

He frowned again. After the horrors he'd faced, no wonder he had temporary amnesia. That we could reconnect as lovers before those traumas pushed to the surface was a gift. Helena had been right.

I ran a daring finger over where a particularly long thick welt had disfigured his back. Ric bucked away like a bronco again, then his face registered shock. "You . . . touched my back."

"So?"

"It felt . . . good. My back feels—"

"Smooth and creamy?" I asked provocatively, pushing into a full frontal embrace, running my fingers over the faint smooth tracks of the erased scars, feeling his torso quiver with pleasure instead of flinching away.

He tilted his forehead against mine and cupped the sides

of my face so we were enclosed in our own secret communion, breath mingling between us, warm and intoxicating.

"It wasn't a dream, was it, Delilah? Somehow you kissed me whole again."

"Yes." I inhaled his breath and wafted it back into his mouth on that long sibilant sound, like a sigh. I'd tell him about the Resurrection Kiss later.

"You see ghosts in mirrors, you turn my oldest pain into pleasure, what else on earth can you do, Delilah Street?"

"Love you," I said.

Our kiss right then was a vow. We felt nothing more extraordinary than accelerated human heartbeats. How we both appreciated that. I especially felt relieved. No way did I want to keep passing on Brimstone Kiss side effects.

"So where the hell are we?" Ric asked as our lips parted. "What happened and where are my frigging clothes?"

I hesitated. His clothes were probably rags in the deepest bowels of the Karnak Hotel. To explain that, I'd have to spin an incredible yarn about rogue CinSims, vivified dragons, carnivorous hyenas and zombie mummies, Egyptian vampire warriors, and the sacred and profane underground rivers of Vegas.

Even a man who could dowse for the dead wouldn't buy this whole scenario until he had time to get oriented.

"Look, my dear *hombre*," I told him. "We've been in big trouble and ended up depending on the kindness of Christophe at the Inferno. Until now you were in the healing hands of a doctor and a group of no-nonsense nurses."

"The day shift, you must mean," he qualified. "I think I can wrap the night nurse around my little finger and big—"

I fanned my fingers over his mouth before I got too interested in what he was going to say.

"Serious *professional* nurses, Ric. You need a doctor's

permission to leave here. I'm sure he'll check you pretty soon and dismiss you. Meanwhile, give me your sizes, *amor,* and I can have this fun clothes shopping spree for you in the hotel galleria."

"Yeah?" He frowned again. "The left side of my neck really throbs." His fingers patted the square gauze patch. "What happened there?"

"We're in a suite at the Inferno," I said, going back to his first and easiest question. "Some bad operators got hold of you but we got you back."

"And they kept my clothes?"

"Right. It's a long story, Ric. You need to sit down with something bracing besides me and hear it step by step. Wouldn't you be more effective dressed than wearing an air-conditioned, string-tied, sissy hospital gown when you tell those sponge-bearing, bath-hungry nurses that you're fine and to buzz off?"

He thought about it—the exposure of a hospital gown's open rear slit combined with his back phobia—and nodded.

"Don't spend too much, *chica*. I doubt you'll get what I would."

"Oh, no worry. I'll just load up on Elvis T-shirts and Hawaiian shirts and Bermuda shorts. Cheap, fast, and they show off your legs. That's so you."

"Delilah!"

I quick-kissed him good-bye and escaped before he could ask too many more questions.

While I dashed into my bedroom to snag my handy messenger bag, a morning nurse came out from her bedroom. I asked her to call the doctor, saying that Ric was awake and restless.

Then I skedaddled, telling Quicksilver to watch on the

way out and keep an eye out for Grizelle. I winced to think of how Snow's potent Brimstone Kiss had boomeranged to put the risen Ric in mortal danger from Snow's shape-shifting bodyguard.

That's another reason I wanted Ric ambulatory and out of here. I didn't want either of us depending on Snow's "hospitality" now that he had a bitter personal reason to hate us both. A man who can raise a centuries-dead dragon from its ashes may not be a master vampire but he sure was something dark that decent folks should frown on.

I tried to make my passage through the hotel a low-profile slink. I was doing fine until I had to cross the casino area to get to the shopping arcade called Beelzebub's Boutiques. That was the Inferno Hotel, a relentless theme park of evil.

A small pale dog came yapping after my heels.

That so reminded me of my lost Achilles that I played the sucker and paused to look.

This dog was taller than a Lhasa. It was a curly-haired white dog with gray touches on its forehead and perked ears like a center-parted toupee. I recognized the wire-haired terrier with a sinking heart and a soft "Damn."

"Asta? What are you doing here?" I asked fruitlessly.

The dog danced around me once, then bounced a few steps away and paused so I would follow.

He wasn't Lassie but I knew exactly where he wanted me to go.

I gave up and followed Asta back to the Inferno Bar, where his master, Nick Charles, debonair detective possessed of the best pencil-thin mustache of his era and the Inferno house CinSim, held forth.

Nicky stood beside a willowy woman with a side-parted thirties hairdo in tight Marcel waves. The curls broke into adorable fluff at her sharp chin line. She more leaned than sat on a bar stool. She had thin arched eyebrows and wore a chic, dark, slim day gown bowed and ruffled around the shoulders.

I would kill for that dress, and then I'd have to kill again to be thin enough to get into it.

"Delilah," Nicky greeted me, with a devilish arched eyebrow.

He took me aside to mumble in my ear. "Are you by any chance responsible for my new condition of domestic bliss here at the Inferno Bar? It does cut down on my cigarette-lighting for attractive women tourists."

I sighed to indicate my plea. "Guilty."

And I had three times the reason to plead guilty. I'd talked Snow into giving Nicky his two CinSim better halves a while back. Here was walking, bouncing, barking evidence that Snow had lived up to his word. Great, I'd just condemned him to Living Hell. Although it may have been his natural element.

Lighten up, Irma told me. *The Family Charles makes a helluva better Inferno Bar attraction than Nicky feeling low-down and solo. You think the guy tourists won't flock to witty, winsome Nora like the dames go for Nicky? And that Asta is too cute for words. Snow owes you for peerless marketing moxie. Again.*

I'd just let his probably immortal back be sliced to chopped liver to restore Ric's. The pure profit motive wasn't enough to overcome Snow's enmity now. Interesting to contemplate what physical torture he would consider sufficient repayment. And now he knew my weaknesses . . .

Still, I doubted he'd use Ric against me. The lead singer of the Seven Deadly Sins had too much pride. No, it would be between him and me only and it would not be pretty.

Perhaps not even survivable. For me. Snow wouldn't want scars for scars. He'd want what I most feared he did. My soul.

"Why the glum face, Miss Delilah?" Nick Charles coaxed me. "Here's a fresh Brimstone Kiss. It's the new In drink."

I couldn't help recoiling.

"Ah, too fiery a concoction even for its inventor, but just the thing to loosen the tongue of my pal, Rick Blaine. We're fellow film barflies from way back. I quite agree. I prefer dry and subtle. Speaking of which, you have favorably impressed the CinSim Consortium. You definitely ought to be in pictures." He winked.

That reminded me. The Inferno's infernal floating mirror-ball surveillance cameras would soon pinpoint my whereabouts. Better keep moving if I didn't want to be zapped with Seven Deadly Sins lightning.

I blew a farewell kiss to Nick and Nora. Asta, who was now perched on a bar stool, wagged his stubby tail. The trio made a sophisticated film still in living black and white.

I kept on a direct line for the Devil's shopping zone.

Once there I could window-shop the world's finest clothing brands for my baby. Nothing too good for his rehabilitated back or my sensitive fingers.

I found a shop selling Zimmerli Swiss men's "furnishings." "Pagan style" briefs in finest cotton, a red silk iridescent shirt, silver satin tie, dove gray sport coat, and charcoal slacks.

Ric would leave the Inferno ready for a road show company of *Guys and Dolls*.

I hesitated at bill-paying time. Snow had promised Helena that anything Ric or she needed would be "on" the hotel.

Nope. I had three fat checks coming for my snoop work from Hector, the CinSims, and Howard Hughes. Technically, I'd also been hired by Snow to discover the identity of Loretta Cicereau's ancient vampire lover boy, but I'd taken my blood money, and how. I charged the clothes to my credit card, glad I could put Ric in glad rags on my own ticket.

I circled the bar on my trip back upstairs and arrived to find Quicksilver waiting and my things packed in the same suitcase and sturdy sacks Godfrey had sent from Hector's place.

Ric was standing with the doctor, a CinSim with a vague smudge of dark beard that lacked the brunet perfection of Ric's dusky jawline.

"Do not bend, spindle, or mutilate this young man for the first day or so," the doctor advised me. "You could still drill to China through that neck wound."

Ric grabbed my suitcase, then my newly freed hand, and rushed after me and my crinkling shopping bags into my bedroom.

As soon as the door closed, he flung the hospital gown to the floor, standing as nude as Adam and almost as unmarked, except for having a navel.

"I finally caved and let those nosy nurses give me a frontal sponge bath, *chica,*" he admitted, "so I'm fit for new clothes."

I dug out the underwear, not tighty whities and not boxers, but something smooth and close-fitting in between.

"What the hell are these?"

" 'Pagan' briefs. European. Expensive."

"*Dios!* Trust women to go for freaky underwear."

He pulled them on and they were all they could be, from my viewpoint.

I'd looked him over good. No vampire tsetse fly or leech bite scars, just the faint silvery rays on his back. He paused to turn his head over his shoulder to the mirror and view his back in wonder while I pulled out and undid the packaging on his new ensemble.

The Holy Family was much appealed to, along with other saints and martyrs, but Ric was finally clothed in my selections and looked like a million dollars. For a Vegas gambling shark.

"Not bad for a speed run," I said. "I wish Helena could see you now."

"Helena? My mother the shrink? She—? You—? Delilah?"

"I love you with your jaw dropped but we really, really want to leave here, pronto. I'll explain it all once we're at your place. Or mine?"

"My place," he said absently, tying a perfect double Windsor in the pricey silver Italian silk tie.

Now I understood why he was the "freaking best-dressed Fed" I'd ever seen, as I'd told him when we'd met in Sunset Park. Now I realized why he always craved a silky skin of posh clothing.

It wasn't vanity. It wasn't snobbery. It was urban survival for someone who'd had to develop a skin of sandpaper way too young.

I smiled. Ric was busy asserting his druthers. Let the little things ease him back into his post-Karnak nightmare life. We'd handle the big things later.

Chapter Fourteen

WHEN I DROVE Dolly under the porte cochere of the nearby coach house at 4:00 P.M., Godfrey was waiting by the driveway.

How long had he been there? I wondered, primed to feel guilty about Ric's and my late, leisurely lunch at the Bahama Breeze at the juncture of Howard Hughes Center Road and Parkway near Paradise and Flamingo. That's where and when I explained my and Helena's hit-and-run cross-country trip. I even promised Ric a Vampire Sunrise soon.

My tale bemused and amused him. He was also too unquestioning. I realized Helena's therapeutic hypnotism had put her in the back of his mind so that I could remain up front to tend and pamper him. My respect for her tripled.

The restaurant was so very Vegas, and the piña coladas were almost as good as my homemade cocktails. They even allowed Quicksilver inside for a grilled steak kabob . . . as long as he ate it under the table and from my skewer.

When we reached the estate, Godfrey was unruffled.

"Good day, Miss, Master Quicksilver. Splendid to see you back, Mr. Montoya. I am posted here to take your belongings, Miss, and establish Master Quicksilver at the cottage. We presume you will drive Mr. Montoya to his place of residence. Should you require a change of costume, this bag will suit your needs."

He took our paper shopping bags and handed another to Ric in Dolly's passenger seat.

Quick jumped out of the backseat and ran to the top of the Enchanted Cottage's semicircular stairs, barking once in protest at being left behind as I drove back out on Sunset Road.

Ric suddenly slapped his forehead with a palm. "Say. We need to pick up my Corvette."

Omigod! I wasn't about to stimulate bad memories by breezing past the Karnak's parking lot for a look-see. Maybe Ric's gal pal, Captain Kennedy Malloy of the LVMPD, could check into that. I imagined a delicate and unpleasant conversation:

"And why can't Ric Montoya deal with getting his own car from the Karnak parking ramp, Miss Street?" Malloy would ask in icy disbelief.

"He's still recovering from my raising him from the dead," I'd reply. "It's best he doesn't deal with the little things for a while."

"And *I* am a 'little thing'?"

Actually, like many women in authority, she was way more petite than I was.

No, asking Malloy to retrieve Ric's car wouldn't work. My best bet for that was my friends, the parking valet demons. They went crazy over vintage rides and Ric's bronze Stringray was one, if not as venerable as my own Dolly.

I texted Ric's home address to Hermie at the Karnak and requested the car's "discreet" return to his home address garage. Ric must have parked the Vette on the Karnak grounds and demons had an infallible nose for Old Detroit metal. Foreign models just didn't do it for them.

What I really needed to find out was what Ric's mental wheels could remember.

"Worry about your ride later, *hombre,*" I purred in a kittenish way I'd picked up from late-night TV movies. "You look good in my passenger seat for now." Was I turning into your usual manipulative fatal femme or not?

His hand smoothed the red leather interior. "I'd rather drive."

"When you're better."

"I can get better?"

I grinned to hear that cheeky optimism back. Ric was pretty quick with the quips for a dead man. My hands tightened on the big steering wheel with the finger indentations sculpted on the underside. I had a lot of verbal tap-dancing on the truth ahead of me.

We soon reached his rambling house in an established Vegas gated community. I parked Dolly inside the courtyard, so Old Mexico. At Ric's Alamo-massive dark wood front door I suddenly realized he'd been found naked. No house keys.

"Ah, we're still missing your personal effects," I told him.

"No problem."

His fingers tapped out a pattern too quick to see on the security keypad. The heavy door jerked ajar as the system beeped. Ric's short-term memory might be AWOL, but he recalled the important things. I was glad to be one of them.

The house was cool and dark, shuttered against the peak late-afternoon heat. We turned on lights as we went through the public rooms right to the bedroom and into the master bathroom beyond.

"Sorry, Del," he said, yanking out the impeccable knot he'd only put into the new tie a couple hours before. "I really need a shave and a real shower. I feel like I've been through . . . I don't know, been crawling through some rank slimy jungle for hours. Like my skin is crawling. Except for my back, of course."

He lifted me to sit atop the long bathroom countertop and began to take off the clothes I'd just seen him put on. I was beginning to get why men went to strip clubs.

The slip-on shoes and silky socks went first, then the men's bedroom "butler" stand got the pants, shirt, and tie.

"You really like these things?" he asked of the briefs.

"Ah, yeah." Trust the Swiss to engineer underwear to its most smoothly structured second-skin state.

Ric touched his neck bandage just below the beard line, then picked up an electric razor that looked like a Martian spaceship probe from *The War of the Worlds.*

I put a hand on his wrist. "Some like it rough."

Actually, I wanted to get past the settling-in process to the thing all men hate: talking it over. I'd probably have to sleep with him first, which was fine with me.

He hesitated, then put down the razor and turned his bare brown back to me.

"You already knew," he said.

"The other night, when I slept over in the den. I woke up first. You'd turned over in your sleep."

"Damn! I never do that."

"It was my fault. I can't sleep on my back so you forgot to keep your back out of the light."

"I thought you acted kind of . . . weird that morning."

"Never try to fool an ex-FBI man." I ran a finger down his shoulder blade.

He shut his eyes in remembered past pain and present pleasure. "So when and where'd you get the Midol touch, *paloma*?"

"Every miracle has its price."

"My mom must have told you what and why. She swore it was just between us when I was ten years old."

"You were a child and she was acting as your psychologist. Things change. People change."

"You changed me."

"Superficially."

"No. You changed my past. You *replaced* my past with whatever you did to me last night. I'd be a fool to resent that, but I need to know what and why, just as you did."

My fingers plucked the faint silver skeins of scars on his back like a harp, sending shivers of sensual pleasure through his frame.

He caught my wrists in his hands, then in a one-handed grip.

"No, Delilah. You don't play me to distraction. I know I'm foggy about a lot of things. First a shower, then bed, then you spill your guts. *Sí?*"

I laughed as he pulled me off the countertop and tugged me toward the shower. It was one of those glass curves with a tiled wall and floor and sprays versatile enough for a car wash.

"I'm still dressed!" I objected, but I kicked off my casual mules as I went with him.

"Then you'll have to get all those wet things off when we're done. I'm not letting you loose to work your wiles. Trust me."

I couldn't stop laughing as he turned on the water. I shut my eyes to the warm tropical waterfalls of modern plumbing.

After all I remembered going through, and all he couldn't remember going through, that simple chlorinated city water seemed to rinse our skins and souls clean.

Ric peeled me out of my sopping top and jeans until I

was as naked and free as he was. Well, except for the silver familiar. It had curled down into a big toe ring, either shy or savvy about staying out of the way. Anyway, our impromptu coed shower had us both feeling safe and happy, even though that could never last.

"My bed this time, a real bed?" Ric asked. "You can be on top."

Beds were my bête noire, thanks to childhood nightmares. I couldn't bear to lie on my back, feel pinned. But if Ric was my bed and lay under me . . .

When we waltzed into the bedroom, smooching, and I finally dared really look at his bed, I melted like a shelled M&M.

The sheets were black satin, all the better to set off my Snow White skin. The many piled pillows were encased in blue satin, to set off my ballad-black hair and blue eyes.

Now I could harbor no doubt this man was as terminally crazy about me as I was about him. Color-coordinated bed linens, can you dig it? I shut my eyes. This felt like a continuation of the Inferno bridal suite wedding night, when I kissed my comatose prince whole and awake again.

"I've wanted you here for a long time," he said. "I guess you can tell."

"It's only been weeks, Montoya," I reminded him as I pushed him down, under me. Ric could sweep me away like a swooning bondage princess or let me ride him like a Valkyrie. What a guy. Thanks to Helena's shrink insights, I understood that his sexual versatility was adapting to my conflicting needs for both trust and independence . . . surrender and control.

Say, maybe I could accomplish another bit of sexual healing, as the song said.

I had to shut my eyes to block the image of his dead-to-the-world body crawling with black leeches and blue-winged tsetse flies feeding on his genitals as well as every inch of skin.

His ready erection then at my presence was *his* miracle, not mine, and I blessed his foster mother (yeah, she'd approve) for giving him this pleasant, delayed return to reality. Maybe I could extend it.

I glimpsed a familiar glint behind his head and pulled away the color-coordinated pillows.

"You have a *mirrored* headboard, Montoya?"

"I bought it before I knew you and about your mirror magic," he protested.

But his protests, however sincere, were too late. I'd spotted the chrome border and churchlike spires at the top framing the beveled mirror squares.

"This is so tacky," I said. "You have really gone over to Vegas glitz. Hunt-club Virginia bluebloods would be shocked. Stay right there."

I raced into the master bath and the huge closet, snagging the sky-blue tie and a similarly smooth, silky black one to match the décor honoring moi.

Irma was trying to urge me to tasteful restraint, but that was exactly what I had in mind.

He'd been found in the Land of the Book of the Dead, slumped half sitting against a wall, his wrists in chains above his head.

I reappeared with the ties swagged around my hips entwined with the double glints of my own hip chain and the silver familiar. Belly-dancing gear was Ric's Achilles' heel.

"Delilah," he said, his voice both a warning and a goad.

"Stay right there," I answered, unleashing the ties and looping them around his wrists and the headboard spires. "I'm going to kiss you all over until you beg for mercy."

The map of his face and body bites was burned into my memory. My Brimstone Kiss lips were going to visit the site of every atrocity, erased maybe, but still needing a sensory remodeling. Pleasure where pain had been. So simple.

He took it for an erotic game. That showed how far I had come, repressed Kansas orphan me. I could seduce Ric into taking this healing necessity that admitted how deeply he'd been lost, how close he'd been to a tortured-to-death vampire victim, as Delilah's naughty little bedroom improvisation.

That we were here, able to make love and deceive ourselves, just a little, to get us through the night, testified to our mutual loyalty. I untied him just as playfully as I'd confined him.

"Don't stop now," he complained as his arms wrapped around me. "I'd love to do this same thing to you." His luxurious, probing kisses punctuated a list of druthers.

"Here, *paloma* . . . on my midnight black sheets . . . your white naked body on your back . . . I'd make you moan . . . like you made me moan . . . when you made my back . . . your personal paranormal playground . . . and my old scars . . . my new erotic zone."

Oh, oh, oh. I so wanted what he did. I was almost climaxing before his arms lifted my torso so he could impale my soft center and take me for a wild ride on a bucking bronco, my long hair whipping around my face and neck like a mane.

Ric was *back,* stallion-strong, loving me more than ever. His release matched mine and justified everything. For the first time, I felt less soiled by the Brimstone Kiss. For the first time, I felt a throb of inner peace that I had taken and given that potent kiss in such quick succession.

Everything was getting back to what it'd been Before.

Before the Karnak Hotel vampire Pharaohs had lured Ric into their power.

Before I risked my free will and traded Snow the addictive Brimstone Kiss for Snow's help in rescuing Ric.

Before my attempts at the Kiss of Life, aka CPR, failed and I resorted to a last, passionate farewell kiss . . . tainted by the brimstone of compromise yet containing the new gift of the Resurrection Kiss.

That scenario was a lot for one Latin lover to absorb so I concentrated on our reunion and union, until we collapsed on each other in waves of fulfillment.

"This is wild," Ric said. "I have this whole new erotic zone." He wriggled his back into the satin sheets as I laughed.

"But," he added, "I don't remember anything from early that afternoon a week ago when I went to check out the Karnak until you were tongue-lashing my back with your velvet lips last night. How'd you find Helena anyway? Why didn't she stay?"

"She said what you needed was me, *hombre,* and she was right. You'd mentioned your father's full name once. Philip Burnside. I'm a reporter. Once is enough." I considered. "Not with everything."

"Nope. Forget it. No more sex until I know what's going on from A to Z," he threatened, getting up to leave the bed and the bedroom. He showed me his naked back without a qualm. I wished I could be as forthright about what he wanted to know.

He returned with a bottle of *roja* wine, no brand I recognized but a vintage as red and smooth and warm as blood. We drank it out of big bubble glasses as we leaned against piled satin pillows the color of my eyes.

"Do you remember anything about your kidnapping?" I asked.

"Was that what it was? I, um, remember heading to the Karnak Hotel and Casino. Grisly Bahr had alerted me by phone that someone from there had just contacted the coroner's office with suspicious questions about the male corpse from the Sunset Park grave."

"And you didn't pause to tell me where you were going?"

"Bother you with a slender lead at an established hotel?"

"You'd just lectured me about keeping current on who was doing what, where. In fact, I was trying to call you that day to say I'd checked out the Karnak the day before and it was crawling with vamps."

"I found out soon enough, but I don't remember much yet. So what are they like?"

"As old as the ancient tomb paintings and as eternally young-looking. I'd only gotten out, and that barely, thanks to my mirror magic skills. I didn't realize until the next day that the folks in charge were obsessively interested in the zombies you pulled out of the ground at Cesar Cicereau's Starlight Lodge."

"You're saying that my raising the zombies to protect you in the mountains last month tipped these Karnak vampires off to my, um, talent?"

"Yes. You saved my skin from being mounted in the werewolf mobster trophy teepee."

"Why should these Karnak vamps care? So I stopped another Vegas hotel mogul's hit squad. You'd think they'd thank me."

"I'm sure they would have, had you cooperated. They want someone who can raise really old vampires, the ugly, ruthless bloodsuckers, not the modern half-and-half kind.

We both know how you feel about raising the dead for other people's gain."

"I will never sell bodies and souls into slavery again."

"Admirable. I will never starve again, or eat turnips again." His grin showed I'd lightened his dark mood by evoking Scarlett O'Hara's famed turning-point vow. "Holy Hathor, Montoya! You must have made that all too clear to the Karnak vamps.

"They decided to induct you into their club so you'd want to do what *they* wanted. When the expedition from the other Vegas hotels found you, the Karnak vamps had sucked you dry, Ric. They'd used every bloodsucker they had access to, even leeches and vampire tsetse flies. You were—"

He shook his head. "I don't remember anything after arriving at the Karnak lobby. I recall a huge hyena-headed statue of a god I'd never seen or heard of before in the main check-in area."

"They'd already ID'ed you, as they had me, and were waiting to pounce. Luckily. I doubt we'll ever know what kind of tête-à-tête you had with the terrifyingly self-absorbed Twin Pharaohs who rule the Karnak."

"Twins?"

"Kephron and Kepherati, two of the most incestuous brother-sister royal twins the River Nile ever birthed. It's a long story, but I found archaeological evidence on the web that the ancient Egyptians had vampires among them."

"Naw. Their culture keyed on death and resurrection, life and the afterlife, true, but I've never heard of Egyptian vampires. Anne Rice had an 'immortal' mummy running around World War I England in one novel, but I don't think he sucked blood. The Egyptians are almost the only ancient world culture without vampire lore."

"No more."

"Quoth the raven?" he asked, leaning forward to kiss me long and deep and totally without fangs.

"Poe's raven was carping about '*never*more.'"

"No more, nevermore, what's the diff? I'm okay, you're okay. We're so more than okay together."

I wished I believed that as easily as he did. It was indeed all too easy to soften into his arms and strum my fingers over the silvery scar strings on his now sensually tuned back and celebrate life and love and libido.

"Then how did you know where I was and what was going on?" he asked when our embrace took a time-out.

Eternal ex-FBI man, asking questions. The habit of intellectualizing would probably save his sanity. I smiled and resumed my narrative.

"The clue I'd found was that some Egyptian tombs, from the most ancient and lost to the most celebrated finds of modern times, including King Tut, contained a weird potted artifact of a gilded headless animal hide hanging from a lotus plant."

"Headless? Like the 'bone boy' in the Sunset Park grave?"

"Mentally acute and decidedly not dead," I said, smiling. "That's *my* boy."

"This 'artifact' was the symbol of beheaded vampires in the Egyptian tombs, the *proof* that even pharaohs like Tutankhamen could be vampires?"

"I thought so. Meanwhile, the Peter Lorre CinSim at the Karnak has many shared movie ties to the Humphrey Bogart and Claude Rains CinSims at the Inferno. He'd seen me captured, and then escape. He must have realized your capture was act two of the royal twins' ambitious scenario. When he saw you being held and forced to suck winding cloths, the 'better angels of his being' emerged from behind the creepy criminal roles and came to the rescue."

"CinSims have 'better angels'?"

"A theory of mine. I think the actors are taking over the roles. It was an incredible string of events. The Karnak's Peter Lorre 'Ugarte' *Casablanca* CinSim somehow managed to break his venue moorings and get a physical token I'd lost at the Karnak to me at the Inferno Bar as a veiled warning.

"He did it using the Inferno's Humphrey Bogart 'Rick Blaine' CinSim, who broke free of the lower-level *Casablanca* key club and got to the William Powell 'Nick Charles' CinSim at the Inferno Bar. Nicky somehow tipped off his 'cousin' William Powell CinSim, Godfrey, at Hector's estate. Who told me to get to the Inferno Bar to pump Rick Blaine of all the things he didn't think he knew."

"Gosh, Delilah! I need one of those star maps of Hollywood, Las Vegas–style, to follow this scenario."

"Consider it as a CinSim chain reaction, and damn efficient in its dysfunctional way. Trust me. We've got a long ways to go before we understand the hows and whys of CinSims.

"Anyway, I was called to the Inferno Bar in my best thirties velvet gown to evoke Rick Blaine's film ladylove, Ilsa/Ingrid Bergman. I picked his brain like a noir femme fatale.

"When the Inferno's Rick Blaine physically produced the case of Lip Venom I'd unknowingly dropped during my escape from the Karnak, I realized *someone* at the Karnak wanted me to go back there, bad.

"I also realized that you weren't answering my calls because of the usual Vegas Strip cell-phone dead zone, but were actually missing. That's when I finally grasped that the Royal Pains had been much more interested in your zombie-raising act than my minor mirror magic."

"This is," Ric asked, "where Christophe and his rock-star persona's Brimstone Kiss come in?"

Ouch. "Right."

"I've heard of the Brimstone Kiss," he said dismissively, the way even the best guys sometimes don't get girls with long-distance but potent crushes. "Heartthrob singers always sucker the fangirls with some sexy stage shtick."

Nobody does it like Snow does, Irma singsonged softly in my ear.

I gritted my teeth and gave Ric a palatable song-and-dance.

"Exactly right. Only, Snow has some ulterior motive for kissing strangers. He takes it semi-seriously and insisted I accept the infamous kiss if I wanted his help invading the Karnak and springing you."

I hoped I'd sounded casual enough.

"Some freaking stage kiss?" Ric asked. "You'd think a rock star could get whole harems of a lot more than kisses in the dressing room every night."

"It's like a job application. The dude thinks he's going to find Cinderella or something. I didn't pass the glass lip-lock test."

"He kissed you? You let him?"

I didn't think Ric was ready for the potential multiple orgasm part yet. Maybe never.

"You know I've never been the groupie type. I admit I found it pretty humiliating and sure hated the idea of kissing another man when I was rounding up a rescue party for you, *mi amor.* But it proved worth the hassle. Ric, he raised a dragon from its ashes to help take down the mummy legions!"

"No big deal. I can raise zombies. So back to this kiss thing—"

"That *was* a big deal. I really, really didn't want to be unfaithful to you but I guessed he was the only Vegas mogul who could or would save you."

"I can see you were between a rock and a soft place. A kiss is just a kiss," Ric consoled me, ironically quoting the song from *Casablanca*.

"Not Snow's," I admitted. "The mosh-pit women who get it are forever addicted to trying to get another, but they never do."

"Women go nuts over those rock idols."

"Once was enough for me, since it got you back."

I didn't mention how very specifically it got him "back." From the dead.

"I can dig the bastard would want to kiss you but it's awful petty to make a guy's girlfriend give out just to revive a dead dragon and take on a pack of vampire mummies."

I laughed, as he meant me to do, glad this iffy confession was over.

After all, a kiss is just a kiss unless it's a key to immortality.

Chapter Fifteen

"BASTARDS!"

The deep-toned bellow beside me sounded like a cry of the damned from Hell.

It was Ric, visiting the Land of Dream and finding out-takes from his recent all-too-real nightmare of capture, torture, death, and revival.

He'd sat up, sweeping off the black satin sheets and reaching out to throttle unseen attackers. "Hell-born bastards!"

"Yes, but you escaped them. You're free now." I tried to soothe but sounded ineffective even to me.

"*They're* not free," he shouted, pushing out of bed and scrabbling for his clothes in the dark.

This was a walking, talking nightmare. I felt for my own shed clothes alongside the bed.

Ric was heading for the bedroom door, mumbling about car keys.

I stumbled after, barefoot, pulling on my jeans as I went and sticking an arm through my knit-top sleeve. Wherever he was going I was going with him, but not bare-chested too.

The door to the garage was already slamming shut. I rushed through to hear the garage door grumbling as it lurched upward and the driveway security lights came on automatically. Ric's house had the latest "smart" gadgets.

Whew! Hermie had literally "delivered" already, keys and all. The Vette engine roared into hot-throated life. I yanked open the passenger door and jumped in just as Ric shifted gears, backed out, and turned into the street with a banshee engine howl.

The garage door and lights were closing down, computer-controlled.

The low classic sports car was controlled by a driver who was a nightmare walking, with a crazy woman riding shotgun on what promised to be a wild ride.

Funny how when you save someone's life you don't want him to throw it away.

"Ric," I yelled over the whine of the four-hundred-horsepower engine. All those powerful hooves were almost striking sparks off the pavement. "Where are you going?"

"The bastards," he growled, increasing our speed to over one hundred, I'd bet. The side windows were open, so I practically had to hold my hair on . . . until a silver net of a scarf materialized to do the job for me.

I figured if my silver familiar was not panicking but being practical, I should be too.

I stopped trying to rubberneck and read the speedometer needle. I eyed Ric's fierce profile instead as we took a freeway on-ramp at high speed. His eyes squinted against the wind but they were open, and the car *varoomed* up Highway 95 dead center of the lane, as if it ran on a track instead of costly vintage gasoline.

"Where are we going?" I shouted.

"To Hell," he shouted back.

Oh, well. As long as this wasn't just an aimless race to nowhere . . .

At this hour of the night we met only a few lonely big rigs heading south. The low-slung Vette was surprisingly solid but did a little stomach-churning boogie as the semis tried to suck us into their slipstream.

Actually, if I hadn't been worried about Ric's state of mind, I've have enjoyed the heck out of this furious fun-house escape trip.

By now we were so far from anywhere anyone wanted to *be from* or *go to* that the desert was a blank black canvas. We saw only what the headlights revealed.

It was like cutting the dark with a butter knife, or a bronze bullet.

Without warning, Ric braked hard and spun the small steering wheel. The Vette did a TV chase-scene 180 and stopped.

We were facing back into the night we'd dissected with speed, a ton and a half of low-slung Detroit steel, and Ric's justifiable nightmare fit of rage.

We both sat there panting, feeling the cool desert wind curry our hair with its sagebrush-scented fingers.

In the distance, something howled.

"Coyote," Ric said, finally looking at me. "Not wolf. Even the werewolves don't come way out here to hunt."

His hands were still strangling the small steering wheel. I understood what the car represented to him, the same thing that Dolly meant to me. Choice, refuge, and escape.

I looked nervously behind us. No headlights coming. Ric seemed calmer here. He was desert-born, after all.

"'Bastards,'" I repeated. "Were you thinking of capturing El Demonio and his cartel crew?"

His head snapped to face me. "Helena told you all the current specifics of that? What else did she spill?"

We would either go soap opera here, or not. "Lighten up, Montoya. You are such a trial for us mothering types. Of course we talked all about you. She even gave me sex tips."

"Jesus, Del!"

He looked so shocked I almost laughed. "For *me,* not you. Seems she could tell I was an uptight virgin who didn't have a clue."

"Not so much lately," he said absently.

"So, who are the 'bastards' that drove you out of a nice warm bed with me into the desert dark?"

"Not 'who,' what. I just remembered that part."

"The tsetse flies and leeches? The biting and draining?"

He was shaking his head even as I suggested that, as if his torture and temporary "death" were trivial matters already far behind him. I hadn't yet told him he might have been clinically dead, though.

"No, nothing to do with me," he said. "I risked that sort of thing every time I went to Mexico the past year."

His casual confession made me shudder in the chill night desert air. No wonder Helena was concerned. Ric had been flirting with a rematch with El Demonio and his henchmen for years. A wimp he was not, at least not on his own behalf.

His eyes closed, I could see in the dashboard uplight, holding in the brown contact lens. I had so much more to confess to him. Better do the rest gradually. Ric was replaying some horror other than his hours in the hands of the Karnak vampires, something more painful for him than any physical abuse.

I laid my arm along the seat back, stroked my fingers into the soft hair at his nape. "Tell me, *amor.*"

He shivered this time, a frisson of present pleasure overlying the just-past horror that had gripped him.

"I only glimpsed it, like a flash of some ungodly circle of Hell. The people, the numbers and numbers of people, and so many of them children."

I waited.

His eyes opened as he faced me again, features contorted by rage and disbelief. "*Children.* Do you realize what that means, Del? This goes far beyond a few tourists disappearing at the Karnak recently."

I nodded. "They were prisoners?"

"Yes, and now that you've told me about the vampires, I realize they'd been captive for years, maybe decades and centuries. They were penned like cattle, food stock for an entire buried civilization of vampires. Bred to feed the future since far, far in the past. Bred to reproduce and replace themselves. Virtually naked, filthy, fed to be drained and finally cast away, mindless as zombies, barely sensate."

He described a scene of the damned in Hell.

"Surely," I suggested, "their dainty pharaohships don't sip from unclean stock? Did you meet them at all?"

"I dreamed it all again. I was caught in some endless gray underworld and taken before their thrones. The splendor you describe around them is a blur. They wanted me to tell them how I raised the dead. Since dowsing is an inborn talent, it's not a translatable skill. They didn't want to hear that and had me taken below again, but not before a pair of crocodile-headed guards held me immobile and the pharaohs each drank from the vampire bat-bite scar on my neck."

This time *I* shut *my* eyes. That damn boyhood "vampire bat bite."

"Those ancient, noble vampires are spoiled and lazy, Del," Ric said, knowing I blamed myself. "It was the easiest point of entry. After sharing a bloody kiss they blotted their lips on a linen square and watched as I was dragged away. I think they always get First Blood when there's a mass feeding, after the victims have been cleaned and stripped for the real bloodbath."

"No wonder you tried to outdrive your dreams," I said.

Glancing again into the side-view mirrors, I saw only darkness in the distance. It was as if everything living in the night had drawn away from our presence and the matters we discussed and the fates we'd escaped.

"They've got to be destroyed," he said matter-of-factly. "All of them, all the profiteers and string-pullers who exploit the supernatural-human struggle to come to terms with each other. I don't care if they're some corporate 'Immortality Mob,' the Mexican crime cartels, our own rogue human citizens, or subterranean vampires. You say a 'coalition' of Vegas bigwigs organized a rescue party for me? That could be promising. How'd you manage that?"

"You know. I started with Christophe and the Brimstone Kiss."

"Smart, I see that now." Ric grinned at me, happily innocent of how deeply I'd felt the price I'd paid. "It takes a bastard to shut down a city of bastards. He could be king of this town if he wanted to. Guess he can't surrender the stardom and those idolizing mosh-pit groupies."

"I'm sure that's an inducement to someone with an ego as big as the Convention Center," I said, nervously, glancing again to the side-view mirror.

Two tiny yellow eyes flashed far and wee in the darkness behind us.

"Maybe we should get going," I suggested.

"We're okay."

"You've done this before?"

"Yeah, when things get to me. Usually I drive until I'm out of gas and then walk to the lights to get some."

I looked around at the enveloping dark. "What lights?"

"There are always lights somewhere in the dark if you keep going long enough and walk far enough."

"Uh, very philosophical, but those headlights are closing in on us from behind. Even if they're not, I do not want to meet whatever would have eyes that big and move that fast."

Ric glanced to the rearview mirror above the dash.

"Just a deadheading semi driver speeding."

The headlights swelled to the size of fireballs. "Ric!"

I squinched my eyes shut, braced my feet, and hunched my shoulders, anticipating a rear-end collision. Jeez, after all we'd gone through we'd be bug juice on the front of a massive grille. At least no one would suck us dry. I wondered if Grisly Bahr would ID us . . .

Ric floored the Vette. I was slapped back so hard and fast in the seat the wind was sucked out of my chest. We accelerated to max in what felt like five seconds flat. When I glanced in the side mirror the two paired headlights were shrinking down to bug size themselves and my heart was pounding for nothing.

"That was a rush," I commented.

"Nothing like a near miss to make you feel alive again," Ric said, letting the car slow down to twenty miles over the speed limit.

Was I going to argue with anything that made him literally feel alive again? Nope.

His hand on my inner thigh promised that I'd soon be feeling very live again myself. We had lots to think about: Vegas supernaturals and politics, the nature of Hell in world mythology, revenge, death, destruction . . .

Was it any wonder that making love, not war, came out on top? At least if I was.

Chapter Sixteen

THE PAST FEW days' events gave me much to think about as I drove Dolly home to the Enchanted Cottage late the next morning.

Ric wanted to use his discreet law enforcement contacts to investigate if word of the Karnak vampires was drifting around.

That would mean his checking with Captain Kennedy Malloy, but the rivalry was more on her side than mine. I was okay with it. Ric also swore that, no matter what he found out, he wouldn't go back to the Karnak without me. Not that I was crazy for a return engagement.

So we'd agreed to switch roles: he'd take the investigative lead for the next day or so; I'd get some R&R.

I welcomed time on my own. I needed nothing so much as the fast-food jumbo burger and fries beside me to share with a joyous Quicksilver, then to take a nice long nap until late afternoon.

Quicksilver had hated being home alone while I was out cavorting with Ric. After I awoke, I tossed something to sweat in over the hip-slung silver familiar, donned light tennies, grabbed Quick's chain leash, and we headed for Sunset Park.

Quicksilver bounded along the curving red-clay packed path ahead of me as we jogged. By now the western mountains were softening the sunlight. Day workers had gone home along with night-attraction-seeking tourists. We had the park pretty much to ourselves. Soon I was panting and Quick wasn't. Who was the dog here and who was the master?

I slowed to a walk as I watched him bound onto the grass and weave among the trees with their individual plaques commemorating the dead. I don't know why people could memorialize loved ones in the park, but it was a nice touch. At least there weren't actual bodies under the trees, like the old bones Ric and I had uncovered here earlier.

Sunset Park was peaceful at six in the evening, off the traffic noise from Sunset Road. I welcomed returning to daily routine. Even the silver familiar had stretched into a chain so fine I couldn't feel its eternal presence for now, especially with Quick's heavy-duty steel leash chain looped twice around my hips until I needed it again.

I felt as happy and secure as the old Wichita, Kansas, Delilah Street, a dedicated career girl with a house, a dog, and a future . . . before a vampire anchorman and a jealous TV-station weather witch blew all that away. I picked up my pace to keep an eye on Quicksilver, now a flashing gray form a hundred yards ahead.

I loved watching his bounding gait off leash and pounded after him, past a bench hosting a flash of flowery pastel orange and blue.

Wait a minute!

I stopped to trot back to the bench.

Sure enough, my old pals Chartreuse and Flamingo from mobster Cesar Cicereau's cast of werewolf flunkies were sitting there, looking hollow-eyed.

They weren't pretty to begin with, these late-middle-aged guys with sagging abs, thinning hair, wrinkles, and warts. Werewolves or not, they displayed that insane desire of some older human men for rainbow-colored leisure wear. Maybe it was liberating after a lifetime limited to the blue, beige, gray, brown, and black of men's clothing.

Me, I wore a cherry-red terry-cloth shorts and tank top jogging set—but I'm a girl, so they tell me.

"Were you gentlemen expecting me?"

"And your big dog too," Tangerine said, nodding at Quicksilver charging toward us like a pewter bullet.

"We have orders to escort you to the Gehenna," Baby Blue explained.

I missed the earlier nicknames I'd given them the first time they kidnapped me: Chartreuse and Flamingo. Kinda like Starsky and Hutch or Brad and Angelina.

Quicksilver skidded to a stop beside me, his shoulder hard against my hip, teeth bared to display his panting tongue. The Izod shirt twins backed up.

Werewolves had a major advantage over vampires when jousting for control of Vegas in the 1940s. They could look and act purely human for all but three nights a month. Sunlight-allergic vampires were out of action sleeping for twelve of every twenty-four hours.

On the other hand, werewolves were just ordinary mobsters most of the time, not monsters. That was a disadvantage when they needed to get tough with a woman who had a huge wolfhound-wolf-cross dog looking on. Quicksilver was *always* half-wolf—24/7—in a city that rocked around the clock.

"Um," said Tangerine, "no dog this time."

"Tell *him,* not me."

"Um," said Baby Blue, who did happen to sport watery eyes of that shade, "we are not putting the bag on you, Miss Street. We are just offering a chauffeur service at Mr. Cicereau's beck and call."

I spotted a charcoal gray stretch limo purring in the

parking lot. Much better than the dingy white van they had hustled me and Quicksilver into before.

I glanced at Quick. His eerily human blue eyes were regarding me with unarticulated agreement. He could pace that limo on Highway 95 if he had to. Ordinary wolves can outrun cars at street speeds. Quicksilver had a turbo in his tank that put him in the speed-demon range, like a cheetah.

"And why should I accept a ride from two guys who dropped to all fours at Starlight Lodge last month and tried to run me down and tear me apart?"

They eyed Quicksilver, each other, and then me.

"Look, Miss Street, we were there, yeah," Tangerine admitted.

"And we did the Change. Had to," Baby Blue said.

"But we're just small stuff," Tangerine added. "We were hit-and-bit late in life. We're only good for a little wild game or chicken-chasing, honest."

"Nothing human," Baby Blue added. "We're late converts. Never got the taste. We never would have laid a fang on you."

"Never would have had a chance, either," I pointed out.

"True. We don't even get near the, uh, kill. The alphas throw a few tidbits to the fringes. That's us. That's all we get."

"'Tidbits'?"

"Not so much bone and blood," Tangerine explained eagerly. "Just some organ meats like any human can find in the grocery store."

"Some organs make pretty grisly fare," I pointed out. "Hearts, livers. We humans aren't like turkeys with hanging neck giblets to suck off and distribute in blood gravy."

"*Eeuw.*" Baby Blue was quick to defend. "We don't get those big, important organs thrown to us, no siree."

He glanced desperately at Tangerine. "Just the useless bits, like, uh—"

"Spleens," Tangerine put in. "Not even needed in live humans. Three-to-six-inch little sausage things like you'd put in a bun."

Quicksilver must have enjoyed the Pastel Brothers' verbal tap-dancing act, because he pushed his fanged muzzle close to their crotches and growled.

They paled in unison and shut up.

"You guys have a lot in common with Quicksilver. He likes to chow down on little sausage things too."

They back-stepped both physically and verbally. "Look, Miss. This is a friendly let's-just-talk sort of 'meet,' honest. It's not even Mr. Cicereau who sent the limo. It's Mr. Sansouci."

Sansouci? Had there been a palace coup at the Gehenna?

Now I was getting interested. Sansouci was Cicereau's right-hand man and not voluntarily. Cicereau had tried to use me and—when that hadn't worked out—kill me. He'd offed his own teenage daughter decades ago, so I had no doubt about his murderous capabilities.

Sansouci, on the other hand, had a certain hard-bitten self-interest I could work with. "Hard-bitten" was the right expression. I'd recently learned he wasn't a Gehenna werewolf but a daylight vampire, a new breed that hankered for a new dawn of cooperation between vampires and Vegas humans: voluntary long-term blood donors rewarded with exotic vampire sex.

"Mr. Sansouci, he—" Tangerine began and then faltered, eyeing his compadre.

Baby Blue gathered himself, shut his eyes, and bit the bullet. "Mr. Sansouci said we should say . . . please."

We all four kept shocked silence. That was simply not proper mob protocol for human or werewolf.

I shrugged. "I'm not dressed for a meeting and I need to get Quicksilver home. He's been on twenty-four-hour duty lately and might snap at the wrong spleen among your crew."

"Fine." Tangerine sighed in relief. "We'll give you two a lift to Nightwine's place and wait for you to get ready, like a, um, date. The boss isn't quite ready to see you, either. Right, Marvin?"

"Right." Baby Blue bolted for the idling limo and opened the back door.

Quicksilver bounded inside to check it out.

"Watch the claw marks on the leather," Tangerine cried. "Mr. Cicereau nips off ears for that. Sir."

I ducked to follow Quick inside. "You boys *know* what Quicksilver nips off."

They shuddered in tandem and piled into the luxurious upholstered cavern behind the solid black window between us and the unseen driver.

Little Red Riding Hood had never dreamed of a classier ride, with two werewolves and an Enchanted Cottage at the end of it. And no grandmother, except maybe Caressa Teagarden way out at Sunset City.

Chapter Seventeen

FIRST THING I did when I got inside and alone at the cottage was to call Ric. I'd learned my lesson.

"Cicereau sent a limo for you and said 'please'?" He chuckled. "Now I *really* don't trust him. Anyway, I've found a quirky little lead at the morgue. Keep your cell on vibrate and on your body at all times."

"Any place special I should keep it?"

"Don't tempt me with interesting options. I'm a sick man."

He sounded perfectly fine, except I was starting to find his waking mental blank on his Karnak ordeal a bit eerie. Was Mama just a shrink or a head-shrinking witch doctor?

While I showered upstairs with Quick watching our "guests" in the driveway below, I mused aloud about the proper attire for a meeting with a chastened werewolf mob boss. I was curious if the Enchanted Cottage's newly emerged and still invisible lady's maid had the skills of a consulate advisor in a foreign country.

I emerged from the shower.

Hanging from the chrome dress fixture I'd bought at Wichita's Prairie Rose dress shop when it went out of business in the Crash of '08 was a black sixties pantsuit. It had wide bell-bottom legs and a riding-style jacket over a white ruffle-cuffed and neck-ruffled blouse. Retro Edwardian. Very Mrs. Emma Peel of *The Avengers*.

One couldn't get more properly kick-ass than Diana

Riggs's Mrs. Peel, so I happily donned it along with a pair of square-toed, gray patent-leather sling-backs. The shoes were also highly kick-ass. Metal cleats underlay those sturdy square toes.

The silver familiar chain looped itself thrice around my neck, dangling a sinister six-inch white rhinestone hand with each finger dipped in a pointed marquis-cut scarlet rhinestone "fingernail." Butler and Wilson from the days of lovely '80s excess.

Grrrr. Snap! My, what big claws I have.

I pulled my black hair into a low ponytail at my nape and reluctantly decided against wearing a fedora. Vegas was *not* fedora country. Though the pantsuit wasn't pin-striped, it broadcast a nice air of Broadway musical mobster, so when the Devil tries to "drag you under by the sharp lapels of your checkered coat" you can do your own dragging back. Cesar Cicereau, not I, was going to be the dragee at this meet.

I'd learned as a TV reporter that dressing for the assignment unconsciously positions people—and now even *un*humans—to act according to *your* scenario, not theirs.

The outfit, though modest, had another tactical advantage. Sansouci, a highly heterosexual hunk, would fall like a ton of testosterone for this shady lady maybe-dominatrix outfit.

Score two for the Enchanted Cottage's anonymous personal closet shopper.

I went downstairs to make sure the kitchen witch had refreshed Quicksilver's water and food bowls. He'd come inside to greet me, and now laid his handsome head on graceful, deerlike forelegs to sigh dramatically.

"You're a good dog," I told him, "but these big tough

werewolf bad guys get so twitchy around wolfhounds. Me and my Mrs. Peel pantsuit can handle them."

"GEHENNA" WAS THE Jewish version of Hell, a place where both soul and body could be destroyed in "unquenchable fire," if I remembered the Gospel of Mark from Our Lady of the Lake Convent School religion classes.

Here in Las Vegas, the Inferno Hotel had copped the "unquenchable fire" theme-park look. The Gehenna had settled for deeply, darkly, dangerously, enticingly menacing.

The sprawling hotel-casino crouched on the flat landscape like a supersized Bruce Wayne batcave or maybe a charcoal-colored, glassy tidal wave frozen in mid-storm-surge. It made wolfish gray into a direr shade of black.

The limo paused at a side entrance. I strode past bracketing musclemen, through a row of glass doors, and into the cool shadowy interior, my eyes momentarily blinded.

Blinking fast put two more hunks of wolfish muscle and Sansouci into focus between them. He was pocketing the tiny earphone that had announced my arrival.

"I'll escort Miss Street from here," he said, taking my upper arm in a grip part courtesy and part custody. "You're not carrying," he noted, eyeing the sleek pantsuit and not-so-sleek me in it. I'm more tennis player than fashion model and stand almost six feet in heels.

For answer the ruby fingernails of the glittering hand on my ruffled chest morphed into scarlet snake heads and hissed. Sound effects were a new manifestation of the silver familiar, in operation only since our subterranean march on the Karnak's undead minions just days ago.

The memory made me shiver a bit.

Sansouci wasn't scared of big bad red rhinestones. In fact, he eyed them with a glint of vampire lust.

"Vegas does keep our hotel-casinos freezing," he said, smiling to detect my involuntary shiver.

Sansouci was a couple inches taller than I, broader and more muscular. With his forest-green eyes and his black hair strafed with silvery highlights, what a handsome dog he was! No wonder I'd taken him for a member of the werewolf mob, not a vampire.

"You know that Cicereau hates me and it's mutual," I said.

"Then why did you come?"

"Because you said 'please.'"

"The flunkies said 'please.'"

I shrugged his hand off my arm as we stepped through verdigris and copper doors into a private elevator. "And I wondered why Cicereau sent forces to aid Christophe. They don't strike me as brothers-in-arms."

"They're mortal enemies," Sansouci confirmed, "but thanks to you we've found a more worrisome breed of immortal enemies right under our noses."

I smiled tightly. *Sansouci* would give me credit. He was actually a stand-up guy for a bloodsucker. Cesar Cicereau was a Vegas founding father. He gave no one credit.

This elevator car was a lot more elaborate, and forest-like, than the public ones that led to guest floors and that I'd taken before to Cicereau's offices up top.

Exotic woods with black, white, golden, and red grains as tight as shades of wolf fur were carved into a thick tree-like bas-relief against a dusky, deep amber-tint mirror that glinted like wolf eyes around me. I felt surrounded by an Art Nouveau woodcut in living color, not stark CinSim black-and-white.

So awesomely beautiful! Someone in the Gehenna werewolf pack had the soul of an artist.

"How's Montoya doing?" Sansouci asked as the floors whisked by.

"Better than could be expected."

"I guess his FBI nickname of 'Cadaver Kid' proved more appropriate than anybody suspected."

"You're fishing, Sansouci. I don't take bait. Ric is doing fine and so am I."

"Cesar Cicereau isn't."

The elevator halted but I hit the STOP button to keep the doors from opening. "I should care? He wanted to use me. When I escaped that fate he tried to kill and eat me."

"Those whom the gods cannot use they then destroy."

"The actual quote is: 'Those whom the gods would destroy they first make mad.' "

Sansouci grinned, damnably roguish, Clark Gable–style. I "got" the devoted harem of human ladies who served as his moveable feast with no loss of life beyond what a blood donation site would take.

"You were born mad as a hornet," he said, "so it was hardly a fair fight, Delilah. You won't believe what the Old Man has been reduced to since you last saw him."

"You care? You're a political prisoner. At least *you* said so."

"I care when things happen in this town that are more supernatural than we're used to dealing with." His voice lowered to a mock-wolfish growl. "Can we move on, or do you like being penned in a small steel box with me?"

Oooh, shades of being buried alive with a vampire. No thanks! I hit the red STOP button again so it popped out and the doors slid silently open.

"This is the office level," I noted. "Reached by a different elevator."

"Right. The boss's private car, but the same office,

scene of our martial arts dance in the dark when you first broke in, I still don't know how—"

Good. My mirror-walking talents were still a mystery to Sansouci and therefore his boss. I hustled down the hall, eager to find out what had become of Cicereau.

The office was empty. I paused in the doorway, eyeing the mirrored wet bar that had been my entrance and exit point. To an observer I would have looked like someone hankering for a drink.

Sansouci brushed past me to the humongous executive chair behind the desk, where he stood staring at the computer screen.

I'd sat there when I'd secretly returned to download the 1940s photo of Cicereau with his "family." That had included an infinitesimally younger version of Sansouci . . . the usual towering Vegas chorus-girl arm candy, Vida . . . and Cesar's teenage daughter, Loretta, soon to be his murder victim for the sin of loving a vampire prince, not a werewolf.

"Look," Sansouci ordered.

I reluctantly rounded the desk to stand beside him. Sansouci was equally effective as seducer and slayer. I kept my distance when I could.

The blank black screen I stared at was like the famed electronic billboard in Times Square. Big bright moving crimson letters paraded endlessly across it: ASK DELILAH STREET.

"So now I'm an oracle?" I asked.

"To Cesar Cicereau you are. And maybe his salvation."

Sansouci looked somber but I wanted to laugh.

I wasn't sure about anybody's salvation in the world that existed after the Millennium Revelation, least of all mine, but Cesar Cicereau would be on the bottom of my Most Likely To Be Saved list.

"I don't like Cicereau, man or beast," Sansouci admitted, "but I like what's happening to him even less. It doesn't bode well for our little supernatural playpen here in the Nevada desert."

"'Our?' Leave me out of that category."

He stared at my chest, which didn't need the enhancement of ruffles. The pointed ruby rhinestone fingernails were now dripping pendants of mock blood drops.

So sue me. I was a bit on the supernatural side myself these days.

"The 'Cadaver Kid' truly lives up to his rep now," Sansouci went on, "and you ain't just a wayward orphan *CSI* corpse anymore. Remember, I watched you raise the beloved dead."

That cold shiver hit me again. "Wayward orphan?" Sansouci had been researching my background. Nothing supernatural about that. He'd also been speculating about what Ric and I had been and become before and after the recent rescue mission under the Karnak Hotel.

"You combine the worst of human and super, you know that?" I told him. "Snoop *and* lech. And leech," I added, because it was a handy play on words.

"Also the best, maybe? Just hang on, let me show you why Cesar wants to see you so badly."

SANSOUCI BENT TO touch the screen, banishing my name to bring up a mini-movie.

The scene was so dark it looked filmed in black-and-white. Once the action started, scarlet ropes of fresh, spilled blood whiplashed across the somber screen and even spattered the camera lens. These were outtakes too violent even for Hector Nightwine's gruesome *CSI V* TV show.

I jolted back as if I were a target. "What the hell? This was filmed at this hotel?"

"Security cameras." Sansouci touched a corner of the screen so the scene shrank and became more comprehensible.

A dark shambling figure was churning through five or six uniformed people trying to block its path. One by one the guards were seized, slashed in a major artery, and tossed aside, spewing blood like human fountains.

The daylight vampire did the voice-over while we both intently watched the bloodbath, for different reasons.

"Whatever weapon he's using cuts *down* along the arteries, not across," Sansouci pointed out with creepy expertise, "cuts through tissue and muscle and bone. Maximum blood. Wasteful."

Sansouci sounded clinical but I saw him bite his lip. Then lick it. For a vampire, this must resemble watching the Roman Circus, bloody stimulating and even entertaining.

The last guard standing wheeled to run. In an instant the man's face did a 180 turn over the shoulder, eyes popping. The huge shadow bent over him as jets of arterial blood flared into a hellish halo over the victim's head.

A limp lump of fabric and flesh was tossed aside as the marauder moved on, out of camera range.

My pulse was pounding. This was mass slaughter and the site was clearly deep inside the Gehenna.

"Don't the hotel security cameras move to follow intruders?" I asked.

"Yeah, but it learns. After this, it batted down the other cameras like King Kong grabbing airplanes from the top of the Empire State Building."

"What, or who, is it?"

"Some hellish new supernatural. It got all the way to the public areas before the alarms went off. It must have retreated, or hidden. This is the second incursion in twenty hours. The first almost caught Cicereau alone in his office, staring at the 'Ask Delilah Street' message that's taken over his computer."

"He can't think *I'm* doing this?"

"He doesn't think; he fears. He does believe you know something about what's going on."

"No, I don't. So I might as well leave now."

His hand caught my upper arm, way too tight this time. "No. *I* think you may know something about what's going on too. You're staying and talking to the boss." His expression softened. "Besides, I *know* you'll enjoy seeing him again."

I jerked my arm away, mostly because he finally let me. That's what I liked about Sansouci. He was a thug but he didn't overplay the role.

Now he had me curious.

"Delilah," he added, "you're a major player in this town now."

Huh? I didn't try to translate that. Sure, I'd freaked everybody out by seeming to raise Ric from the dead but maybe they just hadn't tried CPR on him. And they hadn't possessed the magic of the Brimstone Kiss once removed.

Why the hell hadn't Snow tried that supernatural kiss thing on Ric himself? Afraid of being labeled gay? That was such a delightful new way to mentally slander Snow that I hardly paid attention when Sansouci hustled me out of the office back to the elevator.

I MULLED OVER the murders on the security tapes while we were whisked up another few floors. Las Vegas kingpins were addicted to heights far above the madding crowd.

The taped scene was disturbingly brutal. Werewolves relished a chase and vampires liked to linger quietly over a fresh drink. This marauder had a relentlessly machinelike air I'd seen in action before. It reminded me of something, but the link stayed vague.

The elevator opened on the foyer to Cicereau's penthouse.

I entered another elaborately carved and gilded chamber of stylized tree trunks thick enough to form a prison wall.

Here we also faced six disturbingly lupine guards, hairy enough to resemble hulking Victorian gentlemen with sidewhiskers, say the Mr. Hyde side of Dr. Jekyll.

These weren't the fully human Cicereau pack members who usually faced the public. Nor had they been sent to Christophe as "soldiers" for the war against the Karnak crew. These were Cicereau's paw-picked bodyguards, the weres who never fully reverted to human for some reason, like the half-were biker gangs on the Vegas streets.

That thought reminded me of my least favorite fledgling half-were, Vegas cop Irving Haskell. He was not among this elite pack yet, thank Larry Talbot.

In fact, I wished I was facing a tormented, self-hating werewolf like the "Larry Talbot" persona actor Lon Chaney Jr. had pioneered. In 1941 *The Wolf Man* classic horror film portrayed the title character as all angsty dude, with my devoted CinSim and all-around character actor, Claude Rains, playing his father figure.

Back in 2009, the film was remade with Benicio Del Toro in the wolfman role and Sir Anthony Hopkins in the Rains part. Goes to show you the old thriller classics had more universal appeal than critics at the time thought.

Changing into something worse than you thought you were is a major psychic nightmare of the human condition.

Unfortunately, Cesar Cicereau felt no regrets at having

to tear out human throats as often as I got my periods. He was in his inner sanctum, a bedroom with three rock-hewn tiers leading up to the huge round bed.

A semicircular plasma TV faced the bed with my name up in lights on it, in red LED moving dots, like the computer screen below, only Times Square bigger.

ASK DELILAH STREET.

Like Howard Hughes in his scraggly late-life incarnation as a vampire, the stocky, fleshy-faced Cicereau would not enhance an orgy movie set. Especially now that I could see the beads of sweat on his unshaven upper lip from twenty feet away.

He growled when he spotted me, clawing the olive-green brocade coverlet with fingernails so ragged they snagged the expensive threads. Otherwise he resembled your stereotypical mob boss: middle-aged, constipated with power, and about as attractive as week-old corned beef and cabbage in a Dumpster.

"Okay," he barked at me. "Talk."

A sudden flutter in the treelike lattice of vines above his bed made me look up. I spotted Phasia twining her fluid fey form snakelike through the thick leaves. Even higher above, I spotted her "sister," Sylphia, whose body glimmered like a glam-rock eye-shadow counter at Sephora.

The pair had sweet unearthly faces and skinny Barbie-doll-like limbs. No larger than eight-year-old human children, they were apparent adults of their kind. Phasia's pearly skin had a snakish pattern, as Grizelle's black human skin showed a tiger-striped one.

I'd never seen either fey sister shape-shift into snake or spider, but they harbored characteristics of both.

I wasn't surprised to look farther into the room's bordering shadows to see Madrigal, the Gehenna strongman magician, also on guard with his performing familiars. Things were bad if Cicereau was trusting to magical guardians rather than to his extensive wolf pack.

"I have no idea why my name has shown up on your personal and public hotel electronics," I told the boss. "I'm just a paranormal investigator. Maybe you need an exorcist."

"You hit it on the spot, sister. That's exactly what I need." He eyed me hungrily. "Get out," he ordered the werewolf guards. "You too."

I felt Sansouci's custodial hand drop away. The thick carpeting was too cushy for footsteps to be heard, yet I sensed the vampire retreating as silently as the werewolves.

Only Madrigal remained. Our glances crossed but we remained equally expressionless. It wouldn't do to remind the erratic Cicereau that we had known each other, however briefly. The mob boss would no doubt be reassured to know that the fey sisters, at least, hated me the way tween groupies hate a rival for a boy-band member. Madrigal was *theirs*.

Cicereau began jabbing at a gigantic remote control device with dozens of buttons.

"This is what I've been seeing for two damn days anytime I look at any screen in the whole damn hotel."

I turned to watch the semicircular screen behind my back. The upper two-thirds of a human figure appeared, a young girl wearing shades of blue. She talked too, in an accusing baby-doll voice.

"Delilah knows what you did, Daddy. I've been telling her *everything* so that soon *everyone* will know. You had me killed, your own daughter. You slaughtered me and my first beau. Poor Prince Krzysztof. You hated that my boyfriend was vampire but I'm only half werewolf. I had a human mother. What was so wrong about our love? Only your hatred. Delilah knows everything, Daddy. I told her it all."

I watched in frozen disbelief. Thanks, kid. I help find your forgotten murdered bones in Sunset Park. I listen to your vintage sob story in my home-turf mirror, and you snitch on me to your mob boss father in living LED.

Take it easy, whispered Irma. *Cicereau wanted you here because he can use you. Otherwise he'd have offed you without asking questions. Find out what he needs.*

"Yeah," the mobster crooned as if he'd overheard Irma. "That's what my darling daughter would be broadcasting on every TV screen in the hotel if we'd let her. We've had to shut down the Sports Book section," he added indignantly.

Uh-oh. That's where all the lucrative sports bets were made, an area of cushy seats like the world's biggest home theater. Multiple screens ran every football, baseball, basketball, soccer game, and horse or car race in the world. The bets were major.

Cicereau muttered on. "Vengeful little brat has been haunting all my most profitable venues. Even the slot machines are going nutso. You know those video poker machines with the gloved magician hands and dancing wand the tourists love to watch?"

I did. I loved to watch 'em too, truth be told. It was so *Salagadoola mechicka boola bibbidi-bobbidi-boo!* Disney *Cinderella* fairy godmother. I loved the way the animated white gloves and wand turned tricks on the slot machine screen like a chicken-ranch brothel baby on speed.

"I know the machines you mean," I conceded. "Cool."

"Not so 'cool' if the magical gloved hands are grabbing cash out of the tourists' hot little paddies, or even going for their necks and trying to throttle the life out of them."

No more than Las Vegas casinos and other gaming hot spots did every day, I mused as he ranted on.

"If you know so much, Miss Delilah Street, aka Maggie, maybe you know how to get my dead daughter the hell out of my hotel and my life. The sixty-years-buried dead have a lot of nerve showing up where they're not wanted and where they ought to damn well know that by fucking now."

Yes, he was a callous monster of a mobster and I personally would love to see him hounded to the gates of the nearest madhouse by Daughter Dearest.

However, I was in a much more vulnerable form than she: physical and mortal. My first problem was figuring out why she'd dragged me into her family revenge fantasy. Second issue: Why was she showing up here and now?

"It's bad enough," Cicereau groused, "I got a freakish serial killer loose in my operation. I don't need some long-gone daughter giving me public lip."

He was right. He was caught in a pincer attack between the living undead and the dead. Any bad publicity on either front could cripple his operation. Who wanted to check into a hotel where an unstoppable invader could skewer your carotid artery or the boss's dead daughter could show up in *Debbie Does Dallas* on your hotel room flat-screen and take all the fun out of X-rated?

Cicereau pointed a smaller remote control at me.

"I was willing to bring you into my hotel family to make hay on the Maggie craze. Now my crazy daughter is taking over all my venues and taunting me with your name, Delilah Street. You will either rid me of this ghost or you will *be* one. In about five seconds."

He pulled yet another remote control device out from under the covers. A pearl-gripped Uzi. What you might call in Paris a d'Uzi. It was way over-the-top showy but no less effective.

"I need absolute privacy," I told him, "and a single screen where Loretta and I can speak girl-to-girl."

"My office computer? She screwed that up too."

"No, that's too 'you.' What's the most secure screen setup in the hotel?"

Cicereau frowned, then bellowed, "Sansouci!"

He appeared in the bedroom door.

"You heard that?" Cicereau said.

Sansouci nodded. Vampires had supersensitive hearing? Maybe.

"And?" Cicereau aimed the Uzi at his high-end hostage, but what use was an Uzi against an immortal vampire? Guess Cicereau didn't know that I knew Sansouci's real breed.

"Eye in the sky," the daylight vamp said. "I'll take her there."

"Not a bad idea but, shit," said Cicereau, "you do realize that bitch daughter of mine could use the security surveillance system to broadcast her wild charges over the whole hotel?"

"Then we need to get there fast." Sansouci took my arm again, which I was beginning to like when it involved a quick exit. We swung out the door and out of direct Uzi range into the hall.

"Can you exorcise that ghost in the machine?" he asked.

"I can try."

Trouble was, did I *want* to spare Cesar Cicereau the juvenile justice he so richly deserved from his murdered daughter?

Chapter Eighteen

All Las Vegas hotels have wall-to-wall security cameras. Nowadays many are mobile, even nomadic. Before one overblown holographic glass block is laid, the building's skeleton is festooned with hidden camera links. Many newer ones are wireless.

Central control areas are scattered throughout the structure. Sansouci led me to one hidden center and ordered out all the resident spies.

It was just me and him and walls of color and black-and-white screens showing monitored areas, the casinos and shops, elevators, pool areas, even hotel rooms. I felt like a Homeland Security operative.

"You need to expel Loretta," he told me. "If she uses you to get herself broadcast over the entire hotel snoop system we're both dead. You for real, me for a few more centuries of indenture."

"Why'd you get dragged in on this?"

Sansouci's smile was both rueful and sinister. "It's a game Cesar has played with me for decades. He likes me in the target zone. He knows he can't kill me but he can add to my indenture."

"He does that with Madrigal too."

"Yeah? He also wants to sucker you somehow. His daughter's ghost he'd just like to exorcise."

"I'm starting to wonder if she *is* a ghost."

"What else would she be?"

"I get that she and her lover were not of the 'same' supernatural derivation. I understand they alienated both sides of the vampire-werewolf war to control Vegas as it became a hotel and gaming hot spot in the nineteen forties. What about the thirty silver dollars thrown on the still-embracing dead figures?"

"Exactly what you suspect," he said, "to show the lovers were Judases to both sides. The werewolves included an early design of an Inferno Hotel chip as a message to the vamps that they planned to own this town."

"Loretta and her six-hundred-year-old vampire prince were killed by her father, but why were the methods so brutal? Bullets and castration, rape and stabbing. Loretta's a vengeful spirit, sure. But . . . with, I'm beginning to think, ambitions and unsuspected abilities. You never really did her wrong, Sansouci. You just watched. You might still be able to negotiate with Loretta."

Sansouci's hand indicated the static scenes on the dozens of spy cameras. "Nobody can undo yesterday. That's not negotiable. Call her, but don't let her broadcast."

For some reason, my high-profile necklace thinned and slid down behind the neck of my blouse to go undercover as a hip chain.

Call and control Loretta. Easy to say, less easy to do. I was working with emotional plastic explosive, ectoplasmic explosive with a lot of bones to pick. Her own.

"Loretta," I said softly, envisioning the girlish apparition from the Enchanted Cottage hall mirror, wearing a blue taffeta forties gown. Puffed sleeves, flattened bodice, slender waist. She was a prepubescent Disney Snow White with the light brown hair instead of my potent midnight-black locks.

And so she appeared in a flash, a tender pastel vision

of color superimposed on the serviceable black-and-white scenes of the surveillance cameras. I wondered why they still used some of them, instead of all color.

Loretta took the opening line. "Delilah! You came when I called."

"Of course I'd do that. Did you ever doubt?"

"No, I didn't." She frowned, seeing past me. "Why is he here?"

"He?"

"Daddy's prisoner."

"Your daddy doesn't trust me to talk to you alone."

"And just what have we been doing all these times in your hall mirror?" she asked, giggling. "I'm very pleased with you, Delilah."

"Yes?"

"Well, you got *him* back, didn't you?"

How did she know about the showdown under the Karnak, about Ric?

She gushed on girlishly. "It's wonderful he's alive again."

"Yes," I agreed. *How did she know?* If a ghost thought Ric had been really dead . . .

"And he's so powerful now that he's come back." What did she care about Ric? "Don't you think he will become incredibly powerful?"

"I . . . don't know. I'd settle for back the way he was."

"Well, yes, that too, but I want more than the way he was, I want him back the way he could have been if Daddy hadn't . . . let . . . his . . . pack . . . mutilate him . . . and violate me . . . and kill us."

Oh. We weren't talking about the same "he" at all.

"How they killed you both was terrible," I agreed, switching gears fast. "An atrocity."

"Having his head severed truly killed him. He didn't just die. His flesh rotted to nothing. The coroner nicknamed him 'the Bone Boy,' " she added bitterly.

"Coroners need to insulate themselves from the violence of death."

"He's not a 'Bone Boy' anymore."

"No? That's good."

Sansouci's frown was deepening.

"I want to thank you for that," she said. "You've been very helpful."

"It was nothing," I said. "Once I heard your story—"

She giggled. I was beginning to find the giggle sinister.

"That was a great story, wasn't it, Delilah?"

"Of course I realized that you needed to . . . embellish it to win my sympathy."

"You did? You're smarter than I thought. And I knew you had reason to hate my father."

"Who wouldn't? He kidnapped me like I was a paper doll to cut out and use. And what he did to you and your prince . . ." I eyed Sansouci. He had made me think . . . damn his vampire eyes!

"You've done very well, as I said," she added imperiously, "but you're not done. My darling is back in full physical form—"

The rampaging monster on the security tapes!

"—now *I* want to come back physically too."

I finally got the whole scenario, a sort of *Sunset Boulevard*/Sunset Park movie melodrama of lust and death and resurrection for the unhuman set. How had the Bone Boy been fleshed out and animated? By something the Karnak vampires had figured out while torturing Ric? Loretta was supposed to get her long-dead and even-longer-undead lover boy back over my lover's dead body? No way!

"Yes," I conceded to gain time to think, "the ancient Karnak pharaohs may have developed a way to reconstitute bone into muscle and blood-seeking flesh, but Loretta, you're not a vampire. You were never undead, like Prince Krzysztof. You were a half-human werewolf. I doubt ancient Egyptian vampire rituals can raise the dead, only the Undead."

"*NO!*" She stamped her foot, unseen on camera, but I bet it was shod in a soft satin slipper. "They have the means now. And *you* aren't done! Now you must give me a body, make me whole and mortal, or I'll tell Daddy you brought my Bone Boy back and he'll grind *your* bones to powder with his werewolf teeth."

"Sweet," Sansouci muttered under his breath. "Her father's daughter."

We were witnessing a spoiled rotten, mean-girl supernatural tantrum? That didn't make Loretta Cicereau less dangerous.

I started fiddling with the screen controls, focusing past her to the background where tourists milled unaware of the ghost in the foreground.

Also mixing into the tourist scene were some Gehenna CinSims. Black-and-white cameras were their medium. That's why the surveillance cameras weren't all in color! Jeez. These casino owners are so paranoid. Can't even trust their "unreel" help. I fixed the focus on one CinSim after another.

Meanwhile, Loretta was concentrating on bending me to her wants and needs.

"First, Delilah, get that turncoat half-vamp out of here."

I turned to eye Sansouci with a signature Mr. Spock raised eyebrow. The tables had turned. Now Cicereau's dead daughter was bossing him around.

Sansouci made a sour face but shrugged and slipped out via the gray-flannel upholstered door. He was used to high-handed Cicereau ways. The control room was designed to be soundproof, so now Loretta could speak in total secrecy.

Until, that is, she might decide to turn on the audio-visual systems and we'd take over every mike and screen in the hotel-casino.

She lowered her voice despite our complete privacy.

"I know what happened at the Karnak after the pharaohs recovered Krzysztof. They modified ancient rituals to clothe his bones in muscle and flesh and bring him to life again, Delilah. Once they trapped the man who was with you in Sunset Park when you two linked to find me and Krzys, all became possible. You found me so *he* could resurrect the Elder Vampires."

She certainly thought the world revolved around her undead melodrama.

"How did *you* know Ric was captured?" I asked.

"You think you're the only one who can call a moon goddess Dark Mother? Between Hathor's mirror and the moon goddess Hecate's power you escaped the Karnak's royal vampires. I felt the wind of your passage through ancient corridors as if you were air or water.

"Hathor is the protectress of women in business—as we both are, Delilah. We're businesswomen, you small and I . . . major. The goddesses protect women who are cunning as well as beautiful, as we both are. Well, we both are beautiful. Cunning is not your strong point, as it is mine."

Oho, so now I have looks, not brains. I'd been called worse. By better.

Ric's savvy mother-cum-doctor had helped me see that I'd grown up hating my looks because of who—or what—they attracted when I was a vulnerable preteen even younger than Loretta. As a woman grown I could realize I wasn't responsible for whom I attracted. I could accept that my looks were attractive to more guys than half-vamp greasers. Some of those guys might be bad or some might be good but, either way, more power to me.

So it was out with the half-breed vamp boys and on with seriously complex men like Ric. Or seriously supernatural forces like Sansouci and Snow.

In view of my new take on me and men—leaving out my professional orphanhood—it was fascinating to watch Loretta's devious side appear. Her father's daughter. Sansouci had nailed it. Made me almost glad I'd never known a father.

Loretta's Technicolor image cavorted on every black-and-white security screen. I kept surveying the background for random CinSims. She might claim moon goddesses as her allies but I had my Silver Screen legions to call on.

At least, they had called on me when it came to rescuing Ric. That proved the allegiance went both ways.

I noticed a nervous little guy I'd first seen at the craps table in the background of one screen in which Loretta's image now dominated the foreground.

Could it be? *Yes!* Ugarte from the Karnak, aka actor Peter Lorre from *Casablanca,* was now a floating CinSim at the Gehenna. Was he a plant, or an escapee? You'd think he'd have found shelter at the Inferno with Snow or contacted Godfrey to enjoy Nightwine's formidable protection. Those two Vegas moguls were collecting free-range CinSims for their own purposes.

Or had Ugarte already sought sanctuary with one party or the other and then been reassigned to the Gehenna as a spy? His criminal on-screen persona fit right in with gangsters. Every mob needs a house flunky.

Either way, I'd assumed earlier that Ugarte had made sure I learned that Ric was being held prisoner at the Karnak. In that way, this pathetic doomed con-man character from *Casablanca* had heroically tipped off all the topside Vegas Strip lords to Lower Egypt's vampire legions, undermining their power from below.

As soon as I figured out what to do about Loretta turning me into a hotel-wide streaming message, I'd look up Ugarte and get the story from his own pale-gray Silver Screen lips.

Meanwhile . . .

"Why are you using me to aggravate your father?" I asked her.

"You know what he did to me and Krzysztof. I told you our dead souls bonded with you and your Ric when you dowsed together in Sunset Park to find us. We're your matchmakers. You owe us. Ric has paid us back, though he may not know it, but you haven't."

My fingertips grew icy. Loretta considered Ric's capture and torture "payback"?

"You think Ric's ordeal somehow helped the Egyptian vampires raise your Prince Krzysztof?"

"It wasn't an ordeal. It was an honor to be of such vital use to the sacred entwined pharaohs and their people. And I *know* it did."

"He told them where the Sunset Park bones were kept, is that it?"

The coroner's office location was public knowledge. I could see Ric "giving" that away to conceal his real secret: his inborn abilities to dowse for the dead and raise zombies.

"*I* told them where Krzysztof's bones were," she scoffed, as if I were stupid. "No, they have what they really needed from Ric, and you're welcome to the leftovers."

My hands reached for the screen, ready to seize this

bloodthirsty spoiled brat's wrists, or even more happily, her neck.

Of course my fingers curled as they met solid glass. Although I could see Loretta's image, the medium was a camera, not a mirror, and she was safe from me.

More to the point, I was safe from her.

"What am *I* supposed to 'pay'?" I asked.

"You must give me what you gave him, Ric."

I kept silent but my blood iced in my veins again.

"You must meet me in a mirror again and give me the same Kiss of Life."

"It was merely cardiopulmonary resuscitation. CPR won't resurrect someone long dead, like you, Loretta. You saw me pound Ric's chest to get his stopped heart going again before it was too late. That's a common 'miracle' of the late twentieth century you didn't live to see. I was merely acting as any ordinary emergency tech person."

I was, of course, lying big-time right now.

I had to admit to myself now that Ric had been truly dead. I had to admit that Snow's lingering Brimstone Kiss allowed my "Kiss of Life" to reverse mortality. I'd probably pay for that down the line but I didn't know how yet. Nor care. The intensity of my love for Ric scared me plenty. An unloved childhood was not good practice for mature love but somehow both Ric and I had managed to overcome our beginnings. Our endings were a lot more vague.

Meanwhile, Loretta hadn't bought either my arguments or my lies.

"How will we know you can't revive me if you don't try?" she cried. "Now!"

"This isn't a mirror, Loretta."

"Madrigal has a very special one onstage."

Oops. I'd hoped she hadn't known about the magician's

mirror with its front-surface glass. The blue-tinged glass was an entirely natural substance in the real world that eliminated the slight double image all other mirrors cast. That somehow allowed me to project myself more fully into the "world" beyond the reflections.

I had even left a mindless simulacrum of myself in Madrigal's mirror the first time I encountered it. I wondered, if I did indeed give Loretta what was left of the Brimstone Kiss, would our places be exchanged? Might *I* become the permanent prisoner of Mirrorworld while she walked free?

Whatever might happen was too dangerous to risk, not to mention turning her loose on Cicereau and the Gehenna. Her boyfriend's killing spree had already claimed innocent lives. I began to fully understand Ric's tortured continuing responsibility for the zombies he'd been forced to raise for El Demonio Torbellino during his youngest years.

Looking into Loretta's calm yet demanding eyes, I knew she wouldn't care. She'd presented herself to me as a horribly wronged victim, an abused innocent. She'd made me think we had love and loss in common. She'd been wrong, yet I was beginning to see that Cicereau had killed the teenage lovers the brutal way he did for motives beyond mere paternal rage.

"What do you want," I asked, "besides a restored physical form?"

"Nothing much. Revenge and this hotel empire of my father's. His time has come and gone, don't you think?"

Wow. I had a very romanticized view of parental relationships. I may not have goddesses seriously in my corner but I might have some Olympian-like powers myself.

"Give me a little time," I told Loretta. "I need to arrange some things."

She smiled wickedly. "I can't wait to see you set my father up for a fall."

Maybe, maybe not.

The major problem: she was "in" every surveillance camera in the hotel.

I collected Sansouci outside.

"Any place we can talk in absolute guaranteed privacy?" I whispered. Yeah, it looked like we were nuzzling.

"Cicereau has every place in this hotel wired. The surveillance centers are pretty good, but Loretta's got those now."

"Trusting sorts run in the family, eh?"

"Trust is neither a werewolf nor a mobster virtue," Sansouci said, "so we serve double doses of paranoia here at the Hotel Gehenna. However, Cesar is no dummy, either. His extreme paranoia led him to establish an electromagnetic dead zone, eavesdropping- and I'd think also ghost-proof. Only Cesar and his top full-blood assistants use it."

Sansouci was enjoying breathing hotly in my ear, telling me arcane little nothings, so I called him on it.

"Tell Cicereau in just this very secretive way that *I* need to use it."

"He'd bite my freaking lips right off."

"What a grave loss for the Sansouci Ladies Daily Dinner Society. Tell him."

Although I was worried about Loretta's eavesdropping on my plans I also saw she was overconfident. Getting Krzys back from the dead had her high on hormones and revenge.

I knew that feeling now, and how physically blinding extreme emotion was. In the group homes I'd learned to deaden my feelings to conceal my reactions. Now that I'd found and almost lost Ric I understood the power of honest feelings, and I also had some hot ideas on how to manipulate them.

Bad Delilah!

Chapter Nineteen

BY THE TIME Sansouci and I returned to Cicereau's sky-high suite the daylight vampire had become resigned to bearding the werewolf mobster in his rock-star bed.

Cicereau's private rooms were pretty secure but I'd been able to mirror-walk in and out of his office like a ghost. As an actual ghost, Loretta might share my talents in that regard. I was betting that she didn't have all of them.

Sansouci braced one knee on the crushed velvet upholstered bed frame and conveyed my message from his lips to Cicereau's ear. Really, gold crushed velvet was so seventies! Some old things were just tacky. I'd give Cicereau my interior design advice later.

The mobster howled indignation and actually snapped his currently human teeth. Sansouci retreated fast.

I looked at Madrigal. He was attired, or perhaps I should say *not* attired, in his macho stage gear—Roman kilt, bare chest, metal wrist and upper-arm bands, gladiator sandals buckled up to the knee. He still played an impassive palace guard beside the bed curtains.

The mobster growled at me, eyes glaring under thick gray brows, then nodded at Madrigal, who quickly came to my side. The magician's sharp hand gesture signaled the fey sisters to remain topside in the woodsy ceiling bower. They writhed and hissed their objections but stayed put.

So, with a two-hunk escort of vamp and magic man, I left the suite for the elevators. We jetted down a few dozen floors in silence. Sansouci had pressed no buttons so I wasn't surprised when the car charged past the lobby level and lower yet. I gathered Cesar had an elevator control button on his awesome whole-hotel bedside remote control the size of an organ keyboard.

Once again I was plunging into the lower depths of a major Vegas hotel with an iffy escort. The silver familiar had been an invisible hip chain through my latest negotiations. Now it was shifting to upper-arm bands like Madrigal's, ready to be deployed as weapons if necessary.

Madrigal's muscles and weird sister familiars didn't scare me, but Sansouci had been made, not born, a daylight, lady-sipping vampire. Who knew if under extreme pressure he could revert to a traditional blood-sucking killer in a heartbeat—mine—or not.

Umm, Irma purred in my ear, *we're double-dating at last. I'll be happy to take on the vamp.*

Despite her usual randy suggestions, I was happy to have her along for backup. I was beginning to realize that Las Vegas's new supernatural Underworld was also literal. Despite the spectacular high-rise real estate above the Strip, a pit of hidden vice and danger lurked as deep below, an eternal dark reflection.

What little I'd glimpsed of the Inferno's underbelly was a literal re-creation of Dante's nine circles of Hell. What would a werewolf crimelord's basement contain?

The verdigris and copper elevator doors parted to reveal . . . nothing. A dim musty featureless cellar. We might as well have been poking around in Castle Dracula's semi-abandoned cape-and-coffin storage dungeon.

I saw a lot of crates piled here and there but none in a sinister coffin shape. Vampires, except for the hostage Sansouci, were persona non grata in Werewolf Land.

Our shoe soles ground on a patina of sand drifting over the hard-packed floor. Light came from a leprosy of mosses and lichens on the walls, which glowed like deep-sea life-forms. Some moved. Fungi and slugs and maggots and worms and other writhing things made living mosaics. Like Spanish moss or cobwebs, the growths dangled from the low ceiling to brush our heads and bodies.

Madrigal, bare-shouldered and annoyed, twitched his mighty muscles to dislodge the tendrils. A gaudy collar and cape materialized to clothe him.

"So you *are* a real magician," I commented, my voice echoing.

He shrugged again. "A minor talent. Why does Cicereau maintain an unfinished subbasement?"

"Maybe it's a getaway from urban Las Vegas and its surrounding desert," I suggested. Everything damp, dark, and likely to be found under the detritus of a forest floor thrived down here.

Sansouci walked up to a wall and eyed its glowing upholstery of vermin. He pulled a credit card from his back jeans pocket and used it to scrape off some lichens.

I jumped back, Madrigal with me. His gladiator-style sandals offered an impressive display of muscled calves but his feet and lower limbs were exposed to the writhing grubs seeking a new place to attach themselves.

Sansouci was sensibly shod in ankle boots and, despite my steel-toed seventies slingbacks, I dearly missed my secondhand motorcycle boots.

The vampire's credit card (is that a non sequitur or not?) slid into an uncovered, neat, man-made slot in the wall.

Sansouci grinned.

With a sleek mechanical hum wildly out of character for this creepy-crawly place, a clean brushed-aluminum door panel knifed into the opening as the lichen-covered walls slid back.

The panel unfolded accordion-style to reveal a clean shining expanse. We three walked into a gleaming room, floor, walls, and ceiling all burnished in my metal of power, silver. Entering this surgically sterile box felt rather like visiting a gaudy high-tech crypt. Was this an empty safe or a bomb shelter?

"You should be at home in confined places," I told Sansouci, astounded to hear my voice deadened as if the metal walls were swathed in unseen cotton batting.

Meanwhile, the garage-door-sized mobile wall sealed us in.

"I haven't been confined like this for a long time," he said, turning to examine the featureless space. "Cicereau slipped me the key card when I whispered in his ear, which is keen enough that he'd already heard what we required. This seems ultra-private. What did you want to discuss?"

I turned to Madrigal. He was also pacing the perimeter of our silver box—which was illuminated by its own burnished surface—like a lion caught in a trap.

I'd misjudged his motives. He was intrigued, not intimidated, and passed his big hands over portions of the walls. They opened out into other boxy chambers as he strode along. We were inside some giant's metal origami napkin unfolding in all directions.

"Magic," Sansouci muttered.

"Not my magic," Madrigal answered. "I just have a way with magical stage illusions. Sensitive pressure points lurk beneath all these surfaces. Quite a sophisticated construction. Certainly not made by or for Cicereau."

His words had Sansouci and me feeling along the slick

walls, pushing at points where the shining aluminum seemed to dimple.

I gasped as my particular wall unfolded into a train of compartments.

"It could be a trap," Sansouci warned. "Explore the unfolding distances too far, and you many never find your way back, or out."

"Exactly," Madrigal told him. "Or you may find your way out of Cicereau's service and Vegas altogether, which you look as eager to accomplish as I am, my friend. Too bad you and I haven't talked before, vampire. I took you for just another of my jailers."

"Don't get optimistic," Sansouci growled in good imitation of a werewolf mobster. "I swore in the name of my kin and kind to serve Cicereau."

I wasn't interested in their dueling macho supernatural conflicts of interest.

"What is this place?" I asked Madrigal. "How can Cicereau claim and use it?"

"As best as I can guess, it's fey like the Sinkhole, a remnant from the ancient days of earth beyond numbering. The fey have left their mark in every time and place."

"They're still present and powerful then?"

"Present but remote. Powerful but feral," he warned. "The Dread Queen rules in a court consumed with light. She has no heart, or so my feral fey companions say. They've stayed with me because desert places like Las Vegas repel the fey. I've tamed my assistants enough that they prefer my presence. This place may be a tent the fey moored on ancient earth when it was ripe with dark life."

"Older than ancient Egypt?"

"As old as the stars," he answered.

Sansouci snorted, bringing a welcome clap of reality to

the scene. "What would a greedy thug like Cesar Cicereau have to do with such airy fairy beings?"

"He inadvertently may have built his gambling hell on a focus point for the fey," I suggested.

The vibrant wall I touched felt warm. "We truly could be in another dimension for these moments. Cicereau's daughter couldn't penetrate this unearthly place."

"The fey are secretive and unrevealing," Madrigal warned. "Yes, they'd find the spirits of our own world crude and intrusive."

Convinced it was safe to talk here, I said, "All right. Let's not linger. Could I call Loretta into your backstage front-surface mirror and trap her there somehow?"

"As your own image was once mired!" Madrigal got the idea right away. Then he shook his dreadlocked head. "Intriguing but risky. Your mirror double was vague and dispirited, a shadow suitable for a quick illusion onstage, but no more."

"*Whoa,*" Sansouci said. "You kept a captive image of Delilah backstage? And I didn't know about it?"

"Not your business," Madrigal answered. "Cicereau thought I'd magically conjured the *CSI* corpse, Maggie. He wanted her kept top secret. Then, thanks to Delilah calling her image back from afar, the mirror version, her simulacrum . . . vanished before Cesar could decide what to do with her."

I explained myself to Sansouci, since no one could overhear us except perhaps the Dread Queen and she seemed seriously camera-shy.

"Realizing I'd left another skin behind in Madrigal's mirror gave me a high ick factor," I told him. "I used my own mirror to recall or dissolve it."

Sansouci was eyeing me with disbelief. "You can *project*

and *retract* yourself in mirrors? No wonder I couldn't trap you in Cicereau's office! Yet that fool police detective Haskell suckered you."

Did I mention I blush easily?

Sansouci watched my face, then chuckled. "Sometimes you're such an amateur, Street, yet you keep us hopping." He eyed Madrigal and grinned.

The magician shook his head sourly. "You latter-day vampires are being led around by the wrong bodily fluid. Don't let your libido make a fool of you. Amateurs can get us in trouble with Cicereau, and he's no one to cross."

I caught my breath as Sansouci's angered inner vamp hardened every muscle. His frame seemed to gain a hundred pounds and six inches. Blood rushed to his eye-whites and lips as they peeled back from shining white canine fangs. This was the big, bad vampire who'd fought off the spectral hyenas from the Karnak Hotel.

"You play a dangerous game with your fey handmaidens, magician," Sansouci warned. "Don't mistake the face I show Cicereau with reality. When it suits me, I can still take my humans raw, magic or no magic, fey or no fey."

Gulp, Irma gurgled softly in my mind. *Guess our girly power is a might undercooked to trifle with these dudes.*

Yeah. So I might as well appeal to supernatural testosterone with, uh, reason. Madrigal, no lightweight in the human muscle department, was frowning hard by then and I sensed a minor spell coming on.

"You guys should be allies," I pointed out. "You're resident prisoners. I'm only visiting at Cicereau's invitation, remember? Okay, his command. I'm here to do a job for the head honcho. You want to help and get me outa here, or play Incredible Hulks? You gonna let a couple of pretty women, one of them just a slip of a ghost, get you off your game?"

I would *never* have put myself in league with the dainty Loretta, but after my session with Helena Troy Burnside, I had a fresh appreciation of the power of feminine wiles. Any weapon in an impending paranormal storm.

Astonishingly, they bought my argument. You could visibly see their fury subside. Delilah Street, supernatural peacemaker.

"You want to get rid of me," I reminded them softly, "you have to help me. How," I asked Madrigal, "can I use this fey archeological construct to trap Cicereau's vengeful daughter?"

He nodded, ready to deal. "What's left of fey territory in our post-Millennium Revelation era," Madrigal said, still keeping a wary eye on the subsiding Sansouci, "is like a cloth anchored here and there to our world, each touchpoint held down by a single stitch. I found Sylphia and Phasia in such an accidental juncture. Once they've been discovered by humans, they're no longer welcome in fey realms."

"Like birds that fall out of the nest and humans touch?"

"Exactly. Yet, without a linkage to this human world, they would fade and die."

"You are the linkage," I said.

He nodded. "I freed them but they bound me."

"I may indulge libido," Sansouci said, "but you embraced the bonds of lethal matrimony."

Madrigal's face darkened with bad blood, then his expression softened.

"Many risky supernatural bargains were made on either side of the Millennium Revelation, vampire," he said. "Some better, or more bitter, than others."

Sansouci nodded. I sensed a certain truce born of truth between these two men who were not quite simply men.

They turned their gaze on me with an unspoken unity that made Irma moan unhappily in my mind.

Divide and conquer was no longer an option. In fact, I was actually glad that I'd helped point out their common cause.

"Madrigal," I asked the magician, "can you reach your stage mirror from here?"

He turned, regarding the dazzling silver fractured images everywhere. Then he nodded.

"These all must lead to touchpoints. Sylphia and Phasia have marked my stage area. Here."

He grabbed my shoulders and turned me to face one burnished silver tunnel. I gazed down it and finally saw a simple rectangular frame at the end. Madrigal ran a hand from my shoulder down my arm to my elbow.

"What you see you can find," he said. "Come with me."

I felt him step forward and matched the gesture. The mirror so far away was now rushing right at us. I blinked and turned away, expecting impact, shattering, cuts.

"Damn both you mirror-walking freaks to the Inferno underworld!" Sansouci thundered somewhere back down a tunnel of time and space. "How the hell do *I* escape this Disney action ride?"

I blinked again. Madrigal and I were standing on the darkened Gehenna stage. Only the perpetually glowing bare backstage lightbulb—known for decades as the "ghost light"—was lit.

It illuminated mere slivers of the dark-floored stage, the hanging black velvet curtain folds, the plain silver frame holding a mirror that shone softly blue, like a hologram. The mirror reflected nothing, neither the magician nor myself. It was half in feyland and half here. It was waiting.

Madrigal looked up, so I did too.

Oooh, Irma murmured. *Those creepy feylings abandoned Cicereau and are hanging like Spanish moss from the ropes in the backstage flies.*

"Call her," Madrigal urged.

I didn't have to ask who. "Loretta."

Her slight figure appeared, perhaps three inches high. It sped toward the mirror frame and me, growing to lifesize.

"You're here at last, Delilah," she said. "You're ready to free me, let me loose in my home environment in my revived form. Oh! Daddy Dearest will be so frightened! Me back. And free. Krzys back! Free and in solid form. This is my inheritance, finally mine. Delilah, kiss me. Let me through! Let me into you."

Ooh, Dee girl, the big L smooch is no big deal, Irma muttered, *but I do sooo not want to be possessed. Do something, Delilah!*

I was getting terminally weary of supernaturals in Vegas who wanted my body. I glanced at Madrigal. He was ignoring the wonder of Loretta's appearance and looking up. I saw why. Sylphia was dropping her webs upon the mirror frame while Phasia twined her serpentine body down them to add a sinuous decoration to the plain frame.

The fey webs were propagating, twining the frame and pushing inside, sending tendrils like curls down Loretta's soft cheeks and neck, circling her arms and wrists, glittering, glowing, enhancing, confining.

At first she lifted an arm, enchanted by the iridescent threads falling from above like soft, warm, living sleet. Then they crisscrossed to construct a diamond-patterned veil for her features. She tried to speak but they spun a sugary gag over her mouth. She blinked but they painted sticky iridescent mascara on her eyelashes. She couldn't close her eyes. Her entire slender body was twined, twined,

twined in tender, tensile steel, fey gift wrap and ribbons, until she was a glittering mummified statue, a mannequin from some Macy's Christmas fantasia display window.

The feys' thoroughness and speed took my breath away, as it had hers. Wait. Ghosts didn't have breath, but they could talk. Same way vampires didn't have circulatory systems but males could get it up for sex.

One of those sweet and sour mysteries of life . . . and life after death.

MY CELL PHONE vibrated, and I jumped. A cell phone seemed too modern for a place where I'd watched a ghost bound in a mirror.

Ric! I pulled the thin shell out of my riding jacket pocket and clapped it to my ear.

Instead, Sansouci's voice shouted into my ear.

"I hope you've got that girly ghost banished because—" He grunted as I heard Uzi bullets spray in the background. "Get Madrigal up here too. I was jerked back to the elevator the instant you two deserted me in the aluminum tent. By then that killing machine had made it all the way to Cicereau's—"

A pause, and then I heard the words "freaking bedroom" fading into the distance. I shut and stashed the phone. No time to take a break to call Ric.

Sylphia and Phasia remained coiled around the mirror frame like Art Nouveau nymphs. Madrigal looked puzzled.

"Cicereau and Sansouci need us all upstairs," I told him. "Fastest."

He nodded at the creepy pair, then ran into the wings where all the stage equipment was kept.

The fey sisters shot up on Sylphia's Spider-Girl web into the dark flies, diminishing contrails of iridescence. I cast a final look at Loretta webbed in eerie glitter-bound glamour, a captive ghost. Her mouth had opened to speak and frozen in that impotent, mute position.

Then I followed Madrigal into the unlit backstage area . . . just in time to be lassoed around the waist by a sticky rope of Sylphia's spider silk and jerked upward into endless dark until, beside me, Phasia hissed happily.

Now I was as much in their power as Loretta. They were jealous goddesses when it came to Madrigal's attention and association, and could easily drop me to the floor, which was rapidly vanishing stories below. The theatrical flies seemed to stretch up and up like an enormous elevator shaft. I was rising only by these fey cables, with no solid car to support and protect me.

Before I could fixate on my fears, I was swung into bright light and onto solid carpeted floor where Madrigal waited. There was no elevator car in the shaft, just concrete wall and steel supports. Then I watched a stalled car shuttle past and heard closing doors above. The strongman magician had simply suspended an elevator car at the top of the shaft and climbed the thick cables.

That didn't explain how the theatrical flies had morphed into one of the elevator shafts, though. I remembered what Helena Troy Burnside had said: many people found their native skills supernaturally sharpened after the Millennium Revelation.

So a stage magician who'd found a pair of fey nestlings could become an enhanced actual magician, thanks to these reverse changelings, his assistants.

Madrigal's big hand kept me upright while his agile assistants slithered up the hall walls to the ceiling and skittered down the passage to Cicereau's penthouse door.

I didn't have an inclination to question anybody's transportation methods. The trail of bloody footprints on the lush forest-green hall carpeting made talk unnecessary and time precious.

Hard to believe, but I joined Madrigal in pounding down the blood trail to Cicereau's door to save the werewolf mobster's skin. Wolfish howls were cutting off in mid-shriek.

Madrigal's brute force bounded through the shattered wooden door. A charnel house stench of blood and feces kept the two dainty feylings hanging from the door frame in the hall. Human offal overpowered even their predatory snake and spider sides.

Madrigal and I barged inside. In a split second the scene resolved into a mind-boggling series of gruesome vignettes.

Cicereau and the Uzi were both bloodied, the mobster kneeling on his gaudy bed as if huddled in a foxhole. His six wolfish guards lay gutted on the carpeting, a couple changed into full wolf form, clawed feet twitching.

I swallowed hard, thankful I'd left Quick safe at home. He was always too willing to leap into an unfair fight.

Sansouci, against the wall, had taken his fearsome vampire form. Mouth and eyes foaming with blood, he was straining to contain a huge forceful figure part Beowulf, part . . . mummy, and all monster.

"Krzys!" I cried experimentally. The hulking shoulders and neck shifted in my direction.

Yes, Loretta's Prince Charming had come back to unlife from his Sunset Park bones. The Karnak vampires' mystical methods must have managed to clothe bones with muscle and flesh.

His turning at my call not only gave Sansouci a chance to break a chair back for a raw stake, it revealed a face that was a burning-car-accident patchwork of Beauty and

Beast. Those pale, Polish-blue eyes he shared with Loretta and Quicksilver shone like aquamarines in a leathery skin cobbled together from beaten gold and stiffened gauze. A few gilt strands of hair glistened on his mottled bone skull. His hips, swathed in a transparent linen Egyptian kilt, showed splitting patches of skin over a raw substructure of naked muscles and tendons.

Apparently the new Egyptian art of raising old vampires was still in the R&D stage. Imagine a Frankenstein monster mummy. No, *don't!*

Sansouci was French toast. Cicereau was a werewolf shish kebab and Madrigal and I were about to become either escaping cowards or dead fools.

Madrigal wrenched his head around to eye his startled assistants twining the empty door frame. Violence in fey territory must be the poison and wire garrote sort.

"Save yourselves," he cried.

"No!" I answered. "First make them release Loretta. Can they retract their silken fey bonds at long distance?"

He nodded. "But—"

"Can you darken these lights?" I asked next, eyeing the window-wall opposite all this, the dark expanse reflecting portions of the carnage as if lit by heat lightning, by all the neon wattage of Las Vegas.

"No," he muttered, "I can't darken the Strip. What do you think I am?"

"Useless?" a voice snarled from the wall, sounding strangled in the Bone Boy's huge hands that were all bone and sinew and muscle and no skin and around the daylight vampire's muscle-bulging throat.

Sansouci had come to the Inferno at Snow's call to help save Ric. I needed to return the favor.

"Give me a mirror!" I screamed at Madrigal. "I need

darkness behind a rectangle of the night. Damn Vegas and its overlit arrogance! I need just one door-size patch of darkness for a mirror—"

Madrigal looked toward his fey girls, whose entwined fingers and locks of long hair made them twin Medusas lost in their own reflections.

"Their own binding ritual will release Loretta's image. That's all they can do."

And it wasn't enough. The mob boss's glorious bedroom panorama of the Strip's nightly fireworks would destroy us all. I needed solid darkness to draw Loretta close, to make her visible. Or . . . the windows needed a solid silver mirror backing.

The fey sisters' posture reminded me of something.

Meanwhile, Sansouci had roared and slipped away from the wall and the creature's stranglehold to attack Krzysztof from the rear, driving the jagged rung of the chair-back into his leathery shoulder. A wooden stake wouldn't kill, but if any vampire was left in this risen abomination, it could immobilize him. I didn't dare watch their battle.

My distracted mind fought to concentrate, to sense the whispery feel of the silver familiar on my skin in its precious metal form. Now it was made of Snow's and Achilles' conjoined locks of hair, one a strand that I regarded as an enemy to me and mine and my very mind and soul, the other cherished as a memento of a faithful canine defender. Now dark and light influences had braided into one strand I could consciously command. Maybe.

I called them up and cast them out, away from me, surrendered them. It was as if all my energy and will had turned steely cold and seeped from every artery and vein of my body in an ugly, draining rush.

I could hardly stand, then felt Madrigal's strongman body behind me, bracing mine like an easel a canvas. I felt blank, empty. He was crooning some strange syllables that brought Phasia and Sylphia creeping into the room.

The scent of blood intensified into the metallic tang I'd sensed on my tongue at my first, agonizing menstruation. I felt a sudden, gut-wrenching, and purely phantom cramp in my belly and mind.

In front of my eyes, the familiar stretched into tendrils from my left and my right arms and pooled on the window glass into a spreading surface of bright liquid silver. It resolved into a person-high oval of light against the night's darkness, blotting out all the neon of Vegas.

I saw myself reflected. Standing alone, dressed exactly as I was but upheld by no one, wearing no pair of thin silver leashes on my wrists.

Lilith.

Now. When it least mattered, I saw her, clear and separate. Now, when extinction was a leap and snarl and slash away from all of us in this room that held stalking Death within it.

She wore the exact double of my Mrs. Peel ensemble, except that when she tossed her head her hair pulled free into an untamed mane. Then she was . . . gone.

I lost my breath, my senses, my mind.

Summoned, Loretta levitated into the mirror that I had made, like a saint ascending into heaven. Sweet, pretty murdered and now murderous Loretta.

Her image also was as clear as crystal.

I stepped in front of it.

"Krzysztof," I cried from the heart. "I'm here."

Then I stepped away again.

The monster turned. His wayward gaze fixed on the

vision floating almost fifty stories above the Las Vegas Strip, the mirror-bound image of his lost love.

He made a sound of such bestial longing that every human ear within reach—that is, only mine—must have sensed a pounding heartbeat freeze. Then he lurched in his mad destructive inhuman way toward his beloved.

Three giant steps and the double-strength safety glass fractured like a bad dream. Daggers of mirrored glass splintered, scattered, admitted the lavishly lit night as Krzysztof stepped forty-some stories into the empty, as-yet-unbuilt Las Vegas Strip of his nineteen-forties past and vanished.

I felt the silver familiar rebound on my body like a snapped rubber band, or a yo-yo abruptly recalled, an echo coming back five times louder. I would have fallen from the impact without the literal backup of Madrigal.

His fey assistants came twining his form, each one peering over his mighty shoulders, evoking the huge Strip billboard advertising his Gehenna act.

They gazed at me and purred in concert. They were Madrigal's familiars, I realized, as eerily attached as mine.

I turned to find what was left of Sansouci.

He leaned panting against a wall, bloodied. As I watched he wiped off secondhand gore sprayed from the dying werewolves whose corpses littered the floor. His green eyes had faded to hazel. Did vampires feel something as human as fatigue? He managed to raise a bloody hand as if shielding himself against me or the lights or the hole in the window-wall.

"You are too sucking fierce for Vegas," he said, then coughed up secondhand blood and laughed.

Last I looked for Cicereau. He remained on the bed clutching his emptied, Liberace-glammed-up Uzi, surveying his fallen werewolf guard and those of us left standing: magician and familiars, daylight vampire and paranormal investigator.

"I should reduce your times of indenture," he told Madrigal and Sansouci. Then he laughed too. "But I can't afford to let you go, especially after this."

He addressed me last.

"Good thing my pack failed to kill you at Starlight Lodge, after all. I'll pay what you're worth for this night's work, then the slate is clean and we can all resume being the usual enemies in peace."

"This is entirely your fault," I told him. "If you hadn't killed your own daughter and her vampire lover so brutally it never would have happened. You deserve to see ravaged victims raised and walking back to you. How could you do that to your own daughter? Or your own werewolf mobster ambitions? Now the Karnak vampire empire is poised to resurrect any destroyed master vampire they can find the world over and try a takedown of Vegas and anywhere."

Cicereau stirred on his blood-spattered brocade coverlet.

"I had to make an example of them. I didn't care who Loretta picked for a boyfriend but Loretta was half-human. We werewolves and vampires feared that the unprecedented cross-supernatural lovebirds might be able to reproduce like humans. The unnatural result of such a union would destroy the ages-old turf of our two kinds and no one wanted that. That's why we made a blood pact over their dead bodies."

"You're telling me that supernaturals find half-breeds *un*natural? Werewolves and vampires aren't exactly the Smiths and Joneses or the Hatfields and McCoys for that matter."

"Kind must stick with kind. Family is family in the lupine line." Cicereau's sweat-mustached upper lip lifted in a snarl of disdain. "Vampires are already a mongrel sort, connected only by their unnatural appetites. What makes the werewolf mob invincible is that we are all blood family, not just joined by shedding it.

"Each full moon we shift into our pack form and celebrate our unity. Vampires hunt alone, like the inferior cat. That's why we defeated them eighty years ago for control of Vegas. That's why we will defeat the Karnak nest. Christophe should have burned out the entire lot with his dragon's fiery breath when he raided them.

"Now this vampire empire knows that we know they exist. I hear *that's* all *your* fault, Delilah Street, and you and your FBI boyfriend are another damnably dangerous couple loose in Vegas. So you'd better leave while I'm feeling grateful. Sansouci, get her out of here. And, Madrigal, time to let your pets clean up the mess."

I was too tired to argue, almost too tired to stand. I did manage to walk out of there, unaided, on my own two blood-spattered feet.

Chapter Twenty

THE GEHENNA WASN'T done with me yet.

Sansouci steered me into a guest bathroom near the door to Cicereau's suite and told me to clean up.

In the mirror I saw his point. No chance I was regarding Lilith's image this time. Blood dotted my face, hair, and the jabot of my white blouse. A few swipes with an evaporating soap product cleansed the face and hair. The blouse would just have to pass as polka-dotted. I wiped the blood drops off the gray toes of my shoes and the bell-bottoms of my black pants. The black jacket absorbed dark red and looked fine to the casual glance.

The silver familiar wasn't about to waste its glory on my bloody cravat. It snugged around my hips again, under the pants. I leaned against the green marble sink and called Ric to tell him I was all right and heading home from the Gehenna.

"You sound breathless," he answered.

"I have my reasons, which you'll know when we meet up."

When I stepped out again, an equally gore-free vampire henchman was awaiting me in the entry. Must be a matching boys' room through the opposite door. It occurred to me why a werewolf mobster would provide lavatory facilities at the door to his elegant private penthouse. Must have a lot of messy underlings visiting to report on the latest hits and misses.

"Slick thinking," Sansouci said.

"Yeah. It's pretty obvious why Cicereau's visiting goons would need to tidy up right here at the front door."

He frowned, then eyed the unmarked doors.

"Not these rest rooms. I meant your slick trick, conjuring a hallucinatory exit for the Karnak's revived killing machine. Forty-some floors ought to stop reanimated bones pretty cold. What happened to Loretta?"

"That was just a mirror image I summoned like the one I left behind here for a while. Loretta is still bound in Madrigal's backstage mirror."

He nodded. "I better hustle you outa here before Cicereau forgets he's grateful, and then make sure that mirror trick is holding."

No rest for the wicked, as they say.

We zipped down in the next elevator, picking up hotel guests as we stopped at lower floors. No one recoiled or flared their nostrils, so we must have looked—and smelled—fairly normal, as normal as a silver medium and a daylight vampire could be.

Once on the hotel's thickly tourist-populated main floor, Sansouci steered me through the casino to a gilded cage. I pulled against his one-armed custody at the very sight of bars.

"It's a cashier's cage. Relax."

Sansouci flashed a Gehenna/Magus/Megalith consortium gambling card, a credit card for gamblers. I'd barely glimpsed the holographic image that flipped from an Annie Liebovitz portrait of Cesar Cicereau to a wolf's-head before Sansouci slapped it down on the brown marble counter and slid it through the cage.

The woman on the other side wore a one-shouldered rabbit fur corset and purple-dyed rabbit ears. I guess

"Prey" was her middle name. She batted metallic green false lashes as she pushed a wad of bills under the cage bars.

"Somebody must have hit the jackpot," she simpered at Sansouci. "I get off in forty-five minutes, big boy."

"My women do it much faster than that," he noted, swooping up the stash and handing it to me.

"Ah, do you have a money bag or something?" I asked the now thoroughly miffed cashier.

"Stick it in your—" she began as Sansouci turned me away from the cage into the clatter and chatter of the casino.

He stopped a passing cocktail waitress tricked out as a calico cat. "Got a nickel slot bonanza bag?"

She produced a pink burlap bag into which Sansouci dropped my loot.

In ten minutes of twisting through the milling throngs we finally exited the cold and glamorously dark interior at the hotel's entry canopy.

"While you were irritating Cicereau," he said, "I dialed Nightwine's majordomo."

"Godfrey? You know Godfrey?"

"I know how things work in this town. I figured you'd need a ride." He waved a hand.

That's right; I'd been driven here by limo. My God, there idled Dolly, my '56 Cadillac convertible, shining like a decapitated Black Maria police wagon from the thirties.

I turned, grateful. "Sansouci, you're amazing."

He gave me a rough little shove. "Get outa here before Cicereau accuses you of ripping him off and has you arrested. His gratitude lasts about as long as a five-dollar whore's blow job."

I was feeling the stress of the last couple hours so I

stumbled forward at Sansouci's ungentlemanly push. Why was he irked with me? I'd saved his bacon and his boss's too.

As I neared, I saw the black Caddy didn't have a red leather interior like my Dolly. And ace attorney Perry Mason was at the wheel.

"Godfrey has told me you've been absent without leave for far too long, Miss Delilah," the CinSim Perry said sternly as he leaned over the wide front bench seat to open the passenger door. "I'm taking you straight home, no argument. Now get in."

"No argument," I promised, relieved.

Perry was a CinSim but he seemed to be totally mobile, unlike most, and nobody would mess with him in this town anyway. He was a man of size, with a sterling legal reputation to match. He was also Big Daddy for a lifelong orphan like me. A girl couldn't have a better escort.

As we pulled out of the overlit neon canopy into the blitzkrieged Las Vegas Strip night, I couldn't help studying the Gehenna's exterior perimeter for signs of a resurrected vampire who'd fallen to earth—hard. Thanks to me. I saw nothing but milling tourists, yet in the distance I heard a wolflike wail.

In what seemed like no time, Perry's Cadillac throbbed next to the real Dolly in my Enchanted Cottage's driveway.

"Get some rest," he ordered in his brusque yet kindly way. "Godfrey said you've had a long day."

"Yes, Perry. Thanks so much for the ride."

He leaned across the long leather bench seat to advise me further. "And watch that fellow who walked you out of the Gehenna. He looks like a gigolo."

I laughed to imagine Sansouci's reaction to that. "You don't have to worry, Mr. Mason. I'm a very cautious girl."

He nodded satisfaction as I got out and watched him glide away in engine-growling, shiny-black barracuda glory.

I sighed and turned toward my home, sweet home, aka the Enchanted Cottage, wanting to hit the shower, put on some blood-free clothes, and relax.

Then my cell phone vibrated. The famous Strip dead zones were sure working now.

Why did I have a queasy feeling? Could the wolfish wail have been a distant chorus of screaming police sirens I'd heard as Perry Mason had chauffeured me away from the Gehenna?

"Delilah!" Ric's voice was easy on my ears but not the urgent note in it. What was the expression that so fit Sansouci tonight? No rest for the wicked. I'd been wicked enough tonight to impress a werewolf mob kingpin and a vampire . . . and make a permanent enemy of my first mirror BFF, Loretta, now my new Best *Fiend* Forever

"Where are you?" Ric and I asked in tandem, then laughed.

"I just now got home," I said.

"I bet you had a lot to catch up on after . . ." He paused, probably aware of others close enough to overhear. "After our latest assignment," he finished in lower tones. "Listen, I know it's late but I need you at the coroner's. Grisly Bahr called me over for a private talk about some missing corpses. Now he's got a supernatural pile of mystery meat coming in fresh from the Gehenna. And where've you just been?"

"Uh, the Gehenna."

"I figured the dead meat is no mystery to you."

I decided not to mention I was actually the chef on that one. Not yet, at least, until I knew what officialdom was doing.

"No."

"Better keep that between me and thee," Ric said. "Kennedy Malloy is en route to Grisly's place too."

"Sure I should show up at all?"

"Why not?"

"Captain Malloy liked you first."

He laughed. "She's a professional associate, that's all."

"To her, so am I."

I may be new to the dating game but I knew enough to realize that even smart guys like Ric could underestimate the depth of a woman colleague's interest. Few decent guys were out there. Lots of competition for them.

"I've been getting some flashbacks," Ric said in a lowered tone, after a pause, "and some flash-forwards maybe too. You really okay, *chica*? I had a bad feeling an hour or so ago."

Yeah, well . . . I'd been getting multiple bad feelings about then too.

"We'll have a one-on-one later," he added. "After our date at the coroner's."

Actually, I couldn't wait to see what Grisly made of what was left of Loretta's risen Prince Charming turned avenger. It was even possible the fall hadn't, ah, killed him.

BEFORE SEEING RIC, I needed a quick shower and change. Dried blood was *not* the latest shade in streetwear, even in Vegas.

I turned to the steps leading to my charming arched front door and only then noticed Quicksilver's gray fur blending into the aged wood. He sat there on prick-eared alert, his neck ruff fluffed and his blue eyes half closed in that mute, rebuking look smart dogs get.

His black nostrils flared to inhale the invisible traces of blood and gore from my clothes and skin.

How dare *you have fun without me?* his guard dog look and posture screamed, in the best canine form, of course.

"I suppose you want to shower with me too?" I asked.

He stood and shook out his thick, silvery coat, then grinned.

"No, you don't. Stay down here and guard Dolly. I need to make tire tracks to the coroner's office as soon as I'm decent and dry."

The grin allowed a long pink tongue dangling room, reminding me that we were now twins in the healing department.

"And don't drool any stray saliva on Dolly's leather upholstery!"

Inside, I first had to stash my cash from Cicereau in the . . . uh, okay . . . the open floor safe I spotted in the parlor.

"Thanks," I muttered to my resident guardians.

Then I rushed up the steep stairs, shedding clothes as I went. I hopped in the hall to kick off my gray sling-backs and wriggle out of the bell-bottoms.

I'd resolved to avoid looking in mirrors for at least a day but still glimpsed my frenzied hopping in the tall mirror at the hall's end.

No bound and gagged Loretta, thank the mirror goddess, but another figure hopping there in eerie time with mine. A naked Lilith, putting *on* what I tore off.

Just too bizarre! I fled into the bedroom and the bathroom beyond it, toward the sound of pelting shower water, thank the secret pixie or who- or whatever had turned it on!

In moments, pink water swirled around my bare feet in the shiny hole-pierced drain, reminding me of Snow's pink ruby collar gemstones and matching eyes behind the dark sunglasses.

Argh! I didn't want to remember any part of Snow, particularly his presumably bleeding back. Still, if anyone deserved to suffer on Ric's behalf, it was Snow, who'd *charged me* a personal price for saving Ric's life.

Wait. He hadn't saved a thing. I'd done that. He'd taken his blood money—i.e., my kiss—for the mere attempt at a rescue mission.

Which had worked. As his supposedly enslaving Brimstone Kiss had not.

So why was I furious?

Stress, Delilah. Irma's voice soothed me like a slippery bar of soap stroking my shoulders. *You're just stressed.*

And seeing Lilith in my hall mirror donning my discarded clothes doesn't help, I railed at Irma. Who does she think she is? Besides *me*?

She doesn't have me, Irma soothed.

But she has my clothes and she's done it before! That's what got me accused of being the Snow groupie killer on that hotel security tape. It was Lilith, not me, on the scene, and I'd be judged crazy if I tried to say that.

I wrapped myself in one of the huge coat-tree-hung towels that dried me from ankle to armpit in three steps, then stood thinking on the plush bathroom carpet as the wet soles of my feet sank in. Something else sank in.

In that inadvertent Inferno crime-scene security-camera shot Snow had held back from the police, Lilith had been wearing the same striking vintage evening ensemble I'd rented only a few hours earlier at Déjà-Vous, the costume shop Snow owned.

That I'd tried on in the Déjà-Vous *dressing room mirror.*

Lilith could "'nap" the clothes from my own image in a mirror! I stomped out into the hall. She/I were a set of overlapping images, one towel-draped, one wearing the blood-worn clothes I'd just dropped to this very floor.

They should have been lying there, puckered and empty. Corpselike. The floor was dry and clean.

Back to the bathroom.

Mrs. Peel's freshly cleaned and pressed "Carnaby Street" sixties suit and ruffled shirt hung from the clothes rack. Lilith wasn't *stealing* my look, she was duplicating it.

I shook out my mane of wet hair and felt a jet stream of warm air riffle it like a blow torch. Did a demon hairdresser come with the place, just now announcing its presence in an emergency? Maybe the Enchanted Cottage was only three-fourths Disney and one-quarter imp. Or vice versa. And the mirror could be as much my enemy as my friend, as Loretta had so recently proven.

I nodded my head slowly, speaking not exactly to Irma or to my invisible dresser or to Mrs. Peel's empty suit.

"Makes sense. If I'm wearing this outfit and I saw Lilith jumping into it, my mirror image can duplicate any wardrobe item of mine reflected in a mirror to masquerade as me."

Not to worry, Irma purred in my inner ear, *she copped the unwashed, used clothes. You aren't exactly the same at all. What a stupid skank!*

By then I was redonning the outfit, not pausing to consider its blood-drenched recent past. The Enchanted Cottage was just doing its job: putting the best, freshest face on everything that had been tainted.

There was only one thing it couldn't counter: the mischief unwanted guests like Loretta and Lilith could get up to in the front-surface glass of my hall mirror.

Quicksilver was already perched on Dolly's passenger

seat before I could get the keys out of my messenger bag and open the driver's-side door.

"What have I told you about jumping over the door when the window's down?" I demanded. "Okay, be snarky."

I fished his sunglasses out of the humungous glove compartment. Dogs love convertible rides but the desert wind is too drying for their naked eyes. And the glare of the Strip at night made sunglasses a good idea. Besides, Quick liked turning heads.

I donned round Audrey Hepburn sixties shades myself.

Dolly's engine purred like a kitten en route to the coroner's. Surely my sixties duds revved her fifties Detroit heart. To my mind, clothing stopped being cool in the seventies and drowned in the gaudy, trickle-down Reagan eighties.

When I got to the low morgue building off Charleston I noticed that Nightwine's nearby soundstage was still grinding away. My heart lurched and clutched to see Ric's bronze Stingray next door parked beside a white Crown Victoria that had to be Captain Kennedy Malloy's ride.

No wonder poor Dolly lurched and clutched while I put her into park and turned off the engine. If it wasn't Lilith trying to take my place in the mirror, it was Captain Malloy trying to move in on Ric.

"Watch here," I told Quicksilver, rushing inside. Some people are just dying to get into the morgue and I was one of them right now.

The receptionist, Yolanda, sniffed as she handed over my ID card. "Mr. Montoya came inside with the police captain a half hour ago," she informed me. "You may be too late."

"Nobody's left yet," I pointed out, "unless the corpse we're all here to see took a stroll."

Her nose curled. "*Ugh.* I hear three techs fainted moving

the remains into the autopsy room. Care for some Vicks?"

"Thanks, but no thanks," I said, smiling in the name of getting along with the clerical staff.

Patting Vicks VapoRub on the nostrils is a cop trick for masking the stench of death. I have to admit I was nervous. I'd never before attended an autopsy for a revived dead body I'd been responsible for killing again.

"Murder" had become a very loose term in the post–Millennium Revelation world.

A wide-eyed tech assistant (just like I'd recently played next door) issued me the regulation latex gloves and Plexiglas visor at the autopsy room door. With an unnerving sense of déjà vu, I joined several similarly accoutered people gathered around a stainless steel table.

It was like walking in on my longtime nightmares, only *I* was one of the weird beings surrounding my supine self, not the body on the examination table.

Perspiration stippled my entire body like a rash. Why had I ever thought I could do this? Stroll up to something I'd tricked to jump out a window? Guilt was such an iffy element nowadays. Had my desperate act blasted all hope from Loretta's previously presumed innocent heart or had I stopped a monster in its tracks? Did I have the right to dote on the sight of Ric standing alive and well near the fallen jigsaw remains of Loretta's Polish prince?

"Autopsies are off-limits for civilians," Captain Malloy noted from behind her glinting transparent mask.

I readily turned to go, but Ric stepped up to capture my elbow and stop me.

The clear plastic face guard blurred his mocha skin and coffee-dark hair and eyes, but I couldn't fail to recognize the rolled-up ivory silk shirtsleeves and tailored buff-colored slacks. He was Mr. Suave even around an autopsy table.

"Miss Street may have seen the victim alive," he said.

"She can ID *this*?" Malloy jeered. "I thought I'd spare a civilian embarrassing herself." She stared at Ric's fingers making comforting circles on my elbow.

I took a deep breath.

Yeah, lady, Irma taunted on my behalf, *he's pretty familiar with the lay of her land. Too bad, loser!*

Irma made me smile inside. She was always in my corner.

I walked closer to the table to regard my victim, pushing aside both childish nightmares and adult guilt.

Had Captain Malloy been trying to do me a favor! The broken and tangled form was less human than a robot graveyard. I saw only twisted pseudo-flesh over raw muscle, not Loretta's idealized and romantic undead lover. Nothing of him had been revived but the bones and patchwork covering, and the brain had been a mockery.

This repellent conglomeration of flesh and bone had been raised only to become mindlessly murderous, perhaps reviving its last mortal, defensive impulses. Not its fault, but also not a reason to spare a killing machine.

"What a puzzling mélange," Grisly Bahr said, his fuzzy caterpillar eyebrows arching like inchworms. "Although I spot a lot of shiny nostrils in the room, Miss Street, the amateur among us, was right to abstain. The mentholated Vicks was unnecessary, folks."

Besides giving me an "A is for Amateur" scarlet letter, making all the police pros present hate me, Dr. Bahr was also stating the oddly obvious. This blob of monstrous mortality smelled more of sunbaked asphalt than decaying flesh.

"I got a call from the meat wagon," Captain Malloy noted. "What brought out the civilians?" she asked Bahr, eyeing me and Ric.

Oooh, she must be mucho mad about you being here, Irma whispered in my ear.

Ric wasn't going to tolerate official snootiness goring his associate.

"Dr. Bahr had called me on another matter involving the bodies found in Sunset Park a few weeks back," he said formally. "Miss Street had been present for that discovery, so I suggested she meet me here."

"Not expecting a crowd, I'm sure." Malloy sounded sour. "Or a bizarre new body. I wish losing gamblers would leap off the Hoover Dam instead of a Strip hotel for a change."

She folded her arms over her dark blazer, reminding me of the faux uniform suit I'd worn to D.C. A trim blonde looked more icily official in navy blue than a buxom brunette, I observed.

"It's not a despondent gambler," I felt obliged to tell her. "It's the male vic from the park. Any sign of those original dry bones?" I asked Grisly.

He shook his head. "Just fragments and powder here now. I'll have to analyze every component. What was the height of the fall, three hundred feet? Any identifiable face?"

"You wouldn't want to see," said a new voice.

Malloy's constant frown deepened as she turned to spot Sansouci entering, gloves and visor in hand. "Another party crasher. I suppose your presence confirms this individual died at the Gehenna."

"Yup. My boss wanted to make sure the body got here . . . safely."

"As if." She didn't need to say more. The body could hardly be more destroyed. "I'd think Cicereau had better errand boys at hand than a gigolo."

Ouch! Irma gasped. I found the comment telling.

"Get out, Sansouci," Captain Malloy ordered with contempt, "along with Montoya and Street."

The resulting silence got intense. Sansouci looked ready to break out the fangs again and I was wishing for some.

Ric, Mr. ex-FBI Coolio again, took us both in hand, my alter ego and me. His hand on my elbow propelled me and Irma to the door.

"Time to visit the snack zone," he said, "while the pros get their teeth into their new corpse."

Sansouci followed.

THE SILENCE AS we three withdrew was mutual. None of us easily swallowed orders to retreat.

Once we'd hung up our visors and discarded the latex gloves, we passed through some heavy stainless steel doors. Sansouci and I followed Ric, down a hall exhaling the delicate odor of decay to the employee rest area, where soft drink and snack machines lined the walls. It was otherwise empty.

"You guys know each other?" I asked, surprised. Sansouci had seen Ric during the Karnak rescue but Ric had been dead to the world in a very real sense then.

Ric nodded slowly, measuring Sansouci's breed and steel.

"The FBI keeps mug shots and files on all the Vegas principal players. I still have access."

"'Principal players'?" Sansouci mocked. "I'm just Cicereau's lieutenant."

"That how you know my girl?" Ric's tone wasn't searching for steel now, it was showing it.

"Yeah. I like her too."

"Am I going to have to do something about that?" Ric asked.

The scent of testosterone in the innocuous break room overcame the potent ozone formula that quieted the reek of decay. Some said it was just Febreze. I knew enough to keep my mouth shut for once. Irma didn't.

Dueling dudes! Over us! This is a first, girl, relax and enjoy.

Whoa, Irma! "Relax and enjoy?" That's what sexist men in the bad old days advised women facing a rapist to do, I told her. I don't need to be anybody's prize.

Aw, guys gotta do this stuff. Don't enjoy, then, but relax.

Sansouci pulled out a plastic chair and sat down at a flimsy matching table, crossing his arms over his impressive chest. "Nope. Not while you're alive."

Somehow that settled things, even though Sansouci and I knew that condition was ambiguous.

Ric had already moved to the garish wall of steel food dispensers, poised to feed dollars into drink slots. "Anybody want anything?"

I shook my head but the guys had Red Bulls. Of course. Having been shooed out of the autopsy room by a woman, they had to macho up again.

"Sounds like you annoyed the homicide captain," Ric told Sansouci after we sat at his table. "What's her issue? Any untimely expirations you might have had something to do with besides the current remains?"

Sansouci shrugged. "Malloy? Hell hath no fury—"

—like a woman scorned, Irma breathed. *This Malloy broad has her eye on both Ric* and *Sansouci? Her taste is way too like ours.*

"Yours," I said aloud.

"Our what?" Ric asked.

"Ah, I meant Malloy's dating druthers is *your* problem, guys. Come on, Ric, don't so look innocent. You know she likes you. Apparently she liked Sansouci once too."

But I couldn't believe it even as I threw out the pretended distraction, though I'd rather have Ric and Sansouci getting territorial about Kennedy Malloy than about me.

Malloy had wanted to be one of Sansouci's daily dinner dates? I couldn't picture a high-ranking police officer willing to be some vamp's midnight snack or lunchtime lay, even if she had nothing to lose but a few ounces of blood.

"You doing all right now, Montoya?" Sansouci asked Ric to change the subject.

"You were in on that Karnak action?" Ric asked in turn, surprised.

"Yeah. Cicereau volunteered some forces when Christophe rallied a rescue party, thanks to Miss Street here."

"I need to hear all the details," Ric said.

"Delilah didn't tell you?"

Ric took in his use of my first name. "We had other things to discuss first, but now I'm all ears. Shoot."

"It was pretty awesome, man," Sansouci said. "Christophe has unsuspected resources."

"Not unexpected by me."

"You may have been Mr. Suspicious FBI Agent Man, but you were out, uh, cold at the time."

Sansouci eyed me nervously. Ric had been more than "out cold." Cicereau's man didn't know how much I'd told Ric.

"Look," Sansouci said after a big ice-breaking chug of Red Bull. "I don't know what anybody else thinks but I figure we're all sitting on a fire-ant pile of ancient evil that makes a few Stripside touches of the Apocalypse look like a Punch and Judy puppet show in Sunset Park.

"To save your sorry ass, Montoya, your lady here

helped expose the whole shebang. That got a bunch of powers along the Strip stirred up to go and kill a tombful of ancient Egyptian immortals, which is kind of ironic if you think about it."

This was such a hokey recital I expected Sansouci to pull out a cheroot and strike a match on his spurs to create a smoke screen.

Ric seemed unconvinced but a good interrogator is always tricky to read. "So this body tonight—?"

"My turn," I said quickly. "That's what the Egyptian cartel at the Karnak wanted with you: raising poor dead Loretta Cicereau's slain boyfriend from the bones. Meanwhile, Loretta's ghost had been working on me in my mirror after the same thing. She wanted her beloved Prince Krzysztof brought back to life. The Karnak's royal vampires wanted it more."

"Why?" Sansouci asked.

"Think about it. He's a six-hundred-year-old vamp. Apparently most European vamps of that 'superstitious' era are permanently staked and beheaded, and moldering immobilized in unknown graves. The Egyptians must have been working on some potion or rite over the centuries that raises vampires from even the bones."

"My God," Ric said. "When I got here Grisly showed me the empty gurneys where the Sunset Park bones had lain. You mean," he challenged Sansouci, "that hunk of once-biological . . . material in the autopsy room was . . . *grown* from those bones by a nest of ancient Egyptian vampires?"

"Yeah, and they needed you to do it. You have some kind of resurrection mojo? That certainly explains—" Sansouci shut up as I kicked him hard in the shin under the table. "When your girlfriend figured out where you were and why," he resumed, "she needed an armed expedition to pry you loose. Everyone in charge seems to think the excitement is over but the Bone Boy killed some tourists and a half dozen of Cicereau's wolf-boys tonight. Unless someone stops those crazed mummies gone wild we'll all be bloody gauze-bait."

"The werewolf mob only looks out for its own," Ric said. "Why'd you care?"

Another long silence, during which Sansouci smoldered and Ric matched him glare for glare.

"Ask your lady friend," Sansouci snarled in a wolflike way that confused the real issue. He stood, practically pulsing with conflict and resentment.

Ric leaped up. "What does Delilah have to do with it?"

"Because it's all about *you*."

"Not here and now," Ric said. "Why do you know more about it, and her, than I do?"

Sansouci, the coward, took that for an exit line. "Listen. I have to report back to the boss. Ask your lady."

He finished the Red Bull as if swilling the last of a rare blood vintage. Of course only I thought of that image. "I'm sure she can fill you in on all the gory details."

With a bloodthirsty grin, he swaggered out.

"Kennedy Malloy must have lost her mind," Ric muttered. "That guy is Thug Central. She'd risk her career for a few nights' stands with a *werewolf*? He must be some salsa dancer at Los Lobos."

Poor Ric. He had so much to get caught up on.

"Do you think Malloy can dance?" I asked as we dumped our trash and headed into the empty halls of the truly dead.

"Not like you can now that I've taken you in hand," he said.

"Speaking of which, we need to fox-trot back to Quicksilver and Dolly. You can follow us to my place. Poor Quick's been feeling as left out as you lately."

"So much has been happening," Ric said, not aware of the half of it.

I'd have to fill him in fast. His powers of dowsing for the dead were the heart of everything horrible that had happened to and around him. It wasn't right to keep him an ignorant accessory to the biggest and baddest news to hit Vegas since the Millennium Revelation.

I couldn't afford to spare Ric anything at this point, not even the fact that I was now a stone-cold killer.

Of the Undead.

Chapter Twenty-one

IT WAS LATE—MIDNIGHT—when I buzzed my gate open so Ric could park his car in the Enchanted Cottage driveway. I then stopped Dolly at the big house and told Godfrey I was home safe and thanks for sending Perry Mason to fetch me from the Gehenna earlier.

Hector Nightwine, of course, was glued to one of his surveillance screens as well as a classic film, so I was being polite and updating him at the same time.

Besides, it suited me to let Nightwine think Ric and I were settling down for a nocturnal reunion at the cottage. We were, but I had plans more radical than romantic.

Meanwhile, I deserved some R&R: Ric and Roll.

After I drove around to park Dolly, I found Ric sitting atop the semicircular steps leading to my front door. All the driveway lights were on.

At the bottom of the shallow stairs, Quicksilver sat in his alert "at ease" position, a furred statue in gray shading to silver and beige on his paws and face, blue eyes sky-clear. His upright ears and grave expression matched Ric's posture of calm watchfulness.

The only thing supernatural about this scene was the obvious truce that had been declared between my two devoted but overpossessive defenders.

Gosh. A boy and his dog. *Aww.* Made me very suspicious.

Ric rose to open Dolly's heavy door before I could

gather my messenger bag from the red leather seat. Quicksilver was there just as fast.

"Really rough day earlier at the Gehenna, I take it?" Ric asked.

I leaned against Dolly's side. "Rough enough."

"I've got some things to report too, but it can wait until we unwind," Ric said.

Quick was not ready to roll over and snooze after being left out of the action all day. He padded backward and went belly-down into an excited play-bow. Our morning run had been interrupted, and how.

"We decided to get some exercise while waiting for you to drive around," Ric said. "The lights back here are bright enough."

He glanced at a stick lying on the flagstones beside the stairs. They'd been *playing*? Please!

I handed Ric my messenger bag. "Take this in then. I'll give Quicksilver some quality time out here."

Quick gave a sharp, impatient bark.

"You'll hear all about my commission at the Gehenna in a few minutes, both of you buddies," I told Ric.

Actually, this man-dog détente pleased and intrigued me. I needed time to digest it, as I did the Ric-Sansouci meeting. A lot of my assumptions had been kicked in the gut today. I couldn't believe that Loretta had tried to trick and use me and would happily risk Ric's life to get her dead vampire lover back and that Cicereau might not deserve quite the level of her vengeance.

"What are you up to?" I asked Quick as we sat together on the stairs.

Can a dog shrug? Quick turned his head to the side and scratched idly at his wide black leather collar. I owed him a classier neckpiece, but those silver discs on the collar had a way of shape-shifting like my silver familiar. I'd decided to leave bad enough alone.

Speaking of which, my silver familiar had split into two heavy silver wrist weights. Somebody hinting I'd neglected my resistance program since hitting Las Vegas?

Who'd had time to join a gym when she was serving as a supernatural punching bag? Yet I'd tied the treacherous Loretta up in knots and turned her dad into a client and Sansouci and Madrigal into my assistants.

I noticed at the morgue that Ric was looking and acting same-old despite his ordeal. Now he and Quicksilver were newly in tune. Life was looking good, even though I'd forgotten to refresh my sunscreen when I took Quicksilver to the park that morning. I could feel my face and arms prickling now. I would probably be shrimp pink for my intimate midnight supper with Ric.

I let Quicksilver into the cottage after typing the secret keypad code Godfrey had given me to disable the security and spy cameras inside the cottage.

I ambled inside after him, hoping for Enya on the sound system, a cool fresh drink and a hot fresh guy.

Instead I heard the roar of the crowd. Ric was planted in the parlor on the leather easy chair, feet up on the ottoman, watching some baseball game on the big-screen plasma TV. Quicksilver had plopped down beside him.

Men and dogs and chasing balls! Ric lifted a tall glass glittering with condensation. "Gatorade. Pitcher was on the kitchen counter. I assume you're going to change out of that adorable but slightly butch outfit."

Jeez. Woman comes home from a hard day of ghost corralling and the men of the cottage are too laid-back to pamper her.

I pounded up the stairs to find the hall mirror blacked out even from my reflection, and the resident "helpers" were in fine form. The wrist weights slunk down my own form, uniting in a garter just above one knee. In ten minutes I was out of my Emma Peel outfit and powdering my sun-pinked face and arms with the pale cooling mineral powder on the dressing table. Black Irish skins are too pale to tan, but we sure can burn.

A turquoise gauze halter jumpsuit hung from what I'd named the "designer brownie" hook. With bronze high-heeled sandals and a rhinestone bib necklace to enhance my décolletage, I was ready to blow away my complacent males downstairs.

When I got back down, though, Quicksilver was nowhere to be seen. The mute TV was a reflective black glass mirror I avoided looking into. I didn't want to remember Lilith right now.

I entered the Victorian parlor to find Ric waiting for me by the fireplace with the anticipated drink. I blinked to see it was a Vampire Sunrise.

"I thought *I* had a 'smart' computerized house," he said, "but your funky cottage shakes cocktails, bakes popovers, twice-bakes potatoes, sears filet mignon just-right rare, and coddles crème brûlée."

"It's enchanted, not funky." I sipped a stiff belt of my Vampire Sunrise, courtesy of the kitchen witch, and felt every muscle in my body and each brain cell in my head turn into an enervated noodle.

Ric finished me off by standing behind me and massaging my bared shoulders.

"*Mija,*" he whispered into my overheated ear, "the Inferno bridal suite is cushier than cardinal sin but I like Casa Delilah a lot better."

"You're really all right?"

"The doctors say I won't be able to join you and Quicksilver in a five-K run for a while, until my blood and stamina build up, but otherwise, I'm fine. What about you?"

"Hungry."

He whisked me and my drink to a small table in the corner set with all the aforementioned dishes in peak hot and cold condition.

While we enjoyed our romantic dinner for two, a couple dozen questions ran through my head. I imagine Ric had three dozen. I decided to take the Red Bull by the horns.

"Sansouci is right," I said as we finished our creamy desserts.

"He certainly seems cozy with women of my acquaintance."

"Woman, singular. I had no idea until tonight that your starchy homicide captain had a weakness for vampires."

"Are you crazy? Kennedy Malloy hates all things supernatural and Sansouci is Cicereau's head goon, a werewolf."

"So everyone thinks." I leaned forward over the last of my drink, the scarlet grenadine at the bottom. "I discovered that he's a vampire and not just any vampire."

"Vampires are vampires." Ric watched me carefully. "Aren't they? And what's he doing fang-in-fang with the werewolf boss?"

"Sansouci's not a werewolf. He's a vampire hostage. It all goes back to the mob war for Vegas in the nineteen forties. The werewolves beat out the human mobsters from Chicago and L.A. as well as a vampire organization with French roots, of all things.

"When Cicereau's daughter played Juliet to a vampire Romeo, all the supernaturals feared an 'unnatural' alliance and the possibility that half-human Loretta could produce vamp-werewolf offspring. Each side, werewolf and vampire, agreed to their deaths and exchanged hostages to ensure that the status quo stayed in play: Werewolves lucky seven, Vampires zero. That was more than seventy years ago and it's held so far, although our discovering the Karnak vampires could put a real kink in the balance of power."

Ric sat back, stunned. "I feel like I've been out of action for a year. You've dug up an amazing amount of dirty supernatural secrets since you hit town."

"I was an ace paranormal TV reporter in Wichita, remember? We're very thorough in the Midwest."

I leaned forward again. "Seriously, Ric, when we found those sixty-year-old murdered bones in Sunset Park, we hit the mother lode for every hidden influence in Las Vegas. The minute that happened it became all about raising those dead bones. Cicereau's daughter, Loretta, began appearing in my mirror, playing the victim and seeking my sympathy and help."

"So she's a very vengeful ghost?"

"Yup, and the Karnak vampires have been in hiding for decades, centuries, maybe millennia. Now they're hungry to raise really old vampires, not the modern variety like Sansouci, whom they consider degraded."

"Just how degraded *is* Sansouci?" Ric asked, a possessive male gleam in his dark eyes.

"You mean to Kennedy Malloy, or to me?" I asked, demure.

"Delilah, don't tease."

"He may seem tame, but I have a long history of not trusting anything with fangs except my dogs. I'm using Sansouci as a source, not vice versa. He's a new breed of vampire, one the vamp mob of the forties had hopes could eventually go mainstream in society. They'd been working on that strain for almost a century, even before the mob war for Vegas, which they lost."

"A mainstream vampire? How?"

"You saw it. Sansouci gets around 24/7. He's not handicapped by having to hit the dirt for twelve out of every twenty-four hours. He takes his blood in small harmless doses from consensual humans. Yeah, exclusively female. Wouldn't you? Kinda grazes, the way women on diets are encouraged to consume."

"Delilah, you're being wicked!"

"Glad you think so, Montoya," I purred. "I'd like a really rich nightcap upstairs when all this major revelation stuff is over.

"But," I added, going for an even better gleam in his eye.

"Yes?"

I got serious, knowing he was right that I'd been leaning too much on Sansouci as a snitch.

"First, I think we have to find out what's happening at the Karnak since the other hotel owners raided them on our behalf."

"You're talking a return raid of two," Ric said.

"You all right with that?" Like I didn't know.

"Totally."

"The twin pharaohs aren't going to take this lying down like royal mummies in their caskets. And I want Quicksilver along. The royals keep a semisupernatural pack of really wicked hyenas. We need Quick's supernaturally superb canine-lupine senses of smell, hearing, and sight. The Royal Twits will never expect us to rush back in where humans would fear to tread."

Ric paused, looking at me as if I'd grown a second head. "And here I thought you'd be too protective to want me to go back."

"I figure you'd go back anyway. Better with me and Quick. I remember the lay of the land and he can smell it. Besides, he's major PO'ed about being left out of our adventures recently."

He eyed the dog, lying alertly by the parlor fire. "He's been jealous of me. Of you."

"That's why he's so good at his job." I couldn't tell Ric quite yet the dog had recently taken on a six-hundred-pound tiger for him, for me.

"You want the love or a first-class partner?" I asked.

"I want to go for both."

"Quick," I said.

The wolf-dog clicked over on curved nails.

"Shake," I said, just kidding.

Trained dogs did those tricks. Quick didn't.

He jerked his fanged snout in Ric's direction, then mine, and howled until all the hidden cottage pixies or whatever squealed and fled the building.

They'd be back, and so would Ric, Quick, and me.

In the best-case scenario.

Chapter Twenty-two

ANY REASONABLE PERSON would expect a hot bedroom scene to follow the life-threatening stress I'd faced at the Gehenna tonight and Ric's return to walk-around good health.

Yeah, me too.

We nuzzled naked in my four-poster bed long enough to drive Quick out an open window to patrol what was left of the night.

And we came mutually . . . to an agreement that we'd better save what was left of our strength for our covert assault on the Karnak in the morning. Make war, not love.

Ric went home early the next morning and returned to the cottage wearing undercover black, a heavy Kevlar vest lacking only the big white letters, FBI, and high-top butt-kicking rubber-soled boots. He applied black camo face greasepaint from his kit bag once here and was much impressed by my Assault on the Karnak ensemble of steel-studded spandex patent-leather catsuit and matching crotch-high boots.

My silver familiar had assumed the form of a Wonder Woman brow coronet. When the silver familiar had the chutzpah to mock me I actually felt stronger.

"New bling, huh?" Ric teased, his forefinger touching the central five-pointed star. "One way to keep the hair out of your eyes for battle."

Quick wore his usual thick fur coat. I'd noticed that the

silver circles on his black leather collar changed to represent all the phases of the moon: full, quarter, and half. Today they were almost at the full. His pale blue eyes were all black iris. When he grinned, it was to display a lethal mountain range of jagged teeth. I almost glimpsed a diamond glitter, but maybe that was his magic healing saliva.

I texted Manny's Demon-phone for him to meet Ric, Dolly, Quick, and me in the Inferno entryway at 10:00 A.M.

The lure of Dolly's chrome and horsepower and a big tip had Manny paying another parking valet to take his place while he ferried us to the Karnak parking garage. From there we'd sneak into the Karnak underbelly on our private commando mission.

I drove Dolly directly there, Ric and Quicksilver safely hidden in the car's hearse-size trunk. Facing the Karnak vampires still didn't faze him, but Ric had been nervous about this trunk part of the plan.

"NO OFFENSE, DELILAH," he'd whispered in my ear when Quick's furry back was turned, as if that would do any good with those sharp, pricked wolfish ears, "but he *is* your dog. I'd trust him with your life, but not, uh, my back. He's really possessive of you, not that I blame him. One session of playing ball doesn't mean he wouldn't snap mine right off."

Ric didn't know Quicksilver and his magic saliva, delivered by licking, had healed him not just once, but twice. From some supersensitive canine sense, Quicksilver had moved Ric up to Priority One after his Karnak ordeal and my supernaturally successful Kiss of Life efforts.

He hadn't been present at the Inferno when I reluctantly accepted Snow's Brimstone Kiss in the first place. Grizelle had been, and for me that had been one tiger and one human female too many for witnesses.

On the other hand, the canine/lupine breed depended on judging friend or foe by crotch sniff. When Quick had first met Ric, he'd made clear that if he didn't like how Ric treated me, the "spleen" would be the first to go.

Obviously my hundred-and-fifty-pound adopted shelter doggie had never had a sexually active human companion, or any human home.

It took those observant and rare wolfhound-blue eyes only seconds to figure out that Ric might look like he was attacking me, but in a welcome way. In those first awkward moments, both man and dog had been a bit uneasy with each other. Perhaps I should say, a "bite" uneasy.

Now I was asking them to make like littermates in the cavernous trunk of my car, which even then was not roomy enough for Ric when it involved getting down with doggie breath.

"Quick and I are a team, yes," I told Ric. "So are you and I. It's time we merged the K-nine operation with the human one. I'm counting on you guys to get along for the sake of the mission. Right, Quick?"

A short, sharp bark of agreement.

"Ric?"

"Some of my best friends in the FBI had hairy backs, and they had my back too."

"Then let's go kick Karnak butt."

"SHE'S YOURS AND Manny's if we don't come back in twenty-four hours. Or so," I told Hermie as I handed him Dolly's keys when we met at the Inferno drive-through. "I figured you and Manny would do anything for Dolly. And me."

Manny was off parking Hermie's personal '66 Mustang somewhere dark and deep in the hotel garage.

"You boys would have to ferry her back and forth between the Karnak and the Inferno," I added, "but Hell could use a new Charon franchise these days anyway."

I slid into the passenger side of the bench seat, knowing Ric would seethe at the idea of my letting a minor parking-valet demon behind Dolly's wheel before I let him drive her. I'd owe him a long desert drive in Dolly after this expedition. With benefits.

Hermie was in tears. True, they were purple and sizzled. I knew he was more blown away by my bequest of the car than fearful of any dread outcome by which he would get it. I was still touched as we zipped up the Strip.

Hermie drove Dolly to the lowest level of the Karnak garage and parked her in a dim, specially tagged area where she'd be safe and Ric and Quick could exit the trunk like shadows. God, their names rhymed! I hadn't realized until now.

I was still grinning when I sprang them from Dolly's trunk.

"OK, boys?"

They couldn't wait to jump out and stretch. Nice muscles, furred or not. Ric smeared my face with black greasepaint. In our skintight black outfits with the war paint I bet we looked like rogue Cirque du Soleil cast members.

"Come on," Hermie prodded. "This is a top-secret route."

He led us to an elevator door cleverly disguised as a fire hose installation panel.

The lower you went in Las Vegas these days, the closer you got to hellishly intemperate zones. Sweat started trickling down my back. My steel-studded pseudo "wet suit" was living up to its name. At least the catsuit was a strong second skin with first-rate protection against fangs, venom, and weapons.

The elevator was the size of a large upright coffin or a royal mummy case. Ric and I squeezed in, black on black, Quicksilver between us, panting up a storm.

Ric and I grinned at each other. Our shared inhaled doggie breath carried a faint overtone of fresh blood.

We shrugged. Carnivores Are Us.

The letter on the single button on the gilt panel was a weird hieroglyph, a star shape with five lines rayed out. It could represent a human with a wide stance and wide, welcoming arms.

Oddly, it recalled the famous Leonardo da Vinci figure of a man with radiating arms and legs symmetrically splayed to contact the edges of a circle. The Circle of Life. And Death.

Quicksilver frowned, salivating without compunction. Healing was the last thing on the lupine half of his mind.

I glanced at Ric. His features were as focused and intent as a hunting falcon's. If a human being could salivate, this was it.

"Where are we going?" I asked Ric. He must have rambled in the belly of the beast deeper than I had.

"I don't know. I just bet I'm going to enjoy it."

"You figure your instincts will lead you back to those lost souls?"

"Yup. That vision of Hell haunts my dreams, and I dowse for the dead on instinct. Maybe I can detect the dying too."

So here we were: one woman, one resurrected man, and one rescue dog with "gifts." We might be up against the entire immortal Egyptian empire, but we were ready to rock and roll.

The only thing we weren't willing to do was roll over

and play dead. We all had a lot at stake. *Oops.* Bad expression.

Quicksilver thirsted to confront his ancient hyena enemies.

Ric ached to destroy anyone or anything that preyed on innocent victims.

I needed to redeem the unhappy pasts of both my partners, man and dog.

Chapter Twenty-three

THE ELEVATOR DOORS opened on deserted halls depicting the eternal Egyptian decorative combo of earthly and afterlife paradise and a passage through the murky underworld separating these two desirable states.

We all paused, awed. Ancient oil lamps cast an ambient glow like the high-tech, ultraviolet-filtering low lights museums use to shield irreplaceable artworks. They illuminated everything.

The hundreds of thousands of ordinary humans who produced the Egyptian culture's prodigies of architecture, art, writing, and religious complexity for their time and place were almost supernaturally gifted.

Add to them a vampire's eternal life and strength and they were terrifying.

They always say, "Don't look back."

That's what someone somewhere sometime must have told Dorothy Gale after she got back from Oz, I bet. Dorothy, don't look back! Don't see the curled toes and striped socks of the Wicked Witch of the East lying dead under your tempest-tossed house. You didn't kill her. Fate did. You can't afford to feel guilty in a land where Wicked Witches will eat you alive.

Irma was playing Greek chorus to me at this moment.

Girl, don't follow that yellow brick road. They play for keeps here. Death is the game, my pretty, and those ruby red slippers of yours? Take another gander. They're black butt-kicking boots. No pretties here but us.

I looked around at the large jars and linens, deciding we'd arrived in a mortuary temple storeroom. I'd been boning up on ancient ways along the Nile since my first foray "way down in Egypt land," as the old spiritual put it, where Moses told Pharaoh, "Let my people go."

I glanced at Ric, trying to picture him as the Charlton Heston film version of Moses. I saw a bit of the liberator but not the asexual religiosity, thank goodness.

Quicksilver growled as Ric did a rapid visual survey.

"Great stuff for the tourists," Ric said, "but my dream featured the deep, dark, down and dirty parts. That's where we need to go if we're going to free anybody from being kept as enslaved food for an aristocracy of immortal vampires."

Ric's glimpse of enslaved vampire food kept like cattle in cavern camps overrode the memories of his own torture for now. I was thankful for anything that banished such pain. Still, how could we three rescue "herds" of people who'd survived thousands of years beyond their time?

He must have explored far beneath the royal pomp and circumstance areas of the Karnak's inner necropolis to have discovered the vampires' human food supply before he'd been captured and became it.

I shivered inside my warm catsuit. Helena's therapeutic intervention still dampened Ric's bad memories. What would happen when they fully exploded back into his consciousness?

If he remembered his torment, would he also remember I'd kissed him back from apparent death, or the brink of it? Would he love me for doing it? Or not. Love me or loathe me? I was becoming a person with either friends and lovers or enemies, nothing in between.

Did I really want to awaken every morning in a city like Las Vegas with its hidden underworld of blood, lust, greed, and death? Did I want to call a glittering playground built upon the exploitation of so many victims home? Maybe we all do that, unknowingly. That was the trouble with the Millennium Revelation. Nobody with eyes and a brain could pretend to be ignorant and innocent anymore.

Rats. That made life hard but . . . maybe more worth living? Or not losing, at least.

I nodded at Ric. "Lead on, *amigo,* and we'll follow."

We were a team, yes, but sometimes one had to take the initiative. He moved forward with the bold caution of a point man in a SWAT operation.

So far we'd only intruded on the lavishly decorated corridors of an ancient Egyptian tomb. Although the chambers and halls we passed were empty, we never had a sense of being alone. The eerily lifelike painted bas-relief human figures on the walls ensured that. In shades of red, yellow, blue, and green, the people alongside us were forever frozen in their daily occupations of work and pleasure, their black-outlined eyes always facing the viewer and on us.

The hieroglyph of their god Horus, an ever-vigilant open eye, supposedly had inspired the watchful "private eye" logo of the first and most famous private detective agency in the world.

The nineteenth-century U.S. Pinkertons' "We never Sleep" motto and open eye symbol had set the PI standard ever after.

So in the shadow of sloe-eyed, life-size Egyptian hunters and courtiers and pharaohs and boatmen and handmaidens and beast-headed gods, Ric checked every corridor each way.

A pulsing muscle in his cheek caught the light of the ancient lamps that allowed us to proceed without using our small, high-intensity flashlights.

Some seductive perfume in the smoke-wafting oil blended with the dusty, dry air and snaked almost physically through these chambers and narrow passages that angled up and down without stairs.

Ric always took the downward path.

Claustrophobia? Oh, yes. I had it.

Yet this grandiose tombscape also felt seductively peaceful, even intimate. All those white-garbed silent figures we passed seemed to acknowledge us in our somber cat-burglar black as we stalked images of their daily lives.

Were they Egyptian frieze angels on eternal watch, cast in the exquisite concrete of their long-dead culture? A TV reporter learns to look for visual metaphors. These pleated linen, wing-shaped kilts and skirts and capes seemed celestial and reassuring.

Except that talk of "dead" cultures was a mind-blowing concept now that we'd seen some still "lived" on . . . undead.

I was glad to spot no throne rooms or the beautifully neurotic twin sibling pharaohs I'd encountered on my first visit.

Truthfully, I hoped never again to glimpse them or their court musicians and armies of animated mummies and tomb-painted legions leaping off the walls to battle intruders like us.

Nor did I ever want to see again that dank, undecorated dungeon reached by some underground mirror of the River Nile, where Ric had been tortured until virtually every drop of his blood seeped into thirsty undead throats.

I still wasn't clear how the hellish river under the Inferno Hotel, doubtless the Styx, connected with a new supernatural Nile. Did moving water resemble a literal bloodstream in this Millennium Revelation world, linking cultures current and ancient, as well as lusts as old as time and as new as the latest cell phone model? At least this section of the Karnak's lower depths was dry and so far deserted.

The lamplight cast Quicksilver's canine profile ahead of us. His sharp snout and ears reminded me of Anubis, the jackal-headed god of the dead. His entire body stiffened in warning, ears pricked even farther forward, eyes staring, shoulder muscles quivering.

I put a containing hand around his collar . . . and pulled back stung fingers. The silver circles dotting the wide black leather were pulsing like overheated hearts, hot enough to raise coin-shaped blisters on my fingertips.

Oh my.

Ric's warning grip on my upper arm dimpled my steel-studded catsuit. We formed a linked trio in an instant, each in physical touch, all on high alert. I felt battle resolve amplify and echo between us like the drumbeat of a common heart.

We faced a darker opening, with no hint of hanging oil lamps beyond it.

Ric stepped through. We all did.

Our eyes slowly adjusted to a subtle twilight.

Gone were the lavish decorations. We stood among a thick convention of pillars like the towering black basalt ones that surrounded the Karnak Hotel entrance on the Las Vegas Strip.

These pillars, though, were of more human height, only twenty-some feet high, and made of humble yellow stone. So thick they still seemed squat, the forest of supportive pillars upheld a cavernous underground area we could see no end to.

"A royal basement?" I asked in a whisper.

The vast space with its unseen distances reverberated my three words into a muddled chorus from perhaps a thousand lips, losing all meaning in the process and becoming a rasping hiss.

I clapped a hand over my loose lips.

Too late to rethink and shut up. I'd already roused a native. From around one fat pillar popped a bizarre figure like an ancient Egyptian jackal-in-the-box.

It was half my height. I felt Ric's grip ease at that fact.

A growl reverberated into a pack of hellhounds as my dog brushed past us. Quicksilver wasn't standing off. To him, short stature was no sign of weakness. His canine grin became a widening maw and the long, low, gargled growl in his throat made a more menacing warning than any hundred rattlesnakes could broadcast.

"Aha!" cried our challenger, stomping his bare feet on the sandy stone floor and pumping his chubby hands up and down like an annoyed toddler. "Dance music at last in my deserted domain! Who goes there? Who comes to greet Bez? Man or beast, or pretty woman?"

Except for Quicksilver, who continued to growl into the creature's curly-maned, blunt feline face, we were speechless. Ric and I had been primed to face insanely bloodthirsty vampires from a civilization that, in the search for eternal life, had invented the most death-centered culture in the ancient world.

Instead we meet a stumpy, grumpy figure from a fleabag traveling circus?

"Well?" this "Bez" demanded again, in perfect English. "I've been waiting centuries to see natives beyond my prison doors. Are you man or woman? I can tell by the hyena breath that this rude individual at my level is a beast."

Quicksilver whined a question and suddenly sat on his haunches. The creature had passed his acid test. It bewildered rather than awakened his combined canine and lupine instincts.

"To answer your question. We are all three," Ric said.

I remembered that the lion-bodied, human-headed sphinx had offered a riddle to all who passed in some old fable.

"Ah, but is she pretty?" came another query.

I couldn't fault Bez for asking. My black hair resembled the shoulder-length wigs both men and women wore in ancient Egypt. My camo-streaked face was missing elaborate Cleopatra eyeliner. And I didn't wear a long tight skirt.

"What's it to you?" Ric asked, not intimidated.

The figure did a clumsy somersault directly into our path. "Nothing and everything. Pretty women are a specialty of mine. Ugly ones too. As you may notice, I have no claim to beauty myself."

I eased out my held breath and scanned our otherwise still-unpopulated surroundings.

No, no incoming spectral or physical hyena packs. No charging zombie mummies. No terra-cotta-skinned warriors armed with spears, battleaxes, bows and arrows. No royal gold chariot bearing twin male and female pharaohs braced for battle.

Just this impish squat figure blocking our passage.

Well, had we met our one Munchkin in this murderous Land of Egyptian Oz?

Was he—and I noticed the operative organ, rampant and outsize, that confirmed it beneath his round belly—a chubby Cupid-like court jester? His head was at about my waist level and, given his lascivious grin, I was not really comfy with that, even in a fully covering catsuit.

His legs and arms were all hairy muscle and his face surrounded by curly hair and long beard. He was a jug-eared, lion-maned, Egyptian-collared and kilted, rotund creature, both jovial and sinister.

I couldn't decide if he was a pet or a demon.

From Quicksilver's continuing blend of whimper and growl, he was as confused as I was.

Not Ric. He'd pulled out his boot knife, a wicked eight-inch blade, and aimed it at the navel on the jolly little pot-belly, just above the too-obvious male member.

"Aren't we the pretty foursome?" the creature demanded, unfazed and preening. He leered at me. "I bet you bear a tattoo of my image on the inside of your thigh, if you're the pretty lady."

Ric's fist had him up in the air by the bunched beaded collar, dangling. Ric kept the powerful kicking legs two feet from his tensed torso, doing no harm.

"What," he demanded, "have you to do with this lady's thighs?"

"Nothing! And everything! Good sir. Fine sir. Gentle sir. I will give her sweet childbirth, that's all."

"Thanks, but no thanks," I said. "You think I'd wear a tattoo of your person on my flesh?"

He shrugged and appealed to the dog.

"It does look too wet and slippery to hold ink," he conceded of my thigh. "Yet many ladies do and are the better for that. I should introduce myself so you will explain your most fascinating selves.

"I am Bez, cousin of the goddess Bast, lion cub in some guises, otherwise humble domestic servant, protector of households and the birthing process, and licker of lady parts when invited."

Quicksilver went to his belly, stretched out his legs, and fixed his canine jaws and eyes on what delicate bodily part—as with Cicereau's goons in Sunset Park—he considered the creature's "spleen." One leap and . . .

Ric shook the little man. I realized Bez was a dwarf. Ric's personal history of childhood slavery would keep him from hurting anything with a childish aspect unless he was dangerously and personally challenged. Bez might be many things, even dangerous at times, but now he was merely a friendly and curious obstacle. Ric's frustration must be immense.

"What are you doing down here?" he demanded.

"What your gentlenesses must also be doing down here," Bez said. "Exploring maybe, patrolling. The Lands of Their Joint Majesties are minor above, but major below."

"You're a guard dog of sorts?" Ric asked.

"A guard god. Yes, a humble one, or I would be much closer to the throne room. But, really, sir"—his oversized head leaned inward—"if you yourself do not harbor millennia of blood tastes, you'll much prefer these empty, natural caverns, home to those who would practice the old ways but also have no way to defend their preferences, alas."

"The *new* ways," Ric said, "require legions of cowed and unwilling blood donors, indentured for centuries, being born and dying for one reason only: to be food."

"Food. Ah, yes. One of my favorite things. I admit to a lion-size appetite despite my small size. I must say I like being of this elevated stature your gentle grasp permits."

The bizarre head that combined features of a chubby man and a lion looked from right to left and back again.

"However, since I am charged with the safe passage of life from mother to child, and most of these born here are meant to be drained, ultimately to the death, I suppose I am obligated to help any liberators rash enough to venture below. I saw you captured here, man-stranger. Your valiant fight gave me hope my people might someday face a kinder fate. If you could use a guide to the Underworld, I would volunteer myself."

Ric lowered Bez to his chunky legs with a swallowed curse.

"All right for now, Shorty. I'd not seen your like down here, during my brief and, as you state, violent earlier visit. You seem harmless enough."

"And nice to see *you* again, sir. Harmless? Always my major advantage, sir, among a very formidable pantheon of predatory-headed gods," Bez said with a bow. "It's true I'm partial to the ladies but my role is guardian, which leaves me stranded at a lot of portals while others have all the fun."

Ric was still dubious. "Such as inspecting women's thighs, no doubt."

Bez peered mischievously around Ric at my dark-clad legs. "She wears no linen sheath but I sense the female. No tattoos of me? Not a one?"

"Alas, no tattoos at all, *especially* of you," I answered.

"I am considered a lucky charm."

"But you're not Irish," I noted. There was something leprechaunish about him, also Puckish. He was also clearly Egyptian, although oddly so.

"*Eye*-rish?" he echoed me. "Does that have something to do with the Eye of Horus, which never sleeps? Speaking of such, I advise moving on. Like the River Nile, to move is to make new and in moving one is safer than still water.

"So speaks Bez, the guardian."

RIC CLAPPED AN arm around my shoulder as we and Quicksilver followed our cavorting guide.

Despite Bez's assurances, we all kept looking left and right, back and ahead, keeping a 360-degree eye on our surroundings. The area did indeed seem deserted, though we figured from Ric's seeing hundreds of corralled people down here that some nasty people herders must lurk ahead.

Ric leaned near so I could place my whisper for his ears only.

"If such a creature as this Bez can exist here, perhaps it's a safer zone."

"Don't count out Coyote," he growled back as deep and low as Quicksilver.

"Coyote?" I was lost. Didn't he mean hyenas? They're the African—and now new-ancient Egyptian—variety of canine.

"Trickster god," he hushed back.

Oh, Irma whispered in my inner ear. *I've heard of that dude. Well known among Native Americans in the Southwest. Remember that trickster gods are two-sided coins, Dee. Sometimes helpful, sometimes definitely not!*

I nodded, puzzling Ric, who didn't know I'd never outgrown my childhood invisible friend. In fact, I had two invisible friends now, counting the Invisible Man CinSim at the Inferno.

I was always happy to know that Irma and her strong survival instincts were aboard. When she came out to chat, it boded well. Bez might be a guardian god but I packed a guardian goddess.

Speaking of goddesses, I felt the silver Wonder Woman coronet melting down my cheekbone and neck, a cool thread snaking down my torso to wrap my left thigh. Oh, no! The silver familiar was faking a Bez "tattoo" on my leg. *More* subtle mockery? Snow might claim the amulet's activity was only driven by my own conscious and subconscious, but I knew he'd get a vengeful kick out of my skin being marked, even temporarily.

I had to stop worrying about what Snow might or might not do to me now that I'd really done him wrong. It was messing with my mind at crucial times.

Think, Delilah, don't let guilt grab the steering wheel from you!

I didn't need Irma to goad me on this subject. I was far too aware of what Snow had done to me and I had done to him. I was concluding neither of us came out looking good from that juvenile, supernatural one-upmanship contest.

So I reconsidered the familiar's latest shift on my epidermis. That damn mobile silver hitchhiker might consider it vital to mark me with Bez's sign of protection. I surely wasn't a pregnant woman in need of a mystical midwife. I *might* surely be a mortal woman requiring supernatural Egyptian protection in the coming hours.

MEANWHILE, I HAD *two* keen hunting dogs for partners.

"I recognize this stone forest." Ric pushed past Bez to palm-stroke a shoulder-high scratch on one massive pillar. "I used my fingernails to etch my path."

"Hieroglyphic cookie crumbs. Good thinking, Hansel."

I rushed ahead to another marked pillar. The faint marks on the exposed fresh stone stood out down here, even in the eternal twilight glow.

"Naughty, naughty!" Bez cried, dancing after us as if his bare feet trod hot sand. "The royals don't want any graffiti but their own on their walls and pillars."

Ric and I caught each other's glances, then laughed. We had reason to scoff at the royals' rules after enduring separate capture by them. Being considered trespassing graffiti artists tickled our senses of humor and survival.

When your life is on the line, there's no sense going down sniveling.

Quicksilver demonstrated the same spirit by stretching his six-foot length up a pillar and dragging a front fang along it. He turned to grin at us. A crooked line like a faint lightning bolt was his mark.

That sky-set signature was more than appropriate. I noticed the silver circles on his collar had swollen into almost full-moon roundness down here. Did that mean he sensed the lurking presence of his canine cousins, the royal hyena corps? I hoped not.

"How'd you get this deep on your own?" I asked Ric.

"I trapped myself in a mummy case-guarded hallway near the hotel levels. I only descended a few levels to reach the royal throne room for a disdainful interrogation session. The Twin Royals had nothing on Captain Kennedy Malloy of the LVMPD in the disdainful department, I must say."

Ric eyed me sideways, amused. Little did he know he owed his two coffee-dark irises to a contact lens I'd slipped into the one that had turned silver.

"Kennedy isn't as possessive as you think," was all he said.

"Maybe not, Mr. Tequila Smoothie Montoya, but *I'm* a lot more possessive than *you* think."

Ric hadn't been conscious to see me poised to battle Grizelle's huge tiger form to the death.

He smiled ruefully. "I lucked out to get this deep unchallenged. In the desert you learn to move silently, so the rattlesnakes don't strike. We don't want to linger down here. The last time I did that it didn't turn out so swell. So, no, I didn't take your handy dandy elevator ride down, I just followed the yellow sandstone road."

When I lifted my eyebrows, he swept his rubber sole

over the yellow sand covering the limestone. "These paths go down stories and stories, like the staircases in the London Tube. Ever been there?"

"Nope. No Tubes in Kansas except for funnel clouds. When were you in London?"

"A couple of years ago when I was still with the FBI. Some very old bodies that needed finding were buried deep."

"I bet."

Apparently our new guide didn't want us dawdling. Bez did several handsprings past, popping upright to bar our way again.

"I am Bez," he announced again. "I am only a minor god. Some say I was imported from Nubia, a lesser being, but I am an offspring of the Nubian lion-god."

"Impressive," Ric said. "One of Hercules' twelve labors was to defeat the Nemean lion."

"I can add to that," I said. "Samson wore a lion skin and was also said to have defeated a fierce lion, but Delilah—"

"—trimmed his mane," Ric finished with a grin. "Hey, little big guy," he said to Bez, "you do realize you're traveling with the mighty Delilah?"

"Ah, no. Thank you for the warning. One would not wish to lose one's mane to the mighty Delilah."

Almost ready to giggle despite our surroundings, I pictured myself carrying oversize shears in my duty belt holster, the kind I'd once found at an estate sale, used at newspapers in hot-lead typesetting days to cut across copy paper with one swipe of giant blades. Delilah Street: the Amazon scissors queen.

A few good slashes to curtail Samson's God-commanded locks had made the biblical Delilah's reputation. I intended to slash whatever needed it and a lot more than hair.

Bez was dancing on impatient feet again. "One must not idle. We must pass these unmoving pillars to arrive elsewhere."

Quicksilver was the first to follow Ric's sinuous path forward. In several minutes we'd woven between a couple blocks' worth of lavishly decorated pillars. I was gaining new respect for Ric's inbred desert survival skills. He must have been hard to capture. Only being outnumbered by hordes of Egyptian vampires probably had accomplished it.

Plus, he'd penetrated the heart of their evil empire, if you hankered to use old movie-serial terms. My first visit here had just brushed the surface. I had no talents the Egyptian vampires could use, so they hadn't tried that hard to keep me.

In retrospect, I found that rather insulting.

By now the spare stone underground vastness had developed a foul smell. Quicksilver's black nostrils were flaring with distaste. I recognized the unhappy combined reek of stale meat and fresh excrement.

Ric caught my eye and looked down. The sandy floor had darkened, like the ground of a bull ring, as if with blood.

No. It was damp. With water.

I didn't hear any fresh-flowing stream like the underground rivers used during the Inferno invasion of the Karnak. We were in a very different section. This was seepage from below.

Bez, who'd paused, gargled distress low in his throat, the feisty lion cub. Quicksilver echoed him.

"We're near the . . . encampment," Ric warned me. "You can smell the human occupation."

I inhaled deeply. Yes. Blood, shit, and tears. My heart

clutched. As a paranormal TV reporter in Wichita, I'd covered a couple of brutal cattle mutilation sites in the boonies.

Cows made such pathetic victims. Large, bulky creatures, they were never built to run away like horses. They'd been fashioned to graze, essentially as helpless against serious, or even supernatural, predators as housecats and backyard dogs.

Why did these harmless animals allow savage mankind to make them into domestic slaves? Into beasts of burden and consumption? I'd never understand what domesticated dogs and cats got from their association with a creature as abusive and bloodthirsty as man, whether up to his one final death . . . or now, to supernaturally extended lifetimes far beyond the single death allotted ordinary animals and less cannibalistic humans.

What would I give to live?

I knew what I'd give to keep Ric living. Almost anything.

"Almost" was a weasel word. I'd probably give my life, then some trickster supernatural might give me more lives and what would my "sacrifice" have been worth? Caring so deeply about another person was new to a wary woman who'd until now invested emotion only in speechless animals that couldn't reject her.

Just days ago I'd considered an unwilling kiss the ultimate price to pay in terms of sovereign personal freedom. Now . . . it wasn't that simple. Now I knew I could kill as well as kiss.

Quicksilver rubbed his consoling muzzle against my hand. I'd give up a lot before I'd lose him, too, but living life only to stop its inevitable losses didn't seem to be a winning game after the Millennium Revelation.

"Delilah," Ric whispered from ahead, his single word slithering between the stone pillars.

I realized I'd let him get out of sight . . . and Bez too.

Quicksilver and I rushed through the crowded pillars, following the scent of herded humanity. Ric was striding ahead into the stench-ridden air, sure and determined. Quicksilver and his supersensitive nose pushed past me to trot in Ric's wake.

Thanks to the intense perfumes the ancient Egyptians used, I'd never scented true life in the Karnak Egyptian underground, as Ric had. He didn't just find and sometimes raise zombies, he knew the scent of the human flesh that had made them, even if it was decaying.

I was also aware we were approaching the place where Ric had been captured before. Quick sure smelled danger, dashing back to circle me, then ahead to Ric, shifting his keen, sky-blue eyes this way and that, hunting imminent enemies.

THE PILLARS ENDED unexpectedly. We stood below overarching stone ceilings dripping icicle-like stalactites down to form mirror-image stalagmites reaching upward, like lacy stone cathedral spires reflected in a lake. They created an outer fence of frozen stone and glittering minerals from the ancient salt sea that once had covered the Nevada desert. They made a shining canopy that turned the everlasting twilight here into an eternal dawn.

I turned in a circle, gazing up in wonder at a Notre Dame cathedral of subterranean stone that offered soaring arches above, now that we'd passed the pillared forest.

In the massive swoop of stone roof my imagination traced giant veined dragon wings. No Seine River flowed nearby, only the tears of the earth falling downward and piling upward to the stone points of the wings, anchored like tents or fey touchpoints on the ground.

When I'd slowly come back down to earth to follow Ric's stare to level ground, I realized the breathtaking beauty above only made the horror below and ahead of us even more stomach-clenching.

Dark cave mouths yawned open to background a festering crowd of gathered human figures. I saw the crowded, stinking masses prisoner beyond a deep pit. There was nothing ancient or Egyptian about that scene.

On the rim of the pit, caveside, lay gnarly gnawed bones and black-green piles of melting ooze. Picture your refrigerator after a week of disconnection. The stench of rotting meat and vegetation made a Dumpster behind an abandoned food store smell sweet by comparison.

What kept these people where they were? With tentative strides forward, we four finally stood staring down into the apparently bottomless pit separating us from the milling mobs across the way.

I edged closer behind Bez, easily seeing over him.

From the twenty-foot-wide pit that separated the cave dwellers from our party I heard a harsh, scaly stirring deep below. Imagine King Kong dragging his knuckles over an iron mine.

"Viper pit?" I asked no one in particular.

"Not snakes, but other creatures of the Nile banks," Bez said. "Insect life once teeming near the great river are set on guard here to protect the precious, self-generating food source."

Knock out the fancy language and you had the Karnak State Fair Cow Barn, only it never emptied out all year 'round and the "moat" was patrolled by creepy-crawlies.

With a jolt, I realized that the prisoners' front rows were

all children, the adults behind them. Their skins presented a patchwork ranging from darker to pale colors and all wore rags of tattered mummy winding gauze.

This close I noticed that the "children" more resembled Bez. I doubted Ric had. A brief glimpse of this scene had stirred his rescue genes. He hadn't yet encountered Bez and realized that the prisoners were petite ancient Egyptian adults and even smaller dwarves combined with—I blanched—some tall, pale folks in shredding knit tops and shorts . . . the occasional kidnapped tourist.

That dozens of stubby fingers clutched the rags of the taller bedraggled figures behind them was even more heartbreaking. Worst of all, I discerned a few of the "adults" cradling packages that were probably babes in arms.

"They're still here," Ric breathed, as if hoping such a nightmare couldn't be glimpsed again.

He knew better, and so did I.

Beside me, Quicksilver sneezed and boxed at his wrinkled snout. To his sensitive canine nose, the very air we breathed was a torture of noxious, yet carnivore-tempting scents.

It was hard to imagine the immaculately clad Egyptian aristocracy, vampire or not, venturing down by the caveside to pierce and suck these filthy throats. Expecting a smidge of nicety from a ravening vampire was probably a romantic twentieth-century fantasy the Millennium Revelation hadn't debunked yet.

Ric had evaluated the whole nauseating setup. His expression showed how impossible this rescue mission was, even as the tourists cried, "Help!" and the smaller adults, dwarves, and children called out in no recognizable language but need.

Though Ric's obsession to return here was crystal clear,

what two humans, a dog, and a lesser Egyptian god could do for these lost souls was muddier than the banks of the River Nile in ole Egypt Land.

Small, smudged fingers reached across the twenty feet or so between us. Oh, lord, the last thing I could deal with at this moment was unclaimed orphans. And *more* ancient Egyptian vampires and gods.

Yet those ancient syllables called for aid.

Then I realized the most chilling fact of all.

They were not beseeching Ric and me and Bez, but someone—or something—behind us.

Chapter Twenty-four

We all turned around with a grim sense of foreboding.

I glanced at Ric and Bez, then looked to what they were staring at. The same thing I was. Nothing. Just the same-old, same-old decorative pillars.

Quicksilver sat still, ears on alert, a frown furrowing his canine brow. Then I looked *up* the pillars instead of just *at* the stone on my eye level.

This front rank displayed more than a wallpaper of earth-tone painted hieroglyphs carved into their sandstone surfaces. My eyes followed the ground-level vertical lines of cinnamon-skinned legs and traveled up to discern the subtly incised shapes of huge heroic figures marching fifteen feet high across the several pillars behind us. From the collared necks down, they were the traditional human. From the necks up, they bore the heads of animal, reptile, and insect.

No vegetables, thank goodness.

A glint of gold to my right made me turn that way.

Oh. Ah. Anubis.

Ric grabbed my arm at the same moment. "All these impressive figures must be Egyptian gods, but who and what is the black guy wearing enough gold to be the sultan of Brunei?"

On a pillar far down from where our party had broken through the front lines, thus making a surprise appearance, stood the most spectacular pillar sculpture of all: not cinnamon-skinned, but the muscular night-black human body of jackal-headed Anubis, god almighty. This was a giant version of the gleaming statuette I'd seen at a St. Louis museum. His sandals, kilt, armbands, headdress were all bright gold against his smooth, Nubian-black stone skin. The jackal head's sharp black nose and tall, perked ears made Anubis the most impressive animal-headed god in a pantheon that included gods and goddesses with lion, cow, hawk, crocodile, and cat heads.

"Anubis," I whispered in awe.

"Wanna bet," said Ric, "Anubis drove the most awesome dune buggy on the beach in his day?"

Anubis was king of the pillar gods down here, no doubt.

"Along with Osiris, he was the head god of the dead," I explained. "He specialized in embalming and protecting the dead on their journey to the Underworld and Paradise beyond if they were found worthy by Osiris. Osiris ruled and judged, and was the one to pass muster with. Or else."

Anubis obviously meant a lot to the people penned together across the pit, but such commoners were often unable to afford mummification. While we gawked at the spectacular figure of Anubis, Bez stationed himself before another pillar down the line.

"Here he is, here he is," Bez's joyful voice broke through our joint bedazzlement.

Bez's small figure already looked distant, but he was only eight pillars away, gazing upward with a grin.

"Come here," his gruff voice ordered. "Anubis is pretty and more powerful, but here's the only one who can help us, and them!"

A stone god could help us? Ric and I exchanged dubious glances as we hurried to examine Bez's friend. We saw another fifteen-foot-tall Egyptian man, the only one not wearing an animal head. This guy stood in a shallow boat, and if he could climb off that stone carving, he could indeed help us. I stood transfixed to see the magnificent carving up so close. On this huge scale, the low-relief carving was quite deep, cut an impressive four inches or so into the stone.

I have to admit I've always prided myself on being a sensible girl. I'd never been a sucker for a boy band or rock music idol. Still, examining these half-naked ancient Egyptian wall studs was getting on my nerves. Was this a minor side effect of the Brimstone Kiss? Was I starting to become a hunk connoisseur at this late date?

Wowsa! Irma agreed. *Does he play bass lute? This boy definitely needs to go electric.*

I decided to act the reporter and objectively dissect the mystique. I'd never regarded these Egyptian male art figures as sex objects, but "dead" was no longer the negative it had been before the Millennium Revelation.

Whether depicted as a vibratoriffic nine-inch-high statuette or much larger than life, I had to admit they were impressive, always posed in action, one foot ahead of the other in mid-stride.

Knife-sharp pleated, white-linen kilts set off their native BC tans. They sported the deepest richest tans since George Hamilton, a terra-cotta pigment coursing with life. They always presented their powerful facial profiles, with "maned" wigs brushing broad shoulders that emphasized slim hips.

Front-facing kohl-outlined eyes seemed to look directly at the observer—you, the lone chosen girl in the mosh-pit crowd—despite their aloof, sideways posture.

They fostered the Brimstone Kiss groupie's eternal hope: If *only* you could get this ancient hottie to look your way, he'd be lost, or at least interested.

This particular dude stood in a boat and held a staff. His headdress featured the sinuous upright form of a cobra with neck fanned for striking. I knew this "uraeus" was a royal or godly symbol. A star incised the sky on each side of the cobra-surmounted headdress.

No question, this guy was a stone star.

Immobile stone. What was Bez thinking? How could he help us free the penned prisoners? A god this size could have ferried them away with those bulging biceps for many return trips and still have left behind teeming masses yearning to breathe free.

Too bad. He was pretty but not useful.

Another glint of gold in the low light made me contemplate the Hunk Afloat on the Boat again.

Yes, that fugitive glitter came from his form, perhaps high-karat gold touches applied to his wrist and ankle bands, and the wide collar over his shoulders. Why did *he* merit the only gold work on a pillar god besides mighty Osiris, this mere boatman who didn't even rate an animal head?

I traced the thin glimpses of gold into actual curved links and *that* woke up my Bette Davis eyes. The boatman was *chained* to his wall! Was he too a prisoner, like the wretched humans in the caverns?

I'd never heard of a chained figure in Egyptian mythology, granted a scant online education in the subject. I knew the Greek god Prometheus had been chained to a rock with an eagle eating his liver for eternity for the sin of bringing fire to humankind. What could this guy bring to us?

Call me an optimist. I figure if I've never heard of something, it might have possibilities. I'd never heard of Cadaver Kid Ric Montoya before coming to Vegas a few weeks ago, for instance.

And look where *that* had gotten me.

Maybe thinking of Ric had snared his glance. He nodded as if reading my mind.

"Time to improvise, Del," he said.

He nodded at the dimly glittering wall décor. "You like this guy's looks?"

"I like his size. He could pole vault that staff over the pit or stomp what's down in it."

"He's just another pillar poster boy," Ric said with competitive male disdain.

"You didn't see guys like him leaping off the walls to stop your rescue party from getting to you."

"Guys that tall?"

"No, our size, but I figure anything that's kept in chains beneath the Karnak might be willing and able to help *us*."

"Couldn't hurt," Ric agreed. "What do you—?"

I'd been really good at obstacle vaults in Our Lady of the Lake Convent School's despised gym classes. Hey, I'd already leaped onto a golden chariot and stone horses' backs during my first visit to the Karnak.

In a moment I was three feet off the ground swinging on Boat Boy's ankle chains, then I scaled his staff to a swagged wrist chain six feet up. The deeply incised figure provided plenty of crevices.

I heard Quicksilver's nails scrabbling to gain purchase on the carving, but it offered footholds only to me. The heroic scale of these Egyptian monuments would delight a newbie rock climber. I dangled from a wrist chain that had looked braid-fine from ground level.

In reality—such as reality was in the bowels of the Karnak—the chain was oversized enough for my fingers to close around the links.

I pumped my legs to get my momentum going. Soon

I was swinging on the chain, the pendulum of my body weight exerting many times its actual force to pry a link loose.

Of course, padded gym blankets didn't lie below, but solid stone.

I felt a stomach-churning drop as a link released and I swung back and forth on one wildly whiplashing end. My scrabbling feet found no holds other than the pleats of Boat Boy's kilt under the navel and over the, uh . . . well, I understood why Ric was hollering my name like a panicked school principal watching a prank.

The chain link finally pulled free, and so did my grip. I plunged, braced to land hard. Instead, I was caught with a tooth-shaking impact in a pair of brawny, bare, brown masculine arms.

Ah . . . not Ric's arms. He was wearing chin-to-sole undercover black.

I'm a rather brawny girl myself—five-eight and fully packed—but this guy had me covered, crushed to his warm Indian clay chest, bringing a dull red flush of annoyance to Ric's hovering face.

"Thanks," I said into the man's liquid sloe eyes, living eyes. "I'm good."

I wriggled down into Ric's steadying custody.

The wall behind my recent landing pad was the same, the engraved god was on his pillar, and all was right with the world, except the broken chains were still swaying.

And Boat Boy was now standing right here with us, six-some feet of living ancient flesh.

Bez jumped up and down in manic glee.

"Shezmou, my brother, I have been alone on guard for so many millennia, helpless to succor my kind as their blood flowed thick into the vermins' throats."

Apparently, his fellow dwarves had fed the royal vamps since cobras became hair ornaments around here.

Bez remained a puppet on a yo-yo string, dancing and declaiming.

"O Shezmou, my very *big* brother, how good it is to see your handsome face and form standing in human shape on solid stone again.

"How good to know you will snap off the heads of the evildoers as ripe grapes at the harvest.

"How good to see that you will cast them into the eternally grinding press to again make the bloodwine of Egypt's gods run red along the Nile."

All well and good, but was Shezmou into liberation politics?

FOR THE FIRST time, I understood why the Egyptians depicted their gods as either twenty-foot giants or doll-size statuettes.

Shezmou in fleshly human form stood about six and a half feet tall. All the Karnak Egyptians I'd seen so far were on the five-foot-zero side. His self-proclaimed "brother," Bez, was a shrimp.

I wasn't sure what rules of form gods had to follow, but this fellow's well-tanned painted version still stood at eternal attention, appliquéd to the pillar. If he had been the statue brought to life, he could have crushed us all.

So the Shezmou who'd caught me in the bride-carried-over-the-threshold grip that had Ric developing lockjaw had to be an avatar, the living human-form incarnation of a god.

For now, he seemed more interested in taking in the scenery than in me.

"Bez," he said, warmth cloaking his deep, mesmerizing

voice, as he glanced down. Or frowned down. Although Egyptian wall paintings depicted musicians and dancers, the faces were all similarly stylized. No Quicksilver grins on these folk.

"You are as plump and mischievous as ever," the descended god noted of his baby bro. "Who are these strangers in our land? Who are this serpent man and woman and the pariah dog of strange coat and aspect? And what unfinished tomb is this?"

Okay, Bez's introduction had been a bit ominous with all that flowing blood stuff, but this guy was hitting political incorrectness on all cylinders.

"The dog is no feral pariah," I said, despite the tight grip of Ric's hand on my arm advising diplomatic tact. "Quicksilver is a mighty warrior who could scent a"—what did Egyptians hate? Ah, who?—"an enemy Hittite and track him to where the Blue Nile trickles into crocodile spit."

My knowledge of Egyptian landscape and history until recently had been limited to corny old films about that old Roman Empire soap opera trio, Caesar, Antony, and Cleopatra. Two guys and a gal always provided tried and true dramatic fodder. And guess what we have here, folks? Except for the dog and the class clown.

Shezmou grunted favorably at Quicksilver, whose slavering teeth were positioned over the thankfully veiled "spleen" of his linen kilt.

"A hunting hound, I see. Forgive me. I did not notice the collar in that thick hyena-like neck pelt. Our most prized hounds are lean and flat-coated, but this creature's head, ears, and jaws are more related to our noble and powerful Anubis."

We'll take it! Kinship with the jackal-headed usher of

dead souls is a great recommendation for Quicksilver in this culture. Meanwhile, Shezmou was regarding me with initial disfavor as well.

"This form felt female in my grasp but twice the weight it should be. That black, utterly concealing gown feels of the slick of decay rather than the radiant white of linen woven so fine a dancing girl's tattoos may be sighted through it."

Well, pardon me for not being reed-of-the-Nile bulimic!

Somebody ought to report those wall babes in their totally ass- and thigh clinging cellophane sheaths. Pity I forgot to put Spanx thigh-smoothers under my steel-studded catsuit to conceal unsightly bulges, like muscles and a skeleton.

"If I hadn't had some heft," I pointed out, "like a well-honed weapon, Your Lordness of the Bloodwine, my weight wouldn't have broken your chain to set you free."

He looked up at the still-vibrating separated golden links.

And frowned. Again.

"True, but who is this Nubian?"

Ric was Hispanic in camo black-face but that was going a little far. How to explain a man wearing head-to-toe undercover black in a context this disoriented god five thousand years out of his time would understand?

"I'm here to protect her." Ric's vibrant basso vibrated the sandstone under our feet, and particularly under Shezmou's big bare feet.

For an instant I hallucinated a silver flash striking like a knife blade from Ric's single contact lens–shrouded eye. Eyes were very significant to Egyptians. I guess I could be forgiven for imagining things. This was a rather hallucinatory place.

Shezmou stepped back, holding up a peaceful palm with a five-pointed figure tattooed in its center.

"The woman's weight broke me free," the liberated god said, "and I am satisfied. I care not whether she and her companions be Nubians or Hittites or Nile asps."

This was a relief, in a way, but why did the Karnak Egyptians, from royals to god, speak English, even if it was weird formalized English? Had they been watching late-night TV movies too? Or PBS? Maybe not so far-fetched.

As one of the first cultures with written language, they had the interest, and their own language was fading. I'd read that Cleopatra was the first pharaoh to bother speaking Egyptian in three hundred years, the latest in a line of Greeks whom Alexander the Great appointed to rule Egypt. By then Egypt was a conquered territory.

Could the vampires have gone to ground beneath their own desert sand centuries ago? Possibly to escape Roman persecution back in 50 BC, as Christians had later? If so, they might speak their own language among themselves but learn the dominant language topside too. Plenty of time to do it.

I'd seen that the mystical rivers of both Egypt and Christian culture flowed beneath the Las Vegas sands. Might the vampire empire have been here, isolated and inbred, even while empty desert was becoming "Vegas!" seventy-five years ago? Imagining the Egyptian vampires as the second immigrants to our shores, only subterranean, after the Native Americans was a bit of a stretch even for my inquiring mind.

Speaking of "stretch," Shezmou took one three-foot stride away from our party, then one long stride back.

"What a pleasure to be active again. My vintages of strong and sweet red wine will once more nourish the blood of pharaohs."

Ric spotted an opening for a skilled interrogator and jumped into it.

"Obviously, you're a mighty warrior," he said, "but a wine connoisseur as well?"

"Wine." Shez turned, a slight smile on his face. "This is the jewel of the Nile. Only the most perfect soil must be found to grow the grapes that will surrender their sweet juice in the wringing grasp of the wine press.

"Many white grapes bleed a weak and pallid ichor, but the precious red grape oozes only the sweet crimson wine that soothes a proper pharaoh's throat and gives him the strength of a lion, my divine godhead.

"My vintages are much treasured. When I turn my press on the olive and other fruits of the earth, I squeeze out sweet scent and unguents for the living and dead. My concoctions soften living skin, sweeten its scents in the sun god Ra's harshest rays, drive away biting insects, and prepare the dead for their passage to the Afterlife."

This softer side of Shezmou was intriguing after Bez's intimidating introduction. Still, I didn't miss the implications some of his words branded on my brain: "the precious red grape oozes only the sweet crimson wine that soothes a proper pharaoh's throat and gives him the strength of a lion."

If this didn't refer to a pharaohnic taste for blood from the git-go, I was Cleopatra's asp!

While I was connecting the mythological dots, Shezmou's measured pacing had grown more impassioned.

"I remember now! So many ungodly scenes have passed

before my motionless stone eyes all . . . these . . . years. They grow sharper in my mind and heart and belly and in my sacred eye."

His 3-D human form did come with two eyes, both dark and gorgeously outlined, Johnny Depp pirate-style. His dramatic gaze surveyed the surrounding pillars. Then they lifted to take in the yawning upper reaches of mineral salt-sparkled stalactites that had dripped down from the long-lost seas above our heads more than three million years ago.

He was beginning to understand that his confinement had lasted centuries and he lofted his fists like Bez. Shez's infuriated shadow cast a far taller and broader darkness than his dwarfed brother.

"I have been held impotent through all these dynasties, while *they,* the *unnaturally* eternal of our kind, have perverted our rites and our people? While they have become . . . cannibals . . . to dine again and again on these helpless ones and even the most precious and protected of my small brother's kind!"

His luminous, black-outlined gaze drifted to Bez, tenderly.

"Is it not written by the sage Amenemope? 'Mock not the blind nor deride the dwarf nor block the cripple's path; do not tease a man made ill by a god nor make outcry when he blunders. Man is clay and straw, the God is his builder. The Wise Man should respect people affected by reversal of fortune.'"

"Amen," Ric said.

I recalled that dwarfism was common among the ancient Egyptians, including royal families. Even King Tut's tomb included a funeral gift showing a female dwarf with bowed legs and clubfeet.

I was finally seeing the big picture, all the implications of the god-occupied front bank of pillars.

Bez had been left below as a harmless watchdog and his

brother's image chained because, being Anubis's headsman—and since beheading was the only method they knew to kill vampires—Shezmou was the only god who could judge the utterly secret culture of vampire Egyptians who were suspended between life and afterlife.

When Bez goaded me to free Shezmou, he awakened to see what endless generations of a vampire ruling class had wrought.

Why had my act of breaking the chain freed Shezmou, though? Could anyone have done it? I hoped so, because I wanted as little power and its obligations as possible.

At least, thanks to us, Shez was back and poised to take action at last. I hadn't seen any mobile gods during my first two visits to the Karnak, either during my personal escape or the aggressive military mission to free Ric. The real god had been down here, large and impressive and made of stone. Upstairs on the Strip level the impressive twenty-foot-high statues of the gods were the tourist attractions, gaudy and impotent.

With Shezmou finally on the loose, Kephron and Kepherati, the Twin Pharaoh vampires who'd separately tormented Ric and me, were about to become hyena leavings.

Ric and I eyed each other. We could always use powerful allies and were sitting pretty. One of us didn't agree.

Quicksilver growled and shied away when I put a comforting hand on his head. His pale blue irises were almost all black pupils now, black moons set into his skittish eye whites, like a reverse of the night sky.

He trotted off, leaving us alone with the two living Egyptian gods, and went to scout the forest of stone pillars.

Good. He could guard the perimeter while we parlayed with our unusual new allies at the literal gates of Egyptian Hell.

Chapter Twenty-five

SHEZMOU STRODE BAREFOOT back and forth along the deep, wide trench that kept the captive vampire meat isolated and helpless.

In the pit, the deep-set mysterious guardians vibrated and sizzled like living maracas. Who or what they were I didn't dare imagine. Ric and Bez and I watched Shezmou with varying emotions.

Bez was still bursting with pride and triumph. He figured the Big Guy was back. I still didn't see exactly how that would save anybody. Curse and kill rogue Egyptian vampires, sure.

I didn't need cheerleading to feel as trapped as the folks opposite us. On second thought, Ric and I agreed that Shezmou was the merely mortal persona of a god who'd sacrificed size and strength to come to life. Such gods could be slain and sacrificed, maybe to rise again in an afterlife, but rarely can they do their worshippers and believers any good in this one.

"It's like a zoo exhibit," I murmured bitterly as I stared across the sinister abyss toward the people scenting freedom and milling about without hope, except for the tourists pushing forward to stare at our bizarre party. "Monkey Island. The Great Ape 'enclosure.' The breeding program for the Egyptian Vampire Dynasty."

"This explains the missing Karnak tourists," Ric said, his expression grim.

"Those poor tourists!" Of course, they expected us to help them. "I can see the terrified whites of their eyes from here. It must be like being abducted on *Lost,* or imprisoned on Dr. Moreau's island of cross-breeding human-beast experiments. Judging by their small size, the other prisoners are at least descended from the ancient Egyptians. They buy into this mythology, this pantheon of animal-headed supergods."

"You sprang loose one of the most dreaded, apparently," Ric said, eyeing Shezmou, "even if he has some old-fashioned ideas."

He shook his head and sighed.

"I never saw these prisoners clearly when I was here before, Del. I must have been sandbagged fast after getting this far. It's nuts to think you can 'free' members of an ancient race.

"I know keeping them prisoner for generations is wrong, but who am I kidding? A former FBI agent isn't Moses, and these are *real* living Egyptians. They don't want to go anywhere. They want to stay here. Maybe even as victims. The world is a food chain and has been for thousands of years. Who am I to say it has to stop, anywhere, anytime?"

"Hey." I shook his arm until his grease-paint camouflaged face turned my way.

No wonder Shez took us for serpents in our high-tech "skins" and black war paint. Not all bad. Serpents were wise. And stealthy. And had an unfair but useful bad rep.

"Listen, Ric. I didn't rub albino nose with Christophe to preserve your life and freedom just to have you renounce your desert Savior complex. Obsessive do-gooders like you and me are hard to come by."

"It's called simple survival, Delilah."

"Survival is never simple, Ricardo."

He leaned his forehead against mine. "You noticed."

"So now we're here in no-man's-land again. Now what?"

"We've got Quicksilver," Ric said. "I no longer underestimate that dog's mojo. We've got Bez, who must be a world-class ankle-biter if I've ever seen one, and this Shazam character. We five could take on a lot. I just don't know how we're going to transport a couple hundred vampire-abused semihumans out of here to any shelter or safety."

"Maybe we could work up a new Cirque du Soleil show around them."

He smiled palely at my joke. "Freedom means nothing if you don't have any real role to play or work to do. I can shuffle risen zombies off to 'jobs' on desert ranches from sunrise to sunset. They're really only automatons until I free them totally. And don't think the ones I raised to save us at Starlight Lodge a month back aren't weighing on my delicate conscience. I hate to see people used and abused, but it's also pretty bad to be *under*used."

"Boy, you've never worked very long for a major private corporation, have you? I suppose that's why you left the FBI. Come on, Ric! We can't get anybody out of here, including the Lord of the Type AB Wine Cellar, unless we figure out how to do it ourselves."

My pep talk was all too timely.

A new maraca rumba was heating up in the distance, not just in the pit below our feet. As I'd feared, rousing Sleeping Beauty, aka Blood Boy, would not go unnoticed for long in the Egyptian underworld.

THE CONSTANT SCRABBLE of creatures in the pit had played background to our presence here.

I'd pictured millions of beetles piled atop one another clawing to climb sixty feet to reach the cavern floor.

I'd been thinking of the dung beetles represented in probably millions of scarabs in these five thousand years. Dung beetles were as sacred as cats to the ancient Egyptians. Their skill in rolling balls of dung to feed their massive underground broods provided symbols of renewal and resurrection.

Scarab amulets were placed over mummy heart sites. They'd become a modern jewelry object. I could deal with them.

"Aieee!" Bez cried in horror. He shrank as close as a child to me while we viewed the massed, writhing beetles in the stinking pit below.

"Such relentless devourers," he moaned, "of skin, hair, horn, furs, feathers, and mummy wrappings. They can enter the snuggest tomb to disfigure the dead and make them unfit for eternity."

At his words I ID'ed the little buggers. So these weren't the sacred scarabs, aka dung beetles, of lore and jewelry design. These were a nastier sort. Who hadn't watched a *CSI* episode where a swarm of flesh-eating dermestid beetles picked skeletal remains clean in the forensics lab?

"Away, foul Apshai," Bez shouted, his voice echoing. "Even the Book of the Dead abhors your very name."

What a gruesome alliance nature and the Karnak vampires had devised! If the beetles were inadvertent guards who held the people of the caverns captive, they themselves were also prisoners of the pit, living by picking flesh from the animal and human bones that eventually fell into their innumerable midst. Maintaining a "herd" of slowly sucked-to-death vampire victims was not a neat or humane process.

Now I heard the distant click of more than the imagined billions of beetle legs and pincers behind us. Worse, although the noise echoed off the walls of the pit below, it came from the forest of pillars, from far at its rear.

And it was gathering momentum, like oncoming rolling legions of millions of glass marbles streaming through the thick-set pillars, striking stone and caroming off, spinning along the gritty floor on an incline, gathering incredible mass and speed.

Ric and I turned and froze, heroes in a B-movie horror thriller.

Bez jumped up and down, one fist filling his wide mouth as moans of warning and despair tumbled past his knuckles. We were too stunned to check out Shezmou, but spotted a silver-gray streak zooming toward us like a ground-bound meteor.

It was Quicksilver as I'd never seen him before, running with ears pinned flat back, tail straight out to avoid drag, all four paws seemingly off the ground at once, heading our way.

Behind him came the rolling thunder of an army of oncoming foes of no description we could imagine. We spotted a low muddy-brown tide scraping through the pillars as if carrying thousands of twigs in its path, coming flash-flood fast.

It burst through the last rank of pillars into the clear area before the pit, revealing a ground-hugging army of brittle brown forms, fanged and clawed, of all lengths from one foot to fourteen or fifteen. A carpet of moving, mummified crocodiles.

My silver familiar had gone reptile in reply, snaking a braided rope out of each of my catsuit sleeves and then filling my palms with a cold metal whip butt.

I was no Lash La Rue or Indiana Jones, but my instinctively lifting my arms to repel the odious menace sent out coiling ripples of thick silver "snake" chain that tangled in stubby crocodile legs and caught in their brittle ridged scales.

I was lassoing lethal luggage. Each spasmodic jerk of my arms spun a zombie croc over the pit edge behind us.

The hissing and scrabbling below met falling crocodiles. Up bellowed a powdered red fog of beetle shells and mummified crocodile scales like a steam engine pouring out smoke.

Near the pillars, Quicksilver jumped atop a twelve-foot-long running croc. His snapping jaws seized the dried skin behind its long-snouted head.

Quick's four clawed feet dug in as his weight pushed off the thing's back. The creature skidded straight for the pit, massive tail lashing as I captured it with a silver whip coil so Quick could leap free of the powerful club.

Bez crouched to grab the baby crocs under two feet long by the tail and fling them into the instant garbage disposal behind us, now seething with the death and disintegrating agonies of small, live beetles and huge mummified predatory Nile crocodiles, two species once sacred to the Egyptians.

Crocodile rodeo one wild ride at a time wasn't going to stem the lethal tide or keep us from plummeting into the rift with our scaly attackers.

I thought about Ric, then I felt powerful hands curl around my shoulders from behind, bracing me.

I glanced back in gratitude, or farewell, to discover Shezmou behind me. I started to wrest away but he lifted me by the shoulders and set me aside.

He set me aside.

Hell, no!

Just then I felt someone else behind me and hands slide down my arms to my hands, covering them.

Ric.

I glanced over my shoulder again and gasped. The battle had dislodged the contact lens I'd installed to hide his postresurrection silver iris. It was not only fully revealed, but the white of that eye had gone bloodshot.

His hands tightened on mine until I thought the bones would crush. I looked down. His fingertips were oozing blood onto mine and down along the silver whips, which were expanding and twining into a net—I remembered my silver familiar morphing into a net scarf during that wild Corvette ride—suspended above the solid carpet of writhing crocodile mummies.

That giant net settled on them like a cape. Where it touched, mummified corpses turned to powder, to carnelian dust. As new oncoming crocs rushed over it, they too disintegrated into a cloud of rising dust.

I also remembered it took drops of Ric's blood to raise a zombie, and now, apparently, to kill them.

A CHORUS OF coughs behind us proved that this literally poisonous cloud had also enveloped the weakened captives. I was most concerned by powdery contaminants puffing up from the pit as disintegrating crocodile mummies met and smashed beetle shells.

Some beetle varieties did carry toxins. Although flesh-eating beetles were guiltless that way, we were likely inhaling their dried excrement too. Aw, nice.

I checked Ric's face, imagining what millennia-old dust formed of crushed insect carapaces and reptile scales would feel like lodged behind a contact lens. Burning hell. Luckily, the action must have jolted out Ric's sole contact lens without his ever being aware I'd made sure he wore one. I'd have to update him on that at the first opportunity.

Shez and Bez, being gods in demigod form, were apparently immune to mortal reflexes like coughing and tearing up. Quicksilver, now a Redcoat from head to tail-tip, barked out hoarse canine coughs.

Meanwhile, the wondrous carpet of chain my silver familiar had spun, augmented by Ric's strange new silver vision, lay powdered red too. The pattern reminded me, with a chill, of Sylphia's enwebbing prison spun to contain Loretta Cicereau in Madrigal's magical mirror. Right now one pissed-off werewolf mobster's daughter wasn't my immediate worry.

As the last dust settled, the silver links disappeared along with any trace of the mummified crocs.

Ric's hands were clutching what had changed from silver whip butts in my hands to Wonder Woman wrist cuffs above them. The blood around his nails and knuckles had dried and was flaking off. It was as if everything here must ultimately desiccate and die.

He cupped a hand over his silver left eye.

"God, Delilah! A dagger of ice-cold glass stabbed my eye, then some barrier flew away, small and dark, like a crow's wing in the corner of my vision."

An ice-dagger in his Brimstone Kiss–altered eye? My anxious girly heart fixated on the Hans Christian Andersen fairy tale where the Ice Queen thrusts a sharp cold hook into a boy's heart and that icy control grows in him until he rejects his childhood friend and true-love-in-waiting . . .

God, girl, Irma kicked in, *I'm all for true love and mineral powder bronzer, but get us out of this sandstorm of dried ick pronto!*

"Ric, you just lost a contact lens I installed when you were unconscious at the Inferno. Um . . . it's cosmetically necessary. I'll explain later."

Twenty feet away, Quicksilver braced his feet and shook himself from ears to tail. More red dust rained onto the stone floor to dissipate into motes. Quick had recovered his cool, northern colors of gray fur and blue eyes.

Bez dusted off chubby hands, making us cough again. "Good work. That was like the elder days, Shez, when we gods weren't all living by rules cast in stone and hieroglyphs."

"Indeed," Shez agreed. "I cannot wait to resume my old role, though, toward these new-style and decadent ruling Egyptians. They relish my bloodwine and scented balms and perfumes but have neglected to worship my other role as a winepress of sinful souls, where I stood as Lord of the Blood beside Osiris, as his chosen headsman."

Ric and I checked each other's understanding and pulse rate, wary of our associate's new blood-lusty attitude. Almost everyone with a smattering of Egyptian knowledge knew Osiris was the God of the Dead. His "headsman" must be a pretty bad fellow. What had I let loose on the Karnak and Las Vegas?

"A 'winepress of sinful souls'?" Ric asked Shez, getting to the nitty-gritty.

"So it is written in the ancient texts now known as the Book of the Dead," Bez explained with reverence. "He"—pointing to Shez—"is to be worshipped and dreaded. He is the Lord of the Blood. When evil souls try to slip into the Afterlife he slaughters them, wrenches off their heads, and throws them like grapes into the press to make bloodwine for the pharaohs."

Ric had gone silent. For once I didn't want to break the tension with a quip.

"It is written," Bez went on like any true believer quoting from a holy book, "that *he* rules in the night of the burning damned, and of the overthrow of the wicked at the Block, and of the slaughter of souls. It is *he,* Shezmou, the headsman of Osiris, who cuts them up, Shezmou who has boiled their pieces in his blazing cauldrons so that Unas can eat their words of power, can consume their spirits. Unas is mighty, but Shezmou is the Lord of the Slaughter."

I had no idea who this Unas was, and from what little I'd learned of the Egyptian pantheon, they'd had three thousand years to fine-tune an enormous number of gods and functions.

So I didn't doubt that Shez, exacting winemaker and perfume connoisseur, had a dark side I'd never want to meet in person.

Also, though, I figured Ric and I could sure use it now.

Chapter Twenty-six

QUICKSILVER DID SOMETHING then that I'd never seen or heard him do so impressively before.

He sat on his flanks, aimed his nose at the distant cavern ceiling as if it was a midnight sky, and howled long and mournfully, the hair of his hackles lifting thick from his shoulders.

That primal wolfish cry gave me goose bumps all over.

Beneath his warning aria of soulful animal passion, like the low growl of a snare drum, came the onrushing clatter of another faraway wave of attackers, that rolling of a million marbles along every inch of stone in the forest of pillars between us and escape.

The way I figured it, we were just the antipasto, a tasty display of tidbits between the oncoming vampires and their habitual prey beyond the pit behind us.

Ric moved to my right side and Shez to my left with Bez beside him.

Quicksilver finished his spine-chilling howl by staring straight into my eyes. His expression had never seemed so human. I read anguish there as if it mirrored my own feelings. The wolf-dog looked as if his instincts were being torn in two, between his canine loyalty to me and the ancient demands of his lupine breed.

Spinning away, he ran flat out for the first line of massive stone pillars, directly into the oncoming clatter.

I couldn't imagine what form of mummified zombies would overrun us next. Then a thick, dark shadow filled the gaps between the pillars, an oozing wall of flooding sludge eight feet high with a glint of gold near the top, froth atop the water.

Quicksilver leaped up against the first charging wall, six feet high, catching a golden lasso in his jaws and pulling the darkness down.

I gasped to see a massive mummified bull body crash sideways, pulling its harness mate with it. The sound of their terrified and angry bawling rang off the pillars.

Quicksilver had vanished under the black, rising dust of their fall. As the wooden-wheeled light chariot the bulls had pulled crashed into its fallen coursers, the wooden chariot shaft attached to the yoke between the bulls' horns broke loose, splintering into a massive rough-pointed spear.

The Egyptian charioteer, a mere extra in the royal scheme of things, catapulted onto that ghastly weapon, transfixing his chest as his head and limbs thrashed.

I winced at this bug-on-a-pin sight. The driver had been no cannon-fodder mummy, but a true man, a living version of the ruddy-skinned, black-wigged men immortalized on tomb walls. His wrist- and armbands of turquoise and carnelian reflected the light as he wriggled.

I spied another flash of flying gray fur. Quicksilver was bringing down another ponderous pair of mummified bullocks. Zombies were driven beings, not always controllable. Time after time a lead chariot fell between the stone pillars as others piled up behind them, causing chaos if not death.

Rich male laughter drew my eyes to Shezmou. The Lord of the Slaughter must be enjoying the rout, and the carnage.

But when I turned, the laughing man was Ric.

"Zombie chariot draft teams," he was saying, his hands spread with triumph. "These bulls I can handle, O Great Royal Vampire Fools!"

And *he* strode forward as the mouth between every pair of pillars became clogged with falling bulls and tangling chariots.

Quicksilver was still acting as a one-wolf pack, hurling himself at every path between the pillars to distract the bulls like a rodeo clown, spinning his lean torso in midair, driving them off-balance.

In Quicksilver and Ric's wake came Shezmou, laughing like the Jolly Green Giant shilling for frozen peas, wresting off the head of any charioteer he could find and hurling them like soccer balls into the pit.

I was as confused as my familiar. My mind and emotions truly must control it, because I could feel my silver cuffs tightening and loosening on my wrists, generating heat and a new, molten-metal uncertainty at what form to take in this kind of battle.

Maybe we were just superfluous, like little Bez. The two guys and Quicksilver seemed to be handling all comers. Shez had moved on to wrenching off bull heads and hurling them two-armed into the pit.

I heard a new hard-driving metal clanging, remembering the sacred rattles called sistrums, which resembled chef's whisks with broken wires.

Over a fallen pair of headless bulls came leaping gilded hooves, six living gold-harnessed gazelles pulling a golden chariot bearing the twin pharaohs, Kephron and Kepherati, side by side.

I stared at the twins' petite, royally decked out forms and their delicate faces, each as exquisitely modeled as that signature Egyptian artifact, the bust of Nefertiti. One might almost concede their miraculous eternal survival was worth the cost of millennia of innocent blood.

Kephron was holding the bow while Kepherati pulled fresh arrows from the chariot's side quiver.

Kepherati handed her brother-spouse the feathered arrow and smiled, showing dainty vampire fangs. Kephron drew back the bowstring, his grimace showing larger fangs. He aimed . . . straight at . . . oh, me.

My conflicted wrist cuffs swelled into a solid silver spear shaft in my defensively lifting fists. Ah, not a great defense against a well-aimed arrow.

Quicksilver's racing form came snaking between the twelve pairs of oncoming gazelle hooves. Unlike the bulls, they were too many and too agile to overturn.

Those sharp, flying hooves could kick my dog to death!

Kepherati dropped her next arrow to jerk the left rein and pull the gazelles horizontal to the pit, coming abreast of me as Kephron let his arrow fly.

Somehow Quicksilver scrambled out from under the gazelle hooves, but he was limping . . . oh, God. And he still raced toward me as he so often did in Sunset Park.

I sensed Ric shouting, "No!" and saw him riding a dark wave, an animated headless bull he was driving straight for the gazelles and the royal chariot.

Quicksilver charged me, knocking me to the dusty stones. The royal arrow sped toward me just as fast.

I heard a violent huff of escaping air. Quicksilver and the arrow flew out over the pit together and down, down, down into a rising red tornado cloud of beetle and crocodile dust.

I knew there was sound all around, but I couldn't hear it.

All I could hear was Shezmou's nearby triumphant laughter as he tore off another foot-soldier head and threw it into the pit and final judgment.

After my dog.

Chapter Twenty-seven

I CRAWLED TO the edge of the pit and pushed forward to stare into the blinding, choking dust.

"Del!"

Ric had dived atop me, defending me but also holding me back. I made my fingers into claws and held even harder onto the crumbling stone edge.

"Quicksilver! He's down there, Ric!"

"I saw."

"Did the arrow—?"

"I don't know if it struck him," Ric shouted as chaos sounded around us. "He knocked you below the arrow's arc, but he had to overshoot the edge to do it. He vanished with the arrow. Shezmou's head-tossing is keeping the pit dust stirred up. You can't see a thing. It's like looking for a window into a muddy river. Get up, Del. They're still trying to kill us."

"I can't just—"

Ric pulled me half upright, turning me away from the pit. All I could see was the headless carcass of a fallen chariot bull behind us, the mummified bull Ric had animated long enough to charge the royal chariot. He dragged me to it.

Like Custer and his men facing the Sioux at Little Big Horn, we hunkered down behind the slain mount. Peering over that huge but now fragile barrier, we could see the still-linked gazelles racing away, reins and harnesses trailing, into the maze of pillars. The Twin Pharaohs' golden chariot stood marooned where it had rolled to a stop in front of the stone forest, facing the pit.

The Twin Pharaohs stood as still as the pillar figures in their gorgeous, golden toy, armed but isolated figures, leaders cut off from their troops and even retreat.

Quicksilver had accomplished that as well as saving me from their arrow.

Meanwhile, packs of fully physical hyenas poured through the pillars to surround and guard the royals, snapping formidable jaws that could sever bone. And the sandals of spear-bearing foot soldiers slapped stone as if stomping scorpions while rushing over the fallen bull-drawn chariots to engage Shezmou and Bez in the space between them and the pit.

I braced my arms and used the silver staff to pull upright. Apparently the familiar had known I'd shortly need literal support.

Then the forward charge faltered. Shezmou and Bez had been recognized. Gods might seem human, but true Egyptians had no heart to fight them.

Shez stretched an imperious arm and staff to the assembling warriors. Spears arced and fell useless at the feet of our new friends. The warriors' god-driven fear made them pile up on each other, halted like the waves of the Red Sea before Moses. Attackers stopped, quieted, and became audience.

Shez paced back and forth in front of his should-be worshippers and their feral pets, challenging them with fists and roaring voice, letting his opinions be known.

"Who has kept Shezmou, headsman to the mighty god Osiris, chained and mute all these centuries in this low, unembellished place, neither tomb nor temple?"

Shezmou raged on. "It is my duty to help my lord Osiris administer the Land of the Dead. I separate the damned from the saved. You unnatural rulers, paired in your perversions," he thundered at Kephron and Kepherati. "You dishonor the gods and land by dining on your kind.

"True, I am the subject of the Book of the Dead's 'Cannibal Hymn.' That is my privilege for making bloodwine of evil souls. Drinking their bad blood is my duty. Mine alone! I am the god! For millennia, you have not allowed your soiled souls to make the sacred transition through the Underground to the Afterlife.

"I, Shezmou, will crush your fanged heads like rotten grapes overripe on the vine. So come, feel my vengeful grasp, taste my wrath. Die the ultimate death you have averted for so long and deserved for so long. Before you touch yet another of these Children of the Caves, you will feel your own eyeballs spurting away like seeds and your heads rolling speechless into the pit."

An awesome address, but even hyenas that have been granted both physical and spirit form are still merely brute beasts at bottom and not responsive to oratory, or to those who look like mere men and would be gods.

The massing hyena packs broke into the eerie hooting calls of their breed, then dug in their low-slung rear quarters and leaped forward to drive the puny men, midgets, and women into the choking, festering pit behind them. If we could hardly breathe at the brink of it, how could Quicksilver survive at its unguessed bottom depths?

He was a supernaturally smart dog and devoted to me, I told myself, but that hadn't kept Achilles from contracting fatal blood poisoning from biting a vampire in my defense back in Kansas.

Neither hoping nor mourning was any longer an option.

As the wall of caterwauling hyenas leaped at us, I had to join Ric and Shez and Bez in repelling the repellent. No matter how much my heart called to Quicksilver in the fuming pit behind me, instinct and comradeship made me stand my ground and face whatever the immortal pharaohs could fling at us.

"*Delilah!*" I seemed to hear my name screeched. "*Delilah-aha-ha-ha-ha-ha-ha-ha*!"

My braced silver staff shivered at the impact of one furry chest. I did as Shezmou and Bez did, used the animals' charging weight to fling them aside so they plunged into the pit. I felt like I was stabbing Quicksilver over and over.

Sounds of growling and snapping echoed off every stone surface. I glanced up at Shezmou's pillar, hoping his bigger-than-life image would step from the stone to turn the tide of battle. But what was etched in Vegas, stayed etched in Vegas. At least the god's man-figure had more than mortal strength.

Ric was holding his own in casting hyenas to their howling deaths below. I was startled to glimpse a silver aura around him as he caught a hyena neck in his bare hands. I'd glimpsed our conjoined multicolored auras in his bathroom mirror the first time we'd made love. This was war, not love, but I sensed a new link between us.

The hyenas' small dark eyes blinked shut against a metallic flash that pierced them. They seemed limp as he cast them away. I almost felt sorry for these cousins of Quicksilver.

No, wait. I'd looked them up. Hyenas were related to cats and mongooses, not dogs. I hurled with fresh zest.

The charging line of vampire warriors behind them was nothing to feel sorry for. How awful to see those calm, noble wall visages flaunting jaws that could drop inhumanly open, showcasing fangs as overdeveloped as a sabertooth tiger's on a smaller, though no less lethal, scale.

Instinctively, we four had made a line, with Ric and Shez turning sideways to guard our flanks. We were slowly being forced forward away from the pit, making us harder to push in, but also in more danger of being surrounded and overrun.

My arms and legs ached almost beyond feeling from wielding the solid silver staff. Its weight was starting to hurt me as much as my enemies. And the familiar was showing an aggravating lack of innovation. Why didn't it morph into a rocket launcher, for instance, so I could take out the oncoming lines of warriors bursting through the stone pillars?

Ric and Shez had moved forward to shelter Bez and me. Our flanks would be history any minute now.

Us too.

Perhaps Shez and Bez couldn't die, but Ric and I certainly could.

Weariness must cause hallucinations. I watched a feathered arrow arch over our small force into the massed ranks, felling a warrior, whose prone body in turn felled two more.

More arrows in quick succession, graceful and swift, snapping into flesh and bone with a low, razor-like zing.

Only the royal pair had borne bow and arrows in their chariot. Had their men somehow taken the empty pole and worked the chariot around behind us?

An oversize Egyptian warrior fought his way to my right side. Not Shez, but almost as tall. He wore the same black, braided wig, the forerunner of modern dreadlocks. Had another pillar god escaped the stone to become an avatar? Which one now?

I dared a glance to muscular Egyptian-brown leg and hip under a kilt covered with rich turquoise and carnelian beads. Across his bare brown chest a sling held a full quiver to his back. Silver-tipped arrows from that quiver flew so fast over Shez and Ric's heads that fallen Egyptian vampire warriors piled up as high as the toppled bull carcasses.

What ancient Egyptian god-made-man was *this*? I scanned the pillars, but found no massive human-headed figure other than Shezmou's. The demigod's bow action kept him in the strict profile of the tomb paintings. He wore no uraeus or headdress as Shez did.

Still, his silver-tipped arrows stopped the vampire hordes like holy water in a seventies Hammer vampire movie.

If the new guy's silver-tipped arrows didn't actually slay the vamps, it didn't matter. It slowed them long enough for Shezmou to leap forward like a starving hyena, twist off their heads, and throw them in the pit. Neat. His ancient modus operandi echoed the later European method of killing the immortal pestilence.

Silver certainly empowered others besides me. Maybe Ric and my conjoined talents had called this silver-armed warrior. My silver medium, mirror-walking, CinSim Silver Screen–loving ways made me an unpredictable player on the Las Vegas Supernatural Follies stage, even to myself.

I could only hope the dog I'd named Quicksilver had picked up some of my quirky powers with the pale precious metal or harbored more supernatural ones of his own than I had ever dreamed . . .

Chapter Twenty-eight

MANPOWER MUST BE a nagging personnel problem in every culture.

After several strange high-pitched syllables echoed against the distant stone ceiling, any warriors still standing circled the golden chariot. Twelve took up the fallen harness pole to play gazelles and bear the doll-like figures of the royal pair back into the dark safety of the stone-pillar forest.

"*Hah!*" Shez trumpeted, shaking a fist at the departing troops. "All blood and no guts, you foul vampires! It is an honor to lose your head to my bloodwine vintages. They feed the true pharaohs who will rule in the Afterlife as on earth because they do not ache for the false immortality of bloodsuckers."

He laid an appropriately bloody hand on Bez's shoulder. "Well fought, little brother."

Then he regarded Ric and me. "You both wear the black of Anubis's honored jackal-headed form, so I will call you the Foreign Children of Anubis. I thank you for freeing me for such a long-overdue dinner."

I turned to thank the other descended god on my right. He was gone. I gazed into the stone forest. Many men with terra-cotta-colored skin had vanished there only moments ago. Was our sudden ally a rogue vampire? Could the Royal Pains have rebels in their ranks?

I finally forced myself to turn and walk to the rim of the pit. The red dust was still settling, like ancient earth quieting. No sound from below sounded like claws scrabbling for purchase on a long climb upward.

Ric's hands on my shoulders were bracing. I sensed his shared sorrow descending on me like an invisible cloak.

"Well." Shez came to us. "I have much work here, I see. Of course we must all take ourselves away before the cursed bloodsucking breed regroups and returns."

"You're a bloodsucker too," I pointed out.

"I am a demon lord and a god. I am also a jealous god. No one, not even Pharaoh, should usurp my role. But if you, my friends, wish to kill some scavenger dogs or rabid warriors with the fangs of cats, I will joyously end them all by harvesting their heads for my winepress."

He frowned as he gazed across at the silent herds of human vampire fodder.

"Bez, my little brother of the lion, many of those are your kind. Are we to leave them for future devouring? Granted, I thirst for souls to judge after such long captivity, but these creatures have been preyed upon by their own cannibal kind and there should be some appropriate afterlife for them, although not the fine attendings due a Pharaoh and the high priests and royal figures of our true ancient Egypt before it was corrupted."

"That Shez is certainly long-winded," Ric whispered in my ear.

Gods are probably all that way.

Which made me think of the God of the Old Testament, the devious and nervy biblical lady I was named after, and other interesting things.

First, someone had to get these literally innocent bystanders out of here. Where? They were human but had become a hidden race beyond its time. Though the many dwarfs among them had been easily accepted by the true

Egyptians millennia ago, even modern America was still behind that culture in accepting what we delicately called the "differently" abled.

Aren't we all "differently" abled? I sure was, and I didn't know the half of it, because I'd not yet caught up with my *CSI* autopsy-table double, Lilith.

I glanced at Ric, disconcerted by seeing his bare, silver-iris eye. That would not play well on the Strip. We needed to get him undercover again.

I stared into the pit. I'd saved Quicksilver's life once, in Sunset Park, where I'd adopted him when he faced death within hours at the pound. I would scour this city below-ground and aboveground until I found him.

Or I would come back and sift this noxious pit until I found his ashes and I would make Snow raise him from those ashes, like the dragon Gargouille.

Not that Snow would lift a cuticle for me now, after what I'd let happen to him. Still, I was sure he'd take my soul for vengeful laceration in trade for a favor if he could get it.

Ric stared with me into the pit, then looked across to the miserable figures swaying like penned animals.

"You've done a good job of throwing the evil souls to judgment, Shezmou," he told our ally, "but what about these age-old victims of their immortal hungers? And the few of our modern people who were forced into their same bondage? Can you imagine the hell it must be for these innocent new victims?"

"I need not imagine anything, Foreign Child of Anubis. I know Hell well. Your point is as true as your courage in coming back here."

"These new allies freed you," Bez put in, coming to tug on the larger god's wrist cuff.

"I can do nothing!" Shezmou roared, vexed. "Osiris is my lord and these people, however wronged, have no one available to prepare them properly to journey to the Afterlife."

His anger was also an expression of his powerlessness in this case.

I lifted my face from gazing into the pit. If Quicksilver was down there, dead or not, he was doomed along with all the other genuine humans in the place.

If Osiris wouldn't help them all . . .

I looked at the pillars.

I thought about my name.

I needed a Samson. Shezmou had pulled down a lot of vampire evil, but the innocent survivors needed to be pulled into paradise.

"Delilah," Ric said.

I could hear the anxiety in his voice. Don't worry, Ric, I thought. At least I'm walking *away* from the pit for now.

I stopped before Anubis's truly awesome gold-and-black figure. Maybe I could free another god. His jackal head was assuredly canine.

"O mighty Anubis," I said, adopting Shezmou's formal language. Gods tend to care about such things. "You gentle the soul through embalming and guide it on the long journey of judgment to the Afterlife. Surely, anything still living here deserves gentle judgment."

I heard my companions' feet shuffling nervously behind me. I'm sure they thought me mad, talking to pillars.

"Surely you raged in your stone heart, standing here witnessing the rise of the vampire dynasty for millennia, watching a noble race who worshipped you turn predator and turn your godly figures into crass commercial mockeries high above us.

"O mighty Anubis," I continued, "haven't the cuffs of precious gold around your ankles and wrists and mighty shoulders been chains to keep justice from being done to thousands of loyal Egyptians who've lived the lives of beasts and cattle for centuries?"

I felt the silver familiar sliding back around my brow and growing heavy, much heavier than a Wonder Woman coronet. More like a uraeus on an ass-kicking Egyptian headdress. It was almost too heavy for my neck, but I kept my head held high and sympathized with the longest-reigning queens of England, Victoria and Elizabeth II, for doing this in their eighties.

A figure silently stepped to my right side. I didn't dare turn my burdened head, but out of the corner of my eye the shape was about the height of my earlier silver-arrow shooter.

The blackness I sensed told me it was Ric, and his left iris was still a naked silver from my Resurrection Kiss. Maybe together we still had some resurrection magic. Ancient mythologies shared the same roots, after all.

"O mighty Anubis, I, Delilah, call on you to become my Samson who is Hercules who is the sun god Ra, and to bring this perverted temple down!

"I call on you to sweep all the deserving Egyptian souls in it into the great river on the journey to a long-withheld Afterlife. And I join my freeing silver to your eternal gold so that all foreign human souls—"

It was like dealing with a demon, I sensed you had to say it just right with a god or your soul would wing off to the wrong party.

"—and—" I was about to say "canine," but those oddball attack hyenas might still be around to confuse things since they were a muddled breed and gender already "—so that all foreign human and *lupine* souls may return to the Land of the Living for their natural, or supernatural, spans."

I almost said "Amen," but bit my tongue.

My hand reached out to meet Ric's. Then I just wished with all my freaking might on Shezmou's double stars.

First came the distant thunder—like being under a major city subway system. Then a shrill whine whispered through the forest of pillars. I felt cold and Ric's hand became ice. All the gold on Anubis's ebony form glowed and then paled to silver.

I heard a roaring rush of water. The stones under my feet began pulsing. Water. Where would water rush?

Dropping Ric's hand, I turned so fast I felt my silver headdress falling, then looping around my shoulders, light as air.

I turned back to the pit. The edges were crumbling and the people in the caves were sinking, but like feathers wafting down.

What had I done? I raced to the pit edge. A flash flood of silvery clear water was rushing through, rising higher, sweeping everything and everyone away.

The pit edges contracted, like a healing stone scar, sealing everything in, mummies and bodies and souls.

"Quicksilver!" What had I done?

I had no time to bewail anything more.

Shezmou grabbed one of my arms, Ric the other. They lifted me off my feet and hustled me into the now quivering pillars.

"Wait for me!" I heard Bez huffing and his quick running steps behind us. But no pattering Quicksilver claws.

The pillars were grinding now, toppling behind us like dominoes. A gray fog of black stone-dust enveloped everything and I had to shut my eyes. How could Ric and Shezmou keep running, except one of them was a god?

Then everything went silent.

RIC'S HAND WAS still squeezing my right arm but my left was free. I opened my gritty eyes to see a glint of sliver. The familiar had morphed into a Wonder Woman coronet-shaped wrist cuff. I blinked at Ric's camouflaged face. The black streaks were now dusty gray.

He touched my bare forehead. "You lost your crown. What we saw down there and what you did were amazing."

I looked around. Dim. Low-ceilinged. Abandoned except for some hulking bulls. No. SUVs.

"We're in the Karnak parking garage," I said. Croaked.

Ric nodded.

"Just us?"

Ric nodded.

"Quicksilver?"

He looked away.

"Shez and Bez?"

He looked back and shrugged.

My eyes were adapting to the low-level light. Three forlorn figures were leaning like dazed winos against a parked Jeep.

"And them?"

"Tourists with amnesia. I've called Kennedy Malloy to fetch them. We need to be long gone. Fast."

I got it. My plan had worked. For a few freaking minutes, I'd been a goddess, or at least a femme fatale.

Now I was . . . just so damn sorry I'd failed to save another dog. I shook off Ric's supporting hand. I could stand on my own, dammit. I always had.

"I'll probably bruise," I grumbled. "I could get a restraining order on you for that."

He grinned at me. "Hey, Del. We're alive and so are the tourists. Your invocation worked. So maybe that 'lupine' soul is still out there working his way home."

"Or only half of him. I should have also said 'canine' back there, but hyenas are such a confusing breed."

I was being such an ungrateful bitch. It was better than the alternative, and I figured Ric knew that.

Chapter Twenty-nine

"I CAN DRIVE in Vegas Strip traffic," I told Ric.

"You're upset."

"That's why I'll drive."

We were sitting in Dolly near the Karnak parking garage exit. Manny the demon had put such faith in our return he'd left the keys behind the visor.

The elevator that had whisked us down to People-eater Central was just a blank concrete block wall now. Kinda like my emotions. I suppose the Royal Twins had already disabled the route. They may be ancient and incestuous, but they owned and operated an up-to-the-minute hotel in post–Millennium Revelation Las Vegas, which had always been more trendy and over-the-top than anywhere.

Where could we go but home? But this Dorothy didn't want to leave Toto behind with some ghost of Elvira Gulch.

"Delilah," Ric said, "I'll do anything to get Quicksilver back for you. I can get a Homeland Security raid set up at the Karnak on the pretext of illegal Middle Eastern nationals. Something. I can pull strings in Washington."

I believed that last part. But . . .

"It's all gone to never-never land, Ric. You saw it. The caverns, the pit, the pillars, the people. Everything tumbled down. Gone."

"Never-never land was a whole new world, Del."

"What? Like over the Rainbow Bridge? I don't believe that shit. I'd believe almost anything of this crazy new world, but not that Rainbow Bridge fairy tale. Quicksilver is gone! You saw it."

Ric stopped looking earnestly at me and stared ahead at the blare of daylight beyond the dark we idled in. "I understand I was pretty 'gone' myself at the Karnak."

"And I didn't give up on you when everybody said I should, when everybody *said* you were . . . you were—"

"Dead."

"Well, just how dead are you now?"

"I don't know. I almost wish I was so I didn't have to see your heart breaking like this."

"Don't say that!" I was so vehement it scared me. Him too.

He put his hands over mine, which were colder than ice. The silver familiar had handcuffed me to Dolly's super-sized steering wheel, as if sensing I'd run back into the garage's maze to pound on the concrete walls until my blood ran down them and they'd turn into an elevator to take me back to where I'd lost Quick.

"Maybe the dog has nine lives," Ric said, "like a cat. He's paranormally talented, after all."

"He was weakening, Ric. Didn't you see it? That heart-broken howl he gave when he sensed the rotten royals and their minions coming? I could see it in his eyes. Something was wrong. He knew he wasn't coming out of there alive."

"So he stayed and fought and saved your life, Del. That's the best he could do and he wanted to do it. You know how hard he fought."

Well, now I was crying in front of someone like a stupid eight-year-old, which I'd never done when I really was eight.

"It's all right," Ric muttered into the hair over my ear.

"He's always been special. I'm sure he could have ridden a piece of flotsam out of that pit river."

The silver handcuffs had melted away with the release of my tears. Maybe there was a reason people didn't fight them like I did. My freed hands felt my chest and found a fine silver neck chain dangling a locket. I was afraid to find out what kind of hair it held now.

"First Dog of Underground Las Vegas, huh?"

"I can convince Captain Malloy to put an all-points bulletin out on him."

"How? She likes you plenty; me not so much. Why would she help hunt my missing dog?"

"I'll say he witnessed a crime. Attempted murder. Well, he did. The force has an animal psychic consultant now. Even one for CinSims. Gotta keep up with the Millennium Revelation times. I'll still comb the city for him, Del, night and day. Whichever time it is now, out on the Strip."

That's right. We didn't even know what time it was, except mourning time.

"Me, too," I said, turning the ignition and putting Dolly into gear. "I'll look everywhere."

I didn't say "forever" aloud.

RIC HATED LEAVING me alone in the Enchanted Cottage that night but it was well after midnight and I couldn't tolerate either sex or comfort yet.

I gave him one of my gray contact lenses for camouflage until he could buy some brown sets. Ric accepted my vague excuse of a "small anomaly" because he knew I was too heartsick to explain anything. He should always carry spares, I told him, because of his active lifestyle.

"You mean fighting zombies and mummies and vampires and werewolves and assorted other supernaturals?"

I nodded.

"And then there's you and me in bed."

My smile was faint, although I did wonder if his silver iris would affect any intimate action too.

"Seriously, we need to discuss this eye thing of mine," he murmured after kissing me good night on the cottage steps like the prom date I'd never had, sweet and simple.

I nodded, too weary to speak, and he kissed me again.

The cottage seemed unbearably empty, but I'd asked for that. I stopped at the mantel, cupped my hands around Achilles' vase, and laid my cheek against the sandblasted five-toed imperial dragon on the slick black surface.

"I don't even have a vase for Quicksilver," I whimpered aloud.

Lord! That was lame! The cottage's many helpers remained undercover. Upstairs, I changed my indestructible patent-leather catsuit for a roomy tee and went to bed. When I couldn't sleep after an hour, I called the main house.

"Miss Delilah!" Godfrey answered. I guess CinSims never sleep. "We were worried by your long absence and much relieved to see Mr. Montoya bring you home safe."

Nightwine and his obsessive security and voyeur issues!

" 'Safe' is a shaky concept, Godfrey."

"*Ahem,* yes, indeed. Mr. Nightwine was about to have his three A.M. cup of cocoa. Is it possible you'd care to join him?"

"Cocoa? Nightwine? What is it really, Godfrey?"

"I don't know, Miss, but I would ensure that you get the finest Colombian cocoa."

"I don't know. I'm not in a . . . good mood."

"What a pity, Miss."

"I *would* like to see you."

"As I you. You're always a welcome sight."

"Godfrey. Quicksilver is gone."

There I was, gone again myself, with the silence long enough for Godfrey to sense my strangled sobs.

"I will instruct my master to be . . . careful. He is really a lonely individual, you know. Always outside looking in."

I was still alert enough to notice that Godfrey had not called Hector Nightwine a "man." A lonely man. It was a common phrase. Of course, Godfrey was a proper butler and tended to formal phrases.

Still . . .

Where I couldn't in good conscience keep Ric up late tending my wallowing state, I had no trouble bothering Nightwine. In fact I'd enjoyed it, back when I'd been able to enjoy anything. There I went again! I needed to knock myself out of this depression if I was going to look for Quicksilver in the morning.

I dressed in a gray workout outfit and slipped across the dark yard, not looking toward Sunset Road. Godfrey met me at the kitchen door, still attired in his butler's eternal white tie and tails.

Can you say a guy looks radiant? Maybe, if he's a Cin-Sim. That silver nitrite they used in the process of making the classic black-and-white films offered a vibrant array of silvers and grays along with deep, dark black. To Depression-era audiences of the 1930s it whispered "security" and "elegance."

Okay, maybe Godfrey wasn't "radiant." With his slightly wavy hair and pencil-thin mustache and evening dress, he was elegant, though.

"I am most distraught to learn that Master Quicksilver is absent without leave, Miss Street," he said immediately. "I am sure that all involved will correct that situation as soon as possible."

"I intend to tear this town apart looking for him and Ric will too, but Quick plunged down a pit underneath the Karnak Hotel in defense of my life, and it doesn't look good."

"A pit? *Pish.* A mere sidewalk crack for a canine-lupine of Master Quicksilver's brain and heart. You mark my words, Miss Street, he will return from his misadventure smarter and stronger than before."

"You're not talking any miraculous return over the Rainbow Bridge?" I asked suspiciously.

"Rainbow Bridge? Far too tame an exit for the likes of him. Or you, I think."

"*Hmph.*" I wanted to snivel but Godfrey was so bracingly sensible and formal that self-pity just didn't work in his presence.

Which was good. I hated self-pity. I just couldn't accept losing another dog who'd died in my defense. And I wouldn't now.

"The master is awaiting you in the study."

Nightwine didn't have an "office." He had a study.

Godfrey led me up the back stairs to the main rooms and Nightwine's lair. Just the idea of matching wits with the carnivorous old fox was perking me up.

Godfrey announced me and I entered to the sight of Nightwine in a nightcap. It was claret-colored velvet with a gold tassel nestling against his black-bearded cheek.

He also wore a satin-quilted-lapel burgundy robe and all in all resembled an Edgar Allan Poe Santa Claus.

"Dressed informally, I see, Miss Street," he greeted me. "I am glad to note that you agree that mourning isn't called for. You must keep yourself busy while we conduct the search for your delinquent dog."

" 'We'?"

"Well, of course. You and your shadow, Lilith, are valuable employees of Nightwine Productions. I have extensive security contacts in Las Vegas beyond the limits of my estate. Nightwine Productions is the most powerful global digicast network in the post–Millennium Revelation world. The scenes of your recent cameo on *CSI V: Las Vegas* are brilliant, if I say so myself. You definitely have a career ahead of you in film if you will but follow my instructions."

Now was not the time to tell Nightwine *I* was using *him,* not vice versa. Once I determined whether Lilith was alive or dead and could interview her in either state, in my mirror or real life, my "acting" career was over.

Today's psychotic paparazzi and groupies made any public or unusual private life hell. With the ghost of twice-bereaved Loretta mirror-caught in fey chains of my doing, I really didn't want to try mirror-walking right now or staying on this topic with Nightwine.

"I can't believe you'd search for Quicksilver for me, Hector."

"*Tut-tut,* my dear," he said, inadvertently reminding me of my painful Egyptian encounters. "We can't have our budding star moping around in shapeless gray long johns. Nothing is too good for a Nightwine Productions starlet. And you share my fondness for CinSims. Really, we are so *simpatico* that we should consider marriage."

I was about to gag when he added, "Sadly, I am a committed bachelor."

Jeez, Irma said, *Vegas is crammed with guys who like to look and not touch. Lucky for us, in certain cases.*

"I'm sure," Hector went on, chewing something amiably, "that the Cadaver Kid will be on the case 24/7, and you'll be looking high and low. However, I'd advise you to occupy your mind with other matters."

"I don't have any cases at the moment."

"I'm sure something will show up. It always does. Or you can join me for meals here at the house."

I would never again be able to watch Nightwine chow down on his constant exotic snacks without hearing the crunch of beetle shells and mummified crocodile hide in every bite.

"Thanks," I said, rising quickly. "I'll see what I can do."

WHAT I DID was rev up Dolly and drive the mostly empty desert highways like Ric until the sun came up.

When I wasn't puzzling over how to retrieve a loved one who had been swept away by Osiris, God of the Dead, to the Egyptian Afterlife, I estimated the hours since Quicksilver had pushed me out of the arrow's way and vanished into the pit.

I was somewhat consoled that Shezmou, grateful to me for freeing him, had viewed Quick as part of my party of friends and witnessed his heroism. Surely he would speak up for Quicksilver on the other side. If the fall had killed Quick, perhaps his spirit would remain in the Egyptian Paradise, where afterlife was supposed to be luxe and full.

No way would our pal Shez twist off his head like a cork out of a bottle of blood wine. He was just a dog, for Pete's sake. Well, not "just" a dog.

Ric called the next day with frequent progress reports on his efforts.

A police search warrant led to a blank wall. The Karnak onyx horses and golden chariot couldn't be budged to reveal a lower level.

"I'm hunting the Sinkhole tonight," Ric said during his last call of that long day. "It's been playing hard to get lately, though."

"I'll come with you."

"No, Delilah. Keep to your usual haunts, in case he finds his way back."

I saw the logic, but hated returning to the Enchanted Cottage and the word "haunt." Once there, I discovered a fish and macaroni TV dinner in the microwave from the witch. A warm bottle of beer sweated slightly on the kitchen table.

The place's aura had turned tepid and stale to reflect my numb state of mourning. If Delilah was anxious and unhappy, the happy, dancing supernatural staff would let her stew in her own self-pitying juices.

I ate some, sipped some, and went up to bed again, pausing to stare in the front-surface mirror at the hall's end. Wary, I wondered if fey-bound Loretta Cicereau would appear to berate me for what she'd regard as my betrayal.

Blank. Nothing. Not even my enemies could be bothered with me in this state! The silver familiar had shrunk to a thin, weak wrist chain, and pinched.

I dragged myself into my bedroom and crawled under the light, thick comforter that always modified its temperature to what I required.

That, at least, was working. I didn't sweat or shiver. I just fell into a deep dark sleep. Almost twenty-four hours gone, I thought before I zoned out. *Quicksilver, come back!* my mind screamed. Irma didn't even show up to echo my despair. It was like I was becoming a ghost, fading to everyone and everything I knew.

Even Ric, God help me . . .

Chapter Thirty

I AWOKE, EYES wide, staring up at the white canopy on my four-poster bed. Oh, my God! I'd somehow done what I've never done since a child.

I had turned over *on my back* during sleep.

Panic made me gasp, drawing heaving breaths. This must be a dream. I checked both sides of the bed. No goggle-eyed alien spectators gowned in white fenced me in.

I rolled onto my side so fast I almost got sweatsuit burns. In the dimly lit room, my eyes adjusted to scan the high, peaked ceiling and the dormer window where Dracula had come calling a couple weeks ago.

No sinister CinSim waited there for admittance, although the window frame cast shadows on my bare wood floor. Nothing loomed above me, or outside the bedroom to threaten me.

I drew deep, calming breaths and read the luminous dial on my nightstand. Five A.M. *More* than thirty hours. I whimpered my pain.

A shadow from the window vines twitched on my floor like a dark star twinkling. I looked down, around.

Oh, God! Oh, Shazzam . . . Shamu . . . Shezmou! Oh, oh, oh, Osiris!

I scrambled half up in the sheets.

I saw—blink—the gray form of a dog sitting guard beside my bed. He was stretched out on his belly, gazelle-graceful paws straight forward, haunches gathered in back, head up . . . and what a head.

It was a sphinx in the Egyptian wiglike headdress and uraeus, wearing no ears and muzzle, but the face of . . . Lilith!

How did I know it was Lilith and not me? Because the right, camera-side nostril bore the icy star sparkle of a blue topaz stud. I'd dumped that bit of bling when I'd discovered it made me a marked woman.

Quicksilver and Lilith had merged into a bizarre new form?

This must be a dream!

I turned over on my stomach, curled my fingers into the bottom sheet, and muttered, "This is a dream," afraid to crawl out of the covers and find I was in my alien abduction nightmare all over again.

SO YOU OPEN your eyes. The room is flooded with daylight and your sweatsuit has huge damp spots under the arms and across the back and the floor is sunny and cheerful and empty of both night-visiting ogres and angels.

And it's just real life again, swallowed by a loss you won't admit.

It was also late afternoon, I discovered. Why had I been out so long? I wouldn't call my previous state "sleep."

My bedside cell phone had three messages. I rang Ric back without listening.

"Del?" He sounded like he was talking on ice, so careful.

"Yeah. I was . . . sleeping."

"Good!" Much too hearty. "Just rest, Del. Since Malloy's warrant didn't get anywhere at the Karnak, I, uh, visited your last satisfied client."

"Nightwine?"

"Cesar Cicereau. He lost his first team of werewolf guards the other night, as you well know, but he can volunteer a second crew."

"*Cicereau* is gathering a hunt party for Quicksilver?"

"Yeah. He says his werewolf pack can track the true wolf blood in your mongrel wolfhound now that the moon is full. Sansouci and I are taking them underground."

"The moon is full?" I'd been underground myself too long to notice. "You and *Sansouci*? Don't tell me . . . Snow is in on this too?"

"Christophe? He's doing his nightly rock idol riff as 'Cocaine' per usual. This has nothing to do with the Inferno. No, Sansouci, Cicereau's go-to guy, says that freako cop who hassled you, Haskell, hangs out at a biker bar. We can 'persuade' him to take us to the latest location of the Sinkhole. Stink finds stink.

"Del, are you there? Awake?"

Not really. I hadn't realized how many *un*likely suspects would be willing to help me find Quicksilver. Now I was thinking some of the methods might be *subconscious*. My previous night's "dream" may have been a message: to find Quicksilver I had to find Lilith, for real and for once and for all.

"Good hunting, Ric," I wished him, signing off.

I didn't know where I was going, but it would be somewhere.

I ripped off the ripe sweatsuit and took a shower. I opened my closet door myself for once, grabbing jeans and knit top and my customized cop duty belt. Cowboy boot–style mules for my feet.

Dressed, I went to stand before my hallway mirror. Just me looked back. I wasn't fooled.

"Lilith, you bitch," I said, "you taunt me with glimpses of your image on film and in my mirror and then you have the nerve to show up in my dreams at the worst moment in my life, in my own bedroom, glued to my dog, the best dog in the whole damn world. Any of them.

"He's missing now too but he'd never desert me. Maybe you can lead me to him somehow, so I'm going to find *you* before another day goes by. Just saying."

VOWS ARE DRAMATIC motivators. I still needed a concrete trail to follow.

I went downstairs to use the laptop in the study/office (unlike Hector, I don't have room for single-purpose areas).

Why hadn't I ever explored the *CSI V: Las Vegas* website before? Maybe it had felt like a creepy combination of vanity and voyeurism.

Of course, Lilith's autopsy segment was available for download. My shaky hands hit the arrow and I sat back to see my "dead" body—what was the famous T. S. Eliot line about the night? "Etherized like a patient on a table."

That was how I really pictured Lilith, etherized on a table, helpless, dead. "Maggie," the lone maggot, wriggled onstage briefly and then the star-making performance was done and gone.

I forced myself to play the entire two minutes, then reran them. Behind Lilith's bare body, I spotted the blurry, out-of-focus scrubs of minor players like myself.

How little it took to make a star these days: a freaky YouTube video. I could move from "maggot *CSI*" topics to a "maggot art" page. There, the pallid fly larvae were dipped in harmless colored paints to writhe random strokes on a page, later sold as "art." Was self-expression now the domain of brain-worms as well as human brains?

I was thinking one of those resident tequila-bottle worms, being obviously uninhibited, might have a smashing creative career as an artist with the right manager.

Actually, the brains behind the maggot art project was an entomology expert who aided law enforcement on handling insects as crime scene evidence. Even my own "Maggie" was immortalized by the Nightwine media empire.

A click elsewhere on the *CSI* site produced the tape of Maggie and me doing our garbled version of a graveside soliloquy. TV reporting had made me an effective line reader. A tear was wandering, maggot-wise, down my nose when the segment ended.

Get it together, I ordered myself, to cut Irma off at the pass. I hit my bookmarks on the ancient-Egypt sites. Sure enough, Shezmou was there exactly as I'd seen him, under several less pronounceable spellings of his name, Shesmu, et cetera. His being a blood demon and Lord of the Slaughter was a constant, though.

And Bez . . . his name was spelled only one way: Bes. You'd never want to call him "Bess," though. Bez was the phonetic version and much better. The sight of his curly mane of hair and beard and genial Bert Lahr Cowardly Lion face made me feel another almost labor-pain wrench of loss for Quicksilver.

I wondered where the two forgotten gods were, now that the underground food pens were history. Had they retreated back to their pillars if Anubis had left any standing?

Deliberately leaving tragic memories of the Karnak, I switched to my email, two screens full of unopened email, mostly Nigerian in origin.

I started deleting with a vengeance, then blinked and checked my Delete file. There it was: brimfulbabe@snowkissedsluts.sup.

Dot-sup was a new URL address, pronounced "soup," to handle the explosion of supernatural websites after the Millennium Revelation. Those not in the know pronounced it "sup" as in "dine." That was also appropriate for our new supernatural population of vampires and werewolves and such.

Brimfulbabe@snowkissedsluts.sup sure sounded like a Snow groupie user name. I skimmed my new mail list. Among the "AWARD" and "FOR YOU, DEAREST ONE" subject lines were several slugged "Graduation."

It had been ages since I'd graduated from anything, so I checked the email addresses. Yes!

Amazed, I recognized such user names as infernobait, stonedonsnow, snowgasm224, cocainiac, snowkissedslut, all at a new web address, kissedoffsnow.sup.

The Snow groupies were having a weaned-off-the-Brimstone-Kiss graduation ceremony tomorrow night and they wanted me to be valedictorian. Self-esteem had won out over the one-time multiple orgasm kiss and doomed hope of ever getting another from Cocaine the rock star.

I felt the first rush of positive emotion since Quicksilver had vanished into the beetle pit. Maybe I should attend, I thought, teary eyes blurring the screen. Maybe I'd really helped these women. Maybe they really liked me.

I opened a few messages to make myself feel better. And got another bolt from the ethernet. Lilith! They'd found mention of the Seven Deadly Sins rock band and lead singer Cocaine on lilithluvsluci@brimstone.sup. They'd emailed her to attend their "Solicitous" get-together.

I couldn't ask for anything more in my quests to find my double as well as figure out who'd killed the Snow groupie behind the Inferno Hotel.

Well, one thing more. I could wish that I was still as

pure as the driven "Snow" when it came to the Brimstone Kiss. I was not the innocent anti-Kiss crusader who'd organized this groupie self-help bunch a couple weeks ago.

Since then, I'd taken the Brimstone Kiss myself, under duress. I hadn't had an orgasm, much less several, and I'd never become addicted to anything afterward but shame.

Still, I was a fine one to talk now, and that's just what they wanted me to do.

Chapter Thirty-one

I'VE BEEN CALLED nervy a few times since I'd come to Las Vegas only weeks ago. Actually, I'm liking it. Kansas Delilah could have been called determined but never nervy.

Tonight I felt nervy in a bad way.

Despite having faced off a few fistfuls of major mobsters and monsters lately, I approached the deserted Strip shopping center with icy fingers and damp palms.

Only one storefront was lit from within. Funny that this fluorescent sign of life unnerved me more than a fey power touchpoint or a fully packed zombie mummy tomb underneath the Karnak Hotel. I was only going to confront a roomful of mostly middle-aged women.

Imagine, a bunch of ordinary mortals had my knees knocking! The silver familiar seconded my cowardice by shrinking to thread-fine chains and taking cover under my "*CSI V* as in Vegas" black tee.

A good thing I'd paused at the Enchanted Cottage mantel to push Caressa Teagarden's funky green-stoned ring onto my middle finger. It might either draw my "twin" or simply underline any "up yours" gestures I had to make in traffic. Just kidding. I'd never do that to Dolly. Some road-rager might mar her perfect hand-waxed-by-me black finish.

I left my adopted cop duty belt locked in Dolly's vast empty trunk with an unwanted memory picture of Quicksilver's concealed ride-along there. To ensure a low profile, I'd even parked the huge '56 Caddy before a closed dry cleaning establishment. That was six doors down from the array of small, high-mileage late-model cars lined up in front of the unlabeled storefront like a gang of motorized roller skates.

I'd worked hard to become nervy and shameless all my life, but now I had a major case of Cringe.

The emails flooding in since yesterday had begged me to show up tonight.

"We *need* you there, Delilah," they typed in twenty-some messages. "Graduation Day wouldn't be the same without you, without the one who started us on a New Path."

Oh, Lord. I sounded like some cheesy online soul-saver.

They'd even kept up the rent on the former Weight Watchers space, meeting here daily under their own will-power, they told me.

Why? They'd actually bought into my hokey gambit of substituting dark chocolate kisses for white chocolate kisses to symbolize their resolve to grow beyond the addictive memory of Cocaine's unforgettably sensual Brimstone Kiss.

They had determination, chutzpah, heart.

There was only one bluebottle in the ointment. Me. While they'd been meeting and weaning themselves off the addictive smooch, I, Delilah Street, anti–Brimstone Kiss crusader and the liplock liberator, had become a Brimstone Kiss veteran myself.

Whining that I'd been forced to accept the fatal kiss to save a life . . . swearing that I didn't get one fattening, illegal, or immoral thrill out of it, honest, especially not a—*gasp*!—multiple orgasm, not even one teeny tiny singular orgasm . . . nothing except . . . some insignificant, way less than minor, mild body-to-body stimulation even an automated statue of a Greek god at Caesars Palace's fountain attraction might have been guilty of . . .

I paused before the kind of glass-paned steel door that had led to a lifetime of various small businesses, swallowing hard. Swallowed pride really does leave a supersize, almost lethal lump in the throat. Ironic that Snow, as lead singer, Cocaine, for the Seven Deadly Sins, had adopted the role of Pride.

I'd rather have faced six half-were gangs like the Lunatics, three pyramids full of zombie mummies, even a seven-course meal of Hector Nightwine's creepiest favorite things than know that I was something worse than the worst unhuman, a hypocrite.

Still, I couldn't knock the feet of clay out from under my fervent converts just to salve my corroded conscience.

I pushed inside.

And was greeted by Partee Central and a blaring boom box.

The usual metal folding chairs filled half the room, but had been pushed askew to make room for conga lines of women hip-swinging to a familiar music list: all the upbeat numbers from the Seven Deadly Sins albums. (The SDS was one of the few rock groups still popular enough to have best-selling albums.)

I recognized some of the Haves and Have-nots, Brimstone Kiss–wise, from my one and only meeting here, but they were all mingling. There was a mosh-pit, luau, Richard Simmons vibe to the crowd. Even my bruised conscience and sorrowing soul couldn't help nodding to the beat.

Giant brandy snifters on long folding tables along the walls shone bright silver with wrapped white and dark chocolate kisses. Punch bowls held cola-dark brews and milky concoctions floating ice cubes. Both wafted a hard-liquor lure.

"DEE-lie-lah!" a woman's voice hailed me.

Three others manhandled me into the conga line, hands on hips. It would have been churlish to ignore the mood.

How could those Snow-obsessed women languishing for an unheard-of second Brimstone Kiss from the rock god have become these joyous voodoo babes?

They one-two-threed me onto a metal folding chair and gathered around. Two came from the adjacent kitchen bearing armfuls of roses that were plunked into my unsuspecting custody like fragrant floral babies.

One bouquet was white roses, the other a red so dark and delicious it was almost the brown of bitter chocolate. Now I was not only seated and surrounded but armless and trapped. My defensive instincts twinged, but the roses' mingled scents were as heady as incense.

"I don't get it," I shouted into the chaos. Wasn't I here to give a girl graduate pep talk? "What's this about?"

"About *us,*" a woman with thick curly dark hair shouted. "About you."

"We are finally *free,* girl," another voice cried. I glanced to a black woman sporting a gorgeous platinum-gray pixie cut. "Thanks to you. Come on, it's time for the show."

"Show?" I blinked when they swept back their chairs to leave an even wider aisle. A bare-chested ghost strutted into the cleared area.

"Oh."

A Snow tribute performer wasn't what I'd had in mind as an antidote, I thought, as a karaoke machine started blaring a Seven Deadly Sins number.

The guy began lip-syncing to a portable mike and making the rounds of the circle with eye-level pelvic thrusts at every stop.

Omigod, this was tacky. My noble attempt at liberation had ended in blatant, bald female lustulation? The *guy* wasn't bald. *Nooo,* he lashed his long white wig around while slinging his hips like a hash-house waitress. I was *so* embarrassed. I was sure the hair had been designed for a Cher impersonation.

And this guy had it all wrong. Close up, the not-waxed chest had sticky coils of thick clown-white theatrical greasepaint in a moiré pattern. Anybody who'd been in the Seven Deadly Sins mosh pit (not to mention close-up and too personal with Snow himself) would know that lightning-strike scars were his chest tattoo of choice, or not-choice.

And the rhinestone-jeweled fly featured enough cat's-eye-green gems to equip a litter of Grizelle's cubs . . . when anybody in the know, like me, realized that the stones and colors on Snow's performance catsuit fly were all warm and kinda pulsing semiprecious scarlet, amber, and hot pink. (Now that I saw the imitation and thought about it.)

In fact, that imitation was heading to my chair as the guy started ripping the front snaps loose on his leather shirt. Snaps?

The fly was next and so was I.

I finally got it. This was a Cocaine tribute *stripper.* I squeezed my eyes shut just in time and thought of England. And my own situation and failings.

I was a prisoner of personal freedom.

Tangled in tacky.

Gratified by my liberated ladies.

Horrified by my own backfiring hubris.

Humbled.

Humiliated. Again.

At least when I opened my eyes the number was over. The cheap Cocaine clone finally had boogied out the rear kitchen door to a late-night performance at the Idolanimator Club, I was breathlessly informed, as if I would ever go there.

I handed the ladies single roses until my arms were empty. The twenty-four formerly addicted Cocaine ladies folded away their five-dollar bills and shut their purses and leaned back in the folding chairs breathing heavily, exhausted by liquor, libido, chocolate, and dancing.

I sighed relief. Those were fairly harmless failings in the Millennium Revelation's brave new world.

And then I noticed the figure standing just inside the front door.

Tall. All in white. Ghost-white. Eyes like those alien visitors of my nightmares. Big, black, shiny. No, just sunglasses. Arms folded on shirted chest. White silk Armani suit hiding snow-white scars and no gaudy zipper flies.

Himself. The unhuman of the hour. Cocaine. Snow.

Here in person, to take my ladies down.

I glanced toward the kitchen exit. That door was shut.

The women did what women do: they arranged the chairs in tidy rows, they folded the tables. Some grabbed brandy snifters of wrapped silver kisses as others emptied the punch bowls' ice water into the kitchen sink and prepared to tote everything out.

Everyone did her clean-up duty; everyone got a rose and some got leftovers as a door prize. Except there was one more door to pass. To the victors belong the spoils.

Speaking of spoils, he virtually blended in with the almond-white walls all such places have so that whatever happens inside them remains colorful and memorable.

I had a bad feeling I'd consider this one of the most colorful and memorable nights of my life. Not in a good way. I thought only *I* had sucked in my breath. No such bad luck. I heard a dozen deep inhalations and then that number doubled. My Brimstone Kiss sisters had finally noticed who blocked their exit route.

Ai-ai-ai, Chiquita Banana, Irma breathed in the back of my mind. *You are up against the Big Kahuna.*

Bastard! At the very moment when twenty-four individual triumphs of self-control and willpower were reverberating through this plain room, when I was daring to think I might have done some good, even if the outcome was a trifle tacky, up the Great White Cobra raises its lethal head and hisses.

Okay, so I tend to exaggerate. I always was too passionate about my work and too methodical about my passions.

I folded my fingers into my fists, feeling my nails make half-moon indentations all along my life and love and head lines.

The women halted en masse, seeing what I'd seen.

It was an impasse. Past versus present. Charisma versus self-esteem.

If I could have drawn a gun, I would have.

But my empty arms were still laden with a fragrance of roses and regrets.

The woman nearest the door started moving, a stolid middle-aged woman with a pure Mayan profile. She came even with the White Chocolate God.

Chocolate had been invented in the jungles of the step pyramids of the Maya and Aztecs of 1100 BC. I'd done a feature on that for WTCH-TV in Wichita. The word meant "bitter water," because fermented cacao tree seeds produced the flavor.

I waited and watched.

"Candy kiss?" she asked, proffering her brandy snifter.

"Dark or light?" he asked in that reverberating stage basso.

Okay, I told Irma. I'd cave and say, "Which do you prefer?"

"You take your chances," the woman answered.

Nah, Irma said. *You'd be as contrary as she is.*

He reached in and pulled out a tiny silver foiled pyramid with a curl on top. Cute.

The woman left.

The next woman sashayed up. She'd been watching.

"What do I get if you guess which color candy my brandy snifter holds?" she asked coquettishly.

"One less kiss."

"Oh, yeah? I can sell all of these on eBay for big bucks if I say you passed your eyes over the contents."

He waved his hand over them.

"*Gracias!* 'Cocaine-approved.'"

I couldn't believe it. Each woman passed with his blessing, pleased as . . . Cocaine punch.

I don't suppose it surprised anybody that I was last. Alone. Forgotten even by my own acolytes.

Passing him on the way out was the hardest thing I'd ever contemplated. He was so cool, so urbane. So uninjured. So not the vengeful god.

Those attributes made me hate him more. Or maybe it was me I hated. That damn silken suit reminded me of Ric's shining scar-smooth back. I'd only won that triumph at the cost of a few, last lashes to Snow, but those had been knowing.

I knew he'd suffer and had decided to sacrifice his skin and his pain for Ric's redemption. He'd known it, and, worse, possibly had leashed his guardian, Grizelle, to allow me to make my choice.

It's easy to fight for someone you love. It's much, much harder, I was finding, oddly enough, to wrong someone you hate.

So I knew, as I moved slowly to the door to face the enigma that was Snow, that he could be hurt and that I had been willing to do that.

No wonder he'd shown up here to undo my amateurish attempt at do-goodery. I knew I should apologize. I was too proud, and too ashamed.

"I guess," I said, staring at the middle white button on his silken white shirt, "I should have expected you to show up and undo my self-help group."

"Did I?" he asked.

"Well, they were mesmerized."

"*You* are mesmerized. They all left. Didn't you notice? Now you know they're truly free, as you might describe it. Dark or light?" he asked, holding out knuckled fists.

"Chocolate. We're talking about chocolate."

"Of course. And your chocolate won. Congratulations."

"White," I said. "No, I mean dark."

He smiled and opened empty fists. "Sorry. You'll have to buy your own. Such an interesting world, where dark is good and light is bad. Again, I congratulate you."

"But . . . you've lost all these women, all these devoted groupies. They're content with high-calorie substitutes."

"Are you?"

Oh, shit, he was right. No.

"So you've won," he said again.

"You act like you . . . wanted them to move on?"

"Exactly."

"And like I did just what you wanted me to do?"

"Exactly."

"Even to the . . . damage?"

He paused. "It wasn't unexpected."

"You're saying I've been manipulated into wronging you? That's truly wicked. I hate that worse than anything."

"Sometimes it's necessary to sacrifice your pride."

I'd known he'd claimed that seventh Deadly Sin from the first time we met. I just hadn't known that was my biggie too.

"I'm—"

I thought back to the religion lessons at Our Lady of the Lake Convent School, horrified, recalling the thirty pieces of mob silver Ric and I had found in Loretta and her prince's Sunset Park grave. Were they meant for me in some weird way?

"I'm some predestined Judas?" I asked, aghast.

"Delilah will do," he said with a smile I wasn't sure reached his eyes because of the dark sunglasses, which suddenly turned into mirror shades so I saw myself small and convex in them.

I wasn't sure, either, whether his powers had morphed the sunglasses, or my own mirror magic. So either he was a sadist, which I wouldn't argue except *I'd* hurt *him,* or I was a masochist. Either way, I knew letting my guard down would be fatal to something, my life or my pride.

"Samson took pride in his strength," I said, "but he lost it."

"So you've won," he said again.

"If pride is *your* cardinal sin." I remembered that a church cardinal had slain the medieval dragon Snow had recently raised.

"We have so much in common," he whispered.

I had to lean close, and up, to hear.

There was something I had to say, and it was very hard. I could barely whisper.

"I'm sorry."

He bent nearer. I felt icy heat and a heavy, sinking heart. Were our breaths mingling? Did I sense subliminal tremors of tension in us both? Can he give any kiss but the Brimstone Kiss? Did Lilith take it too? If so, what happened? His face tilted away, so did his lips a breath away from mine. They brushed the sides of my hair.

"What did you say?" he asked.

He was going to make me say it again. "I'm sorry, and apparently also a hypocrite."

He straightened, laughing.

"Welcome, Delilah Street, to the unhuman race."

He laughed again and I heard real joy.

"I couldn't," I started to explain . . . something.

"*Shhh,*" he said. "You'd better let me go, or you might be sorrier."

"*Me?* Let *you* go?" I was keeping him here? No.

"The woman walks away," I said. "That's the whole point of this group."

So I turned my back and did.

All I could think as I did my walk-away was how much I'd like to rip the expensive clothes off his back.

Not because I'm a hopeless groupie but because I really have a need to know how guilty I should feel about him. Snow is enough of a bastard to have wiped the whiplashes away like lipstick and he'd never tell me. Or even Grizelle.

Some men just love a good catfight.

I flexed my tense, aching fingers.

Me too.

Chapter Thirty-two

OF COURSE THE point in making a dramatic exit is not to be seen again. And to not look back.

That's the whole point of pride, too, and why it's a sin.

I walked into the kitchen. Not one laggard was left. They'd all faced and passed the night's surprise bogeyman with a lot less drama than I had—I, the founding mother of this exclusive club.

In fact, I hadn't passed him at all.

Nor had any of them approached me or slipped a billet-doux into my sweating palm to offer a tip on Lilith. I'd forgotten all about her until I tangled with Snow. And the groupie murder? I'd been too surprised by the hoopla to think about that, either, although I now had all their freshest email addies.

Evening score: Snow, 10; Delilah, 0.

The kitchen smelled of cola and punch rinsed down the stainless steel sink. The rear exit was an industrial-strength door with a push bar and bold sign, warning: EXIT ONLY.

I hadn't brought my messenger bag, just jammed my car keys into my low-rise jeans pocket. They were always a pain to worm out . . .

I eased the door wide with my back, bracing my feet to hold it open. Once out, I couldn't get back in. The story of my life in Las Vegas, in reverse.

While one hand was jammed alongside my right hip

dueling jagged steel key edges, the big door slammed shut, ramming me in the rear. I hopped outside just in time to avoid crushing.

Nobody was outside to have pushed it. Not even the wind.

Attar of Rose's lime juice and older, uglier scents helped me spot a Dumpster tilting against the building's back concrete block wall like a grounded garbage scow.

Only a faint pink-gold glow made it back here from the front parking lot lights, giving the Dumpster the odd illusion it was outlined in mercurochrome neon.

That's Las Vegas, city of illusions and delusions.

I'd have to hike around the whole unappetizing rear area to get to Dolly up front, if I ever got her keys out. That's what I get for buying tight jeans to wear to Los Lobos werewolf disco someday with visions of Ric jamming his hands down my back pockets during the slow dances.

I didn't know which felt tighter, my jeans or my conscience, and I wore the same insecure mules as when the Bela Lugosi CinSim Dracula had hijacked me from the Enchanted Cottage. Then I noticed that one edge of the luridly lit rusted Dumpster was accessorized with a leaning human figure.

Quicksilver's loss came back with a double stab of regret. In Las Vegas these days seeing a "human figure" is no guarantee of anything. I could use a partner with serious nose and fangs right now.

Oooh-eee, Delilah, Irma joined in with gusto. *You've managed to maroon yourself in dead-end limbo with who knows what. Maybe you'd have been better off in the front parking lot, down on your knees applying first aid to that Snow character's bare back with your tongue.*

That's disgusting! Shut your mouth! I told her.

Irma had been getting on my nerves lately and I didn't need any help in that department.

I dug deeper for the keys, their spiky prongs my only weapon besides my wits, which had been AWOL lately. A shiver along my spine told me the still-hidden silver familiar was expanding its reach to act as either defensive or offensive weapon. I couldn't tell whether it was ashamed of me too, or just being sneaky.

I scuffed forward. Retreat in this city is certain death.

"Can I help you with anything?" I asked.

The likeliest suspect here was a wino hunting dregs in the tossed liquor bottles.

"You can help me with everything," a husky voice answered.

Wrong answer. It was too knowing, too challenging to be a stranger's voice.

"Did you send the message that you'd located someone I'm interesting in finding?" I asked. Was some anonymous groupie going Deep Throat on Lilith?

"Maybe. Depends on the message you got."

Why did I think a simple evening run to a Strip shopping center to meet rock-star groupies didn't require the presence of Ric, or the marines?

I cleared my throat. "I was after information on a murder of a Cocaine groupie at the Inferno. I don't suppose you'd know anything?"

"I know everything," the hoarse voice answered.

I bet. It sounded honed on sandpaper, neither male nor female, human nor unhuman.

The figure was slumped so close to the Dumpster side I couldn't tell if it stood on two legs or three, in shoes or boots, on cloven hooves or big, shaggy paws. The head was a spiky mystery that could be too much drugstore gel or demon spines. Today's street punks often resembled arcane night terrors of hundreds of years ago.

And *why* was my armed duty belt locked in Dolly's truck? Was it because I didn't want to scare the Snow groupies? Or did I just not want to look "hippy" in a former Weight Watchers venue? Or was I just sexist enough to think that a bunch of women weren't dangerous?

Could I actually be hoping that Snow was still hanging around to taunt me further?

You gotta resolve that bipolar thing you got going, Irma suggested throatily.

"I know," I snapped aloud at Irma.

"You *know* who I am and why I'm here?" the figure growled back. "I don't think so, Delilah the Dog Slayer."

How did—? Never mind, it was exactly the right thing to make me wince and lower my guard. "Who are you?"

"You'd never guess in a thousand years, and certainly haven't in twenty-four."

"So you know how old I am. So what? It's public record."

"I'm not."

A scrape of leather sole on back-alley grit warned that the figure had stepped away from the Dumpster and toward me.

The stiletto of light that edged the hulking metal caught the stranger in its glare, cutting a foot-wide swath across a death-pale cheek down to the black-leather-booted calf opposite me. I recognized the footwear.

Mine.

Studying the opposite figure, I recognized pieces of my height, hair, build.

"The late, great Lilith, I presume," I managed to spit out past the rapid hip-hop rhythm of my heart. "I'd heard you might be here tonight. Why show in person only now?"

"You were getting too close."

"And the Dumpster? How could you be sure I'd exit through the rear?"

Even as I asked the question, I wished I'd been wearing Lilith's version of my ass-kicking motorcycle boots to use them on my own rear. *Snow.* He'd been *stationed* at the *front* to drive me out the *back*.

Was I really that predictable? More important, did Snow work for Lilith or vice versa? I waited for Irma to chime in with theories and further critiques, but she kept mum.

"The Dumpster," Lilith answered slowly, like a Big Sister spelling it all out to the middle-grader, "is 'our place.' It's where everyone else thinks I am you and you know I'm not."

"Did Snow grab that security tape showing you in my clothes clobbering his groupie to protect you?"

"You think he'd protect you?"

"If it suited his purposes."

"Which are?"

"Dubious. He *did* give me a copy of the security recording of the scene. Much as you might like to have me taken for a murderer, you only knocked out the groupie. She was strangled later."

"That still leaves you a suspect."

"Unless I can prove *you're* still alive and at large."

"Is that why you've been snooping around the *CSI V* autopsy set?"

"Or are you not dead, but Undead and still looking for victims? Why did you wear the same Déjà-Vous outfit I did that night?

"I might have, like, gone to Déjà."

"In a pig's eye! You went there in its dressing room mirror. You copped my clothes, my look, even as I was putting them all together. Just to put the blame on me? Was that why? Still, how could you know that the groupie would accost me inside the Inferno Hotel? Did you follow her to the Dumpster after that? She must have thought you were me and tried to steal another 'souvenir' of the hair Snow had touched."

"So many questions, Delilah. You really were a TV reporter in the boonies like you claim."

"Kansas isn't 'the boonies,' it's the heartland, and I was a pretty darn good reporter there."

There was light enough to see Lilith roll her eyes, flashing as vivid blue as my own.

"Oh, come on!" she said. "You've got to admit Vegas has a much better and badder class of supers. This is the Big Time, kid."

"I'm not used to being talked down to by my mirror."

"Liar!" It was an ugly accusation but she seemed to be laughing at me. "You get lots of back-talk through mirrors, including from the bad little werewolf girl. And speaking of mirrors, yes, that's where I get most of my Delilah-brand rags, not from any fancy costume shop, not even Déjà-Vous."

She'd confirmed my guess at least.

"So," I said, "if you see me in my hall mirror, you cop my look? Why didn't you let me see you do it sooner?"

"I don't do it very often. Your 'look' is too hicksville. All that vintage stuff. At least your hot Hispanic guy upped the temperature of your wardrobe." I saw her slap the flat of her hand on her jeaned butt, jutted out to catch the light.

I shrugged. I wanted to know the how and why of Lilith's very existence, not her fashion opinions.

"I don't think you killed that groupie," I charged, sounding like *not* killing someone was a bigger crime than doing it. Lilith really turned my head around and my sanity inside out.

"You don't picture yourself—myself—doing it?" she asked.

"No. I know you didn't leave her dead. You might have a notion who did, though. You saw her last."

"Always the unimpassioned investigator, Delilah. You'd think my personal appearance here would rustle up a little sisterly emotion."

"Don't dodge the question, Lilith. Makes me think you do know an answer."

"Maybe it was that creepy guy who was after you."

"That covers a lot of guys in town, unfortunately, from the Lunatics gang to Cesar Cicereau. Given your earlier description of Ric, I assume you're leaving him out of that sweepstakes."

"Definitely. How soon you forget your enemies. I mean that crooked cop who's been slowly rotting off his humanity one private part at a time."

"Haskell! He was there? Why?"

"He knows when you've been sleeping. He knows when you're awake—"

I shuddered at her sardonic words. Lilith was right: like the song also said, you better watch out. In today's Las Vegas, even Santa Claus could be a monster and Haskell certainly was capable of stalking me.

Or *her,* even before I'd come to town.

Just the mention of Haskell's name sent a flutter of likely scenarios through my mind on fast-forward: he'd seen the groupie groping me inside the Inferno that night and . . . figured she was hot and fair game for him? Or . . . Haskell had killed the woman after Lilith repulsed her, mistaking Lil for me and hoping I'd get blamed.

Because . . . Haskell and I had tangled in Sunset Park when I'd first hooked up with Ric (in a purely professional sense). Or, even worse: maybe he'd known and loathed Lilith and took me for her right off. If Snow knew her, she'd had a history in Sin City before I ever came here after seeing her "autopsied" on *CSI V*.

My head was beginning to hurt from calculating all the possibilities.

For sure Haskell would have known where to find the security camera and obscure it while he murdered the groupie. He'd never expect Snow to steal the damning tape of me/Lilith confronting the woman for his own reasons.

I had to recalculate the timeline, and find out where Haskell was when the groupie was killed. His arresting me as the killer certainly confirmed Lilith's story that he'd been around the murder scene that night.

Something came speeding down the service road, something behind Lilith. A four-footed shadow like Quicksilver's bounced off the Dumpster side. The metal banged, a huge, hollow drum.

My heart echoed it as I leaped back from the passing stray animal, hitting hard against the steel door that wouldn't let me retreat. The impact triggered a security alarm with a shrill, banshee scream, not unlike my nerves.

My shadowy double was blending into the darker part of the night.

"Lilith! Wait! I need more info. If you know who really killed the woman behind the Inferno, I need—"

"Sorry, Delilah, I don't stick around for line-ups."

The shadow was already melting into the crux at the eternal juncture of dark ground, walls, night, desert, vision, despair.

"Lilith! You *need* to be cleared as much as I do—"

"If anyone besides you believed in me, that is," the raw voice mocked from the dark. "Anyone official. Sure you're not hallucinating, Delilah? You hear voices, don't you? Why can't you see visions? They'll burn you at the stake yet. But not me. Not me."

The last word came whispered from above, below, nearby, at a deep, dark distance.

So close. Lilith cutting though the night and my doubt like a razor caressing a throat in a cul-de-sac. Not a mirror image. Real. Raw. Unfathomable.

I was surprised that I was shaking all over, from my key ring to the silver familiar on my wrist jingling away like Santa's sleigh bells.

Lilith was real. Light-shy as a vampire. Taunting. Bitchy.

But she was real and she'd been willing to meet me one-on-one-on-two. I lunged away from the steel door I'd jolted that was still unleashing a siren of sound.

Screaming Hell! While I was standing there, stunned stupid about facing my *CSI* double, a live (or at least undead) Lilith, who must have already known for sure I existed, had wisely bolted.

I should too. Talk about dropping the existential ball when it was almost in your hands and tucked under your arm.

I took off running, bouncing off the Dumpster side like the running dog, angling away from the slice of parking lot light, skidding on things I didn't like to think about.

There was one more thing I hated thinking about even more.

Snow at the front door, Lilith at the back.

Were they working together, against me?

Chapter Thirty-three

THE SOUND OF pounding footsteps.

An echo of mine? Or Lilith's? I couldn't picture Snow running to save my soul, or his own.

I raced along a dimly lit row of waste cans behind the closed storefronts. Once I rounded the row's end, I'd have to run even farther in the opposite direction to get back to Dolly. Then I'd need to drive away before the distant police car sirens arrived, forcing me to explain my presence.

The good part was I could honestly play the innocent klutz who'd triggered the alarm, so I was mostly still steaming about Lilith's vanishing on me. At least in Dolly I could cover more ground than she could on foot.

The parking lot lamp at the row's end was growing larger, like the light at the end of a tunnel. A black silhouette inside it was getting larger too.

The image of lurking darkness inside the light was classic suspense movie stuff. I wanted to believe Lilith had had a change of heart and decided to face me.

As a burst of high, mocking laughter echoed off the concrete blocks I ran faster. I didn't expect a sentimental encounter. By now I wasn't looking for Lilith to be a soul sister. Maybe an alibi would do.

After all, she'd known Snow before I had, had even joined the Snow groupies' online community. She had somehow "stolen" my clothing of the moment to play on the physical fact of our identical appearances. Worst of all, she'd been taped knocking out a Snow groupie outside the Inferno in my exact likeness. Accident or plot?

So I wasn't running toward her with open arms, but with my key ring bristling through all my right-hand knuckles. The silver familiar sent chills up my torso and limbs, poised to become the weapon I needed on a millisecond's notice.

Then I realized why my metal familiar was hesitating about choosing a shape. The image ahead of me shrank as I came closer but the laughter reverberated, seeming to isolate my name in a sound studio . . . De-lie-lahahahahahaha. *Dee-lie-ha-ha-ha-ha-ha-ha.*

The thrown-back head, bulking shoulders and thin-legged shadow before me focused into a grinning hell-hound hyena from the Karnak Hotel.

And the echoes of its cackling behind me repeated like a tape loop suddenly sporting eight tracks.

I glanced back to see a pack of the terrifying creatures bunched behind me, coming up fast.

I veered left, away from the lights and the parking lot and my faithful ride and the police cars and the street and the passing vehicles.

My left hand clasped a cold smooth metal handle. When I lifted my arm a streak of neon-pink light rippled over an undulating silver snake. The whip's snap was metal-sharp. A hiss of electric lightning sizzled into the warm evening air.

Good choice. I paused to lash my arm across the oncoming pack. Their unnerving laughter turned to screams of rage as the silver trail slashed *through* their ranks. For an instant they faded, then those ungainly, misshapen bodies took bristle-furred shape again.

I turned to run, the silver whip coiling around my waist to keep me from entangling with it.

Amazing how flat-out flight can get your body zigzagging around anything in your way. I seemed to almost walk over fallen trash cans along the shops' back walls, kicking them behind me into my pursuers like cylindrical bowling balls. The backbeat scratch of long, lethal hyena claws on concrete was a rhythmic counter to the guttural arias of inhuman laughter overtaking me.

My lungs were burning to the point of bursting and my sides felt like some magician had skewered me with a dozen very real sword blades.

For an instant I saw myself reflected in a glass door to interior darkness. The glass glowed softly green from a night-light inside. I glimpsed posters of castles and pyramids beyond the reflection of my form outrunning the night. Close enough to a mirror? Lilith again?

I'd more happily risk plunging through this quasi-mirror as an escape if I wasn't chasing some taunting, unreal image of Lilith . . . I felt the encompassing comfort of the familiar melting as I hurled my body full-speed at the solid glass.

The suspended moment when my feet left the asphalt made me almost temporarily blind, when the sirens and the laughter abruptly ended, when I couldn't feel the familiar at all . . .

Or anything.

Then I saw that my reflection or the image of Lilith had shifted. It was webbed with glittering patterns, the face distorted in a demonic scream. My last conscious sight was the bereaved ghost of Loretta Cicereau. She was as mad as hell and not going to take it, or me, anymore.

Wrong mooove, Irma wailed before she went silent too.

Chapter Thirty-four

I AWOKE ALONE.

Terrifyingly alone.

I searched first for Irma's voice, the last warning I'd heard.

She was gone.

Not silent.

Gone.

You know how some memory, some person, is a part of you even when you're not thinking? Something your mind can always conjure? Maybe it smells like the morning coffee you had first thing at work every morning, or it's a vivid taste like the cinnamon gum you chewed only when you were a kid, or a scent and sensation like a Teddy bear's faux fur you buried your face into at a toy store once, all those traces of memory that go back as far as you can remember.

Irma was like that and she was not here. She had left the room that was me.

So had the silver familiar. Yeah, I'd fought it from the first, resented its source and found its presence creepy. *Not* feeling it at all after several weeks was even creepier.

So what *did* I feel or sense now? First, I hoped my eyelids were shut because all I could see of my environment was that splotchy blackness behind your closed eyes in bed at night.

Second, I didn't seem to be floating but I was definitely horizontal. I broke into an icy sweat when I realized I wasn't inclined to move just as much as I wasn't inclined to open my eyes. Inquiring reporters want to know. For the first time in my remembered life, *I didn't want to know.* I knew I wouldn't like where the faintly reflecting glass door had taken me.

I so far gleaned that I lay flat, on my back, immobile—my most terrifying nightmare since I could remember nightmares—and I didn't feel anything but some level surface beneath me.

Wait. Not quite true. What lay beneath me was stone-hard but not cold, about the same temperature as my body, because I could barely sense it. A deep breath lifted my chest and shoulders against the faintest whisper of a barrier. Something was covering me.

Not clothes.

And not above the neck, so I wasn't a dead body in a morgue—yet.

I listened so intensely I thought my jaws would snap.

Finally, faint as a wisp of wind, I heard or felt motion around me, above me. And, worse than anything, the softest slithering sound below me.

My mind—fearful I'd been transported to the Karnak, whether by my mirror magic or even a physical method while unconscious—sensed more around me than the gigantic Egyptian bulk of the Strip hotel itself.

That was only a gaudy and deceptive gateway to an endless empire buried deep in the sands of time and space. So, with a child's exotic fears, my mind pictured giant cobras gathering here, slipping their faintly sheened coils along a stone floor, nearing, their small evil faces set like poisonous jewels in the broad, flared collars of their scales.

Every lurid film cliché about ancient Egypt assembled on the black screen behind my eyes. I saw and imagined I heard the breathless beat of torch flames in the oxygen-starved environment of the ancient pyramid chambers.

I pictured painted eyes of graceful human forms watching me. I envisioned upright crocodiles marching along with slavering jaws among creatures with the kilted and collared bodies of human bronze gods surmounted by bird and animal and serpent heads clothed in the traditional cloth headdresses.

I took another breath. I could feel and needed to see. Anything was better than six-foot-tall swaying cobras, even mysteriously muzzled royal hyenas I could no longer sense anywhere. Surely they'd be laughing if they were still present. I opened my eyes.

And looked right up into my worst nightmare.

I was indeed lying flat on my back, so I could only look up. I saw a ceiling where all the figures from my imagined tomb frieze floated at crazy right angles to each other. Obscuring most of the paintings was a large overhead lamp, its light focused tightly downward but muted to an eerie glow otherwise, as at a dentist's office.

Figures were indeed gathered around me—pale, mouthless, hairless figures like the mannequins in an expensive, avant-garde department store, with huge black liquid eyes. Three stood on either side of me, motionless.

My fear tripled. I was indeed held helpless in the alien spaceship of my nightmares, or perhaps of my oldest, most buried memories, surrounded by vague silent forms watching me as if I were a bug pinned to a dissecting table. Did they still have those awful high school biology classes where kids had to cut up worms and frogs? The memory made my skin crawl.

This recurrent nightmare of mine preceded that Millennium Revelation year of 2000–2001. I knew I was again Young Delilah, eleven or so. And so scared. So alone. And I knew, even more than before, because Real Delilah was somewhere in here with me, this was going to hurt me, badly. Again.

People think kids don't know what's coming when they lose complete power over themselves, like in a dentist's chair or on a doctor's examination table. Or an autopsy table. But they do, which is why Real Delilah had demanded dentists work with her phobias and let her sit up, why she'd gone to underground clinics for birth control pills to avoid the horizontal horrors of the ob/gyn's sinister stirrup-equipped table, the surety of invasion and hurtful, insensitive intimacy.

Adults think kids are gullible when we're only innocent.

And now I sense myself as a split personality: a kid/adult imprisoned in my past/present and maybe about to lose it all, including my mind.

Okay, Delilah, hang on!

I had that bracing thought just in time. Or was I no longer "I," Delilah, but Lilith on an autopsy table in a new nightmare? An instant after I felt a pain so sharp and yet both alien and familiar I couldn't tell where on my body it had occurred, much less what. I sucked in a monstrous breath.

"Be still," a voice commanded. A human voice.

I let my eyes lower from the hypnotically greenish glass lens bleeding an aura like a halo above me to what—or I should say *who*—stood at the foot of my examination table.

Another unconsciously held breath burst out, surprising me. I saw something impossible yet familiar from *outside* my longtime nightmare: a man's strong-featured face.

He had Orlando Bloom–pale skin, thick black eyebrows, and gel-glossed hair like black patent leather. He looked up from doing something to me I was glad I couldn't see or feel, distracted by my witnessing it.

"You don't want to move when I'm doing this," he said, flicking me a glance. His eyes were dark but the pupils were small and human. Or . . . more like real-life-size cobra eyes, shiny as onyx beads.

His deep commanding baritone had cracked on the word "this." I detected a bit of a British accent. He was irritated with me, that I was awake and had seen him, and that scared me again. I was mute with astonishment anyway, lost in my recurring dream and in this possible rerun in real time.

Nightmares can come true, it can happen to you . . .

The weirdest part was that I seemed immobile without being restrained. Sure, I knew that was the classic paralysis nightmare. I suppose alien abduction victims would say they'd been drugged. And there had been that one piercing pain I'd felt, obviously from a needle, a big needle.

As if answering my speculations, the man (doctor?) lifted a small vial of dark gray fluid up to the murky light. Blood. Mine. What! Freshly drawn blood was bright scarlet.

That's when I recognized my assailant, not only what he was but *who* he was. Oh, he was indeed a doctor, in one sense. Even more improbably, he was also a CinSim standing there in living black-and-white. Yet his backup sextet of masked "alien nurses," although pale, were clearly in muted Technicolor or whatever we see in daily life.

"There's something off about the blood," he declared, almost to himself. "The color, the viscosity. It may not be as useful as his."

Well, of course not! What he held was not scarlet fresh-drawn blood, but as black-and-white as his own figure, which was, oddly for a medical procedure, a white shirt, black necktie, and sport jacket in some grayish tweed.

I took a closer, more focused look at the nurses. White

face masks covered their noses and mouths but what I'd taken for large alien-being "bug eyes" were not exactly that. They were almost black and human size but exaggerated by thick rims of kohl. They looked halfway between the Egyptian women on ancient friezes and modern supermodels sporting ultra-extreme "smoky eye" makeup.

I struggled to sit up. This was getting too absurd to scare me stiff. I could just get up and leave.

No, I couldn't do that. I *was* bound. I pulled against gauze wrist restraints at my hips. My ankles seemed free but I was still as helpless as a kitten up a tree or, more apropos, a sacred scarab beetle on its back.

At least a kitten had claws.

Speaking of which, why couldn't I feel the silver familiar? Why wasn't Irma goading me on with complaints and cheers? I felt oddly shrunken, wondering if that was the first result to a body that was being embalmed, ancient Egyptian–style. What did they do first? Drain the blood? *No!*

Terrified, struggling to maintain hope and sanity, I became my own intentional Irma.

Come on, Delilah! You've fought off group-home bully boys, werewolf and hyena packs. One CinSim and some thoroughly modern human nurses shouldn't unnerve you.

My inner voice sounded soft and weak. I wanted to just go and cower in a corner. I wanted to kick myself again for thinking and feeling that way. What was *wrong* with me?

Nothing, said a wee, small voice.

Everything, shouted voices I'd imagined all around me. "That's why we have to do *this*."

"The blood is the life," the man at the foot of my resting place announced, toasting with the vial of my probable "bad" blood. Hey, it worked fine for me. It was *my* blood! It was *my* life!

And the doc's dialogue line came from an old thirties movie, just like the CinSim.

That "blood is the life" guy had the same hammy tones as the Invisible Man in his mad scientist mode at the beginning of his self-named movie. They all had it, this guy and all the English-y curtain chewers from wee-hours cable rerun black-and-white movies.

I'd seen all those films in the group homes when I didn't dare join the other girls in a group bedroom where the punk boyz would hunt me. Those guys despised and avoided the "game room" with its Ping-Pong table as a place for "losers."

So I hid out there nights to watch old black-and-white films as truly "silent movies" because I didn't dare turn up the volume. I had to stay awake and sit up all night to fend off . . . mad scientists?

No, *boys!* Bad boys. Boyz. They'd been after me before any of the other girls. My white skin, my blossoming "mountains," everything wrong with me. Me.

I was breathing so hard I sounded like a bellows and some distant part of my brain diagnosed it as hyperventilating.

The blood *wasn't* the life. It was death. My death. Bad girls. Bad grrlz. I was one.

That's why I was here, being hurt. I would bleed. I would die and this man, this doctor, would preside.

At least now I recognized him, or his breed anyway.

Doctor. I must do, *be,* as doctor said.

Then another, more terrifying recognition clicked into place. He wasn't just any CinSim doctor, he was the Mother of All Vintage Film Doctors and the Father of the Monster.

Doctor Frankenstein.

Chapter Thirty-five

"WELL," VICTOR FRANKENSTEIN muttered to himself, "if the blood won't do that eliminates the draining process."

I felt the table I was on tilt more level. What was this, psychotic pinball? I realized with another chill that the damn table, and me, had been canted at an angle all along, the better to "decant" all the blood in my body.

Hadn't my earlier online researches revealed that the ancient Egyptian embalmers used just such a technique? Being treated like an antique corpse didn't appeal to me any more than playing a glamour corpse on a twenty-first-century forensics TV show.

"I really don't need you nursemaids anymore," Frankenstein absently told the six weird nurses. "I now have an entire, live body. With such a fresh beginning I can attempt a better resurrection than I got with the Bone Boy. I've never had much luck with assembled parts. The complete body is the key and the blood, not bones, is the life."

The nurses stirred uneasily, or eagerly, which was more than I could do at the moment.

This was an English actor—not today's Colin Farrell or Colin Firth but . . . Colin *Clive!*

The thirties' Frankenstein CinSim extended his monologue to better relish the sound of his own mellifluous voice. The breed just can't resist exposition.

"My royal masters and their minions certainly don't

need any more experience in embalming," he droned over my not-yet-dead body, "so I can hone my resurrection skills. First she must be killed, I think. *Hmmm.* I do find that part a bit queasy-making. I live to create life, not destroy it. I'll have trouble violating that directive. The royals must understand that one does not overcome one's assigned role that easily."

As he maundered on, I realized two things simultaneously. The scared, shrunken part of me that had been quavering on this table had known nothing of the Millennium Revelation and CinSims.

And, second, the part that did was coming back like ghostbusters.

If I wanted the silver familiar back, I had to call it. That couldn't be an ambiguous summons, so any love-hate thoughts of Achilles and Snow's long white locks were out. Besides, after what I'd let happen to Snow, I figured he'd *like* to see *my* blood drained about now.

I concentrated on my stouthearted Lhasa, Achilles, who would have tackled any five-times-bigger hyena on my behalf if he'd been alive. This Egyptian subterranean theme park was a place of resurrection. I'd seen Snow call a dragon to life from its ashes under the Inferno. I figured I could retrieve my late lamented and incredibly loyal dog from the lock of his hair I'd saved from the Kansas crematorium and recently added to the familiar.

This is Millennium Revelation Vegas, baby! Nothing dies here but lame onstage acts.

I took another deep breath while I still had one and called up the look and thought of Achilles with every shred of my bereft heart's longing.

There is someplace even more potent than thoughts of home, and it is the place in the heart where lost loves are enshrined. I conjured Achilles' spirit as hard as a six-year-old kid making a wish, with my eyes squeezed tight and my fingers curled into fists as tight.

Even at six I had stopped wishing for anything, but now I had memories of my love for Ric and the fierce risks I'd taken to save him.

I pictured Achilles bounding to me through foot-high Kansas snowdrifts, his white hair flowing behind him, baring his intent black eyes and long red tongue lolling against small rows of sharp white teeth.

"Ow!"

My wrists felt caught in the vicious steel-toothed jaws of an animal trap tightening like blood pressure cuffs. Then the gauze bindings shredded and my arms pulled free.

I eyed my stinging wrists, which now sported matching Wonder Woman sterling silver cuffs with turned-out, saw-tooth edges. *Ow!* for anyone who tried to grab my wrists.

I looked up to see Frankenstein contemplating a scalpel like Hamlet the skull of his dead court fool. I could kick my unbound feet into Frank's wimpy mad-scientist chest like a kangaroo and be up and outa here in a second.

Oops. While I was busy channeling my dead dog and silver sidekick, the three nurses on either side had pulled down their masks and torn off their gowns.

I gazed upon beauty bare: six sets of sparkling Hollywood-white vampire fangs and snowy banks of dead-white cleavage fit for a plus-size Victoria's Secret catalogue.

The twin silver cuffs melted up my arms and began streaking toward my bare neck.

"Chill, dear," one nurse leaned down to coo. "We're actually your bodyguards."

"Wait," Frankenstein cried as I clutched my winding sheet to my chest and scooted my rear down the stone table away from him. I didn't wait, but spun to get my feet to the floor. I turned to face him across the stone slab with its drainage gutter along one edge.

"Quack!" I accused. "You're not even a real doctor. They called you that in the movie, not the novel. At best you're a wildly out-of-date movie baron and at worst a sniveling has-been."

He stood astounded, maybe shocked to discover that someone else with a speaking role was in the chamber. Spotting the creepy black blood vial resting in the groove at the table's other end, I did an end run around the vampire nurses and snatched it back.

In my hand the true red color blossomed like a liquid rose.

The exit's behind him, Irma cried, back and rarin' to go. *Get us out of here.*

I was amazed to see the nurses filing out behind me through an opening flanked by two giant crocodile-headed statues. Old-time Egyptians were squirts. I lowered my head and ducked through. These passages sure weren't designed for Vikings.

I could sense the nurses running right behind me. The absence of hot, panting breaths on their parts gave me new goose bumps.

Bodyguards? Irma asked. *And I'm Rosie O'Donnell. Scram, please.*

That was the problem. Where to? I had to stop, look, and listen in the deserted passage.

While I surveyed the maze, the brides of Dracula times two were gathering around me, salivating.

"Her heartbeat is so much louder now that she's run," one observed to her sisters.

"I can still smell the fresh blood in that vial," another said, eyes closed with a gourmet's appreciation.

"The doctor said it was 'bad.' "

That wasn't the first time I'd heard that from medical personnel, such as the doctor who'd pumped quarts of blood into Ric's body and treated his wounds. I was tempted to defend the honor and quality of my blood, except that was suicidal at the moment.

"And *he* would be so angry," another vampire nurse pouted.

"Not if the blood was really okay."

"True. We could say she fell and cut her carotid artery open and we could only stanch the flow with our fangs."

"He wanted her alive."

"She still could be. A little."

By then my silver familiar had shifted into a three-inch-wide dog collar around my neck, dangling enough cascading chains of crosses to armor a Crusader.

"Ouch!" a nurse complained, stepping back to hold a defensive forearm against her smoky shadowed eyes. "You're blinding us with all that shining silver churchy hardware. It's very rude to bling us to death."

"Just remember you're 'bodyguards' and get me out of here," I said.

So, like six very busty blind mice, they blinked and took the lead, feeling their way along the dim passage with me clanking crucifixes behind them.

I kept glancing back. Frankenstein was apparently microchipped like all the CinSims. He remained a prisoner of his ageless new laboratory.

The passage ended with a familiar artifact, the chariot "pulled" by stone horses. No ravenous hyenas lingered here now, but I was more than happy to leap into the chariot, armored like a Crusader.

The vampires crowded against the stone horses' shiny, cold sides. I saw one pull on a gold rein that swung from the bridle.

What this ride would be worth in twenty-first-century terms I didn't even want to know. That much gold . . .

Since I had ridden this chariot down into the royal chambers below, I wasn't surprised when the entire supporting floor lifted us all up like a group of Disney World tourists on a disguised elevator.

I *was* surprised when I saw the hotel's marbled main floor with ranks of facing sarcophagi passing and vanishing below.

Then I remembered what my demon parking valet pal had said on my first visit. The chariot marked the entrance to the Karnak Hotel's new high-end condos. Only very high rollers would be allowed to buy into this modern obelisk of chutzpah and wealth on a scale to dwarf Dubai.

I couldn't wait to meet Mr. or Ms. Big when we reached the biggest penthouse in the sky.

Chapter Thirty-six

ONCE THE ELEVATOR stopped, the nurses pushed out the opening doors ahead of me. Hallways led away in a half-sunburst pattern. Directly ahead were gold-sheathed double doors high and wide enough to admit King Kong.

I hoped the big ape was not the next CinSim I encountered. I was in no mood to play Fay Wray, although I was appropriately attired in my bare feet and winding sheet, with the cross-hung chains now a discreet bib necklace at my collarbones.

Even my gaudy familiar had decided to play it close to the vest.

I crossed the threshold as the nurses vanished to either side, leaving me to encounter Ms. Big alone. And she was a rarity indeed.

"Welcome to my kingdom," she said. "I am Cleopatra."

Her "throne room," though, was a lavish modern penthouse suite featuring sprawling leather-upholstered sofas and ottomans you could sink into and glass-topped coffee tables sparkling with art glass decorations from the window-wall light.

I recognized Cleo at once, and, for once, *not* from my long lone nights watching old movies on the group home TVs. I hadn't seen her on any film or any rerun TV channel. She was a creature of memory and the ether, like real Egyptian royalty. She was a Cleopatra for the ages.

Her tissue-sheer gown was a half-circle attached by

jeweled bands at her wrists and upper arms, richly beaded in an intricate rayed design. Gold ribbons radiated from her nipples and the fork of her legs, providing such ineffective coverage the outfit would be banned in Boston to this day. An elaborate gilded headdress half-covered her thick dark hair.

Theda Bara as Cleopatra. Awesome. No footage of this silent-film queen portaying the Queen of the Nile in her first screen appearance remained to fascinate or amuse either lowly masses or sneering film critics. Someone, though, had recovered legendary lost footage to create this CinSim without peer. She was, as much as any moving being could be, even in Millennium Revelation Las Vegas, Cleopatra herself.

I moved my bare feet slowly over the icy thrill of granite floors, for she also was bare of foot, as if savoring the relief from the sandy sun-drenched climate we shared thousands of miles and many millennia apart.

"You are a traveler through the desert and have suffered much misadventure," she said. "My handmaidens will bathe and refresh you."

How could I resist this divinely corny invitation? Was I finally an extra in a vintage movie? Not a desirable corpse for a grue-drenched modern century but a guest in a desert land with an ancient code of hospitality to extend every civility as they had not been bestowed for centuries.

And then they could in good conscience kill me, of course.

But what a way to go!

THE VAMPIRE HANDMAIDENS, now attired in linen sheaths like fifties housewives (except the sheaths were see-through so they probably were Desperate Housewives), guided me through halls and chambers to a sunken pool tiled in lapis lazuli and carnelian.

I dropped the sheet like Miley Cyrus hadn't at that infamous *Vanity Fair* photo shoot. I wasn't worried. I was an adult and this was classy, folks! Art.

Clutching it together had helped me conceal the vial of my blood in my curled fist. Now I laid the tiny tube at the pool's edge before I waded into the limpid water and sank naked under its dubious cover. Wow. Not too hot, not too cold, but just right. A tepid, body-temp tub after all my stress. Perfect.

A wary kid who always used the gym dressing rooms, I'd suddenly shed my inhibitions with my winding sheet. Call it resurrection. Maybe being alive and in possession of all my blood had encouraged me to go with the flow.

Actually, the early-sixties Cleo had been a kind of role model of mine. You figure it: me seeing late-night reruns of the Technicolor Elizabeth Taylor *Cleopatra*: Liz: black hair, blue eyes, white skin. Okay, they said her eyes were violet. I could get contact lenses. Right?

The fanged handmaidens fluttered at the edges of the pool, laying out clothes and jewels. Yes! I so deserved this, and besides, I thought I had the whole scene figured out. Liz wasn't the only foxy chick on the planet.

I stepped out to be wrapped in white linen like the young cowboy on the streets of Laredo, only it was fine-woven white linen as sheer as silk and was a dressing gown, not a winding sheet.

The handmaidens outlined my eyes with kohl and painted my lips red and tinted my finger and toe nails. Just like a free makeover at Macy's.

They scented me with oils and perfumes and smoothed my tangled hair with an ivory comb carved with hyenas and elephants treading on really big snakes. (That ivory kinda bothered me. I used only cruelty-free beauty products at home, what few I had.) And why weren't the elephants treading on those really lethal hyenas?

I wondered which Hollywood Egyptian outfit I'd get and nearly swooned when they produced a filmy skirt and—truly a rare early film artifact—Theda Bara's gold metal bra with coiled serpents for cups and chain strap behind the neck

Okay, I'd been known to decry Princess Leia for having to wear a chain metal bikini in *Return of the Jedi*. Carrie Fisher had objected to her neck-high, wrist-and-ankle-long outfits in the first two *Star Wars* movies, I'd read, but she hadn't warmed up to the gold metal bikini: "When they took my clothes off, put me in a bikini and shut me up, I thought it was a strong indication of what the third film was."

Still, this funky bra was vintage history! Theda Bara hadn't had any such costume nudity or exploitation scruples. If she had, her *Cleopatra* film wouldn't be missing in action to this day. Besides, Ric with his boyhood belly dancer fetish would go berserk if he could see me now!

Sadly for us both, he was safe at home this time, and this was my solo film fantasy expedition. What a kick! I felt like Flash Gordon's girlfriend, Dale Arden, in the hands of the evil emperor Ming. (Look them up; those old movie serials rocked.)

And those thirties action babes always got an extreme makeover before being presented to the Main Man of Power for vague, sinister purposes . . . and then saved by the good guy. A little like Dorothy in the Emerald City, no? Kinda a male female fantasy. Like me sacrificing myself to Snow's Brimstone Kiss before I turned the tables and became Biker Babe and saved Ric.

Maybe I felt so safe running through the clichéd routine because a woman was in charge. Probably a mistake. Women could be soul sisters, then they could turn on a dime like Joan Crawford and Bette Davis and become rival bitches. Maybe like Lilith. Flip a coin and hope it's not silver.

Everything felt and smelled so good, though. I was full-bore me again with my in-board allies—the silver familiar and Irma—operative once more. I was beginning to get what was going on, big time, and who the players were, big time.

I tucked my precious blood vial into the only safe place in this scanty outfit and woman's ally since Eden—my tightly packed cleavage. Ready for my close-up, Mr. DeMille.

If I played along, I would learn much more.

CLEOPATRA WAS WAITING for me in the suite's lavish main room, arrayed on one sofa, but I greeted her again as "Theda" because a film buff knows several things.

One, "Theda Bara" is an anagram for "Arab Death," which was exotic fodder for film magazines in the last century's teens. Today it reflects international terrorism, but that's accidental.

She'd been born not-quite-plain Theodosia Goodman in Cincinnati. She'd made herself into the very first and supreme female film "vamp" to counter those Mary Pickford curly-topped blondes of the day.

Brunette, with Cupid-bow lips and heavy-lidded smoldering eyes, she always played heroines, or villainesses, who thirsted for men's bodies, blood, and/or soul. She was a century ahead of her time, and it's only fitting that most of her film footage is "lost" to this day.

All that remain are fading black-and-white photos of her in gowns so risqué they went down in film history, even if she herself is just a fading footnote now. And here I was sitting in a duplicate of one of the most scandalous, a metal bra.

As femmes fatales go, Theda was definitely out of style. She was wearing the most revealing Cleopatra outfit ever, an exquisitely embroidered transparent silk robe that covered the three major juicy bits with stars that radiated five gilt bands of decorative ribbon. I couldn't help gaping at the decorations.

Her figure was not twenty-first-century. She was small up top with most of her weight between waist and knees, a leftover of the Rubenesque days of yore we women all longed for, when thighs were queen instead of liposuctioned.

Me, I was better balanced, but no skeleton, and I intended to stay that way.

"Would you like some beer?" those bee-stung lips asked.

I knew the ancient Egyptians relished the stuff as much as NASCAR fans—in that searing climate, you'd be crazy not to. Thanks to Shezmou, I also knew that Egypt also had vineyards of the gods.

"Wine, if you have it."

"White, or red?"

Shezmou's bloodwine of pharaohs had intrigued me. White sounded common. I decided to stand out.

"Red."

I wouldn't drink it if it was really blood. We sat atop a giant ant hill of vampires, after all. Somehow, though, I felt secure up here, as if it was neutral territory.

Theda waved a serpent-braceleted hand. I heard the bare feet of my fanged nannies padding away.

My silver familiar transformed into twin upper-arm-twining cobras to duel her golden jewelry. Theda and I gave each other our most mysterious, serene gazes.

I waited for my well-earned wine.

Chapter Thirty-seven

EVER HEAR THE saying, "Pride goeth before a fall?" That really seemed tailor-made for Snow with his internationally successful rock band, his swooning fans and groupies, his Lucifer-ambitious Vegas hotel and subterranean kingdom of CinSims and dragon ashes.

Well, this time *my* pride was about to "goeth," and fast.

I heard the padding bare footsteps of the returning handmaiden nurses. I lifted a languid hand for my goblet of wine.

And got a Lalique angel glass in my hot little palm, glowing cherry-dark with red, red wine.

I reared back to regard my server because across from me Theda's Silver Screen pale gray complexion had become parchment white from diademed forehead to sandaled toes. Not to mention the midsection cellulite.

He was an Egyptian hunk in the burnished terra-cotta flesh, with that Michael Phelps Olympic hero of the Nile build, broad-shouldered and slim-hipped, hairless and muscled from collarbone to bare sandaled foot, except for his gorgeously bewigged head.

I accepted the wineglass from the proffered tray, of course, and watched Theda do likewise. If anything, she looked more surprised than I did.

I took it Shezmou was not the usual wine steward in these parts. I was happy to see him slipping into his other, less drastic role.

He greeted me with the same steady, flattering courtesy I could expect from Godfrey.

"These garments you wear are modern and overgaudy but they become you, Deliverer of Shezmou, though they would not much serve you when facing the abased immortal servants of the fallen pharaohs."

"You know each other?" Theda sat up to take notice. I was getting the house sommelier service while Shez ignored Her Royal Aspness.

"Were you responsible for the sublime scents and silky oils of my bath?" I asked him.

Shez bowed his godly head. "While I am indispensable to the rites of embalming and the judgment of the dead, I most enjoy serving the living with the soothing administrations of my sweet wines and rare oils. How do you find the wine?"

It would have been rude not to sip it, even if it *was* a vital bodily fluid. I was surprised by a taste similar to a light Merlot.

"Marvelous."

Theda stamped her sandaled foot and ankle wrapped in a cobra bracelet that was bound to remain just that, a gaudy gewgaw. Poor thing.

"My wine!" she ordered. "I am Cleopatra, Queen of Egypt."

Shez's Ric-gorgeous brown eyes gave her the once-over I'd get from a put-out Hollywood hairdresser.

"You are a resident CinSim, Orderer of Shezmou. You wear one of my hieroglyphs. My first obligation is to guests."

Of course! The most notoriously revealing gown in the history of film bore *three* five-armed stars signifying Shezmou over the naughty bits. The god guy was a born style maven.

"You'd do really well with your own exclusive shop on the Strip," I told him. "Do you have all the ancient recipes?"

His face stayed beautifully blank. He'd been made a male model ahead of his time.

"Formulas," I prodded, "for your oils and perfumes."

"I would need sesame, moringa, pine kernel, almond and castor oils."

Hmm. I could see the look of the line now: Cleopatra's beauty secrets for the ages. Shez pictured on the label in his boat with two stars over his cobra-topped but noble head. I wasn't sure about getting that moringa stuff . . . I'd groggle it when I got home.

After all, I'd redeemed Shezmou's immortal life and freed him from labeling a pillar in the Karnak underbelly for eternity. Why couldn't he pitch his own private label aboveground in the bustling commercial metropolis along the Strip? I owed Shez a decent future since his past had been so . . . static.

A high-end beauty and wine combo enterprise was fresh marketing. Wait! A wine bar with cosmetics to go. Chez Shez: "Drink in the secrets of everlasting health, beauty, and longevity . . ."

Yes, daydreaming my pet Egyptian god into a beauty brand was making me cocky now that I'd discovered friends in high places at the Karnak's priciest residence tower. Time for serious updating.

"Where is Bez?" I asked soberly.

Shez placed the white wineglass on the zebra-pattern coffee table in front of Theda and turned to me.

"Alas, Deliverer, he was taken to the throne room to be the royal jester. His guardian post farther below was eradicated by us and our allies, as you will recall."

"There isn't a food market there still?" I asked carefully, as Theda stared incomprehensibly.

In her silent-film day, actors did a lot of incomprehensible staring because the action froze as dialogue placards popped on the screen mid-scene.

"No." Shez was emphatic.

What would the Karnak vampires use for food then? I was afraid to speculate at the moment.

"And—" Maybe it was a couple sips of wine, but none of the exotica around me was distracting anymore. "—the great gray warrior . . . hound, was he seen . . . ?"

Now I knew why lushes cried in their beer. Or wine.

"No, Deliverer." Shez remained expressionless. He'd had millennia to master that Godfrey demeanor. "Not along the great River Nile in sky, on earth, or in the Underworld."

I took a deep breath, controlled myself. "But *you* are safe here?"

"Oh, yes. I have an entire floor for my wine and oil presses, my supplies. And, of course, I am free to leave anytime when darker duties with my lord Osiris call me."

"Great," I said.

I felt even safer here now that I'd seen Shezmou. Human "Deliverers" don't get their heads twisted off and he was in no way a vampire.

Still, I thought frantically while nodding and sipping socially. Just who could or would foot the bill for an ancient Egyptian demon god to take up his kinder, gentler hobbies?

"I hope to see you here again, Deliverer," Shez went on. "Your business proposition is most interesting. I do have time on my hands in these latter days."

Shez bowed to me (wow!) and eased out of the room. Whoever had provided Shez shelter couldn't be an out-and-out villain.

Or maybe not.

I heard a discreet clattering noise behind me and turned.

A human in living color was moving toward our conversation group. He had long gray hair and beard and was wearing a striped robe and using a walking staff. With the window-wall light at his back, he reminded me of nothing so much as Charlton Heston as the aged Moses from the 1958 *The Ten Commandments.*

The film had been a Cinemascope Technicolor epic. So this guy was not a CinSim. Nor was he even human, I realized, as he came close enough for me to recognize him.

It was Howard Hughes, dressed as urbanely as Hugh Hefner in a silk-lapeled robe, dragging his IV pole of thinned blood with him like an imitation of Marley's Ghost in chains.

Holy Horror! Imagine. Those two HH-initialed old guys, twins suffering from mogulism and lechery, still going, after all these decades.

A handmaiden nurse scurried to catch up to Hughes and scoot the wheeled IV stand into place next to him when he grasped a sofa back and swooned more than sat on the goose-down cushion. I assumed it was goose-down because (A) he could afford it and (B) the way it swelled up around him bespoke really ritzy upholstery.

Besides, that almost skeletal bony frame needed all the padding it could command.

"Miss Street," he greeted me, or rather, my boobs. "I must say it is an aesthetic pleasure to see that bit of costuming worn by one born to fill it properly."

Theda writhed on her divan and squealed her displeasure.

Hughes ignored her at first, then frowned. "Go tint your nipples or something else vampy."

Theda rose and scurried away, giving me a poisonous look. Another enemy; join the club.

"There goes another secret piece of film history for you, my vintage-film lover." Hughes leaned close enough to whisper. "Seeing the surviving photos of Miss Bara's Cleopatra costuming inspired me to invent the first steel-underwire push-up bra for Jane Russell in *The Outlaw*. Miss Russell also possessed your assets in abundance. Or perhaps I should put it vice versa. So you owe me for your support."

"Laundromats everywhere must curse your name," I told him, unimpressed. "When I was in college, bra underwires were always escaping during the spin cycles and breaking the equipment."

His bony shoulders shrugged. "Progress has its price. My point is that engineering can be applied to the trivial, a woman's undergarments, and to the sublime, a marvel of the centuries, say, an Egyptian pyramid."

I wanted to shrug back but realized that would only incite the undead old lech. I'd thought being escorted here by a harem of nurses and greeted by Theda made this a "just we girls" night or I'd never have allowed the sex-slave pampering bit.

"You needn't fear me personally, Miss Street. I am far too careful to take my blood from any living being and am too old and wise for sex. Besides, Shez is prettier than you; pity he's such a remorseless god. Anyway, do you know how many germs fester in the human mouth?" He shuddered delicately. "I admit I still like to look, but, alas, cannot touch and have not for many decades."

I nodded, almost sympathetically. Even when he'd been alive and first came to Vegas, back in the late sixties, he'd sequestered himself on the top floor of the Desert Inn and bought a local TV station so it would play only the movies he wanted to see, all night long.

How freaky to remember that's pretty much what kiddie me did nights in the Kansas group homes forty-some years later: stay up all night getting hooked on old movies.

I wondered what he feared, what had scared Howard Hughes so much he went from playboy engineer, inventor, filmmaker, flier, and mogul to a crazy, lonely, emaciated, old billionaire hermit?

"Your look of pity is misplaced. I have more money and power than I ever did. Any one of my nurse attendants would rip your throat out at the lift of my little finger and drain your blood for my continual, moving 'cocktail' by IV tube."

"It's not pity, Mr. Hughes. It's curiosity."

"Partly that too, yes. You are annoyingly curious, also lucky I've taken a liking to you. Do you know how long it's been since I've done that? Would you consider a seven-year exclusive contract?"

"You don't make films anymore."

"Are you sure?"

"I guess not. I didn't expect to find you were the literal top man at the Karnak either."

His thin lips smiled, reminding me of dashing forties photos of him looking like Clark Gable's double. I guess a lot of men did in that era. Pencil-thin mustache, fedora at a jaunty angle. They could be the hero, or the villain, in a hundred different enjoyably forgettable noir crime dramas.

"You are always so dependably . . . buoyant," he said, glancing south of my collarbones again. "No one has made me smile in thirty years."

"That's great, HH, but an hour or so ago I was about to become steak tartare for a demented CinSim."

"Frankenstein can be obsessive and he's no engineer, that's for sure, but he demonstrated promise for weird science."

"He's a CinSim escapee from a piece of fiction written almost two hundred years ago as a moral and philosophical fable."

"The point is, he intended to create life. We are now in an era when life can be scientifically helped along at both the beginning and the end of the cycle. And now death can be defeated, by extreme measures sometimes, as in my case, or by something as tried and true as CPR and its Kiss of Life."

His watery eyes fixed on mine. I appreciated the change of focus but wasn't going to say a word about Ric. No one but Grizelle knew I'd accepted Snow's Brimstone Kiss.

"You're saying," I ventured, "that if you'd waited a few more years you wouldn't have had to make yourself into a vampire to stay in business."

"Simplistic, but yes."

"So why let some CinSim loon loose in the Karnak?"

"I own it, for one thing. Yes, I own a lot of things no one suspects I do. Always did. For another, I'm aware that in this post–Millennium Revelation world, the ancient ways might hold secrets of life and death that are every bit as effective and useful as any that modern science can explore."

He sat back. "Drink your wine, Miss Street, not everyone gets a glass hand-delivered by the Lord of Blood himself."

"How do I know it's not sweetened blood," I asked, "not bull's blood, say?"

"Because Shezmou is the god of wine, as Bacchus was for the Greeks. I'm tickled you found and freed him. He is quite the fan, Delilah Street, and proud of his vintages.

The one in your hand derived from a formula many millennia old and the instant-aging magic of a reawakened god."

Millennium wine. That would be a commercial hit too. So would my Vampire Sunrise cocktail, now that I'd discovered the impulsive title was a literal description of up-and-coming vampires in Vegas, from the Gehenna's Sansouci to the Karnak legions.

I sipped ancient wine again while Howard leaned his head back against the sofa pillows. "What impression does the Karnak entrance give you?"

"Those massive inscribed black pillars so close together? They create shade from the sun but their immensity makes you aware of how architecturally awesome the Egyptians were."

"They also obscure the fact that the center of the hotel is the top of a massive pyramid built deep into the sand and stone below the Strip level."

"I didn't see any pointy top anywhere inside the hotel."

"You weren't meant to."

"I see. The Luxor Hotel had already claimed the pyramid as an external image and brand since the nineteen nineties."

"I could have bought and leveled the Luxor and built my own pyramid-shaped building openly here."

"Why hide a pyramid inside a temple facade?"

"You must understand that a pyramid was not just a massive tomb and monument to some old man's ego."

Was that an actual twinkle in Howard Hughes's colorless eye? He snorted with elder glee.

"I do so relish your quaint moralizing stance, Miss Street. Quite takes me back. That has been so long out of fashion. My revolutionary undergarment got *The Outlaw* and Miss Russell's bust delayed from public release for two years, but when it finally came out it took down the old Hayes office blue-nose censorship."

"*You* were the real 'outlaw.' "

His rat's-nest-haired head bowed. "How you make me wish I was the man I used to be. You are as gorgeously waspish as Katharine Hepburn."

"You dated her?"

He merely smirked.

"I *mean, she* dated *you*?"

"Kate was an innovator too."

I'd actually started to succumb to his tattered charm . . . until I remembered he'd had the gorgeous Vida attacked and turned by a vampire merely to provide an attractive vehicle for his own conversion to Undead.

Playboys weren't real men and they really were playing for keeps when it came to satisfying their own wants.

"She didn't much like me, either, in the end," he noted. "But men like me don't care about trifling emotions. We see the future, and you and I are sitting atop it."

"A huge ant hill of ancient hubris? The Egyptian royals have about as much substance and depth as the Nile at its lowest level before the flood. Granted, the civilization and its beliefs and rites were elaborate and impressive, but it's dead and gone except for these ghastly bloodsucking relics."

He shook his head.

"I told you not to underestimate the pyramids as showy tombs. They were really ancient experimental laboratories. 'Resurrection machines,' as some scholars put it. They were after that most prized human goal: eternal life. Call it science. Call it religion. It exists in every culture and every time period.

"Dead bodies are buried, mummified, preserved, marked, and noted. That is not morbid; it is the expression of an ardent, unquenchable life wish. And I want it not just for my admittedly selfish self, Miss Delilah Street, but for my medical interests. I invented the hospital bed, too, you know."

His piercing look made me fear he'd known about Ric's Inferno recovery room.

"I want what I have—long and active life—for every human on the planet, for every child dying of leukemia and every dismissed so-called senior falling into dementia."

I gulped some more of the Lord of Blood's elderberry wine to calm my latest shock.

Whatever else Howard Hughes may have been and was . . . inventor, romancer, aviation pioneer, real estate king, crackpot . . . I now saw him as a creature whose dreams were as outsize as those tombs of the pharaohs we call the pyramids and that Hughes considered Tinker Toys for immortality.

"Yet," I said, "the aristocracy and upper scribe and artisan classes who'd followed the pharaohs into immortality and vampirism bred herds of generations of true Egyptians to feed on beneath this very hotel you now own and operate. You're responsible for those bloodsuckers."

He gazed at the pale red liquid filling the opaque plastic tube piercing his inner elbow.

"Bloodsucking, like sex or any personal exchange of bodily fluids, is so pre–Millennium Revelation. I plan to convert the Twin Pharaohs to my method of ingesting purchased donated blood. The others will follow their example."

"Methadone for heroine addicts or a 'nicotine patch' for the blood-addicted? That doesn't work very well for smokers."

"I'll find a way to make it fashionable. People of any era fall for that."

I pictured the Twin Pharaohs sitting on their thrones side by side, golden IV poles beside them. Then I recalled the albino cobras that I'd seen flanking the dais in what *you* might call "real" life, but *I* wouldn't.

"You could route the IVs through the uraeus," I suggested, "the royal cobra symbol. Make a daily ceremony of it for the royals and the whole court."

His watery eyes gleamed. "What a swell idea, Delilah. Boobs *and* brains. I always liked that combination, you notice. I may have to hire you full-time. You'll make a moral man and vampire of me yet."

He watched my skeptical reaction. "Don't forget the house toast here at the Karnak, Delilah."

"What would that be, Mr. Hughes? 'To Mummy'?"

He actually cracked another smile, exposing sharp brown teeth that would never sink into a rare porterhouse steak or a neck again. Did I feel another flash of pity for his phobic afterlife?

"Every billionaire needs a court jester these days. No. The house toast on this occasion is to you, Delilah Street, and our continuing business association."

He lifted the clear tubing that conveyed the thin pink fluid that kept him undead. As I raised my glass, he intoned, "You live again, you live again forever, here you are young once more forever."

"I still consider myself pretty young, Mr. Hughes."

"And pretty too. Call me Howard. Those words are not mine. They've been uttered for millennia during the final phase of the mummification ritual. I have made it my own motto."

"You do realize I'm a freelance investigator. I work for whomever I choose."

"You'll find, as you've begun to suspect, that choice is

not what it once was in this time and this place. Still, your mobility and contacts with all the parties in our little war of superpowers here in Vegas make you useful."

He shook his head sadly.

"Only, however, for as long as you're able to please all of us equally, if not all at the same time."

I drained the Lord of Blood's wineglass and rose to leave.

"I'll need to change into my street clothes."

"'Street' clothes," Howard Hughes giggled. He was very old and perhaps a trifle senile.

A CinSim Cleopatra appeared in the doorway to escort me back to the bathing chamber. It wasn't Theda, though, but her nineteen thirties version, Claudette Colbert, glittering in a silver-gray winged metal headdress I coveted so much I could feel the familiar arm cuffs bracing for flight to my forehead, and mentally headed them off. *No!*

Claudette had slinked through that entire 1934 film in gowns of hokey Hollywood glam lamé. She even wore a collar of oversized pearls, not exactly a desert kingdom staple.

Still, I choked back an urge to curtsy and left, wondering how I'd get out of here after I was out of the queen costume and into my own clothes.

As I turned to exit the main room, the double doors leading to the penthouse broke open, both at once.

Now what?

"MORE UNEXPECTED GUESTS?" Hughes gurgled. "For me?"

I turned, braced for a pack of fanged mummies. And me with all my major arteries exposed by my dancing girl outfit.

The silver familiar, restrained no longer, was expanding

into growing lengths of chain mail around my naked midriff, and then it stopped, cold. Maybe my hokey gold-metal bra offended its sensibilities.

I grabbed the nearest weapon, Hughes's metal IV pole.

If I ripped out his IV using it as a lance, tough.

A big brown hand stayed my arm.

Not Hughes's brown-spotted, curve-nailed claw.

I turned back to face the impassive Shezmou.

"Wait," he ordered.

Is that any way to treat a Deliverer?

When I spun back to face the door, I was floored by the oncoming leaping furred length and weight of an attacking royal hyena.

I screamed and fell back against Shezmou. Where's your grateful god when you need him? My arms and hands had lifted instinctively to guard my throat.

Too late! Canine claws scratched my shoulders as a hot wave of animal breath scorched my face and closed eyes. Wet saliva swiped me from cheek to forehead, deafening my ears in between.

My eyelashes were almost glued shut, but I was able to stagger back and open them.

I was waltzing with a huge canine form as tall as myself, my arms pushing off the powerful furred chest.

Someone grabbed the creature's collar at my shoulder height and pulled it off me.

Collar?

"Quicksilver?" I screamed, looking from blue eyes to the brown ones behind them. "Ric?" I looked back and forth again. "Ric? Quicksilver?"

"Where did you find him?" I asked as Quick dropped down to four-legged height.

Both looked remarkably well and even smug.

"More unexpected company," came Howard Hughes's long-suffering quaver. "Nurses! I need you. Shezmou will let them out when this abominably unsanitary reunion is over. Send in the crime scene cleaners then."

I heard a fading clatter and cooing, but could not have cared less. The Cleos had vanished too. I sank weak-kneed onto the sofa, running my hand over Quicksilver's furred head and shoulders, not believing he was alive.

He sat, his huge head even with mine, soulful blue eyes fixed on me.

"I thought you were . . . you were—"

He whimpered in that understanding way dogs have, and licked my upper arms and shoulders. It was only then that I saw his overeager greeting had left huge red claw marks on my Sunset Park–pinkened skin.

Two long, warm licks and my skin was lily-pale again, even the remaining sunburn erased.

I turned to Riç, who'd sat beside me, and ran my fond hands over his face and shoulders too. He was wearing his Sinkhole five o'clock shadow and weathered gang leathers and felt yummy solid.

"You are freaking amazing, Montoya. You found Quicksilver like you said. You raised him from the dead? How? Where? How did you two find *me* up here?"

Ric eyed my face hungrily, in his own way lapping up my amazement and joy.

"He's still totally mortal," Ric said. "I found *you* once I found him. You always say he could track you through anything. That included the Karnak complex up to the highest floor."

My restless fingers were petting their forms like a blind person's seeing through feel alone. Ric's smooth warm skin, Quick's warm rough coat. I kissed them both, and the Brimstone Effect seemed utterly gone from my lips and my soul. I wondered if my painful apology to Snow had undone its lingering power.

I preferred plain, mortal joy and the reunion we shared.

My fingers curled around Quick's collar, feeling that the silver circles had thinned to the faintest crescent slivers. My other hand skimmed down Ric's back, feeling only smooth unwelted muscle.

"How did you find him?" I asked Ric.

Ric's grin was white as snow. "Actually, Haskell found him in the Sinkhole."

"Half-balled Haskell? That creepy ex-cop who would have raped me if he could?"

"That's a colorful nickname you gave him, Del," Ric said, "but it no longer applies. Actually, *Quicksilver* found *Haskell*. I doubt this dog ever forgets. Haskell threatened to shoot Quicksilver, remember? So you penned up the dog when Haskell tried as much to molest as arrest you at the Enchanted Cottage."

"You caught up with the creep later in the Sinkhole and beat him up."

"Right. Then somebody or some*thing* came along and gave him half a castration. Fast-forward to now. Quicksilver surfaced in the Sinkhole after the gods brought the walls of the Karnak feed lot tumbling down, encountered the bad guy, and finished the job.

"The ex-cop is No-balled Haskell now."

My jaw dropped, which was an excuse for Ric to soul-kiss me. Quicksilver whined and put a paw on my bare thigh. Velvet paw.

This was getting awkward.

"I need to get my street clothes," I said for the second time that evening, and on this occasion no jokes were made on my name. “We need to get down to the Strip and away from here.”

“Agreed; much to talk about away from here.” Ric’s fingers traced the snaky metal coils of my cobra bra. “No need for you to change clothes first. Quicksilver and I are experienced bodyguards and what you’re wearing is just right for my plans for the rest of tonight.”

Quicksilver subsided to his stomach, nose on paws.

“I agree you must leave,” came a deep manly voice. “I will escort you out.”

“Shez!” Ric greeted the demon lord with a grin. “You’re looking a lot less dusty and bloody.”

“All of you also.”

Shez handed me a gilt-embossed Karnak shopping bag filled with my jeans, shirt, and shoes along with a supply of carved carnelian bottles of bath products, and an Egyptian-collared cape.

“I retrieved your articles from the area below. I am Shezmou, maker of embalming oils and rare scents. I am also Lord of the Slaughter. I go where I please here and will until the sun sets forever on the world.”

“Good thinking,” I said, gratefully covering my Rio beach condition with the cape. “Thanks, Shez.”

I checked to ensure I still had the vial of my blood I’d snatched from the embalming table and had tucked into my pushed together cleavage, feeling very Jane Russell.

From the dilation of Ric’s pupils, I looked very Jane Russell too.

We rose, all three, and left with dignity and no fear.

We had a god on our side.

Chapter Thirty-eight

HERMIE PRODUCED RIC's Vette at the drive-up. Shezmou tipped him with a real coin of some kind. It didn't impress the parking valet demon. Hermie shrugged and bowed us good-bye.

When Ric took the driver's seat, he tipped the delighted demon a fifty-dollar bill. Quicksilver bounded into the front seat after me, so I was squashed in the middle, sandwiched by my two dearest and now really nearest.

I looked in the rearview mirror. A sedate tourist couple driving an electric-powered Caddy convertible sixty years newer than mine was flagging the Lord of the Slaughter to unload their luggage.

I couldn't help laughing, as we all left the Karnak, grinning from ear to ear at our escape and reunion, Quicksilver most of all.

It was still dark, so I dug the neon-filtering sunglasses out of the glove compartment and we cruised the Strip in shades like Hollywood celebs.

At the Nightwine estate, Ric pulled his car under the Enchanted Cottage's porte cochere. We went inside, using the door card in my bagged jeans. We installed Quicksilver by his ever-full food bowl and ever-fresh water bowl in the kitchen.

He eyed us in turn, refusing to indulge. He suspected what was coming.

So did my hormones.

Ric took my hand and led me upstairs. I figured I'd soon have my movie-poster body ravished with Rudolph Valentino moves. Or vice versa. Goodie.

Instead, Ric paused mid-stairway. His cocked knee blocked the stairs and me. *Hmm.* Did he have something kinky in mind with me over his knee?

Yeah. Talk, he requested. Imagine a guy wanting to talk first.

I mentioned that.

"That's a talk-killer outfit you're wearing," he agreed, pulling me so close his Gypsy leathers creaked, "but I need some answers first."

I put my arms around his neck and inhaled a heady perfume of leather and bar-smoke and also scented soap traces from both of us. That's my pseudo-Sinkhole undercover guy, pitted-steel rough on top and civilized silk underneath.

"So," I said, "do I resemble that naughty magazine cover that gave you a premature kick-start on puberty?"

"*Sí, señorita.* First, I want to know how you ended up at the Karnak again to get the temple dancer makeover. Last I saw of my Delilah, she was taking down temples, not sending up temperatures."

I nuzzled his five o'clock shadow. It wasn't just makeup. If he skipped shaving twice, Ric was primed to sell men's cologne in *Male* magazine.

"It's all the real thing," I said, pushing my torso against him so he'd get to the action *I* needed.

"Why would that old lech Howard Hughes, who I noticed didn't stick around for introductions after Quicksilver and I arrived, give you highly collectible seduction gear? What were you two doing in the Karnak's condo-tower penthouse?"

"Details, Ric. You don't want to lose the moment with details."

I'd pushed off him so he could fully appreciate my outfit. I felt the silver familiar slipping its form as hip chain, so my torso had started quivering even before Ric touched my skin.

He wet his forefinger (*swoon*) and slowly dragged it across the filmy skirt's top just beneath my bared navel.

"Details," he mocked me. My insides clenched with excitement while his finger pushed into my outie. "Your costume could use a little ring here."

As his forefinger continued its effective navel engagement, a blue-topaz-studded silver ring snagged the tip.

He frowned. "When did you get that piercing?"

"When you weren't looking close enough, obviously, *amor*."

Damn silver familiar was now butting into my romantic interludes instead of hiding out as a discreet toe ring.

"I'm looking close now," Ric said. "What's going on? You at the Karnak again. You in Hughes's harem?"

"I had a misstep in a mirror gone bad. Last night I finally tracked Lilith through the Snow groupies. She and I had a brief one-on-one in a dark alley. Didn't go well and the Karnak hyenas had tracked me there. I jumped through a reflecting glass door. Knocked myself out in a travel agent's office, I think, and ended back at the Karnak."

I made a face, remembering awakening to a situation so like my recurring nightmare.

"Hughes had somehow grabbed Shez after the pillars fell, so was keeping an eye out for me too and got me to the safety of his penthouse.

"Frankly, Ric," I said, not meaning it, since I was going to skip the weirdness of Frankenstein's experimental embalming operation until I knew more about it, "I've worked for Hughes before. He claims he bought the Karnak before he discovered the vampire empire underneath. He's a nonpracticing vamp himself and finds intimate relations too unsanitary to do more than lust and look. He hopes to convert all vampires to his IV-based sustenance system."

Ric snorted his opinion of *that* experiment.

"He's also a CinSim buff like Hector."

"And you."

"And me. Hughes adopted Shez as a personal wine and bath steward. That's how I got the Queen of the Nile makeover. You don't like?"

Ric decided more torture was needed. He wet his forefinger in *my* mouth (*quasi-come!*) to shut me up. Then he traced my bare and ticklish midriff up to the bottom coil of my Hollywood vamp bra. I was writhing like the gold serpents, as much to avoid giggling as to invite more exploration.

His finger followed the coil on my right breast and stopped at the barely covered center. "This doesn't match," he said. "Unusual for you."

I looked down. A pair of silver chain pastie tassels shimmered with motion. *Shoot!* The familiar was living up to its name in triplicate now!

"Ah, no. Ric. Ah, I guess I should mention that some of the silver jewelry I wear used to be a lock of my lost Lhasa apso's coat. It . . . attached itself to me and changes into . . . things."

"Like those silver whips I glimpsed you wielding at the Karnak, and the silver staff? I thought you'd grabbed them from fallen Egyptian warriors."

"Not exactly. Wow. Don't stop doing that! Oh, yes. Definitely."

That roaming forefinger had made a circle with his thumb and snapped my right silver tassel, making it shimmy-shimmy.

"So this silver familiar has possibilities as a sex toy?" he said.

"Yeah, I guess. So do you."

Ric laughed. "Your skin is so soft." He buried his face in my shoulder and hair. "You smell so good."

Shezmou definitely had a future in the personal products industry.

"I know you're not telling me something about your latest adventure at the Karnak," he said, nibbling on my neck. "Confess or we don't go a step farther."

"Excessive force, Montoya! You are such an irresistible interrogator. Okay. I woke up on a Karnak embalming table with Hughes's silly masked vampire nurses circled around. Just like my kiddie alien abduction nightmares. I almost lost me . . . my current self, for a while there."

Ric crushed me close. "Damn. I knew something worse had happened, Delilah. That's it. We're going to Wichita. Social services or that convent school you attended must have records or staff who can identify the originating trauma."

"You sound like your adopted mother the shrink. I don't know, Ric—"

"It might help you find out more about Lilith and your allergy to the missionary position. And, *querida,* I want you wanting me every which *way* we can do it."

I nodded, shakily. "Speaking of which, can we finally do it now? My way."

Ric resumed leading me up the stairs while my insides did cartwheels. He paused at seeing us in the mirror at the hall's end.

Did Lilith lurk behind there, in my own reflection? Was she watching? Was Snow spying on our every move through the medium of his lock of white hair in the silver familiar?

Ask me if I cared.

No. I was heading to my bedroom with my lover.

I eyed Ric's reflection in the mirror. His strong arms around my midriff were holding me up, supporting me. We were about to, yeah, make whoopee and come like crazy.

We were young, mostly alive, and together, despite everyone else's best and worst efforts.

His embrace was so tight, though, that the vial of my blood—stashed and forgotten between my pumped-up Howard Hughes boobs—squirted free. It smashed to the hardwood floor as Ric crooned major somethings in my ear and swept me away from the mirror into the bedroom.

I glanced back at the tiny glittering splotch of blood and broken glass. Maybe not such a good omen.

But, at the moment—*ooh, hombre mío*—who the . . . flying fey cared?

In the distance, a dog or a werewolf howled, or a distant police siren wailed.

Business as usual in post–Millennium Revelation Las Vegas rocked on.

So did we.

Resources

Actors, Roles, Films, and TV Series

The Adventures of Robin Hood (1938)
http://www.filmsite.org/adve.html

Dale Arden [played by Jean Rogers (1936, 1938) and Carol Hughes (1940)]
http://en.wikipedia.org/wiki/Dale_Arden

Asta
(see *The Thin Man*)

The Avengers TV series (1965–69)
http://theavengers.tv/

Theda Bara
http://en.wikipedia.org/wiki/Theda_Bara
http://silentladies.com/Ladies.html (see: The Vamps)
http://www.tartcity.com/thedabara.html

Ingrid Bergman (as Ilsa)
http://www.ingridbergman.com/
(see also *Casablanca*)

Rick Blaine
(see Humphrey Bogart, *Casablanca*)

Humphrey Bogart
http://www.humphreybogart.com/

James Bond (as portrayed by Sean Connery)
http://www.007.info/Sean_Connery.asp

Billie Burke (as Glinda)
http://www.kansasoz.com/infogoodwitch.htm

Casablanca (1942)
http://www.vincasa.com

Lon Chaney Jr.
http://www.lonchaney.com/lc5/jr/lcjrmain.html
(see also *The Wolf Man*)

Nick and Nora Charles
(see *The Thin Man*)

Cinderella (1950)
http://disney.go.com/vault/archives/movies/cinderella/cinderella.html

Colin Clive
http://classic-horror.com/masters/colin_clive

Claudette Colbert
http://www.classicmoviefavorites.com/colbert/cleopatra.html

Cleopatra (1917)
http://www.silentera.com/PSFL/data/C/Cleopatra1917.html

Cleopatra (1934)
http://www.filmsite.org/cleo.html

Cleopatra (1963)
http://en.wikipedia.org/wiki/Cleopatra_(1963_film)

Cowardly Lion
(see Bert Lahr)

Joan Crawford
http://www.joancrawfordbest.com/menupage.htm

Bette Davis
http://www.bettedavis.com/about/bio.htm

Cecil B. DeMille
http://www.cecilbdemille.com/bio.html
(see also *Sunset Boulevard*)

Dracula (1931)
http://www.bmoviecentral.com/bmc/reviews/34-duanesreviews/64-dracula-1931-75-minutes.html

The Enchanted Cottage (1945)
http://movies.nytimes.com/movie/15781/The-Enchanted-Cottage/overview

Carrie Fisher
http://www.answers.com/topic/carrie-fisher
(see also *Return of the Jedi*)

Frankenstein (1931)
http://www.filmsite.org/fran.html

Clark Gable
http://www.clarkgable.com/

Dorothy Gale (played by Judy Garland)
http://oz.wikia.com/wiki/Dorothy_Gale

Gone With the Wind (1939)
http://www.filmsite.org/gone.html

Flash Gordon (played by Buster Crabbe in 1936–40 film serials)
http://en.wikipedia.org/wiki/Buster_Crabbe

Audrey Hepburn
http://www.reelclassics.com/Actresses/Audrey/audrey.htm

Katharine Hepburn
http://katehepburn.tripod.com/

Charlton Heston
http://www.reelclassics.com/Actors/Heston/heston.htm
(see also *The Ten Commandments*)

Howard Hughes
http://www.1st100.com/part3/hughes.html

The Invisible Man (1933)
http://www.geocities.com/Hollywood/Hills/4337/invman.htm

Indiana Jones (played by Harrison Ford)
http://www.indianajones.com

King Kong (1933)
http://www.filmsite.org/kingk2.html

Bert Lahr
http://findarticles.com/p/articles/mi_g1epc/is_bio/ai_2419200675

Hedy Lamarr
http://www.hedylamarr.com
(see also *Samson and Delilah*)

Dorothy Lamour
http://www.tcmdb.com:80/participant.jsp?participantId=107751

Lash La Rue
http://www.b-westerns.com/lash.htm

Laura (1944)
http://www.filmsite.org/laur.html

Peter Lorre
http://www.reelclassics.com/Actors/Lorre/lorre.htm

The Lost Weekend (1945)
http://www.filmsite.org/lostw.html

Myrna Loy
http://en.wikipedia.org/wiki/Myrna_Loy
(see also *The Thin Man*)

Bela Lugosi
http://www.belalugosi.com

Perry Mason (played by Raymond Burr)
http://www.perrymasontvshowbook.com

Ray Milland
http://www.reelclassics.com/Actors/Milland/milland.htm
(see also *The Lost Weekend*)

Ming the Merciless (played by Charles Middleton in 1936–40 film serials)
http://en.wikipedia.org/wiki/Ming_the_Merciless

My Man Godfrey (1936)
http://www.filmsite.org/myman.html

The Outlaw (1943)
http://en.wikipedia.org/wiki/The_Outlaw

(Mrs.) Emma Peel (played by Diana Rigg)
http://www.youtube.com/watch?v=F02llSrNfnQ&feature=related
(See also *The Avengers* and Diana Rigg)

William Powell
http://themave.com/Powell/

Otto Preminger
http://www.reelclassics.com/Directors/Preminger/preminger.htm

Claude Rains
http://www.meredy.com/clauderains/

Return of the Jedi (1983)
http://www.fandango.com/returnofthejedi_40330/movieoverview

Diana Rigg
http://www.nndb.com/people/041/000023969/
http://www.youtube.com/watch?v=F02llSrNfnQ&feature=related

Jane Russell
http://www.lovegoddess.info/Jane.htm
(see also *The Outlaw*)

Samson and Delilah (1949)
http://www.absoluteastronomy.com/topics/Samson_and_Delilah_(1949_film)

Snow White and the Seven Dwarfs (1937)
http://disney.go.com/vault/archives/movies/snow/snow.html

(Mr.) Spock (played by Leonard Nimoy)
http://en.wikipedia.org/wiki/Spock

Starsky and Hutch
http://www.starskyandhutchonline.com/

Sharon Stone
http://www.sharonstone.net

Sunset Boulevard (1950)
http://www.greatestfilms.org/suns.html

Larry Talbot
(see Lon Chaney Jr., *The Wolf Man, The Wolfman*)

Elizabeth Taylor
http://en.wikipedia.org/wiki/Elizabeth_Taylor

The Ten Commandments (1956)
http://www.youtube.com/watch?v=pXyEcMG5bDs

The Thin Man (1934)
http://themave.com/Powell/powloy/films/thman/ThinMan.htm

Ugarte
(see *Casablanca*, Peter Lorre)

Rudolph Valentino
http://www.rudolph-valentino.com

The War of the Worlds (1953)
http://en.wikipedia.org/wiki/The_War_of_the_Worlds_(1953_film)
http://www.war-of-the-worlds.org/

Orson Welles
http://en.wikipedia.org/wiki/Orson_Welles

Wicked Witch of the East
http://oz.wikia.com/wiki/Wicked_Witch_of_the_East

The Wizard of Oz (1939)
http://www.filmsite.org/wiza.html

The Wolf Man (1941)
http://www.lonchaney.com/wolfman.html

The Wolfman (2009)
http://www.thewolfmanmovie.com/

Selected Websites on Ancient Egypt

Anubis
http://www.touregypt.net/featurestories/anubis.htm

Bez
http://www.thekeep.org/~kunoichi/kunoichi/themestream/bes.html

The British Museum: Ancient Egypt
http://www.ancientegypt.co.uk/

The Griffith Institute: Tutankhamun: Anatomy of an Excavation: The Howard Carter Archives, Photographs by Harry Burton (Anubis emblem upon pole and stand)
http://www.griffith.ox.ac.uk/gri/carter/202-p0673.html

Shezmou
http://www.touregypt.net/featurestories/shesmu.htm

Tour Egypt!
http://www.touregypt.net (various articles)

Maggot Art

Rebecca O'Flaherty, creator of the *Maggot Art*™ educational curriculum, consults with Northern California law enforcement and teaches investigators how to recognize and collect insects from crime scenes. (http://www.maggotart.com/about.cfm)

Delilah's Darkside Inferno Bar Cocktail Menu

Vampire Sunrise Cocktail

Invented in *Vampire Sunrise*

"Umm. Subtle yet spicy . . . for modern women like us."

—Psychic psychologist Helena Troy Burnside in *Vampire Sunrise*

6 ice cubes
1½ ounces pepper vodka
½ ounce DeKuyper "Hot Damn!" Hot Cinnamon Schnapps
4–5 ounces orange juice, well shaken
1 ounce Alizé Gold Passion orange cognac
½–1 ounce grenadine

Put ice cubes in 12-ounce highball glass. Pour in pepper vodka and cinnamon schnapps, add orange juice to fill to desired level. Add Alizé. Last, pour in grenadine, which will settle to the bottom. Add ice to drink as it melts, creating a longer and more sensual experience. This drink is no hit-and-run vampire bite.

Albino Vampire Cocktail

Invented in *Dancing with Werewolves*

"A sweet, seductive girly drink, but with unsuspected kick."

—Werewolf mob enforcer Sansouci in *Brimstone Kiss*

1 jigger white crème de cacao
1½ jiggers vanilla Stolichnaya
1 jigger Lady Godiva white chocolate liqueur

½ jigger Chambord raspberry liqueur
(Other brands may be substituted)

Pour vodka and liqueurs except the rasberry in a martini glass in the order given and stir gently. Drizzle in the raspberry liqueur. Don't mix or stir. The raspberry liqueur will slowly sink to the bottom, so the white cocktail has a blood-red base (for a final taste sensation with bite).

Brimstone Kiss Cocktail

Invented in *Brimstone Kiss*

"Sounds like something you'd sip on all night long and I'd knock back in couple slugs."

—Rick Blaine/Humphrey Bogart CinSim in *Brimstone Kiss*

2 jiggers Inferno Pepper Pot vodka
1 jigger DeKuyper "Hot Damn!" Hot Cinnamon Schnapps
2 jiggers Alizé Red Passion
Jalapeño pepper slice (optional)
2 ounces Champagne (for Version 2)

Version 1: POUR all ingredients into a martini shaker with ice. Shake gently. Pour into a martini glass garnished with jalapeño pepper slice. A hell of a drink!

Version 2: POUR all ingredients into a tall footed glass filled with ice. Stir well. Top off with your favorite Champagne. A frothy but potent libation that might lead to pleasant damnation.